RAZE

Raegan of Ruin Book Two

A. L. Rook

PLAYLIST

Killer - Valerie Broussard
Resentment - A Day to Remember
Razor's Edge - Masked Wolves
in the dark - Bring Me The Horizon
My Heart I Surrender - I Prevail
Home - mgk, X Ambassadors, Bebe Rexha
Strange - Silent Child
Messed Up - Once Monsters
Savage - Bahari
Power Over Me - Dermot Kennedy
Issues - Julia Michaels
Naked - Ava Max
Let Me Be Your Superhero - Smash Into Pieces
Kings & Queens - Ava Max
Who I Am - The Score
Bad - Royal Deluxe
These Are The Lies - The Cab
Die For You - The Weeknd
Iris - DIAMANTE
Play with Fire (feat. Yacht Money) - Sam Tinnesz
Killing Me Slowly - Bad Wolves
fOoL fOr YoU - ZAYN
Outside Looking In - Deadset Society
River - Bishop Briggs
Make Hate to Me - Citizen Soldier
Perfect for Me - Justin Timberlake
Make You Mine - PUBLIC
Main Attraction - Jeremy Renner
Until I Found You - Stephen Sanchez
Ashes - Stellar
You've Created a Monster - Bohnes
Monster - Imagine Dragons
My Own Hero - Andy Grammer

TABLE OF CONTENTS

PROLOGUE

RAEGAN

Six Years Ago...

"Raegan, come with me, please."

Chairs screech against the tile floor in unison when Aiden and Kellan stand in protest.

I glance up from my doodling to the classroom door to see what the big deal is. Gordon stands in his white lab coat, clipboard held against his chest. Having one of the scientists call us away during class isn't completely unorthodox, though, it is uncommon. But it's the menacing stare aimed at me that sends a spike of fear into my chest.

Miss Farley looks away from her laptop that's projecting today's lesson on the wall to my friends. "Sit down. Both of you. He only asked for Raegan," she chides them, then addresses Gordon, "How long will she be out for?"

"The rest of the day."

My blood chills, dread wrapping my body with invisible chains. I grip my hand holding the pencil to keep it from shaking.

Two to three hours was the norm. But the entire day?

I check in with my boys. They're my only source of comfort, and I seek my strength in them.

Aiden's eyes narrow on Gordon, but he sits as Miss Farley requested and then gives me a questioning look. I shake my head and turn to Kellan on the other side of me, who's still refusing to sit. His arm muscles jump when he fists his hands.

"Now, Kellan. Or I'll send you to solitary to think over this behavior."

Gordon's eyes are narrowed on him, his lips pursed with annoyance.

"It's fine, Kell." I can't let him read the fear in me or I know he'll go after Gordon. He may wind up in solitary for it, but he'd argue he got what he wanted so long as Gordon is too injured to do whatever he'd planned for me. "I'm sure it's something stupid," I add, trying to dismiss this as anything more than a random training session for my gift.

He clenches his jaw, and I worry he might react anyway, but he nods and drops into the chair.

From the desk behind Aiden's, Jackson is boring holes into Gordon while looking him up and down for clues of what he's up to. Then, as if he feels me looking his way, he brings his gaze to mine. I can feel this repressed buzzing energy from him. Just like Kellan, he'd take on everyone on this island if I asked him to.

I could never do that.

They may let us get away with disobedience here and there by taking things away, or solitary for violence, but I'm sure there's a limit. If one of them were to ever go too far, I don't know what they might do. Which is why I'm determined to never let that happen.

"I don't have all day," Gordon whines in a condescending tone.

I collect my things and shove them in my bag. Dane is at his weekly health check, so he won't know I'm gone until he's released back to class. Whatever it is, I'll just fill them in at dinner or in their room later tonight.

We leave the wing of the manor that holds all the classrooms and enter the science wing. This is where we have health checks, our training, and other tests to learn the extent of each of our gifts. Usually, these are one-on-one sessions since every student's gift is so unique to one another.

We turn toward a staff-only door next to the health room, and Gordon spins to face me so suddenly that I almost bump into him. Frowning, he assesses me from head to toe. Is this because I learned about him and Vera the other night? Am I going to be bullied into staying quiet?

"I'm going to let you in on some of the inner workings of what we're doing here. Vera already told you an oversimplified explanation of our goals, but it is far more than that. Since you did well in keeping your mouth shut these last few days, I'm going to reward you with more knowledge. I think you could be a great asset to GE once you've mastered your gift. This is your chance to show me your commitment."

He looks at me expectantly, and I go with what's safest and nod.

He twists the knob, then pauses to look over his shoulder at me. "I want to make sure you understood what I said. This is a test for you, and failure is not an option. Don't disappoint me."

My stomach churns. What the hell does that mean?!

Opening the door, he waits for me to enter first. It's a simple room with white walls and a black tile floor. One wall has an enormous window to the next room, from my chest up to the ceiling and the entire length of the wall. There are scientific instruments lining the counter along the back wall and a bed with some other health or science-related tools on wheels next to it.

Vera stands in the corner of the room at a computer and a spinning machine on the counter while she stares through the window. She pivots to face us, beaming excitedly until she sees me. "Rae? Gordon, what the hell is she doing here?"

"Watch your tone, *pet*," Gordon chastises. He moves further into the room and sits in one of the office chairs, leaning back and then smiling while peering through the glass to the next room. "She's here to observe only. To see what miracles we're designing. How are you progressing?"

Her lips press into a flat line, but as soon as he asks her about whatever she's working on, her face lights up again. "I'm so close. I know if I can keep at it, I'll get there. How much longer do we have?"

Gordon turns his smile on me. "Why don't you have a seat, Raegan? You'll get a better view from over here."

Vera glares at me. If she thinks I'm going to make a move on him, then she may have lost her mind. They say people in love sometimes lose all reason. Is this what they meant? "Um, okay," I acquiesce. I'm too aware of anything I say or do at this point with his threat still lingering at the forefront of my mind to respond otherwise.

"You have plenty to work with still. Don't stop unless I tell you to," Gordon instructs Vera, and she nods. Her hands are pressed against both the computer and the machine, likely directing them with her gift.

I sit in an office chair and finally look through the window.

Wait...

Dane?

"Are we almost done yet?" Dane's voice appears out of a speaker in the corner of this office.

"Almost, dear," the nurse with him replies, patting his shoulder. "The machine will turn off when the doctor has what he needs."

He frowns and watches the blood from the tube in his arm flow to a machine, then from the machine into the wall. The tube runs through a hole to this side that then connects to the machine Vera is standing in front of.

"What's going on?" I ask Gordon, fighting to keep the panic out of my voice.

"Just a normal health check. We pull blood every week to study it, just as we do you and everyone else."

But that's seconds of a blood draw. A minute or two at most.

Dane's skin pales, and he slumps in his chair. "Stop it!" I jump up and run to the glass. My fists bang against it to get his attention. "Take it out! That's enough!" Only, the glass isn't glass. It's solid and firm beneath my fists.

"That's one-sided and soundproof, so please desist," Gordon speaks calmly when neither of them notices my panic.

I whirl on Vera. Her eyes are closed in focus as her body trembles from the strain of using her gift.

"Vera, stop! You're hurting Dane. Turn the machine off!"

Gordon sighs. "You're failing the test, Raegan. Remember what I said."

"I don't care about your stupid test!" I cry when Dane pitches forward in his chair. There's a beep from the machine, and it stops. The nurse pulls him back upright, and the machine begins to whir and hum again.

He's whiter than a ghost, his lips colorless, and I can't tell if he's breathing anymore. All the monitors he's hooked up to in the room are beeping nonstop.

He's dying.

I grab Vera, trying to pull her from the machine and find a button to reverse the blood transfer. "Give it all back! Give his blood back or he's going to *die*, Vera!"

She grunts and throws me off her. "He's fine. I'm almost there and then he'll be back. Just sit down."

How can she say that?!

"No!" I launch myself at her again.

Vera grabs one of the other machines, and a robotic arm on the counter squeezes me in its grasp.

The beeping stops and changes to a single, low tone.

NO!

My gift bursts free, spreading through my limbs without my control. I grab the robotic arm, and it instantly turns into dust. My hands shake to clear my gift away, then throw Vera away from the computer. I search the machine and the computer for a back arrow or anything that looks like it'll return his blood to him. There's a switch on the machine pressed toward me, and I flip it. The machine beeps, then vibrates as the blood it has collected reverts back through the tubes. I rush to the window and see the nurse performing a defibrillation on Dane to restart his heart.

"What have you done?" Gordon's voice is filled with horror, and

I prepare to accept whatever failure means because there is no test I would pass if it means watching Dane or anyone else die for their ridiculous experiments.

He isn't looking at me, though. He's staring at the ground. I follow his gaze, and my hearts stops.

No. No, no, no, no!

I drop to my knees and crawl to Vera. Her eyes are open wide, blood cascading down her cheeks like thick tears. Her skin is split from the corner of one eye to her lips, colored in deadly crimson. I can't even bear to look at the rest of her.

"No, no, please no," I whimper, tears streaming down my face. "I didn't mean to. I turned it off!" Releasing a choked cry, I touch her face, her neck, her hand. Searching for some sign that she's still alive. That I can fix this. But I know I can't. *My gift destroys.* That's all it does.

I can barely hear Gordon in the background calling for backup.

I collapse on top of her, uncontrollable sobs pouring out of me as I cling to her body. I want to fix it! This wasn't what I wanted. I just wanted to make it stop.

"Vera!" I'm yanked away from her by strong arms. "No! Let me go!" I fight them, desperate to get back to her. To somehow make this right.

"Careful," Gordon warns. "She's dangerous. Put her in solitary until we figure out what to do with her."

A sharp jab hits me in the neck. My muscles relax immediately, the fight and strength leaving me before my vision fades to black.

I'm dangerous.

CHAPTER ONE

RAEGAN

MY WORLD COMES CRASHING to a halt the moment I see her. Maybe Joe damaged my brain when he slammed my head to the ground.

I'm seeing dead people.

But a quick glance at the others, at Dane, tells me I'm not the only one seeing her. It doesn't mean I believe that she's real. It's a trick. An illusion. I *know* she was gone. I felt her last moments.

She looks nothing like the last time I saw her. She's whole; unbroken.

Vera takes in each of us when we arrive with a calculating gaze. There's no warmth or familiarity when she looks at the others. Then she looks at me, and I see it.

The scar that runs through the corner of her eye down to her lips. A scar exactly where I remember her skin split apart.

"It can't be." I must have said it aloud because Vera's hazel eyes—the ones that mirror Dane's—snap to mine. Hatred burns in her glare, and her face contorts in disgust.

I don't entirely blame her for looking at me that way. I would probably do the same to my murderer. Or...almost murderer? I'm still not sure how this is possible.

She faces Dane again. I take an automatic step closer to him at the threat she poses. The threat only I know about, which means I'm Dane's only defense.

The rush of wind and beating of the helicopter blades means she's forced to yell to be heard over it. "Dane! Get away from her!" Her wavy blonde hair is cut just below her chin as it whips around her face in the rough breeze. She's dressed in the same black tactical gear as all of *them*. Even with the GE logo stamped on the front and back in case there's any question of her loyalty.

Dane doesn't bother looking at me. His eyes are glued to Vera like he's afraid she'll disappear if he blinks. He takes a step toward her, and she retreats. "Vera, what are you doing?" His voice cracks with emotion, but he holds it together. "Come here. I'm here now. I won't let anyone hurt you."

Vera shakes her head and takes another step back. "No. *She* killed me, Dane. *She's* the one who destroyed the island. She's a *monster*. I'm not going anywhere near her again."

The other three swing their gazes to me, but I refuse to lose sight of Vera and Dane for even a second. Vera's speaking the truth. It's what I've been telling them all along, and they refused to believe me. Well, Aiden may have taken my word for it, but who knows what's really going on in his head.

I know I should probably keep my mouth shut, but I need answers after everything I gave up by killing her. And now she's not dead. What was it all for?

"You don't look dead to me," I retort.

Dane clenches his fist. I'm sure he wants to defend Vera from me, but he's too terrified she'll run the second he turns away, so he doesn't.

Her face darkens, and there is *nothing* left of the girl I once knew there. "I did die, and you know it. I was lucky someone could save me before it became permanent."

I purse my lips. Something still doesn't sound right. I've heard of people dying and being resuscitated before, but her body was destroyed. It wasn't about getting her heart pumping or oxygen flowing again.

"Vera, come back with us and we can figure this all out. You don't need to be with them," he pleads.

"You're wrong, Dane," she shouts back. "They are the ones who saved me. Who have helped me. Now I'm going to help them. And you can help them, too. We can do it together." Her smile sharpens. "Come with me, and I'll tell you everything you want to know."

"And what about us?" Aiden steps forward to draw her attention. "He's not going anywhere without his brothers."

"You're not his brothers," she spits. "He's mine, and he can go wherever he wants." Vera shoots Dane a pleading look. "See how they want to control you? They're all manipulating you. Come with me and you'll be free."

"Are you kidding me?" I snap at her. "*That* was the most manipulative thing I've ever heard. What do you want, Vera? Just tell the truth for once. You're not here out of any love for your brother. You're here as a GE goon to kidnap Dane."

I reach for his arm. "Dane, you can't trust—"

"Don't!" He yanks his arm from my grip and finally looks at me. His face is pale with shock, his gold-green eyes wide and shimmering with emotion. "I don't want to hear it. I don't care. My sister is alive and I'm not leaving here without her."

Vera smirks at me. "Come on, Dane. Let's go." She extends her hand out, beckoning him to her. To Gifted Enterprise.

To a lab where I know she'll stop at nothing to achieve her goal for Gordon. Even if that means killing her own brother.

Kellan moves between us and Vera, and she takes another step closer to the helicopter. "What's this? No love for an old friend? I thought we meant more to each other than this," he teases.

"Stop it, Kell. You're scaring her." Dane reaches to grab him. Jackson follows behind and pinches the side of Dane's neck. "What are—" His eyes shutter closed, and he drops.

"Dane!" I lunge forward, but Jackson catches him with air so he's hovering a few inches from the ground.

Aiden stands beside Kellan to face Vera. "You know that none of us can go with you when that means going back to GE. But *you can* come back with us. You're still family, Vera. We won't hurt you. You can fight with us or just live whatever life you want. But we all missed you and want you home. *Dane* wants you home and safe."

Vera scoffs at the barrier they've created between her and a now unconscious Dane. Now, there's no way she's going to get him out of here on her own. "You're all fools going against GE. They're fighting for people like us. I'm as safe as I'll ever be. So, thanks, but no thanks." She turns and runs to the helicopter.

"Can you stop it?" I ask Jackson, pointing to the spinning blades. He regards it with the tilt of his head, then raises his hand.

"Stop!" Aiden knocks his hand down. "We can't take the chance if something goes wrong and Vera gets hurt. Just let her go. Knowing she's still alive has to be enough for now."

Maybe they're relieved to see she's alive, but I know that this only means more trouble is coming for us. The helicopter disappears from view, and I'm filled with with an ominous sense of foreboding.

We make it back to the safe house and I bee-line it to Jackson's room with my phone. I'd tried calling Portia and Elias on the way back, but neither of them answered. I need to hear her voice to know that she made it out of there and is okay. Now I'm pacing around Jack's room while the phone rings in my ear for the hundredth time.

"Come on. Pick up. Pick up!" Portia's voicemail clicks on, and I end the call. I switch over to Elias's number. If I had Noah's number, I'd be calling him, too. Any chance that someone might pick up and tell me what's going on.

Why isn't she answering? If they got her out, what could they be doing that they can't take a call?

"Aiden says they got out," Jack says calmly from where he's leaning in the doorway. His hands are tucked into his front hoodie pocket, his hood up and shadowing his face. But the darkness can't hide his piercing blue eyes that are trained on me.

"Then why isn't anyone answering their damn phones?" I snap, frustrated. This entire mission was to rescue Portia. I can't rest until I know she's safe.

I spin around to the escape hatch in Jackson's room that'll take me to the roof. I can start with Hype and ask around if anyone knows where Elias went.

"Rae," a tight voice speaks into my ear.

I freeze. "Elias?! Where's Portia? Why isn't she answering her phone? Aiden said you all got out."

There's a heavy sigh on the other end. "We did. But...whatever they did to her brought back all her memories of the past. Once we left, she gave us all the slip. Left a note and told us not to follow her."

Fear for my friend squeezes my chest. "You're not going to listen, not after what just happened, right? It's not safe for her to be alone right now. Not while GE knows about her."

"Of course not. I'm going to do whatever it takes to get her back."

I breathe a sigh of relief. "How can I help?"

Silence.

"Elias?"

He sighs again, like he really doesn't want to say what he's about to. "Look, Rae. I know you both became friends while I was gone. I told you when our alliance first began that I didn't want anyone under my protection to get involved in this fight. But they kidnapped Portia, and now that she's on the run...I think it's best for her and for the others at Hype if you keep your distance for now. Let things cool off a bit. You could lead them right to her if you try to help, and I can't take that chance."

My throat constricts.

How can I not look for her and make sure she's safe? But what if he's right and I lead them to her doorstep? Just like I had by bringing her to Joe's house.

It's like Dane said. *Casualties by association with me.*

Elias continues. "You have my word that she'll be safe again. Trust that I'm doing everything in my power for her. There isn't much you'd be able to do, anyway. As soon as she's safe, I'll let you know."

The call disconnects.

Portia was my first real friend. Someone I could open up to and share some of the darkest parts of me. And look where I got her. Kidnapped, tortured, and now on the run.

This was why I never stuck around somewhere long enough to make friends. To have any real relationship with anyone. I should leave this city so they can all come back here without worrying about Gifted Enterprise.

But GE wouldn't follow now, would they? Not now that they know Dane is here. And could I leave knowing that Vera is alive and hunting down her brother?

Someone tugs the phone from my hand and slips it into my pocket. Jackson cups my face and angles it to his. He smells like gasoline and blood. Fire and copper. Death.

I take a deep breath and find comfort in it. In him. In what he's willing to do to protect me and the others.

He smirks and then turns my head so he can peer at the head wound Joe had given me. "Don't worry about that guy. We're going to take down GE. And then when it's all done, we'll find Elias and you can be with your friend again."

"You heard everything?" I rasp.

His fingers poke and prod at my scalp, and I wince when he gets to a nasty spot. His smile falls at what he sees or my reaction, and I feel like a wimp for flinching like that. "Mm. Now you know your friend isn't with GE anymore, we can focus on you."

He drags me to his bathroom and sits me on the toilet while he pulls supplies from a medicine cabinet. I stare at the white tile floor. There's a single drop of red on it that makes me pause. Am I still bleeding? I thought it had stopped not long after I finished the congressman.

Another drop joins the first.

Only thing is, the blood isn't under me. It's under Jackson.

"Jack?" Another drop, and another. It's getting worse. "Why are you bleeding?"

He looks up from where he was picking out the supplies and then sees the small pool of blood dripping from the elbow of his hoodie. I try tugging up his sleeve and gasp when I touch it. His entire sleeve is *soaked* with blood.

"Take this off!" I yank at his sweatshirt, too afraid to attempt it myself with how many weapons he stores in it. Thankfully, he does it without hesitation and dumps it in the corner of the bathroom. "Oh my god, Jack. You were shot! Why didn't you say anything? Aiden! Kell!"

He studies the bullet hole in his arm. "Mm. I forgot."

"You *forgot*?!" I ask incredulously.

He shrugs. "I knew when it happened and kept any blood from coming out, but I forgot to keep doing it at some point."

"What's—" Aiden rushes in and skids to a halt as soon as he sees the puddle of blood. He hits a button on his phone and turns away from us. "Come to the address I text you. Now."

Kellan's eyes widen when he appears in the room. "Fuck, beautiful. Is that from your head?" He pulls me into him and starts checking me over.

I push away from him so I can get back to Jackson's side. "Stop it, I'm fine. Jack's been shot." The bleeding has slowed on his arm again, which means he's using his gift to stop the blood loss. That doesn't mean it's going to heal itself, though.

But none of us "exist" anymore. There is no hospital for us. Not just because we don't want them running our blood, but because we don't have IDs or insurance. We would bring up too many questions that we don't have good answers for, and the last thing we need is to have regular law enforcement or the government looking into us.

The medicine kit is already open, so I rummage through it for gauze, tape, and antiseptic wipes. "Do you have a needle and thread in here? You're going to need stitches. And antibiotics. Is there a pharmacy nearby?" I look up from the kit and all three of them are watching me. "Well?"

Why are they just standing around? Jackson could bleed to death if we don't hurry and close the hole in him! Or he could die from an infection.

He smiles and pulls a needle and thread out of the medicine cabinet to hand to me.

"Knock it off, Jack. Cassandra is on her way. There's no need for you to die because Raegan wants to play doctor," Aiden snaps, leaving the bathroom.

I huff and look between the other two.

"Who's Cassandra?"

CHAPTER TWO

RAEGAN

CASSANDRA TURNS OUT TO be a healer who works for Aiden's Guild and is apparently on call for anything they need. For *healing*, they told me.

Her hands stroke down Kellan's chest a third time, and I jump up from the couch. "Is that necessary?" I snap at her.

She blinks up at me, her fiery red hair spilling back over her shoulder. Her eyes are green-gold, the inverse of Dane's. She has a smattering of freckles across the bridge of her nose and along her cheekbones that give her a youthful appearance. If anyone were to look like some sort of faerie, she fits the bill better than anyone I've ever met. And I know Portia.

"Is something wrong?" she asks modestly enough. But the edge of excitement in her eyes as she's touching Kellan is far from innocent.

"Yeah, beautiful. Something wrong?" Kellan questions with an eyebrow raised and the largest smirk on his maw that I'm tempted to stab him for it.

Cassandra's attention perks at my nickname, and she smiles at Kell. "Did you just call her beautiful? That's *so* sweet. Are you guys an item?"

Kellan laughs, like they're sharing a joke between them, and I'm not standing *right here*. "Naw, she doesn't want me like that. Isn't that right?" he directs at me in challenge.

Dane scoffs with obvious disgust from the couch. His arms are folded as he leans as far back into the sofa cushions as he can, one foot arrogantly stepping on the coffee table with his boots still on. There are metal shackles around his wrists, with chains that attach to metal hooks on the floor. He has enough of a radius to go to the living room, kitchen, and bathroom on his own, though he has to leave the door open for the last one, which I found out a few minutes before Cassandra appeared and we both ranted at Aiden for.

This is Aiden's apparent solution to keeping Dane from running blindly after Vera.

I try not to think about why he has chains handy and choose to assume he took the time to make them with his gift.

"Oh, well, maybe she likes someone else," Cassandra guesses and then throws me a wink, like she thinks she's backing me up. Her hand runs down his tattooed arm, and I bristle at the blatant and unnecessary contact. "I could be your beautiful if you'd like." She bats her eyelashes at him.

That's it.

I smack her hand off his arm, not caring if I get Kellan, too. "If you know each other, then you'd know he heals himself and is fine. Why don't you treat the actual patients?"

She gasps and holds her hand to her chest. "Who, you?"

"Yeah, the one bleeding from her head. Oh, and the one with a bullet hole in his arm." I point to Jackson, who I was sitting beside on the couch. He's normally perched on the back of it, so the fact that he dropped to the actual cushions is a warning sign in and of itself. He told me he didn't want Cassandra touching him, and now I know why.

But I told him I wouldn't let her heal my head until he was better. He relented. Barely.

Cassandra peers past me to Jackson, and I can see the tension in her. My eyes narrow at her. "Is that a problem?"

"Of course not." She clears her throat and stands to move over to us.

Something pushes me back, and I fall onto the couch. Jackson smiles tightly at me and takes my hand in his. The moment his hand joins mine, I can feel the violent energy swirling just under the surface. Like touching him has given me a glimpse of what's going on behind the smiles and his cool demeanor.

His eyes leave mine to follow Cassandra's approach, and the feeling intensifies. I squeeze his hand to remind him I'm here. I won't let her touch him any more than necessary. Though, by the look on her face, she can see her death in his eyes if she steps out of line with him.

Instead of reaching for his arm as she had with Kellan, she sits on the coffee table in front of us. "It'll be faster if I can have contact with the wound directly. Do you have any injuries other than the bullet wound?"

"Nothing that won't heal on its own." Jackson smiles darkly at her, so it's more a threat than anything.

"She's already here. You may as well let her heal whatever she finds." I hold my breath as he considers what I'm asking and finally nods.

Cassandra moves slowly to his arm opposite the one pressed against me. Her fingertips make contact, and she checks in with Jackson, who's staring her down but doesn't react otherwise. Not externally, at least.

Her hands close around his arm, and she focuses back on the hole. I peek over at Jackson to watch what she's doing. I'm a little fascinated and a lot envious that they've had this option when anyone gets injured.

After a few minutes of nothing happening, I shift anxiously in my seat. Then the hole slowly closes. Muscle and flesh stitch together until there's not even a scar or mark to show for it. She keeps her hold for another minute, eyes closed, and then releases him like she can't do it fast enough.

"There." Her eyes flick up to his and then immediately drop back down. "You'll need some rest from a healing like that."

"Why?" I ask, bringing her attention back to me.

"My gift only accelerates his body's ability to self-heal. So, it'll be tired from doing it all at once. Some people have slept for days after a healing like that." She tilts her head. "And you have a head injury?"

I nod and shift myself on the couch. She gently presses her fingers over my scalp. Heat trails from her touch to the pounding and stinging area on my head, warming them until there's nothing left. Then it travels through the rest of me in a flood of warmth. The ache in my re-located thumb dulls and disappears. Every scratch and bruise I have fades away like it never was.

When she moves back, a small wave of tiredness rolls through me.

Oh, yeah. I could definitely go for a nap after that, even if I hadn't already been up all night. At least now I can go to sleep without worrying about a concussion. "Thanks."

She smiles and stands. "Right. Who's next?" Cassandra raises her hands and wiggles her fingers. She steps up to Dane and bends down to him. "Ooh, Dane? Do you have anything you need me to rub and make feel better?"

His hands shoot up to block her from touching him and the chains rattle at the sharp movement. "Absolutely not. Now back the fuck up in case desperation is contagious."

She pouts, and I fake a cough to cover my smile.

"Rude," she snarks, though she doesn't even try to deny it. Instead, she turns her focus on the last person in the room.

Aiden is leaning against the dining table and hasn't bothered to join us in the living room the entire time his guest has been here. Kellan let her in and brought her to the couches to look at me and Jack. He straightens when she walks over to him.

"Did you need anything, Aiden?" She pets his shirt and leans into him. When he doesn't immediately shove her back or insult her like Dane did, I frown. I mean, it's not like I care if he'd be interested in her, but is he really letting her touch him freely like that?

"I'm fine, Cassandra. It was only Jack and Raegan who needed your assistance." His voice is smooth and firm. Rather than listen to what he's saying, she seems to melt into him instead.

Her eyes close and she smiles lasciviously. "No, there's nothing too bad, but I can still fix it all up for you." Her hands flatten on his chest and she goes quiet as she works.

Aiden's dark eyes slide to mine. We stare at each other for seconds. Minutes, while she keeps her hands on him and he does nothing.

Then she moves her hands up and around his neck, pressing her chest against his. "There. All better."

He breaks eye contact and reaches up to gently extract her arms from him. "Thank you, Cassandra. For your help and for coming so quickly." He wraps his arm around her back and guides her to the door. "I'll make sure Cibrina is notified of your work tonight."

She spins to face him. "I didn't do this as a job, Aiden. I'm not looking for your money." She cuts a glance at the living area where we're all staring at them. Her voice lowers, but we can still hear her. "I did it for you. When can we...spend some time together?"

He opens the door and they step into the hall before he closes it and I'm left wondering what his answer is. If he wanted privacy, does that mean he's actually setting up a date?

"Please tell me he isn't falling for that." I shove my thumb at the door.

Kellan cackles and sprawls back over the longest part of the couch. "Why? Does it bother you?"

"It doesn't matter," Dane interrupts sharply. His boots slam to the ground when he sits up. "You." His gold-green eyes lock on mine, and he shoves a finger my way. "Talk."

My walls instantly snap up on reflex. I know he wants answers about Vera, but this is a secret I've guarded at high cost.

Jackson leans forward over his knees. He scrubs at his face, probably to wipe away the sleep that his body wants after that healing, and then pushes his hood back now that he's in comfortable company. "Wait for Aiden."

Dane's jaw clenches. He doesn't argue, but he also keeps his glare pinned on me. If he thinks his stare alone will keep me in my seat and I'll answer his every question, he has another thing coming.

I stand up just as the door opens. "Sit down, Raegan," Aiden commands. "We are long overdue for this conversation, and you are not leaving until we're all up to speed on what you've been keeping from us."

My arms cross defensively. I've kept the promise of what really happened to Vera a secret for six years. I've paid for that promise repeatedly. Does telling them mean that everything I've been through and I've done since then has been for nothing? "I promised I wouldn't," I begin, but it sounds weak now, even to me.

If she's alive now, then I can't let them go on believing she's still the girl they remember. They have to know the threat she is to Dane.

"To who? To Vera? Does her being alive cancel any of that out, beautiful? Because we all need answers. Would you rather we get it from you, or from her?" Kellan drawls.

"What promise?" Aiden walks around the couch and stands in front of the TV so he's facing us. "Tell us what happened with Vera. Why did you kill her, and how is she alive now?"

I shake my head. Dane makes a frustrated sound, like he's about to rip into me for refusing to answer, but I glare at him. "She was going to kill Dane," I say, my eyes boring into his and daring him to speak out now. "Vera and Gordon were working on something that involved taking all of Dane's blood. I wasn't able to make her stop and my gift activated on its own." I take a long, shaky breath. "It came out so fast and strong that she was gone in seconds."

His eyes widen, then heat and narrow. "That's a fucking lie. Vera would never—"

"You don't know *anything* about your sister," I snap at him. "Nothing. Did you know she and Gordon were fucking?" His shock is enough of an answer. "That's what I thought."

Aiden's looking at me like he's scrutinizing my expression and every word. He's searching for a sign of a lie to debunk my entire story.

Kellan is slack-jawed. He, at least, believes me with no further proof needed. Jack hasn't moved since I started talking. He's listening intently and taking in everything I'm saying.

"Why would she want to kill Dane?" Aiden prompts, his velvety tone coaxing even though I know he's picking apart everything I'm saying.

"They've found a way to use Dane's blood to access his gift. I didn't know what they were doing with it before, but this morning at the warehouse, Joe had handcuffs that blocked my gift. It felt just like Dane using his gift on me.

"Kidnapping him is now their top priority so they can make more of those. He *has* to stay away from Vera at all costs. I've already seen that she's willing to sacrifice him for GE's cause. Who knows what other lengths she'd be willing to go to now that she's been alone with them for this long."

Everyone turns to Dane. His fists are shaking in his lap as he glares down at them.

Aiden breaks the silence. "Whether you believe her or not, you have to admit that it's not safe to go to her right now. We've known they've been after you, but not why. Now, we do."

"So what?" Dane growls. "They have my *sister*."

"And you want us to, what, exactly? Rescue someone who doesn't want to be rescued?" Aiden tilts his head to the side as he challenges Dane. "We have to hurry in finding those islands to take Gifted Enterprise down. That's our best chance at getting her back."

"Getting her back is the *only* priority now!" Dane shouts, standing and rattling the chains.

"There is no getting her *back*," I murmur, more to myself than to anyone in particular but everyone hears it anyway. Realizing I now have their attention, I continue, "You may physically get her here, but that doesn't mean she'll be the Vera you remember. That Vera, she's gone." If she even existed. How long had she been with Gordon before I found them? How soon after she and Dane were taken from their homes had she fallen for their propaganda?

We'd all fallen for it at first. It was why we'd stayed without a fight. Until Kellan had enough and tried to leave. That's when we all learned that being there was never our choice. It didn't matter that we had good meals, nice teachers, and people who pretended to care about us and what we were doing there.

Prisoners in a golden cage are still only that.

Slaves to their agenda.

Young enough to be groomed into their soldiers.

Dane flips the coffee table with a roar of rage. It flies toward me and Jackson, but Jack flicks his fingers, and it turns to crash against the wall and television instead. Aiden steps out of the way before it hits with a loud *crack* and then falls apart. "I won't accept that! I know she's alive now. I can't just pretend that she's gone and can't be saved if I know she's out there."

"Speaking of being alive still..." Jackson's calm voice slips in. Dane shoots him a glare for trying to change the subject, but Jack just smiles sardonically at him. "I have another...person who should be dead but is now wandering around." He pauses, waiting for that to sink in before he gives us all another reason to fear GE. "If they have someone who can bring people back from the dead, or heal them even after dying, then we have bigger problems to worry about."

"Who?" Kellan asks. He's now purposefully spread his legs out in front of him where the coffee table used to be like he's enjoying the new legroom.

"Thorne."

Aiden doesn't react, but Kellan and even Dane stiffens at the name drop.

"Who the hell is that?" I ask.

"A literal thorn in our sides," Kellan quips.

"An old *friend* of Jack's," Dane snipes, and Jackson's dark smile only intensifies at him.

Aiden sighs and kicks a stray piece of wood away from him. "Someone with connections to GE that we thought we'd killed two years ago."

"And...him being alive is a really bad thing?"

Kellan laughs, like this is all ridiculous to him and that we're not all talking about the many threats we're up against now. "You think Jack got really good since you last saw him, right? Well, this guy taught him all of that. He's a master of wind and air and he can stop you from breathing or slice you to pieces based on his mood."

Well, shit. Add that to Vera and Gordon and we're looking at a powerful evil team of people who are out to get us.

Wonderful.

"On that cheerful note," I begin, standing up. "I'm leaving. Good afternoon, good night, good riddance, whatever you want for a goodbye." Jackson stands behind me and Aiden moves in front of me. "Uh, what are you doing?"

"You're staying with us now," Aiden says calmly, as if that isn't the craziest thing we've said to each other this afternoon. I scoff incredulously and look around at the others for backup, but no one argues with him. I stop on Dane, ready for him to argue, but his jaw tenses, and his lips stay shut.

"Nope. Nuh-uh. I need my space, and I do my own thing. You already know I'm shit at following instructions, so it's much better that we go our separate ways again. I appreciate your help with Portia, but now that temporary alliance has ended."

I push to move past him, but he bands his arm around the front of my waist, holding me back. "I saw how Vera reacted to seeing you. You're just as much a target as Dane is. Only Vera wants you dead, and Gordon is still out there. We stick together now."

I'm shocked that Dane *still* doesn't pipe in on any of this and give him a look for it. He raises his eyebrows and smirks at me.

Asshole.

"Portia and Elias aren't at Hype anymore, either," Jackson reminds me, but I think he's saying it more to fill in the rest of the group. "You won't have as much protection there as you will here."

Aiden's eyes narrow at me. I don't know why. It's not like I owed telling him that. I shoot Jack a quick glare over my shoulder and then shrug like it's no big deal.

"He's also asked her to keep her distance from Hype until things settle," he adds behind me.

Oh. Right. I remember him saying that, but somehow it didn't click that it meant I'd have nowhere to sleep. Just that I wouldn't be hanging out at the nightclub for a while.

Damn.

"Typical," Aiden responds, like there's a bad taste in his mouth. But I don't think it's on my behalf. "He's willing to hide gifted from the world, but as soon as he's faced with conflict, he runs with his tail between his legs."

"He's looking out for Portia," I jump to his defense. Elias has still done more for me than anyone else has, and I won't forget it that easily.

"He's a coward," Aiden replies venomously. "Regardless, you're not safe there. You'll stay with us and lie low for a bit until we figure out our next move."

Fat chance they'll be able to stop me in the middle of the night, so I decide it's better to give in now and sneak out later. I really could use the nap and then I'll peace out after snagging some food, too. "Fine. Where do I sleep?"

"My room," Aiden answers without hesitation. "Since Dane is otherwise occupied on the couch, I'll take his room and you can sleep in mine." I open my mouth to argue but he continues, "Or you could stay on the couch with Dane. I'm sure he'd be *thrilled* to share with you."

"Fine," I say through clenched teeth. I shove past him to the doorway where I'd seen him naked last night just out of a shower, assuming it's the room I want, and slam the door behind me.

Gordon's stylus taps furiously against his tablet while he frowns at me with disapproval. I try again, gritting my teeth through the pain of using my gift as I fight to break the metal pole in my grip. Another crack splits through it.

"Enough!" Gordon yanks the pole away and tosses it to the floor. I jump back from his roughness, but he closes the space in a single step and grabs my arm. "If this is the effort I get for keeping you alive, then

I'll cut my losses and be done with you here."

"I'm trying, I swear! It hurts—"

"Don't lie to me, pet. You didn't bat an eyelash over killing your friend. Or are you saying it's easier for you to use your gift on people?" He releases me and scratches his chin. "Yes, that may be worth a try."

"No. Please, I can't do that."

He sneers as he looks me up and down. "My patience is running thin. Either you do exactly as I say without complaint or—"

His phone rings and, frowning, he answers. "What? I'm busy—Oh?" His lips twist up as his eyes land on me again.

An icy shiver snakes down my spine.

"Yes. Yes, I'll be right there to take care of it." He pockets his phone. "Good news, pet. You get one more chance to prove to me you can be useful. Fail this, though, and there will be no more chances. I'll hand you over to the lab."

I squeeze my trembling hands into fists, hoping he doesn't notice my fear. This is it. If I fail him one more time, I'll be hooked up to a machine for the rest of my life like that room of gifted prisoners he'd shown me. There will be no opportunity for me to find a way to free the others after that. And that's my only goal now.

Taking a deep breath, I ask, "What do I need to do?"

Gordon smiles, and my skin crawls. "You're going to clean up your own mess while showing me you can be a good pet for GE. For me."

He places his hand against the small of my back, and I hurry forward, trying to keep his touch from me by keeping a step ahead of where he's guiding us out of the gym and through the corridor. I'm so focused on avoiding his hand that I don't keep track of where we're going until he stops us. We're in an office of sorts, based on the desks, computers, and people sitting around.

Banging and muted yelling behind a door on the opposite side of the room has everyone's attention. Gordon brings me to the door, his touch lingering on my back. "Get rid of them." I open my mouth with a question, but he raises a finger to stop me. "Ah-ah. Whatever you need to say or do, make sure they don't come back."

They? *My stomach drops.* No...please, don't be them. *Gordon steps back and waves at the door for me to open it. He stands behind it, so it'll just be me and the office in the background.*

I turn the doorknob as the banging intensifies. The door must be thick, because the shouting on the other side is so muted I can't make out the words, or maybe it's because my heart is thundering in my chest and drowning everything out.

Please, please, please, *I pray silently, willing it to be anyone else behind this door.*

The thumping stops once I pull the door back.

Clean up your own mess, *Gordon's words echo back to me. It can't be anyone else.*

"Rae?" Dane lowers his fist when he sees me. His confusion melts to relief, and he lunges forward to wrap me in his arms. "Fuck's sake, Rae! Where have you been? Are you okay? Did those assholes do anything to you?"

I raise my arms in reflex to hug him back but freeze halfway up. I...can't. This is wrong. It's so wrong. I killed his sister. Vera...with these hands...

I look past him to see the others standing there. Jack's head is cocked to the side as he looks at me so intensely that I'm afraid he'll read my secret if I let him. I hurriedly look away from him to Kellan, who's standing just a step behind Dane like he's waiting his turn to squish me in his giant bear hug. And then Aiden, whose eyes are narrowed as he looks from the office behind me and back to me. To my raised arms that haven't hugged Dane back yet.

My arms drop under the scrutiny and Dane pulls back when he notices.

"What's wrong, beautiful?" Kellan pushes up next to Dane, who still hasn't let me go yet.

"Are you hurt?" Dane demands. He looks me over and then adds, "Have you seen Vera? She's been missing too. Is she with you?"

My pounding heart stutters and then crushes in a vise. I can't breathe. I can't think.

Gordon's voice breaks through the pain and whispers, Make sure they don't come back.

I pull myself free of Dane so there's space between us. It doesn't help me breathe any easier, or the pain lessen, but I can't tell him while he's holding me with worry. I can't take comfort in him with what I'm about to tell him.

My chest is so tight that I'm not sure how I'll manage words. I swallow down the tears, saving them for later. I have to do this, knowing that I'm ending everything between us. Even though I'll keep fighting for them, I know there's no redemption for me after what I've done.

"Vera's dead." My voice sounds hollow as the two words I wish I'd never have to say leave my lips. I don't know why I thought I could run from this. That GE would have told them already to relieve me of this burden.

But it should be me to tell them. I did this. On my own.

I grip my pants in sweaty hands to keep from shaking. They can't see me being weak. They have to accept this, accept that I'm the bad guy here, so that they don't try to get me back.

All color drains from Dane's face. "What? That's not fucking fun-

ny, Rae." He starts toward me, and I move back again, out of reach. "Where is she?!"

"She's gone!" I yell back as his panic escalates into my own.

Dane roars and lunges toward me. I flinch back, but he doesn't touch me. When I glance up, Aiden has grabbed him by the arm to hold him back.

"You're not going to get answers by barreling into the office," he tells Dane. Aiden's gaze locks with mine. "What happened?"

"I—" The words clog my throat.

Make sure they don't come back.

Goodbye.

"I did it. I killed her." There's no emotion when I finally get it out. This is the end of the last seven years together. The end of all of us.

Dane's frozen still, his eyes swimming in tears, as he stares at me in shock. "You're lying," he accuses, his voice rough.

Kellan curses and shakes his head, moving around Aiden and Dane to get to me, and I grab the door and use it as a barrier between us. I can't let them touch me or I'll break.

Aiden's hand hits the door before I can close it. "Are you with them?"

"Yes." I steel my nerves to finish the rest that I know will break us. "I always have been."

CHAPTER THREE

DANE

THERE'S FUCK-ALL CHANCES OF me sleeping.

As soon as Raegan locked herself in Aiden's room, Jack retired to his own room to sleep off Cassandra's healing. Aiden and Kellan stayed awake for a bit, each of them trying to talk to me about my sister, but I'm still so fucking angry at everything that I practically bit their heads off for even attempting to have a conversation with me.

If we aren't leaving *right now* to go get her, then I have nothing more to say to any of them.

They would do the same thing if they were in my position, and they know it. If this were Raegan we were talking about, they would craft a rescue mission without hesitation.

I'm absolutely *livid* that we're doing nothing.

Even if what Raegan said is true, none of that matters. She was clearly brainwashed then, and the longer she's there, the harder it will be to break her out of it. But I know…I *know* she'll come around if she's with me. If she can be made to remember our family and that we could have a home to go back to.

Our parents are alive.

Through some dumb stroke of luck, GE hadn't murdered our family after they'd taken us. Not like they had Kellan's. I could have gone home to them after we got off the island, but I couldn't bear to go without Vera. I'd felt like a failure as a brother. I hadn't protected her on the island like I should have. Even if she was older, I still felt responsible for her when we were there. That, and I'd rather not ruin that luck by bringing GE back to their doorstep and testing my chances a second time.

Now that I know she's still alive, there's hope that our family could be whole again. Get her back, destroy every member of Gifted Enterprise until there's not a crumb left, and then we could return home to tell our parents that we're alive. They didn't lose their only two children thirteen years ago.

Hours after Aiden and Kellan retire to their rooms, I'm still lying wide awake, glaring through the darkness at the ceiling. No matter how much my body may be tired, my mind and emotions are wild within me. I've played through the conversation on repeat and what it all might mean. I replay every word Vera spoke to me on that rooftop and what might have happened if we'd just been able to sit and talk without everyone else around.

I just need time with her.

I won't give up on her. Never.

A door creaks open from the hallway, but I don't react to it. If Kellan can't sleep, he'll often go out to tinker on his car, race, or check in at the fight club. Or Aiden might be trying to see if I've cooled down enough to speak to in private. I actually hope for the latter in case I can convince him to remove the chains.

Soft footsteps tap along the wood floors past the couch and into the kitchen. The light of the refrigerator illuminates Raegan in nothing but one of Aiden's few and infrequently worn T-shirts. It barely covers her ass, and when she bends forward to check a lower shelf, her black lace panties are exposed.

I watch her like a man possessed. It doesn't matter that I hate her with every fiber of my being. It's like the ghost of my youth takes control of me in this moment. Just to get a glimpse of what younger me had wanted for so long, now flashing before me like it means nothing. Is she normally this risqué now, or is she dressing like this because she's staying here?

Is it for Kellan? For Jackson? For Aiden?

Well, it's definitely not for you.

With that stupid reminder, I clear my throat and sit up on the couch, curling an arm over the back of it.

Raegan practically jumps out of her skin and gasps when she either realizes I'm not asleep or remembers that I'm here. I'm amazed she made it as long as she did if she's this skittish.

"Come here," I order in a hushed tone so as not to wake the others. I'm not going to have a chat with her from the living room to the kitchen.

Her brow furrows at what I could possibly want from her, but I'm surprised when she does as I ask without a fight. It seems like all she does lately is fight us on everything, so I expected to have to threaten her to get her over here. She tugs at her shirt in an attempt to keep her underwear covered when she walks. I'm tempted to tell her too little, too late, and then ask who she's dressed for, but bite my tongue.

Seeing her alone has given me an idea that's too good to pass up.

I check the digital clock on the cable box and it's nearly midnight. Good.

She stops just out of reach of me behind the couch, and I wonder if she really thinks I'd attack her. Then I remember I held a gun to her head a few weeks ago and let it go. I grab the chains to keep them from making noise and lift them in offering to her.

"Break these off of me as quietly as you can."

Raegan looks from the cuffs and chains to me. "Why?"

My teeth grind with frustration, but I force myself to keep my temper and voice in check. "I thought my sister was dead for the last six years because of you. You owe me this, at least. Let me go find her and fix this."

"Dane." Her voice is soft and full of sorrow, like she's already given up before anyone's even tried.

"Don't give me that. You didn't even try to save her!" I hiss.

She flinches at that. "I didn't mean to—"

"It doesn't matter," I cut in sharply. "What's done is done. This is your second chance. Are you going to take it, or are you giving up on her, and on me, again?"

It's dirty. I'm playing her fucking dirty and I know it. She knows it. But I also don't care so long as she frees me and I can seek out Vera again before it's too late.

She chews on her lips while studying the determination on my face. There's no way that I'm *not* going to go looking for my sister the second I can. She just gets to make the call if now is that time or not.

Raegan glances back at the hallway to make sure no one else is watching or coming out to catch us. My lips curve upward in a smirk when I see it because I know then that I've won. She holds up two fingers. "Two conditions."

I hadn't counted on those, but I'm willing enough to hear them out if they mean getting to Vera tonight. "What are they?"

"This is a *rescue* mission, not a sacrifice. You will, under no circumstances, go with her to any place of her choosing or to anywhere that brings you to GE. Either she comes to you and comes back here or you part ways. Or...escape, more likely. I'm not letting you go just to have you kidnapped by GE."

I have zero plans of returning to GE, where they'd escalated to treating me like a lab rat in the last year of being there. One of the reasons I can't completely dismiss what Raegan said is that there were a lot of times in the last year where they'd been taking more blood than normal from me. One time in particular that stands out.

I would pretend to go with Vera at the chance of getting her alone, but my plan tonight involves drawing her out to me, anyway.

"Deal. What's the second one?"

"You take me with you."

I chuckle without an ounce of humor. "You're kidding, right? Why would I agree to that? I still don't trust you, and Vera wants you dead. You being there just makes it all worse."

Her face tightens at my words, but she can't argue with them. I'm telling her the reality of the situation and why that can't be a condition. "If you aren't going to tell the others about this, then I need to go as your backup. I'll make sure you aren't walking into an ambush and that you get out. I also...owe you more than just breaking you free. I owe Vera, and you, to try to save her, like you said. I know this will never make it up to you or her, but I will do everything I can to get Vera back."

Her words rock the world under my feet and light a fire in my soul. For the first time, I'm speechless. She's surprised me, in a good way, and I didn't think I'd ever feel that way with her again. I merely nod in agreement, raising my wrists again to show I'm ready for these fucking things to come off.

She reaches for them, but I drop my wrists before she can touch them as a thought occurs to me. "Wait. I have a condition too." I lick my lips to prepare what I'm about to say. "You have to swear that you'll never hurt Vera again. Even if she is brainwashed, or evil, or whatever, I have to know that there is no chance you'll try to hurt her again. I can't let you come with me unless I know that. Even if my life is in danger. You promise that you will do everything you can to save her."

Raegan freezes. It's a big ask if she cares about me at all, but I'm not expecting much on that front after the way I've treated her. I'm more worried that she and Vera will have some sort of vendetta against each other that'll wind up with my sister killed again.

The fact that she doesn't agree right away tells me she's really thinking about it, which I hate to admit, but I appreciate. None of this should be taken lightly. When she answers, it's like a lead weight of worry off my chest. "I don't like it, but fine. I won't hurt Vera no matter what."

I nod and extend my hands out again. "Now get these off. They're barbaric as fuck, and Aiden's going to find some spiked glass handcuffs on his wrists the next time he tries to use these against me."

Vera is a technopath. Which means she can touch any piece of technology and make it do what she wants. No typing, no coding experience. Just complete and utter control over technology.

Yes. I've considered the possibility that she was the one who cut the power on the Tower when it was attacked. And why the generators didn't kick on as they should have.

I'm also nearly positive that she's the one who has been blocking my attempts at getting satellite footage of the Caribbean and Gulf of Mexico.

It doesn't make a difference to me whether or not she's involved. People will do anything when they've been brainwashed. And I'm convinced that's the case at this point. The alternative that she's willingly letting kids be kidnapped and imprisoned to become GE's expendable soldiers, all for power, would break me.

I can't even consider that as a possibility or I'll lose it.

Because of her crazy gift, all I do is hop on the web and send out an encoded message I know she'll pick up and only she will be able to decipher. We had our own secret language as kids that we made up together. It was how we coped when we were first brought to the island and were separated by age and gender, so we passed notes. After the first one was found by a teacher, we created our own language so no one could read one of our messages again.

That's what I send out.

Even if someone else stumbles across it, they won't be able to read it to know what it says or who it's from.

Raegan dresses back in her black cargo pants and black shirt, even though there's still blood on them because she has nothing else to wear here at the safe house. I'm also in the same clothes from this morning. I never got the chance to change or shower since Aiden chained me to the floor while I was still unconscious as soon as they got back here.

I'd bitch that Aiden has no trust in me, but here I am, doing exactly what he thought I would.

It is what it is.

We slip out into the alleyway, and I shove trash bags and empty boxes aside to reveal my ride. It's a Harley Davidson Softail Standard in vivid black with shining chrome accents. Aiden has his Aston Martin, Kellan has his rat-rods, and Jackson has his gift. But this? This is mine.

For the rare occasions I get to ride it.

I yank a tarp from the bike and roll it away from the wall so we have room to get on. Raegan's staring at it with unmasked excitement until she looks at the seat. "Where do I sit?" I've never given anyone else a ride before, so this'll be a new experience for the both of us.

I pass her the helmet and pull out a Halloween face mask with neon lights crisscrossing over the eyes and mouth. It's my secondary option to keep my face hidden from street cameras with my hood tugged further forward over it. "Behind me." I shift as far forward in my seat as I can, but I know it won't be enough.

She looks at me like she thinks I'm kidding, so I raise an eyebrow in challenge. Either she can suck it up or walk, but she's the one who wanted to tag along. As if reading my thoughts or the possibility that I could leave her behind, she shoves the helmet over her head and holds my sides when she throws one leg over.

I slip my mask on and hood up as she does it, then lean forward to grip the handlebars. Her entire body, from the side of her head down to the way her legs straddle mine, presses firmly against me, and I start to reconsider this plan.

My body tenses and heats at the feel of her wrapped around me. It brings me back to the movie nights we'd have together. How she would curl up against me or wrap herself around my arm. How many nights had I thought about kissing her? Of pulling her into my lap and giving in to the fantasies that filled my head instead of the movie I was supposed to be watching? The slip of black panties I witnessed tonight intrudes into my thoughts again.

Cursing under my breath, I throw my foot into the clutch to get us going. I don't give her any time to adjust before I take off through the empty city streets. I focus on the wind whipping around us and the cool night air instead, taking every stretch of road at high speed so all my attention has to be on driving.

We make it to the location in record time, but I wanted to scope it out before Vera got here, anyway. I park the bike in the building's alley, and we climb the rickety metal fire escape from the ground to the roof.

It's the roof of an old strip club that shut down before we moved here, but the neon lights still turn on nightly for whatever reason. It stands out in the city and will be easy for her to find, which is just what I want. Raegan eyes the sign glowing red and then looks at me.

"L'amour?"

I shrug and walk around the perimeter. Aside from the giant letters across the roof, there's nothing else. No entrance or exit other than the fire escape along one side. No big air conditioning units or any other sort of obstruction that people can hide behind. Once I get in a full sweep around the edge, I know we're clear. "It was an old strip club."

"Ah. Someplace familiar to you?" There's no accusation in her tone, but I take it that way, anyway.

"The sign is recognizable. That's all. This club hasn't been around in decades." There's a rumor that this is where secret lovers will meet. When they have nowhere safe or hidden to go to be together, they come here. Away from cameras, people, the world.

I don't know whether or not that's actually true, but I am grateful to find no one else here while we are. I'd feel bad kicking them out of their secret spot, but I'd do it.

I sit down in front of the letter O and lean back against it. It could be hours before Vera gets my message and comes here. It could be minutes. I settle in to make myself comfortable for the wait with one leg stretched out and the other bent at the knee to rest my arm on. Raegan steps up to the O and leans against the other side.

"It might take a while. You should sit down."

She looks at me and then back around at the city before she nods and sits next to me. I wish she'd chosen anywhere else to sit on the roof when her proximity has my body hyperaware of her. It pricks at my temper, and I look out over the city to distract myself.

We sit in complete silence for a long time. I would have thought she'd try to fill the silence with something. Excuses. Memories and nostalgia to try to win me over. How else had she tricked the others? I assume it's my turn now and I'll be subjected to her tricks.

She doesn't say anything at all.

Her body shifts every now and again to find comfort on the cold concrete roof and hard plastic lettering, and the moment she does, my entire body laser focuses on it. All I can hear, see, think about is the fact that she's moving.

It's stupid.

The third time she does it, I'm ready to break the silence just so I can focus on anything else.

"Even though she's alive," I begin, my voice rough, "I still don't think I'll ever be able to forgive you for what you did. I still don't trust you."

I keep my gaze trained on the lights of the city in front of me. I don't know what I expect to see if I look at her face right now, but I don't want to see any of it. Not until I say it all.

"I know," she answers softly before I can continue. "And you shouldn't trust me."

Surprised by her admission, I break my internal promise not to look at her. Her bright blue eyes are filled with fierce determination as she looks at me. My chest constricts under that stare, stealing the air from my lungs.

"Because if I had to do it all again, if I were ever faced with the same choice of watching you die or saving you...I would choose you every time."

She smiles sadly and finally looks away from me. I realize I wasn't breathing while she'd looked at me that way and take a deep breath again through parted lips. I pull my other leg up to give myself more privacy, and then grip the fabric at my chest to will my heart to calm the fuck down.

She's doing it again.

It's what I tell myself, anyway, but I also know better than to believe any of that was fake. There was so much conviction in her tone and truth in her eyes that I'd be fooling myself to say that she was lying. It's a jarring difference from how I'd imagined her after Vera died. When I'd pictured her as a traitor or one of the Gifted Enterprise members all along.

She's acting just as she had when we'd been together on the island. When it had been all for one and one for all between the five of us.

She still killed Vera.

Even if it was an accident or her attempt at saving my life. Those reasons are much better than the original ones I thought she'd done it for, but it doesn't change the fact that she took my sister's life away.

"You shouldn't have made that call on your own. You should have let whatever happen to me happen, and then we would have figured it out together. You should have *told* me what was going on with my sister." My tone is steady, belying the storm of emotions raging in me at this conversation.

Raegan huffs and gives a slight shake of her head. "Letting whatever happen to you was letting you die. There wouldn't have been a figuring it out together later."

"I can't believe that Vera would have let me die. Maybe if you had waited a little longer—"

"No!" she shouts, then she shoots me an apologetic look and softens her tone. "Sorry, but no. Waiting as long as I had and trying to get her to stop was already too much. Your monitors were all beeping and going off and no one was coming to your rescue. Either I did something or it would have been too late."

I still can't believe it. I won't. My sister isn't a monster. We cared about each other and looked out for one another.

"Anyway, I was going to tell you about her and Gordon, but she made me promise not to, so she could tell you first. I gave her a week to tell you on her own before I stepped in. And then...well, she died before that happened."

I nod slowly. This part is also hard to believe. "So, she was sleeping with the enemy, huh? That Gordon guy you kneeled for at the Tower?"

Rae makes a face and looks away so I can't read anything else on her expression. "She told me she was in love with him. But I think" – she chews her lip and flicks a brief glance my way to gauge my mood before she continues – "maybe she was...coerced or groomed or whatever into it. GE made out too well under that arrangement. And when he was with her...it didn't look like he cared much for her."

My hands clench and unclench with restless energy and the need to beat the living shit out of this Gordon guy. If any of that is true...I won't need any gift or weapon to destroy him. I'll do it with my bare hands.

"I'm sorry about everything, Dane. I wish I didn't have a gift that killed so easily and that I could have found a better way to stop her. Even if I stopped her without killing her, though, I'm afraid it would have happened again when I wasn't there. So long as we were on that island and she was being controlled by Gordon, she was a danger to you and everyone else."

I sigh and run my fingers through my hair, tugging at the ends that are dyed blond for Vera. Before, it was in remembrance and because I couldn't let go of the past. Now it's something that ties us together again. Makes us look like siblings, because otherwise, it wasn't always easy to tell.

"If she wasn't my sister, I would get it. But she was—is," I correct myself. "I'm not ready to forgive you and I don't know if I ever will be. But none of that matters to me right now. All I care about is getting Vera back and saving her."

Raegan nods. "I promise that I'll do whatever it takes to get her back and save her this time."

We both share a tenuous smile and nod, then fall back into silence.

The sound of something against metal grabs my attention from whatever thoughts I'd been lost in. A quick check on Raegan shows that she's fallen asleep. I'm not sure yet what I heard, maybe something from down below on the streets, so I don't wake her just yet. We've been up here for hours and the sky is lightening. If Vera doesn't show by the time I can see the sun, we'll head back.

Then I hear the slide of a gun.

I dive over Raegan, knocking her to the ground beneath me just as a gunshot sounds. She moans under me and then curses. "Dane?"

I ignore her and look over my shoulder, my pulse racing with hope.

It's her. Vera.

"Vera, don't shoot. I want to talk." I keep my body covering Raegan's while the gun is still aimed our way. I still trust that she wouldn't shoot me. It's Raegan she's after.

"Why is *she* here, Dane? Why are you still hanging around the girl who killed me? She'll probably try again now that she knows I'm still alive."

"She won't. I made her promise she'll never try to hurt you again. I swear to you, you're safe. You can put the gun down." Raegan makes a noise of disapproval under me, but tough shit. I know it puts her at a disadvantage for Vera to know that, but I need my sister to feel safe more than anything when she's with us.

Vera laughs, but it's nothing like the one I remember. It's cold and sends a chill up my spine. "And you actually believe her? I love you, but you're an idiot, little brother. The only way I'll stop pointing my gun at her is if she's already dead. So how about you move aside and I take care of this little speed bump, and then we can catch up like old times?"

Raegan stiffens. Her eyes are wide with fear when she looks at me. She's looking at me like she thinks I'm going to do what Vera wants. I mean, I did say I'd do anything to get her back. Her big blue eyes look up at me and my gut reaction is to hold her tight. My arms tense with the urge, but I don't move to console or touch her.

"No." I look back at Vera. "She's under my protection while she's here. No one is killing anyone tonight. I just want to talk. She can go on the other side of the roof so you can pretend she isn't here, but you have to put your gun away."

"You're an even bigger idiot than I thought if you really think I would let her live after what she did to me. I'm not going to *pretend* anything. Either I kill her, you kill her, or I'm leaving."

Fuck. I knew this was going to happen, but I thought she might look past it enough just to see each other again. I've underestimated her level of hatred for Raegan.

"Please, Vera. I thought you were dead for years. I need to hold you to know that it's really you. We need to talk about everything that's happened. I'll do anything. Just leave Raegan out of it."

"Fine. Come with me then and she stays here."

I close my eyes to get ahold of my emotions and then open them again. "I can't do that."

Vera scoffs and walks away.

"Vera!"

She pauses at the edge of the roof. "Either bring me her dead body next time or be prepared to come with me. Think it over and decide. Don't reach out to me again until you've made your choice." With that, she hops over the edge of the building.

My lungs seize. I leap up and race over to the edge. She's gone. There's no sign of her on the fire escape or on the ground. I breathe a sigh of relief and then collapse to the ground against the edge of the roof.

She wouldn't even talk to me. All because Raegan was here.

Raegan slowly moves until she's squatting in front of me. "I'm sorry. Dane, we'll figure this out." She reaches for me, and I knock her hand away.

"Don't," I snarl and then push to my feet. I shouldn't have agreed for her to come with me. Or I should have had her hide so she could have my back like she wanted. Then Vera might have been willing to talk. How am I supposed to save her, to remind her of who she is, if she won't let me talk to her?

"We're leaving." I start down the fire escape without another word.

She drops from the last ladder right after me and silently dons the helmet and mounts my bike behind me. The drive back is miserable in my head because I can't see any way out of what Vera wants. I don't want to give her either option, but I'm also not going to give up on her. I know I can get my sister back no matter what GE may have done or said to make her believe she's on the right side.

I try to ride my anger out on the rest of the drive, but it does nothing to temper my mood. I practically throw the boxes and tarps back over my ride to hide it while Raegan stands back and just watches me. I can't imagine what she's thinking as she sees me right now, but I'm too fucked to care.

Once we're back in the apartment, she pauses on her way back to Aiden's room. "Dane, we should talk about—"

"Nothing," I interrupt harshly. "There's nothing to talk about. I need some sleep and the others will be up soon making a ruckus."

"Are the others going to know we went out?"

"No. They'll never know." They don't need to know about our deal or about me trying to get Vera back. She nods and retreats to Aiden's room, closing it softly behind her so that I'm left alone in the living room where the sun has breached the horizon and is already brightening the apartment.

Fucking perfect.

Chapter Four

RAEGAN

They'll never know. Famous last words.

The loud and angry swish of blinds being yanked up followed by harsh sunlight instantly wakes me up.

"Get up." Aiden's voice is low and dangerous, like he's trying to keep this quiet, but I have zero intention of listening to him when I feel like I've just fallen asleep. I turn over to put my back to the window and then tug the blankets over my head. "Not only did you free Dane, but both of you *left* the safe house last night. You need to explain what you were thinking. Now."

My eyes remain sealed shut and I try to find the thread of sleep that still lingers in my mind. If I can find it and tug on it, I'm sure I'll be able to fall back asleep. I may have taken a nap yesterday, but it wasn't nearly enough.

"Answer me. They could have killed you. Dane could have been taken. We don't just run around doing whatever we please here."

When I still don't answer him, though I'm loathe to admit his words are keeping me from being able to return to sleep, he snatches the blankets and sheets and rips them off of me. "Get—"

My body curls in on itself on instinct from the bite of cold that's only there because I'd been so insulated beneath the covers. I realize then that he'd stopped talking and slowly peek one eye open over my shoulder. He's staring at me with an odd expression. Then he blinks, and it hardens.

"Is that my shirt?" he asks coolly.

I reach down and snag the sheet to cover myself with while he's distracted. "Sure is." He looks annoyed by that and I pick up a pillow to chuck at him. "Someone didn't let me go back to my apartment. So, rather than sleep in my dirty, bloody clothes, or *naked*, yes, I took your shirt. Next time, I'll keep them on if you're so upset about it. And thank fuck I didn't sleep naked since you have absolutely no regard for personal boundaries."

His deep chocolate eyes narrow at me. "It's my room."

"That *I* was told to sleep in. But if you're going to make this a habit, I'll sleep in Kell's or Jack's room instead. Or the armory." Actually, that last one isn't a bad idea.

"You'll do no such thing." He throws my clothes from last night at me. "Here. It's called a washing machine. Now get dressed so we can chat about what happened."

My teeth click together as the rage at this man burns me up inside. I throw the sheet back and stand, angrily pulling on my pants while glaring at him the entire time. He doesn't break eye contact with me. Maybe he thinks this is some sort of power play, but he holds my glare until I get to my shirt. As soon as I flip it up and over my head, he turns away from me and mutters something. Before he can continue his tirade about last night, I try to shut it down first. "What happened last night is none of your business. Dane is still here, right? And we're both in one piece. So, no thank you, I will not take a scolding before breakfast and coffee." I check the clock on the nightstand and see that it's just past eleven. So...maybe five hours of sleep? It's better than nothing, but I'm definitely grumpy.

Coffee then.

I open the door to leave the room and this conversation behind, but Aiden stalks after me. "What if he wasn't? What if he left while you were sleeping? Just because something didn't happen, doesn't mean that it couldn't have. You can't go running out in the middle of the night, putting all of us in more danger because you don't know how to play well with others."

"Back off."

I startle and see Dane scrubbing his eyes from the couch. Either he just so happened to wake up, or our fight has done it. I'm going to guess it's the latter by the annoyed look on his face. What's the most shocking thing is that he's aiming that ire at Aiden instead of me.

Aiden is just as surprised when he looks at him.

"Leave her alone. I made her do it. If you're going to bitch anyone out, it should be me. But save it for after I've had at least eight hours of sleep or I might punch you."

Aiden looks at me, and I shrug. As much as I'd love to believe he's doing this for me, I know he's just trying to keep Aiden off our backs so that I'll keep helping him with Vera. I walk into the kitchen and start preparing the coffee pot.

Someone comes in after me. I'm expecting it to be Aiden, who might try to whisper his threats to me instead, but when I look up, I see him sitting at the dining table on his phone. Dane is rifling through the refrigerator and pulls out eggs, cheese, and bacon. He doesn't say anything to me, just starts up the stove and makes breakfast.

I think I'd take his jabs right now over the quiet because I don't know how I should act or feel when he isn't saying anything to me. He's harder to be angry with or avoid when he's not giving me his recent poison.

I chew on my lip and stare at the slow drip of the coffee that now feels like it'll take forever to brew. I prefer this machine over the individual cup type Elias has in his apartments, but now I can see the benefit of the speed in getting a single cup.

Kellan emerges from his room and spots the empty living room where Dane is expected to be. He sees us in the kitchen and Aiden at the dining table and shrugs without comment. "Morning, team," he teases with a grin.

He sidles up next to me and peers into the slow but steadily filling coffee pot. "You sleep okay in Aiden's stuffy room?"

I break out into a smile. "I'd have slept better if he hadn't come in unannounced to wake me up."

Kellan clicks his tongue. "Rude," he says loud enough for Aiden to hear him while smirking at him. "You can stay in my room tonight. I can take the couch, since Dane no longer seems to be occupying it."

"She's not staying in any of our rooms tonight," Aiden says, though his eyes haven't left the screen of his phone. I have no idea what he's doing or why he's on it so much, but I've never been attached to a phone before. Maybe you need people on the other end of it to hold your interest. Or maybe he's a solitaire nerd. No, definitely sudoku.

"Oh?" Kellan's eyebrows raise, but there's an undercurrent of something sharp and dangerous there. "And why is that?"

I decide not to get involved because getting kicked out is what I originally wanted, anyway. Being with them in such close quarters is...well, it's bringing up old memories and feelings I'd rather not have that could distract me from my goals. Getting back to my apartment and having my own space and plans will be a welcome relief from...whatever this is.

Dane doesn't say a word, but I can tell he's listening intently to the conversation by the way he's turned the heat down on the bacon and stopped mixing the eggs while he waits for Aiden's reply.

Jackson pops out of his room at the end of the hall. His eyes stop on me for a beat and then he takes a seat at the table.

"Well, since you're all here, we can go over our next steps. Now that we know Vera is working with GE, we'll have to avoid and take better care of using technology." That's easier said than done. Everything runs on technology nowadays. Locks. Starting cars. Security systems. "Which means the Guild members can't return to the Tower today like I'd hoped. The entire building runs on technology for all its security. Since GE knows about the Guild and the Tower, then Vera does, too. We'll need to shore up the stores and supplies at the Guild's current location and make sure any outside access to their utilities is protected."

"How will that stop her?" I ask, genuinely curious.

Dane pours the eggs into the pan in a loud sizzle. "She has to either touch something with electricity to control it, or if it's connected to the internet, she has to know where to look to hack it. As long as she doesn't know where the Guild is hiding and we don't go poking at GE from their network, they're safe from her."

Now that he's said it, I remember her always having her hand on something before it'll do what she wants it to. Good to know we don't have to dump technology completely.

"Okay. And what about that other guy Jack mentioned last night? Who is he to you guys, and how did you piss him off?"

"Why would you assume we did anything?" Aiden challenges back.

I cross my arms with a huff, ready to argue, but Jackson cuts in.

"Thorne created the Guild."

Wait. What? "So, he doesn't work for GE?"

Jackson smiles and shrugs.

Kellan leans over his forearms on the counter between the kitchen and dining room table. "He didn't back then. Thorne was more of a competitor to GE, though he worked with them at times."

"He's working with them again, if he's not actually under them," Aiden remarks. "He knows where the Guild is and then lured Jackson away before GE attacked. That's no coincidence."

"Wait, go back. Did you kill him to get the Guild? And now he's back for revenge?"

Aiden frowns at my assumption. "We didn't kill him for the Guild. We killed him because Jack found out that Thorne was using the members to get him more power. The Guild itself was a sham. He made it look like he was helping them, but he was setting up jobs that only benefited him. Jack tracked us down and got our help in taking him out."

"And are you sure you killed him?"

Kell taps his finger below his left eye. "Jackson drove a knife through his eye and into his brain. He was lights out."

"How, if he's so strong?"

"By working together and having a plan," Aiden answers. "Which we'll do again."

"We're not going to be able to surprise him again like last time," Dane chimes in. "We *only* won against him because he didn't know Jack had turned on him and called us. He didn't know about my gift being able to block his."

Aiden nods. "Which is why we'll be coming up with a new plan. But after we've moved to a new location."

I'm still hung up on the Guild part. "Why take over the Guild after he died? You could have just told everyone the truth and left it alone."

Kellan chuckles. "The Guild still existed without Thorne. Either someone needed to dismantle it or run it. And the first option meant a lot of displaced gifted people with nowhere to go. Aiden stepped up and turned it around. He changed it into what it was always supposed to be, or at least what it had been promised to be from the beginning. A safe haven for people like us."

My eyes connect with Aiden's. Why? Why would he do that now? He'd never cared about anyone outside of our group on the island. When talking about escape attempts or life after the island, it always focused on us. Even when they got off the island, it was a boat with them on it. I don't remember seeing anyone else there.

The scraping of eggs onto plates is all that fills the silence while I struggle to accept what Kell just said.

It bothers me. A lot. And I can't pin down why it's striking such a melancholy chord in me.

Aiden continues his original statement of the next steps. "I'll be going to the Guild to let them know of their extended stay and to help with the security plan. Jack." He turns to him. "We'll be moving to Plan C. Make sure it's ready and secure before we get there." Jackson nods.

"The rest of you, pack up only what you need and any weapons. Stop by Raegan's apartment and she can grab her things. Then meet up at Old Red tonight. We'll be staying there until further notice."

Everyone nods, and I feel like a complete outsider in that moment. "Uh, Old Red?"

Kellan snickers and leans down to whisper in my ear, "I hope you like firefighters."

Eating breakfast at a table with the four men I'd grown up with is...weird. No one talks after Aiden announces their next steps. I'm expecting questions or more details on the plan. Maybe even idle chitchat between them. But it's quiet, aside from the scraping of cutlery on the plates and the sound of eating and drinking.

Jackson scarfs down his plate first and excuses himself for the task Aiden had assigned him. I'd honestly been surprised he was up today after what Cassandra had said. He looks tired, but he isn't acting like it at all when he gets right back to work.

Aiden finishes after him, though he at least takes the time to chew his food. He's the next to leave until it's just me, Kellan, and Dane. Kellan's been sending me smirks throughout the meal. I think he's been finding entertainment in my uneasiness during this whole thing. I almost jab him with my fork in my lingering grumpiness, but

I stand up instead and bring my dishes to the sink. Dane's already there rinsing his and the others', so he takes my plate without a word and adds it to the pile.

"Uh, thanks."

He nods at me. I decide not to push my luck by trying to say anything else to him and stalk down the hall to Aiden's room. I can tell this safe house was built by them specifically for them. They each have their own full bathrooms attached to their bedrooms, but there isn't a common one with a shower. Which means I'll have to use one of theirs.

Since Aiden offered his room to me for sleeping, I assume his shower is the one I'll use. I had yesterday, and he didn't say anything, so I'll take that as implicit approval.

I close both the doors behind me and then start the shower. My boots and pants are off and I'm midway through my top when I hear the door click open. I drop my arms on instinct to cover myself. My top is bunched up over my breasts, but not really hiding much more than that.

Kellan's leaning back against the bathroom door with his arms folded, legs crossed at the ankles, and a wicked smirk, as if he's settled in to watch.

"What are you doing?" The shower is hopefully loud enough to block our voices if Dane is in the living room. What would he think if he saw Kellan in here with me?

"You keep running away from me, so I needed to catch you with your pants down so we could talk." Literally, apparently.

"And you couldn't wait for me to be done in Aiden's room after?"

"Nope. You'd run. Now, you can't leave unless you're showered and dressed, or else Dane will ask questions." His devilish grin widens.

I sigh and yank my shirt down. I'm no prude when it comes to my body and it shouldn't matter since we've already fucked. But that was before he tried to make this about more than sex. Before he tried to make things personal…intimate.

I've long accepted and enjoyed sex for its physical benefits and pleasures, but there was never anything more to it than that. I'd share my body, but the rest? It belongs to me.

"Fine. What do you want?"

He pushes off the door and prowls toward me. I back up immediately, stopping only once I reach the edge of the shower. It's one of those open doorway walk-in showers, with a split wall of glass and then stone around the rest of it. When I look back at him, he's right in front of me.

"I'm sorry," he starts. All playfulness drops as his blue-green eyes look into mine in earnest. "I should have known there was more to it. I knew you cared about all of us. I was blinded by my own selfish feelings that I couldn't see anything past them. Now that I know the truth, that you never betrayed us and it was us, I'm going to make it up to you."

The air between us is thick and hot. I blame the steam of the shower filling the bathroom, but I can't deny the thundering of my heart or the way the oxygen seems to have been replaced by steam and heat. His lips hover mere inches above mine, but he doesn't touch me.

"How?" That's all I manage while keeping my hands to myself.

His eyes drop to my lips and then back up. "I'm going to start by earning your trust back. I will win your heart if it's the last thing I do in this life. You're mine, and I won't ever let you go again."

My heart stutters in my chest and my breathing shallows. "Kell, I told you, I can't—"

"I know." He smirks and drops his lips to the skin below my ear. His breath is even hotter than the air around us and feathers across my sensitive flesh. "Just enjoy my efforts for now and worry about the details later. What it means to be mine is different than what you may think."

He sucks on that spot, and pleasure zaps through me. Then he moves back and turns to leave. I grab his wrist without thinking. He looks at me, his eyebrow raised in question while a tiny smirk perches on the corner of his lips.

"Shut your face and kiss me."

Kellan chuckles and lowers his face to mine. My lips part with expectation, but he stops short. His large hand skates up my thigh and fingers the lace panties I still have on. "Whatever my girl wants, she gets."

Jury is still out on how much of what he's saying I believe, but the cynical side of me is tired right now. I can worry about that later. As soon as our mouths seal together, like two halves of a whole finally being joined, the realist in me goes to sleep.

We've kissed a few times now, but this time is different.

I can't put my finger on what it is about it that just feels more...real. Like Kellan's baring his soul to me in this kiss. I can taste his feelings and his regret over the past. I can taste his resolve to give me everything he's promised.

His fingers tease the wetness between my folds and then push into me. I groan without thinking, and he slaps a hand over my mouth. "Shh..." He laughs softly into my ear. "Unless you were hoping to piss Dane off more than he is already."

"Fuck," I mutter as he runs his tongue down the side of my neck while pumping his fingers in and out of me. His beard tickles and teases my skin, and I shiver at the sensation. "You might have to gag me," I confess breathily, and he chuckles against my collarbone where he'd pulled my shirt aside.

"Get in the shower," he orders huskily. He's already working his clothes off and kicking them to the side. I hurry to follow suit, but there's nothing sexy or smooth about me when I struggle to get my shirt off in a rush.

Kellan pauses when he sees me, eyeing me hungrily, like he's planning out how he's going to taste every inch of me.

"We need to make this quick," I remind him. The shower's already been on for a while. I walk into the water, and when he doesn't immediately follow, I look over my shoulder to find him appreciating my backside, too. "Kell!"

"Don't rush me, beautiful. I've been waiting seven years for this moment. You were already perfect, but I didn't realize how high that bar could go until now."

My scarred self-esteem can't handle that level of compliment, so I let it roll off my back instead of sinking in. "Get in here and fuck me, or I'll take care of myself."

I duck under the spray and let the hot water soak into my skin. I can feel Kellan's presence behind me, like a looming beast approaching its prey. He holds me still between one hand on my hip and his teeth at my shoulder while his other hand roams along my curves to follow the trail of water.

His fingers slide back inside me, stoking the embers he'd started earlier into flames. My head falls back on his chest as I gasp for air. He works my body like he's an expert already. In ways that others

I've been with have never come close to.

"How many other women?" I gasp.

He groans in my ear and his solid length rubs against my back. "Right now?"

It doesn't matter. It shouldn't. Not when I don't have a leg to stand on when it comes to this. But I can't help the nagging need to know how many others got to have this before me. Because none of my past conquests have been like him.

"Yes. Tell me."

Kellan grunts and then his fingers that were inside of me shove into my mouth, and they push my body back against the cool, stone wall. "We have to be quick, remember? Questions later. Right now, I want to see your tits bounce while you ride me like the animal I am. Now, be a good girl and suck my fingers clean or I'll give your mouth another job to do to keep it busy."

Holy shit.

I seal my lips around his fingers to do as he instructed, and he closes his eyes and moans.

"Fuck, you do that so well, beautiful. I can't wait to feel your mouth on my dick." He pulls me back with him until he sits on the built-in bench. I straddle him without needing further direction. Kellan lines himself up with my entrance and then holds it there by the base of his shaft.

His teeth clench, and I can see his muscles tense from holding back. I see what this is now. He's sealing his promise to me by giving me all the control in taking what I want from him.

I sink the barest amount onto him, and my mouth pops open with pleasure. His jaw tightens further, but he doesn't push himself in or move as I take my time. I can tell it's torturous for him, as it is for me too, but in the best way. I use my knees to help me adjust, and then I take him all the way in with a garbled moan.

Then I start to move. I grip his shoulders for balance as I bounce up and down, up and down, releasing harsh pants and soft gasps when it hits just right. I roll my hips on the downbeat, feeling him hit that spot again and again until I can feel my muscles tightening.

Kellan sucks on his thumb and then begins slow circles over my clit. I grab a fistful of his long, wet locks and move in a frenzy, chasing after the bliss that's waiting just around the corner. My breasts bounce and water falls down my curves onto Kell. "So fucking pretty," he grits out as he watches me like he's ravenous for what he sees.

The orgasm bursts through me in a rush, claiming every fiber of my being. I'm weightless for that moment, suspended in time, in life, in every worry that I've ever had, as I forget who I am. A scream claws up my throat, but Kellan's hand is there to block it before I can alert the entire block of what we're doing.

Somewhere in that blackout of time, Kellan lifts and pins me against the shower wall, and takes over. His hips piston back and forth as he drives into me until he shudders and thrusts home one last time. I deflate around him, leaning my head and arms over his tattooed back and shoulders while we both take a minute to catch our breaths.

I needed that.

The water temperature drops from hot to warm in a noticeable dip. "Fuck. How long have we been in here?" I bite my lips to withhold any more noises while carefully extracting myself from his big dick and then find my feet under me.

Kellan reaches over my head for the soaps and starts spreading it over his body. "Long enough that he's probably noticed we're both missing."

Shit. Hopefully, he got distracted by packing or something else. I'd say the television or a video game, but that clearly isn't an option right now. We both finish washing before the temperature drops any further, then towel off and dress.

"You sneak out first and try to get back to your room without him seeing you," I whisper to Kell, and he gives me a look that says we're already too late to hide this, but sure. At least he humors me and does what I ask. I wait to hear his door close and then walk out, feigning nonchalance.

Dane's door is closed, and I breathe a sigh of relief. When my eyes pass over the living room, I freeze. Dane stomps by on his way to his room with a sneer. "Of course, you're fucking. Keep that shit to yourselves. I don't want to hear it. These walls aren't soundproof. And Kellan," he shouts from his door at Kell's, "I didn't realize murderer was your type." His door slams closed.

There goes any afterglow.

CHAPTER FIVE

RAEGAN

THE DOORS TO HYPE are all locked when we get there. It's midday, so the club itself isn't open yet, but the doors are usually open at all times for the residents to walk through from the street rather than go through the back alley.

I bang my fist against the door. "Hello? It's Raegan. Let me in."

"You think he closed up shop?" Kellan muses while scratching at his beard. "Turned tail and ran once one of his people got attacked?"

Dane huffs irritably from beneath his hood. "We should make sure anyone left behind is invited to the Guild for safety. Or they should leave the city, too."

With Aiden going to wherever the Guild members are and Jackson taking care of the task Aiden set him on, it left me with these two to help me pack up my stuff and move to the new location. I told them I don't need any help, but Kellan refused to let me leave the Loft alone.

I whip around to scowl at them both. "What is your guy's problem with Elias? He wouldn't have abandoned anyone."

Kell laughs and leans his forearm against the brick building to cover me in his shadow. "No? I seem to recall he abandoned you. That puts him on my shit list."

I roll my eyes and bite my tongue to keep from reminding him he has also abandoned me in the past. I knock my fist into the door repeatedly. "Hey! Open up! I don't have my key for the back door."

Finally, I hear movement and running footsteps. The door swings open, but I don't get to see who it is before I'm wrapped in a hug. They're bigger than me, though not by much, so I know instantly that it isn't Portia.

I'm not really the hugging type, so my arms remain at my sides and I try to turn my head enough to see who it is. But they're ripped away from me with a snarl from Kellan. "Don't touch her!"

Dane steps up next to me and folds his arms over his chest.

"Fucking chill, man!" Ethan, the Hype bartender who was friends with Portia, shouts. His expression shifts to relief and a smile when it's turned on me. "I'm glad you're okay. No one has seen you since what happened to Portia, and I was getting worried. Come on, we can catch up." He waves me in, holding the door open for me.

Once I pass through, he starts to close it, but Kellan's hand slams against it. "Do we look like delivery boys to you?"

Ethan releases the door but stands between me and the other two. "No, you look like controlling dickheads."

"Guys, knock it off. You can hang tight in the bar while I go up to get my things. I don't need any help." I barely have anything anyway, so it'll be minutes for me to pack.

Dane's eyes narrow at me as if he thinks I'm hiding something from them. What the hell that could be, I'll never know. "Wasn't your friend kidnapped from these very apartments?" he asks instead, surprising me.

"We've beefed up security, so that can't happen again," Ethan snaps.

"Sorry, beautiful, but he has a point. We're coming up with you," Kellan adds, ignoring Ethan entirely.

Ugh. Fine. I sigh and shake my head. "Just give Ethan and I a few minutes to catch up, then." I wrap my hand around Ethan's arm to walk us away from the other two. When I hear boots behind me, I glare over my shoulder at Kellan until he stops. He gives me a nonchalant shrug and a grin.

Dane closes and locks the door behind him, then leans against it.

Ethan and I slide into a booth along the back wall, and I release another sigh. "Hey, are you okay?" His hand touches my arm.

"Yeah, sorry about them. They mean well."

"Do they? It seems like you're their prisoner. I can get rid of them if you need me to. Bryant's just around the corner, and the others are walking the halls on each floor."

I frown at that. Am I? Aiden wants us all to stick together, but if I really wanted to leave, would he let me? Or am I a prisoner to them so they can keep an eye on me?

I push those thoughts aside to worry about later. "We're just running errands together. I'll be staying somewhere else for a bit, so I'm here to grab my things."

His hand tightens on my arm. "Are you *sure* you're okay? Blink twice if you're in trouble."

"Ethan, I swear to you that I'm fine. How is everyone here?" I ask to change the subject.

He shrugs and retracts his hand. "They're scared. They came here for safety and then the danger came to them, anyway. But they'll get through it. We always do."

It's all my fault. If I didn't stay here, if I hadn't befriended Portia, none of this would have happened. I'm the reason GE got a whiff of this place. And Portia.

It also means GE hasn't realized there are other gifted staying here as well.

Even if I'm not sure about staying with Aiden and the others, I at least know I'm doing the right thing by not staying here anymore. They shouldn't be in danger so long as I stop coming here and leading GE to more gifted. Now, I'm itching to get my things and get out of here as soon as possible. "Good. I should go pack up."

Ethan stands with me and casts a look at the other two by the entrance. "Stay safe, Rae. You always have this place to come to if you need it."

"Thanks." I'm tempted to kiss his cheek, but I'd rather not be the reason he gets a fist there from Kellan, so I squeeze his hand instead. I head into the back and the stairs that lead to the apartments. Before long, two sets of footsteps echo behind me.

I punch in the code to my apartment and throw the door open for us. It's still decorated and styled to Elias's tastes, very sleek and modern, with grays, blacks, and whites. The knickknacks are almost all gone, though, most of them having not survived my encounter here with Aiden, so only big furniture pieces fill the space. Otherwise, it looks empty. Un-lived in.

That's me. A ghost in the world who comes and goes as she pleases without leaving any trail. No family or friends to miss me, nothing to my name, not even an ID to prove that my name is my own. I don't have the luxury of collecting or keeping anything from one place to the next. On more than one occasion, I've been forced to abandon whatever I had and run away.

Kellan and Dane look around the room, but there's nothing they'll see or find aside from what the decorators put in here. "Beautiful. Are we in the right place?"

Embarrassment floods my face, and I keep walking through the room toward the single bedroom. "Of course, it is."

I hear the refrigerator door open. "Then where is your food? Or drinks? Hell, there aren't even any condiments. It looks like it's never been used."

It hasn't.

"Just stop snooping and wait for me by the door. I'll be done in a couple of minutes." I crawl under the bed and grab my backpack. It's the only thing that's survived the last few moves. Then I open the closet. I only had one change of clothes normally, which is why the backpack was all I needed. This time, I'd fooled myself into believing I might stay here long enough to have a mini wardrobe.

This is what I get for wishful thinking, huh?

I have a week's worth of clothing in the closet from that recent shopping trip I did. But is it going to fit?

"What is this?"

I jump at Dane's voice and turn to find him standing behind me with his hands in his pockets. He's staring at the closet with his brows furrowed.

"What does it look like? They're clothes," I snap, because that's my defense mechanism for feeling vulnerable like this. It's like my entire life is being exposed in this little apartment. I'm as empty and meaningless as the barrenness of this apartment. Nothing to keep me here, no sign of my existence.

They have two, no, three places where they can live. Each bedroom I've seen so far has been filled with clothes, shoes, books or magazines, video games and movies...*things*. Items that tell a story of who lives there and a little about that person. Proof that they were there.

I grab the first top off the hangar and shove it into my backpack.

"That's it?" he asks, incredulous.

"Like I said. I don't need help. Just wait by the door," I grit out. I have two pairs of pants and one more pair of shoes on the floor, so I roll the pants up and tuck them in, then organize the dress shoes on top. I work the zipper up a little at a time to make it all fit without breaking it.

"Don't you have a bigger bag? Where are you going to put the rest of your stuff if that backpack is all you have?" Kellan asks from the doorway to the bedroom.

I never should have let them in.

They could have waited in the hall if they were going to poke and prod at me like this. "This is it."

His face screws up. Then he looks around the room to see the same story as the living room and kitchen. Nothing but furniture. And a missing headboard. He stalks into the room and starts opening drawers left and right, progressively slamming them louder and louder each time he finds them empty.

I choose not to watch this and head into the bathroom to pack up my make-up and hair things I'd also gotten while here. I sling my backpack over my shoulder and cradle everything else in my arms.

"Give me that," Dane grumbles, stealing the hair and make-up supplies from my arms. "What else?"

"Nothing. We can go," I mumble the words to him, but Kellan hears them anyway.

He's glaring around at the apartment like it's what kept me from buying or keeping things. "Why is that all you have?"

I can see why he'd be confused. It took them an hour to pack up their clothes and precious possessions and get them loaded in the car.

I shrug it off, ignoring the sting of bitterness that burns my throat and swallow it down. "I've never stuck around somewhere long enough to have more than this." I can feel the weight of both of their gazes on me, and when it becomes too heavy, I clear my throat. "Doesn't matter. Let's go."

I'm adjusting my backpack over my shoulder one second, and the next, it's pulled from my arm. Kellan just gives me a look when I open my mouth to argue, so I snap it shut and just hurry the fuck out of this apartment. I can't stand to see them looking at it, at me, any longer.

"Just wait out here for one minute," I tell them, punching in Portia's code.

"We're on the buddy system now, beautiful. No one goes any-where alone." There are two security guards walking this hall that I look at before looking pointedly back to Kellan. He smirks at me. "I don't give a fuck about them. They aren't me, and I'm the one who's going to make sure you're safe."

The door clicks open. "Just stand in the doorway, then. I don't want you in here without her permission." I keep walking in and see that her apartment is exactly the same as I'd found it when she'd been taken. Which means she didn't come back here after Elias got her away from GE. Even her packed bag is still on the couch.

I know exactly what I'm looking for, so I go straight to her bathroom and pull out the drawer where she kept her hair accessories. There's a tray full of butterfly clips and colored tassels that she'd wear in her hair. I take the purple butterfly clip I've seen her wear the most and curl my hand around it.

I may only wind up being a blip in her life, especially now that her memories are back, but she'll always be more than that in mine. I want something of hers to keep me going and remind me of what I'm fighting for. I slip it into my pocket for safekeeping.

Portia would probably lose her mind in *awws* and hugs if she could hear me right now.

I smile at that and then meet back with Kellan and Dane at the door.

"Did you find what you were looking for?" Kell asks, his blue-green eyes searching me for what I've taken.

"I did. To Old Red, now?" I ask, changing the subject. "You still haven't explained what that is or what it has to do with firefighters. If it's sleeping in a fire truck, you can count me out right now."

On the bright side, it's not a fire truck. It's a firehouse.

An old, abandoned firehouse.

In the south side that the rest of the city has abandoned. Buildings that haven't been up to code in years. Overpriced rent. High crime. Underfunded schools. The term landscaping means giving plant life free will to do as it pleases.

That's where we are.

"Please tell me this is just a pit stop on our way to Old Red," I say while climbing out of the car. It's pretty obvious that this is it. The entire building is made of brick, aside from the trim around the roof, windows, and doors. The surrounding bushes are overgrown and blocking windows and the front door, while vines have raced up the side and burrowed into the gutters.

Kellan and Dane get out of the front seats and look up at the massive building. The garage, or the bay where the firetrucks usually go, is three doors wide and a drive-through. The pavement on either side of it joins into a single driveway before it meets the street. "Wait until you see the inside." Kellan grins at me. He opens the unlocked man door and goes inside. The wide garage door in front of us rattles and groans as it slowly lifts from the ground.

As it rises, we see more of Kellan while he pulls on the chain that drags the door up. "Dane, pull her in." He waves at the car once the door is all the way up. Dane gets behind the wheel and drives in.

I'm still rooted to my spot and trying to get a handle on the fact that this is the place Aiden chose for us to go. I see the no technology angle. This place is probably at least twenty years abandoned, let alone updated, by the looks of it, but why not a house?

"Pretty, isn't she?" a husky voice whispers in my ear.

I startle at Jackson's sudden appearance. "Shit! Where did you come from?" He looks up at the tree behind me and then back at me. Of course. Really, I should know better by now. I sigh and answer his original question. "It's nice in an...old-fashioned way, I guess."

Jack stuffs his hands into his front hoodie pocket and smiles at the building. "It's an unexpected hideout and abandoned. But we'll fix her up."

I'm not really sure what they see in this building until I step inside. If I look past the plants that have moved in, the dirt and dust, and broken glass, I can see the appeal. The floors are a rich mahogany, which matches the kitchen cabinets and long wooden beams across the ceiling. There is a long brick wall that runs along one side of the kitchen into the living area. There are meeting rooms, a fully equipped gym, two living areas, offices, a laundry room, and then one entire hallway of dorms. The rooms are only a bed and dresser, but I'm still pleased to see that I'll at least have my own room.

It looks like it was abandoned unexpectedly based on all the *things* still lying around and collecting dust. Pots and pans, old furniture, papers, knickknacks, books...as if people up and left in the middle of the day and never came back.

The walls without brick are blanketed in old, musty wallpaper and cobwebs are hanging like spooky decorations throughout.

The building is old and dirty, but I'm pleasantly surprised when I flick a switch and the lights turn on.

"I called and had the utilities turned on this morning." I startle at Aiden's unexpected voice behind me.

He lowers the metal pole he'd used to hook over a dozen shopping bags until they all rest on the floor, then digs through them. Aiden pulls out a rag and cleaning spray and hands them to me. "We're all on cleaning duty now."

Wonderful.

CHAPTER SIX

RAEGAN

THERE'S SOMETHING THERAPEUTIC ABOUT pulling weeds. I get to use brute force to yank them out by their roots, some harder than others, and after a power pull of ten minutes, I can see the difference I made. That's probably the best part; seeing progress so quickly for my efforts.

I've gone as far as I can with cleaning between yesterday and today. It's now up to Dane apparently to fix anything that's broken, with Kellan's help and Aiden running the errands for whatever is needed. They're doing some updates as they go as well, already adding more light fixtures to brighten the place up and getting fresh furniture.

Overall, the firehouse is shaping up to be a really nice place to live. Even though it's so big, it still feels cozy and warm.

I push my hair from my face and sit back on my heels with a sigh. I've tackled a quarter of the raised garden so far. I think I've earned a break.

Something white falls on the gentle breeze and lands in the bucket of weeds. I fish it out and smile at the paper crane. I twist back and look up at the roof.

Jackson's sitting with his knees up and wrists dangling over them. His full, pink lips are tilted in that smile of his. The one that's sharpened by violence and coated in darkness. I can tell just by the look in his eyes that he's killed people.

We all have. Though some of us more than others. But it's that off-kilter glint in his cerulean eyes that says maybe he's lost count of the stains on his soul. And he's still hungry for more.

Those very same eyes fall on me, and it takes my breath away. Not out of fear, like it should. I'm starting to see beneath his smiles and calm demeanor for what he really is. Jackson is dangerous. *But so am I.*

I climb up the lattice that's mounted on the ground and stretches up to the roof. It's a single story, so it doesn't take me long to pull myself up there.

Jackson watches me like a hawk, unblinking. Like a predator staying completely still so as not to frighten its prey as it hops by without noticing the danger lying in wait. I suddenly want to know what he's thinking. Where do his thoughts go when he's up here, all alone? And what does he think about when he's looking at me like he wants to devour me?

My entire body heats under his attention. Natural instinct tells me to run; to hide when he's looking at me like this. But there's a rush of adrenaline by defying it.

I've also never had anyone look at me the way he does.

I have his undivided attention. Me, the girl everyone forgot or left behind. The worthless failure.

But I don't feel like that when his eyes are on me. I feel important. Special. Powerful. Because while he's a danger to the rest of the world, I know he would never hurt me.

I scoot next to him, wrapping my arms under my thighs and then nudging him softly with my shoulder. "What are you doing all the way up here?"

Jack flips a throwing star above him and catches it between his thumb and finger. "I'm on lookout." His voice is low and calm, but cold. Detached. It didn't used to be that way on the island, but whatever happened to him since then has changed him in more ways than one.

"Are we expecting them to find us here already?" We've been here two days, and only Aiden has left to buy supplies from the small town we're in. We are technically still in the city, but this town was here first and was absorbed by the city once it was built. A little forgotten town out in the woods and just far enough away from the city center to not hear the traffic.

It's hard for me to sleep with so much quiet. Thankfully, Aiden bought us all clocks with radios for our rooms, so I crank the volume up for background noise, and it's been enough to lull me to sleep.

"Not here, no. I have traps set in a perimeter that I'm keeping an eye on if anyone gets too close."

"From here? Can you see them up here?"

He smirks. "No. But I don't rely on sight as much as everyone else."

I frown, confused over that. Then how...?

"I can hear it," he answers my unspoken question. "If any of the traps are triggered, they'll make a sound that I'll hear on the wind.

It doesn't work if I'm too far away or if I'm too distracted. But I can carry the sound to me if I know where I'm looking."

"Jack, that's...amazing. I didn't realize you could do that with your gift. You've really mastered it, haven't you?"

His smirk sharpens to a razor point. He tosses the bladed star up and then flips his hand palm up while keeping it aloft. "These are mostly parlor tricks. I'm nothing compared to the man who taught me this."

"That Thorne guy?"

"Mm. Thorne. I learned control from him. I can control the air around an object or a person and use it to move it as I want. Or even sounds and smells on the breeze. That's it." The throwing star flips and dances in the air above his hand in twists and turns, spinning faster and faster until it shoots into a tree like a bullet from a gun. "Thorne is all about power. He can command the wind itself. Use it to cut you. To trap you. To steal all the air from your lungs."

Kellan had mentioned something like that when his name had been brought up before, but I thought he'd been exaggerating. How do you stop someone who can stop you from breathing?

Jackson peers at my expression, and his smile softens. "Don't worry, little one. I'll never let him hurt you."

My smile mirrors his. "Right back at you."

His blue eyes darken. I swear, if he were a wolf, he looks half a step away from gobbling me up right now. I think he likes that I fight. He wants to protect me, but it's also more than that. The look he'd given me after watching me kill Joe, the kiss...

Maybe he likes to see me shine and win, even if that looks like me fighting and killing the bad guys.

Kellan would rather hide me away and out of danger. Aiden wants me to obey his every command and stay out of the way. Dane, well, he seems to have a foot on either side of whether or not he wants me alive.

Jackson's inner monster sees mine, and we revel in each other's darkness rather than hide from it.

I stare at my hands and think of my gift. Or curse, really. Others can use theirs for good, but nothing good can come from a power that just destroys everything it touches. How can I heal or help people by breaking things? "Now that you know what happened with Vera, has anything changed?"

His head tilts to the side. Like a dog when hearing a strange noise and isn't sure what to make of it. "Why would it?"

I feign nonchalance with a shrug. "I wasn't sure if the story matched up with your trust in me."

He makes a small huff, more a puff of air than a laugh, then takes one of my hands in his. "I've said this before, but you didn't believe me then. There is nothing you can do that will change my mind about you. You are perfect for me, in every way."

A callous laugh barks out of me before I can stop it. "Perfect? You must be mistaking me for someone else, Jack. I'm broken. Weak. The only thing left of me is my revenge on GE. I'm a vengeful spirit at best."

"No." He squeezes my hand and then pulls me against him. He flips us over so he's on his hands and knees over me. His thumb traces something across my cheek, and I realize I must have dirt from the garden all over my face. "You are Raegan and more. They may have broken you to pieces, and some of them may bathe in blood and darkness and pain, but they call to me just as strongly as the pieces you've guarded all this time. All of them still belong to you, make you who you are. Your jagged edges may not fit each other anymore, but they fit with mine."

Jack leans in close, so his pretty lips feather over mine. "I wouldn't change a single part of you, little one. You may have been beaten and broken, but you never gave in. You're still here. And you couldn't have done that without every part of you, even the parts you think are dirty or broken. So yes, you are perfect to me."

I grab his face and pull it to mine. I don't have any words to give him. I tell him with my kiss, opening my soul to his and surrendering completely to him. I give him everything. Even the parts I've hated or hidden away, I let him have it all. He doesn't look at me and picture the Raegan he knew on the island. He doesn't make me feel less than that innocent girl who didn't yet realize how big and bad the world really was.

He's been looking right at me. Seeing me exactly as I am and wanting all of it. The self-doubt, the self-loathing, the monster, and the villain.

I realize that it's the same for me with him. I know he's not perfect or "good" in the way the world defines a man. He's dark and flawed and immoral compared to that image. But I want it all, anyway. I want his sweetness and calm confidence just as much as his violence. We're both stained in darkness, and I've never felt more at peace with that than I do when he's with me.

I drop my hands to the button on his jeans. I can't wait any longer to be with him. This isn't a distraction anymore. It's a base need that we join together. That we line up our broken souls and hold them together for a moment in time where we can feel whole; complete. I slip my hand into his pants and grip his hard shaft. My cunt pulses from that touch alone, and fuck foreplay. He needs to be inside of me right now.

Jack grabs my wrist and breaks the kiss. "Wait," he whispers, his voice so husky and rough, I can almost feel it across my skin. I look up to see why we've stopped.

He's looking around, but I don't see or hear anything that could have broken his attention.

"What is it?" I ask breathlessly, eager to get back to it. My fingers flex around his dick, and he inhales, then closes his eyes.

"Fuck."

My eyes widen. It's rare to hear him swear, let alone with so much emotion behind it.

Jackson sweeps down to swallow me in another kiss that makes my heart race and relieves me of oxygen. It's over far too soon. I'd willingly give him all the air in my lungs to hold on to that kiss. He presses his forehead against mine and pants above me. "Something's not right. I smell fire in the air."

"Just because we live in a firehouse now doesn't mean we need to go put out fires," I tease breathily.

He smirks and sits up to fix himself and re-button his pants.

I will not pout. I bite my lip to keep it from forming, but I know Jackson sees right through me by the look in his eyes and the continued smirk tugging at the corner of his mouth. He holds his hand out to help me up, which I remorsefully take.

"Jack!" Aiden calls out from the ground. Hearing his voice right now almost startles my soul from my body, and my back goes ramrod straight. Thankfully, Jackson is already put back together and standing, and I just look like I've been sitting on the roof with him.

Jackson turns his back to me and bends his knees. "Climb on."

I hop on, wrapping my arms around his neck and burying my face in his hoodie. I take a deep breath and soak in the smell of fall leaves and crisp air. It smells like twilight. That time between the sun going down and full night taking over, where the cooler air moves in, but there's still that lingering hint of warmth from the sun.

He jumps off the roof with me in tow. My heart leaps at the second of free fall, where I imagine us going splat on the ground, but his gift kicks in, and our descent slows so we're carried down gently. Jackson makes no move to release me, but Aiden's eyeing me over his shoulder, and I'd rather not give him more opportunity to slice me open with his cutting commentary.

I slide down and take a step away. Jackson looks at me for it, but doesn't say anything.

"The fire alarm is going off at the safe house," Aiden tells us. "It's probably one of the squatters on the first floor again, but I want to make sure it doesn't spread. We haven't finished bringing everything here."

Jack nods. "I'll go with you."

"Me too," I volunteer. "I can help move whatever's left."

"Then we'll all go to get it done faster," Aiden agrees. "Let's hurry."

The entire safe house is on fire when we get there. Flames eat up the roof like kindling and reach further to the sky. Smoke is billowing out of the broken windows in huge black plumes.

I hate to be the one to say it, but, "I think the rest of your stuff is gone."

Aiden's frowning hard at the building. It's hard to tell how upset he is about it. Was it something valuable? Or is what he lost just a mild inconvenience?

"Thorne," Jackson says out of nowhere.

Kellan curses, and Aiden nods, his face solemn. "It's a trap."

I scan the building for a person. "What are you talking about? I don't see anyone."

"The windows are all broken to let the smoke out. Fire doesn't break windows," Aiden explains.

"And that automatically means it's him?"

"Go. I'll keep him busy." Jack moves toward the burning building.

Aiden steps in front of him. "Wait. You can't face him alone. It took all of us last time to take him down. And we had the element of surprise. We should leave now before he knows we're here."

"He already knows. Either I distract him here so you guys can leave, or he'll follow us."

I grab his hoodie sleeve. "If this guy is as bad as you said, then I'm not leaving you or anyone else here alone."

"Then we'll all stay and fight him together. Either until he's dead or incapacitated enough for us to get away without being followed," Aiden says.

"Fighting to run away, huh?" Kellan punches his palm. "Not usually my style, but I guess we don't have much choice with him."

Dane raises his glowing hand. "I just need an opening to grab him."

Jackson glances at my hand on my gun, then up to my eyes. "No shooting him or throwing anything at him. He'll just deflect it back at you." My hand drops from my gun. Well, shit on a stick. "Come on, he's waiting for us."

Kellan kicks the door down and more smoke pours through the opening. Jackson waves his hand in a tight circle and the smoke pushes away from us. Like an air current flows between us and the smoke and it circles around us and out.

Once we get through the door, there's no more smoke. I look up and see it moving along the ceiling and out the door rather than filling the room. Jack's looking at it with a serious expression, and I know that it's not him doing it.

"Ah, look. The crew's all here. And I see you've found the girl you were looking for, Jackson. You must have thought you'd gotten your happily ever after. Until you learned I'm still alive, I'm sure." The man, who I'm assuming is Thorne, grins, but there's a manic energy to him that twists my gut in warning.

He's standing at the edge of the hole that's been opened up from the second floor and looking down at us. His hair is the blackest black. Matte and dead even in the fire's glow while it's slicked back at the sides. His face is all sharp points and his nose is a bit tweaked, like it was broken so many times that it finally just healed crooked. One of his eyes is a pale blue with a scar straight through it from eyebrow to cheekbone. From Jackson stabbing him, no doubt. The other is too dark to see, but an obviously different shade from the other.

Thorne is wearing a black trench coat that's buttoned all the way up and is moving behind him from an invisible breeze. Or maybe from whatever he's doing to keep the fire and smoke away from this bubble we're in.

Point is, he looks like a super villain.

"I would have come for you all sooner, but GE has some trust issues I had to help them with first. But now it's time I punished you for what you did. The Guild is mine, and I'm taking it back."

Aiden pulls his sword from his back that unfurls like a whip and slams it down. The sharp blades running down its length on either side cut into the softened floor like butter. "We'll make sure to take your head this time. No coming back."

Thorne laughs. It's a hollow, creepy sound that makes me think of an echo in a mausoleum. "Oh, how little you know. I should take your head and mount it in the Guild for everyone to see what happens when you try to supplant me."

Holy shit.

Jackson leaps into the air and throws knives at him, the time for idle threats and chitchat apparently over with. Thorne lifts a hand at him, and a gust of wind knocks Jack and the knives back to the ground.

Aiden's arm arcs over his head, and his sword moves like a snake in the air. Thorne jumps aside to dodge it, but Aiden doesn't let up. His arm keeps swinging back and forth, over and up. He keeps his blade chasing after him, so Thorne's forced to avoid it rather than attack.

I call on my gift, spreading the fire through my arms to my hands and then holding it there.

Jackson appears behind the ex-Guild master, and slashes at him with a longer blade than his usual throwing ones. It catches Thorne in the back and he falls to the first floor. Kellan runs and grabs him, pinning his arms to his sides. "Dane!" he roars.

Dane's already running with his hand outstretched and glowing white with his gift.

I could come at him now, but with Kellan already holding him and Dane about to grab him, I could risk hitting them, too.

Thorne laughs again. "You think I'd be foolish enough to let him touch me now that I know what he can do?" He clenches his hand at his side, and Kellan's eyes widen. He releases Thorne and grabs at his throat, dropping to one knee. Thorne kicks him in the shoulder to knock him down. "And you. You may be tough on the outside, but there's no healing you can do from lack of oxygen."

Dane lunges forward to grab him, but Thorne slashes his arm at an angle in front of him. Dane screams and falls back. There's blood in a line across his chest, like he'd been cut with a blade.

Thorne sneers down at him. "I'll be taking you back with me. You'll only wish you were dead like your friends by the time GE is through with you. If I accidentally kill you, I'll be doing you a favor."

He's too busy looking at Dane to notice Aiden moving behind him until it's too late. Thorne glances up and jumps to the side at the last second, but Aiden's control over his whip sword makes the adjustment and spears through the enemy's shoulder. Thorne glares at it, and then Aiden, who smirks at him and then yanks it roughly out.

Thorne curses and pulls his hand back like he's preparing to throw a ball sideways, then swings it out at Aiden. A whirlwind of air picks up around him. He grunts, and a line of red appears on his cheek. Then his hand. Over and over again, like the air is made of paper-thin blades slicing into him piece by piece.

A hoard of knives race toward Thorne. He swings his arm up to blow them away, but it breaks his concentration enough that the whirlwind releases Aiden and he falls to the ground. Jackson pulls out round after round of blades, slinging them at our enemy.

Thorne sends some of them back at him, but Jackson uses his

perfected control over the air to pull and flip them back at him. His teacher may have all the power, but he's outmatched by Jackson when it comes to control that fine.

He's pushing Thorne back, and I see my opening. I take the longer way around to get behind him and hope that Jack keeps Thorne's attention trained on him so he doesn't notice me. I run up behind the ex-Guild master and dive at him, my hands out and ready to grab any body part to unleash my gift on, but he moves at the last second and I crash to the ground.

He's too fast.

I groan and push myself up in time to see Thorne sneering at me and waving his hand at me the same way he had at Aiden.

Oh crap.

I feel the wind pick up around me, and I scramble to move away from it, but it follows me like my own personal tornado of death.

The first cut catches my arm, and I cry out and grab it on instinct. Then the wind is just...gone.

I look up and see Jack reaching out to it, trying to control it over Thorne. The mini cyclone spins between them in a standoff of who's going to get it. Thorne has more injuries than either of us, but it's Jackson's body that's trembling with the effort to push it back at Thorne. The debris and ash from the floor get sucked up in the current, spinning around midair and struggling between the two men. It picks up speed, and Thorne's eyes shine with triumph when it moves toward Jack.

He struggles against it, but it steadily sucks him into its vortex and exacts its invisible blades.

"Jack!" I rush at Thorne again, but wind throws me off my feet, and I land with a thud on my back, knocking the air from my lungs. I gasp, collecting as much air as I can, and then it's not there anymore. I try to suck in air, but it's like my lungs have seized, and I can't inhale or exhale anymore. My eyes widen with panic. The other three are clutching at their throats like me, and genuine fear slides through my veins. We're completely outmatched.

The air around Jackson is red with his blood, and his face pinches with pain beneath his concentration. Black dots start forming, blocking out bits and pieces of what I'm seeing in front of me. I reach out to Jack, wishing I could break the storm around him.

He drops; the blood falling on him and the ground. My lungs expand, and I heave oxygen through my mouth in painful draws that have me choking in my desperation to take as much as I can. I grab my throat and cough as my body adjusts to having air again, then look up at Thorne.

He's staring at something on his hand with a frown. Then I see the line of blood across his throat. It's thin; had it been stronger, it would have ended him.

Jackson.

Who isn't moving on the ground.

Thorne glares down at him and raises his hand. I remember how Dane was cut down, and I don't think; I run. Even though my lungs burn and my eyes water, there's no time to wait for that. I cover Jackson's body with my own as a shield. I'll do anything to protect him. To protect them.

My gift stirs in my gut, and I draw it out, repeating the same thing over and over like a mantra. *Just Thorne. Just Thorne.* Jackson trusts that I would never hurt him with my gift, even by accident. Even if that's exactly what happened with Vera. I still don't trust in my gift because I've seen it do something I didn't want. But I will trust in

Jackson.

Thorne's hand swings down, and I grab his leg and thrust my gift into him. He screams, and then it cuts off sharply. I look up, and his eyes are bulging, staring down past me while his mouth is wide open. I look down, and Jackson's fist is shaking as he looks at Thorne with unbridled rage and triumph. Did he cut off his air?

Thorne's other foot flies out and kicks me in the face. I yelp and taste blood in my mouth. I release him, stopping my gift the moment I lose contact, and Thorne takes off out the door.

Jack's fist loosens once he's out of sight, and he releases a breath and closes his eyes.

"Jack?" I roll away and shake him. Something smacks down on the ground behind me. I cough and look around, thinking he's come back, but roofing tiles are falling as the room fills with smoke. The fire is spreading back down the roof and onto the building.

I shake him harder, but he doesn't budge. "Kellan?! Aiden?! Help!"

What if they're all passed out?

I stand up and cover my mouth with one arm, but it does shit-all to block the smoke from my lungs or help me see. I choose to grab Jackson's ankles with each hand instead and start dragging him back toward the door where we came in. Blood tracks across the floor in his wake, and I keep praying that they're all superficial cuts.

"Stop, beautiful. I've got him. Get out of here." Kellan appears from the darkness and lifts Jackson in his arms. I think for a second that maybe he's immune to the fire and smoke, but he hacks off to the side and then gives me a kick. "Go!"

I run through the smoke in the direction I think the door was, my elbow out to feel for a wall in case it's too hot to touch with my hand.

The smoke is mostly going up or out in one direction, so I use that as my guide to the door and stumble through it. I keep going until I'm out of the smoke at the next building over.

Aiden and Dane are there, sitting on the ground, coughing. Both are bleeding, one with a single large laceration and the other with smaller cuts all over. Aiden pulls out his phone, but my attention jumps to Kellan and Jackson when they finally emerge. I rush over to Jack and start feeling for a pulse. His chest rises and falls, and I clasp his empty hoodie with relief. "Oh, thank god."

"Cibrina's sending us a van and Cassandra."

Any trickle of annoyance or jealousy is gone when I hear her name. All I feel is relief that she's on her way. "Tell them to hurry. Jack doesn't look good, and the fire department will probably be here any minute."

I keep my grip on Jackson so I can feel his chest moving beneath me. I don't think I'll let go until he's been healed and I know he'll be okay. There's blood all over Kellan from his chest and arms down.

"Are you okay?" I ask Kell quickly, needing to be sure the blood isn't his. But also worrying about that amount of blood, if it's all from Jackson. When he looks at me, his expression is dark and brooding.

"Just fine," he answers, but there's something in his tone that's off. I put a pin in that for later, because a van pulls down the larger alleyway on the other building's side, and it's time to load up.

Chapter Seven

KELLAN

The knife in my hand slices across the back of my arm in a single, clean cut. Pain flares briefly before it ebbs to a stubborn ache. My skin heals itself and then transforms to tight, golden scales. I pull out my phone and set the timer.

Last night was a shit show of epic proportions. If not for Jackson and Raegan, we would all be gone. The fact that I did fucking nothing during the entire fight has me pissed at myself. I've become too careless, thinking my fighting skills and regeneration meant I was guaranteed a win.

Thorne proved I still have plenty of weaknesses that can be exploited.

I've been wasting my latest years at the bottom of a bottle, being as reckless and dumb as I could be. I should have been training. Learning more about my gift.

Does the level of damage to me affect the strength or duration of the scales? Is there any way I can activate them without being injured first? Could I ever turn them all on at the start of a fight instead of a little at a time? Can I hold it for longer than an hour?

I don't know any of that. I didn't care before. We'd had no real fights in the last two years, and I'd gotten cocky. But fighting against the bottom of the GE hierarchy agents is nothing compared to the big leagues like Thorne. How many gifted agents does GE have at his level? Or higher?

"What are you doing out here?"

My heart stutters offbeat, and my cock thickens in my jeans at the sound of her voice. I'm a goner for this girl, and she still thinks she's going to walk away from this city and us after we take down GE. I also know that she's going to do whatever she wants, even if that means going off on her own if she finds herself not liking our plans.

I don't know why she's decided to stick with us since we all found out Vera's alive. To keep an eye on Dane, maybe. Or she actually agreed with Aiden about us working together to get this done. Either way, she's here for the thinnest of reasons that could snap at any time.

I can't let that happen.

"Training." I check the timer to see that I'm reaching the hour mark of this test. Since I'm sitting on a tree stump, I have to look up to see her face. She's in jeans and a plain shirt like me, both of our tops hugging our upper halves like a second skin. Her long blonde hair is down and un-styled. I can tell because her waves are more haphazard, and there are random curls here and there. "You been looking for me, beautiful?" I tease with a drawl.

Raegan stares at my arm and then the timer. Her brows pinch as she tries to figure out what I'm doing. "You're trying to time how long you can hold it?" she guesses, then crouches down into a squat to get a better look at my arm.

Her breath fans across my arm, and I'm gifted with the smell of vanilla now that she's close enough. I'm tempted to grab her hair and wrap it around my fist. Give her something else to look at. My dick stirs at the thought, and words slip past my lips without a filter. "I can go as long as I need to, beautiful. Want to christen these woods with me?"

Her blue eyes flare at the suggestion, and I know she's down for it as much as I am. Fuck. Yes.

I grab her by the neck, pulling her lips up to mine and then lifting her to straddle my hips. She grinds her pussy into me, and it feels so fucking good. We still have clothes between us, and I'm rock-hard. It's all her. She's an aphrodisiac all on her own. The fire in her big, bright eyes. The warm smell of vanilla. Her sharp tongue that can sound so sweet when it's coaxed out of her right. The way her slight frame fits completely inside mine, which makes me want to wrap around her tight.

She tastes like strawberries today, and I've never been so starved for the fruit in my life. Raegan smacks my chest and pulls back. Her pupils are dilated, and she's panting when she attempts to back out. "Is this all you think about? Sex? Everything just comes out dirty to you?"

I grin and smack her ass, then drag her hips over me again. Her eyes roll back into her head as she gasps with pleasure.

"Maybe I just have a sexy imagination."

Raegan doesn't have a chance to comment on that before I'm smashing my lips against hers again. I haven't finished tasting her.

Her fingers dig into my hair and she yanks my hair tie free. My hair falls around her hand, and she grabs it like it's a safety line.

"Crap. What about your training?" She breaks away again to look at my arm, but fuck that.

"We really need to work on your dirty talk, beautiful. Don't worry, I'll carry the ship for now. You just sing for me."

I lift us up, then do a controlled drop to my knees to place her on the ground beneath me. We're deep in the woods from the firehouse with no other buildings or people around.

Raegan's staring up at me with hooded eyes filled with lust and desire, her hair fanned out behind her mixed in the dirt and leaves. My heart misses a beat at the look she's giving me. If I'd ever had any doubt before, it's gone now. She wants me.

She looks so goddamn beautiful spread out before me with a look like that. My soul goes rabid at the sight of it. Mine. I'm never letting her fucking go. She's mine. These looks are all mine. I'll covet them and worship her like the fucking goddess she is of my soul.

I push her shirt up and tug her bra cups down so that they perfectly shelve her round tits on display for me. And then I ravish them. My tongue circles each nipple until they grow to pert points that I can't help but suck and nibble on, eliciting a sharp gasp from Raegan. Smirking, I slide one hand between us, snapping her jeans open in a rough yank and slipping inside. Her panties are soaked for me.

A growl rumbles from my chest. I take her jeans and underwear in either hand, then strip them clean off of her and toss them somewhere behind me. My clothes drag against the dirt when I shift her thighs over my shoulders. I bite her inner thigh, claiming it and her with a mark that will stick around.

She's writhing above me, moaning into the quiet morning air for all the woodland creatures to hear. We should be safe from the firehouse hearing us, but I'm in too deep to give a rat's ass if they do. I'm not stopping even if a bear or cougar shows up. Her voice is like music to my ears, and I wonder what other sounds I can draw from her lips. Sounds I know I'll replay in my head on repeat like my favorite song.

My tongue takes a long, firm lick of her arousal, and I groan at the sweetness of it. "You're going to be the death of me, beautiful. A man could set up camp and feast on you for life with how good you taste."

Her fingers grip the hair on my head and shove me back down. "Shut up and don't stop," she sasses, but it's dripping with a need that tells me I'm still the one in control. I smile against her lower lips, my trimmed beard tickling against her, causing her thighs to clench around me.

I don't have the patience to drag this out any longer, anyway. I've been starved for the taste of her again. I pleasure her with reckless abandon. No nice, gentle, or teasing strokes. This pussy is mine and has been waiting for me to devour it; I won't make it wait any longer. My grip on her thighs is firm as she tries to wriggle away when the pressure becomes too much, but I hold her steady so she can't run away. She'll take the pleasure I'm giving her, and she's going to love it.

Raegan's hand is pulling my hair so tight that my scalp burns. She's not trying to direct anything, though. She's holding on for dear life while she makes all sorts of sounds that tell me I'm playing her body just right.

I dip my tongue inside her pussy. I can feel it trying to clench, but my tongue isn't what it wants. I slide back up and then insert two fingers, pushing them in and out at a steady pace.

Her body arches like a bowstring and then snaps as her orgasm explodes from her. I hungrily devour her sweetness before it can fall to the dirt so it isn't wasted. I shuck my clothing, then remove the rest of hers as well while she's still coming down from her high, and then I line up and drive into her.

She cries out in pleasure, and my voice mixes with hers. My dick glides into her with ease, and it's like her cunt is welcoming me home. I back out and take my time sliding back in. I want to feel every inch of her pussy, especially when it holds me tight and tries not to let me go. It's pure fucking heaven, and there's nothing I've done or felt in my life that will top this.

Street racing, fight clubs, drinking, and smoking. All distractions from what I was really looking for in this life.

Her.

The thought snaps the thread of control in me, and I move in earnest. I lift her ass while her legs balance over my shoulders as I take her at a completely new angle. She's at my mercy with half her body airborne and in my grip, so she has to take every punishing stroke and thrust, as I angle myself deeper, like I'm trying to come out of her throat.

My own finish line creeps up, but I don't want to go until I've felt her orgasm with me inside her. I pull out, then grab her hips and flip her to her front in one swift motion. Her back is covered in dirt and nature, and now I'll get to rub her front side into it, too. Once again, I sheathe myself in her warm embrace.

I run my hand possessively down her spine as if I can press the dirt more firmly into her skin as a form of marking her. Like Simba's forehead is marked with some mud or coconut crap, I'll claim her in the dirt of this earth. I grip her hips in each hand and step up to an unforgiving pace. "Touch yourself, beautiful."

Raegan reaches between her legs and starts rubbing at her clit. I can feel her pussy pulse and clench around me, and I know she's close. I grit my teeth to hold my own back, but it's not easy. Then she screams, and I hear the flutter of wings flying off with surprise at the sound. Her body convulses around mine, squeezing me tight, and I can't hold it anymore. My seed bursts out of me, and I pound it all into her as ecstasy surges through me.

I collapse over her back, holding myself up but resting against her while catching my breath. Neither of us says a word while our minds and bodies come crashing back down to earth and the physical world around us. I know exactly what she'll do as soon as her brain kicks back online, though. She'll run. Emotionally. Maybe even physically. She'll run from this. From me.

I've learned that sex, she can do. She's not shy or afraid of her body at all. It's intimacy she fears.

It's not something I have experience with either. But I want it. With her.

She's the only partner for me. The only woman who I'd gladly give all my time and attention to. Hell, most of my shenanigans on the island were my attempts at impressing her. At stealing her focus away from the others and earning a smile that's exclusively mine.

I gently pull myself free and fall back on my ass, knees up, uncaring that I'm butt-ass naked in the woods right now, sitting on leaves and twigs. Her body tenses almost as soon as I'm gone. As if losing contact with me is what triggers her brain to overpower her body so she can overthink everything.

"Here." I grab my shirt and throw it in her face when she sits up. "You can use it to clean up if you want."

She looks uncomfortable and avoids my eyes, so I take that moment to turn away from her and grab my clothes to put back on. When I glance back, she's nowhere in sight. Did she run that quickly?

Raegan pops out from behind a bush, fully dressed, though her skin is still brown with dirt, and there are leaves tangled in her hair. She holds my shirt by a bit of the fabric pinched between her fingers and behind her.

"I used it. I'll wash it before I give it back."

Like I care about her cum. Doesn't she remember how I was eating and raving about it? I study her for another second, and then realization clicks in. I grin at her embarrassment, and when she only looks more so at my grin, it widens until I'm sure all my teeth are showing. "Did you pee on it?"

"Gross! Stop making this weird! Of course, I didn't. I just...used it to wipe myself...after. It's a girl thing, alright? Just leave it alone, or I'll never have sex with you again." Her face is red as a strawberry, and it's so fucking cute to see her like this that I want to poke her more. But there's also no way I'm letting her think we aren't doing that again. Because I'd really like this to be a regular thing.

Raegan looks in the direction of the firehouse and it's like watching a rabbit tense in preparation to run for its life.

Distraction seems like the easiest way to keep my little bunny from running, so I look purposefully at my arm. The scales are long gone, as I knew they would be, but I sigh loud and clear to grab her attention.

It works like a charm, and she drops the shirt and steps closer to me so she can look at my arm, too. "How long did it last?"

"Probably just the hour, as usual. I don't usually focus on it once it's there, so it's hard to say." Her brow pinches with concern, and I gently flick her forehead to snap her out of it. "Whatever you're thinking, beautiful, stop. I can just try again."

"How long have you been trying to do this?"

"About two hours, although I really can't count the last one since I wasn't trying to keep it active," I drawl with a smirk.

"Is this because of last night?" she presses, and I shrug. "Why? You're already pretty invincible."

My smile falls, and I rub at my beard. "It's not enough. As you saw last night."

Her blue eyes meet mine, and I see understanding there. We're both not happy about what almost happened. Only difference is that I've made it my one goal in this life to protect my brothers, and now Raegan again.

It was all I wanted on the island after I found out my family had been killed. They're the only family I have now.

How Thorne's alive is still unbelievable to me, just as I'm sure it's haunting Jack. I would have thought his entire eye would be gone from being stabbed, and yet there it was. Probably blind as a bat, but somehow intact.

It makes me wonder just who else we're up against in this battle with GE. It's not going to only be Thorne and some suits behind a desk. The possibilities of other gifts out there are endless.

"And that guy trained Jack?"

"Guess so. You should ask him, though. We didn't get involved until the very end. The quick version is that he took Jack in as a sort of protégé after we got off the island." She looks confused, and I realize she still doesn't know anything about what we did after we escaped.

But I'm all in with her now, so I don't see the harm in telling her any of it. Whether or not the others agree is a different story, but I'll keep it summarized so they can fill in any details if they choose to. The stories involving Thorne aren't really mine to tell.

"We didn't stay together when our boat landed. Jackson and I each took off on our own, and only Dane and Aiden stuck together at first."

Raegan's face parts in shock. "Why not? After all you'd been through together..."

I laugh at that, and it's a callous, rough sort that scratches my throat when it comes out. I still can't believe how little she realizes she's a part of us. Always has been and always will be. "I didn't realize it then, but now that I'm looking back, I'm almost positive. It was because of you. We didn't all agree on you, or in that you weren't with us, and it divided us. But yeah." I wave that story aside for another time, if ever. I'd rather not get too deep into what I'd stupidly done in that dark time she wasn't in my life.

Raegan chews on her lip while trying to process all of that.

I yank the knife I'd used earlier free of the stump and slash a fresh wound on my arm. Her gaze jumps to it, and even though she knows I'll heal, I can still read the worry in her eyes when she sees my blood.

"Will you train me?" she finally asks after my scales have come in, and I set a new timer.

I arch a brow. "With your gift?"

"No," she hurriedly answers. "I need to learn how to fight better. I've been getting by with stealth and finding opportunities to my advantage, but once someone knows I'm there, and if they aren't restrained, I'm at a disadvantage. I want to learn how to fight hand-to-hand and with a knife. Even if they're bigger than me."

"Hate to tell you this, but most people are bigger than you unless you're fighting kids or that friend of yours."

She gives me a playful smack, and I grin. "You know what I mean, you prick."

"Why won't you use your gift?" I ask, genuinely curious.

She frowns at the very idea of it. "It's too dangerous for me to use when others are around. I don't want to...you know, friendly fire."

Is she thinking about Vera? I was shocked to hear that Vera had put her brother's life at risk. I was less surprised to find out she'd slept with the enemy. She was clearly uninterested in her other classmates and spent all her extra time training. And yet, I overheard her teasing Raegan about kissing and taking the next step with the boys on more than one occasion. Where was she getting the experience from?

At the time, it had been a passing thought. I had no evidence or other reason to suspect it was true, so I'd dropped it.

Now, it seems like my instinct had been correct.

"That's just practice." I step in front of her so she has to tilt her face up to maintain eye contact with me and take her hands to place them against my chest. There's a tattoo on one side that looks like an animal clawed at it and ripped the skin away to expose the muscle underneath. Then there are fake scales that trail up my shoulder and down my arm to tell a story about me.

She doesn't react since we both know her gift isn't active, but I like having her undivided attention like this. "You need to remember that your gift is a part of you. It's not something made and attached to you. You were born with it. Like two arms and two legs. Stop hiding from it and being afraid. Learn it for yourself. Test its limits."

Raegan pulls her hands away and tucks them under her arms. "It's not another arm. It's a weapon that I'll only use when I have to," she replies stubbornly.

I sigh. "Alright, I'll train you to fight. We'll do it every night after dark. So, if there's anything you were planning on doing today, I'd hurry and get it done because as soon as the sun goes down, I'll be hunting you down to start, no matter what you're in the middle of."

Her mouth parts at my taskmaster attitude, but little does she know how excited I am by the prospect of making her a badass. Grappling with her and potentially fucking during the session is not a bad idea. "Well? Go!" I turn her around and smack her on the ass to kick-start her. She jumps and looks at me with mock surprise and heat in her eyes.

Hell yes, this is going to be fun.

The firehouse is quiet when I finally call it quits on training. The building is huge, so it takes a lot to add noise to it, but it's also a feeling that there's not a lot of life or activity going on in here.

I stride into the large living area and find Dane taking a break from the kitchen backsplash tiles and tapping away on his laptop on the large sectional couch. He glances over at me, his eyes raking over my dirty state, but for once, he keeps his mouth shut about it.

"Where is everyone?"

"Jack's still sleeping. Raegan left a while ago, and I think Aiden went after her."

She left?

My hands clench open and shut at that bit of information, and Dane watches me with a look of disinterest, but it's a show.

"Order pizza for lunch. I'm going to take a shower."

"It's closer to dinner now," Dane argues, like it matters.

I just shrug and turn away to head for the common men's bathroom and the showers. One of the downsides of this location is that the dorms are tiny-ass rooms with nothing more than a bed and a dresser. I feel like I'm almost the length of the room and might kick a hole in the wall in my sleep. The shared bathrooms aren't great, either. At least Raegan knows she has one to herself. It's been unspoken that we won't use the women's bathroom even if she isn't in it.

Depending on how long we'll be staying here, we'll need to talk about knocking down some walls and adding more individual bathrooms. We don't need ten bedrooms between the five of us.

I take longer in the shower than usual to make sure all the dirt and grime is washed away, pull on some sweats, and then fall unceremoniously onto the couch a few feet away from Dane. There are already pizza boxes stacked on the table, so I dip right in to grab a piece and take a bite.

"No bottle?" Dane questions with faux innocence.

I finish my fourth slice and wipe my hands on my sweatpants before turning on a video game and grabbing a controller off the table. "I don't need it anymore." I used it to numb the pain and the emptiness of my life without Raegan in it. But she's here now. And I've found my purpose again.

Like I'd say any of that to him, though, with the chip on his shoulder the size of the Grand Canyon.

"Besides, I need to be fully alert for training Raegan tonight."

He swivels his head at that. "She asked me to help with her fighting skills. You should join us. We haven't worked on that in a while, and I'm sure your technique has suffered." I shoot him a grin. It's a point I've made to him on numerous occasions, even when we were actively training. Everything starts off well and good, but as soon as something trips his temper, it's like everything he's learned goes out the window, and he just throws his fists around to win any fight.

Dane frowns at me but doesn't rise to the bait and goes back to whatever hacking or research he's been doing on his computer.

Huh.

"Something on your mind there, Rapunzel?" He's too quiet. Something's wrong.

"Do you actually care about Raegan again, or is she just your next fixation now that Aiden has put an end to street racing while we're here?"

Now we're getting somewhere. My eyes don't leave the screen as I mow through a swarm of zombies. "I've always cared about her, just like you. She was never anything temporary, and that's not what this is now. I'm done with all the distractions and bullshit I'd been doing before. I'm ready to take the fight to GE, but Thorne proved we all need more work before we can get there."

"I may have cared about her once, but not anymore. She's dead to me." His voice is cold and hard. Even though I know he's just having another temper tantrum, albeit a less in-your-face one, his words hit me like lightning.

I chuck the controller down, and Dane jerks his head around at the clatter. "That's it. I'm sick of your fucking attitude. You heard her say it was an accident. She didn't just wake up one day and decide to murder Vera. Stop acting like that's what happened. And stop taking out all your pain and grief on her for your own fucking issues. She was *sixteen* when it happened. When we still didn't really understand our gifts. We were dumb and didn't push her more for answers back then, and she kept the reason to herself to protect *your* feelings.

"Your hatred of Raegan is a piss-poor excuse for avoiding what you're really feeling, and you need to figure out a way to get over it. Because if I hear you talking about her like that again, I will beat the shit out of you." With those words, I storm out of the room.

CHAPTER EIGHT

RAEGAN

THE TOWER LOOMS OVER me as a monolith of steel and glass. It's unlike any building I've ever seen before in its style. It's not a tall or wide rectangle like they usually are. The front entrance is within a curve of the building, like a very soft and short U-shape that makes me feel like it's welcoming me into its arms. The first few stories are stacked on top of each other, just steel and windows, but once I count ten windows up, it shifts.

Rather than going straight up, the left side starts to open with green courtyards. The first one is the largest, and then the next level up has its own courtyard that hovers above it but a bit shorter to not sit right on top of the other one. And on and on until the courtyard balconies get smaller and smaller, as does the enclosed floor of the building until it reaches the top.

I attempt to break in through a window, any window, but they're sealed on all four sides. I try the front door next, even pulling out my lock-picking kit from Jackson's hoodie pocket—that I'm borrowing—to see if I can get inside.

This building has been shut down since GE attacked it a few weeks ago. There are *Closed for renovation* signs posted all over the place, from the doors and windows to a sign out front. When Aiden had been ready to bring its residents back in, we'd learned about Vera being alive, and he'd stopped that plan. Apparently, this building pretty much runs on technology. From its security system, to doors opening, meal ordering, communications, everything. It's too much of a risk to stay here when Vera could easily lock us all inside.

He'd cut the power to the building and then locked it up so no one would have access to it while it was unoccupied, but I didn't realize how serious the locks on it would be.

My hand trembles with effort in trying to hold down a pin in the lock with my pick, and then it snaps. In the lock.

Shit.

I try to dig it out with my nails but can't get enough of a grip on what's sticking out to do anything. It's staying there. Well, at least that means others can't try to do the same thing, right?

"Do you go out of your way to be a pain in the ass for me, or is this just your natural state now?" a voice that's smooth as cognac croons behind me.

I sigh and drop my head. "Despite what you think, my decisions have very little or nothing to do with you, Aiden." I look at him over my shoulder while still crouched down in front of the door handle. "Did you follow me?"

His brown eyes, so dark that they look black more often than not, give me a hard stare. "Contrary to *your* belief, not everything is about you either." Aiden steps up next to me and grasps the handle of the door I'd just broken. "I was already on my way here when I saw you trying to break into my building. Why is that?"

The pin that was stuck in the lock gets pushed out by his gift and tinkers when it falls to the concrete between us.

He stares down at me, and I feel small beneath him and that look. It reminds me of all the times he'd cornered me in the past to chastise me. Or that one time...when he'd finally kissed me in the library and took my breath away. I'd compared every kiss off the island to his, and they never came close.

Until Kellan and Jackson.

But theirs were different than Aiden's and each other. Just as unique and panty-melting in their own ways.

Wait. Why am I thinking of kissing him?

I stand up to shrink that distance he has lording over me while I'm on the ground. It helps. Not a lot, but it's something.

"I'm here to look for clues. See if GE left anything behind while they were here." What I can't tell him is that there's a chance Gordon may have done exactly that just for me. Because in his delusional mind, he might think he still has some sort of control over me, and I'd actually *want* to go back to him.

The very idea makes me sick.

Aiden studies me, and I know he's trying to read what I'm not saying. He used to be able to do that with me once before, but I've changed too much in our time apart. And so has he. Now, I'm little more than a stranger whose motives he hasn't been able to figure out yet.

Unfortunately for him, he can't read my body language as well as Elias can. And he can't see straight through to my soul like Jackson.

"The Guild floor was cleaned up weeks ago. If there had been anything left behind, it was either found, or it's gone now."

If Gordon had left something, I doubt it would have been recognizable as anything to anyone tidying up. Then it clicks what he just said to me. "You said it was found. Did you find something, then?"

Aiden offers me a cold smile. "There are two rules in life," he starts, and my brows pinch with confusion about what feels like a change in topic. "Number one: never give out all the information."

I wait for him to give the second rule, and his smile shifts to a smirk. He turns the handle of the door, and it opens without any resistance. His words sink in, and I scowl. What an asshole.

He holds the door open for me and waves his hand inward for me to enter first.

"You're letting me in?"

"Better to be here and see what you're doing than have you come back another time without supervision."

Just what I need. Aiden breathing down my neck as my own personal chaperone. My skin prickles with goosebumps at the imagery that came with that, and I scrub at my arms roughly to knock that shit off. Him being so close to me is not hot or sexy. It's claustrophobic.

The more he tries to keep me under his thumb, the more I debate running.

I've been on my own for five years, and I got used to that freedom. There was no checking in with the group about what I was doing or why. I just did it.

He raises his eyebrows at me when I don't immediately move inside. "Well?"

I huff and storm past him to enter the foyer. As much as letting him stalk me through the building pisses me off, I'm not going to pass up the opportunity to look around. I doubt I could get inside if I wanted to. Not unless I was willing to break the door or glass to do it. And I'm not looking to give GE easy access to this building because of me.

The main foyer is big and open, with more windows than walls. There's the security desk right in the middle that you have to pass through before you can make it to the elevators. Since no one is here and everything is off, I walk right through.

"We'll need to take the stairs. I assume you wish to go to the floor where the fight happened?" Aiden asks. I nod, knowing he's probably drilling holes in the back of my head while trying to figure out what I'm expecting to find here. "That's the Guild's main hall on the eleventh floor."

Ugh. Eleven floors up? Why didn't it seem like that many when I came here to rescue them?

He opens the door to the stairwell, and I glare at the flights of stairs. My legs are still sore from Kellan splitting me in half in the woods this morning, but I'd rather stick a needle in my eye than mention that to Aiden. I huff and get started up the long trek.

Aiden doesn't say a word as he follows behind me. All I know is that I'm panting for air when I finally see the big number eleven next to the door and Aiden's staring calmly at me in his navy suit. Is he for real? I must have that very expression on my face when I'm looking at him. "I take the stairs. It's an easy way to stay in shape while still doing other things."

"You're not human," I gripe.

He smirks and opens the door for me. "Yes, that is debatable. But then the same goes for you if that's true."

We enter the eleventh floor, and it's massive. The entire room is at least two stories high, with a hundred feet of the ceiling arched in a dome made of panels of glass in a diamond pattern on one side. There are doors that lead out to the large courtyard. It's like a well-manicured garden of plants and trees, with gazebos and picnic tables or areas of green grass. Maybe calling it a park would be more accurate.

The area under the half-dome is filled with long wooden tables, sofas, cushioned chairs, and even a standalone bar. Once you're back under the rest of the building, the ceiling is vaulted with massive wooden beams. The tables continue into this room up to a large rustic bar and stools. Between doors and corkboards along the back wall, a flight of stairs leads up to a short, open second floor that sticks out over the bar.

Aiden watches my face and then looks around the room like he's trying to see it from my eyes. I guess when something is in front of you day in and day out, it's hard to step back and really appreciate what you're looking at. "This is the Guild's main hall. It's where members can hang out, eat, or pick out jobs. The floors below are the general offices for various businesses, all worked by Guild members. Their apartments are the floors above, and of course, the Loft."

His eyes scan over an area in the middle of the room that's bare. It looks like tables used to be there, but they were probably destroyed in the fight. Aside from some blank spaces like that, no one would know anything had happened here. Aiden slides his hands into his trouser pockets and turns to me. "Now's your chance to look for whatever it is you think you'll find. You have"—he whips his phone from his pocket to look at it—"twenty minutes before I kick you out."

Only twenty minutes? In a room this big?

"Nineteen minutes and thirty seconds," he amends when I don't move.

Fuck a duck.

I take off to the nearest wall and decide to work from the perimeter inward. I check for anything on the floor, carvings on tables, something on a wall. Anything that might trigger a memory of my year under Gordon. I'm expecting the tables to be marked up, carved, or even the rude bubble gum user sticking it under the tables, but there's no sign of it.

There are a few marks and cuts here or there, but they don't look like the work of someone purposefully marking it up with a knife.

What kind of people are in this Guild?

It makes my task that much easier, though, since I would clearly see anything out of the ordinary. Not only are the tables and benches long, but there are a ton of them.

A jingle tune starts up, and I look around to find Aiden sitting at one of the tables and looking at his phone. "Time's up."

Did he seriously set a timer for me? What am I? A child? "I'm sorry, am I taking up too much of your precious time?" I snark at him while still peering under the current table.

"You are. I have someplace I'm supposed to be."

"Then go. I'm not keeping you here." I look up and search around the room to better prioritize where I think a clue might be left.

Aiden scoffs and stands, sticking his phone and hand into his pocket. "I gave you twenty minutes of uninterrupted time to sniff around my Guild. If you haven't found anything, then I doubt there was anything to begin with." I glare at him, and he tilts his head to the side. "What did you think you'd find here? A note from

Gordon?"

My body tenses on reflex, and his eyes narrow when he sees it.

He stalks over to me, and my heart pounds with every click of his shiny black shoes on the wooden floor that echoes through the grand room. I step back when he doesn't appear to be slowing down and fall onto the bench.

Aiden grabs me by the throat and shoves me back until my head meets the table and my back arches. He leans over me until there's no space between us, and his face is all I can see. "Ow," I growl at him, even though it didn't actually hurt. He'd bent me to his will by his presence more than brute force.

"I'm getting really tired of you keeping secrets from the rest of us. One of these days, they are going to get one of us killed because we don't have all the facts. Either you're with us, or you're against us. There is no in-between anymore."

I swallow roughly, and fortunately, his grip allows it.

"I can't keep the others safe if everyone is running off in different directions because of you."

"I have nothing to do with what the others—"

Aiden's fingers squeeze to cut me off. "You are either blind or willfully ignorant. I know you're not stupid. Jackson has been off doing his own thing for you since you showed up. Dane snuck out after Vera with you in tow after you agreed to free him. I'm sure he hasn't given up, and he's planning something else. Then you're sneaking out and poking around my Guild with no explanation."

His lips move to my ear, and he whispers in that velvety tone of his. Like he's telling me a dark, dirty secret. "If I could tie you up at the firehouse to keep you from causing trouble right now, I would. You're lucky you have the gift you do, or else that's exactly where you'd find yourself right now." The smell of cinnamon floods my senses as I breathe him in, and my shameful body reacts to all of it.

His voice. His scent. Even the threat of him tying me up in his attempt to control me has my heart fluttering.

More evidence there's something wrong with me.

His grip loosens, as if he thinks that's the end of it, but I take that opportunity to fight back his fire with my own. "You're never going to control me, Aiden. You and I both know it, and I can see how it tortures you so."

His eyes flare with heat. He pushes me back down with his body, the air between us sweltering as he presses into me and sets my heart racing frantically in my chest. Aiden's hand twitches around my neck, and I can see the battle warring in his face of what he *wants* to do and what he *should* do. We stay in that position for what feels like ages. Long enough that my body tingles and trembles from my unhinged heartbeat and not enough oxygen.

Finally, he releases me. "We'll see," he answers slowly, and it sounds like a dark promise. He steps back, straightens his jacket, and fixes his tie. I cringe at the twinge of pain from the awkward angle I'd been in, but it passes quickly.

"Get up. You're coming with me while I run my errand, and then we'll both return to Old Red."

I'm tempted to be a brat and ask him why—he just really seems to bring that side out of me—but I'd rather not waste any more time if Kellan's going to be training me tonight. I know Aiden doesn't want to let me out of his sight, and I'm also curious to see what he was up to coming here. If I'm to believe he wasn't actually following me.

He leads us to the kitchen through the bar area, and then to the pantry or stock room. He moves some empty shelves aside and inserts a small piece of metal into what appears to be the gap between two concrete slabs. After a click, the floor pops up by two inches. Aiden presses the floor down and slides it to the side, creating enough space for a body to fit.

"There's a ladder. Climb down, and I'll meet you at the bottom." His face is unreadable when I stare at him. His threat of tying me up haunts me, and I'm getting the distinct feeling that this might be his alternative. Lock me away in a concrete box somewhere in the middle of a fifty-ish story building?

"Uh, I think I'll just head back."

"Don't you want to learn my secrets?" Aiden purrs, and a trickle of fear slides down my spine at his threatening undertone.

"Not if you're keeping them in a dark pit of hell. You can have them." I turn on my heel and walk out because. Fuck. That. It reminds me a little too much of solitary on the island, and I'd rather not go through that again, thank you very much.

Aiden takes my arm to stop me. "You're going down there, Raegan. Either on your own or with my help. Don't make this harder than it needs to be."

Oh, fuck no. I yank my arm from him, but his grip doesn't budge, and then his other hand takes my other arm so he's between me and my escape. He pushes me toward the hole in the floor, and my feet push and kick at the floor in an effort to stop moving.

"Aiden, wait. Wait. Wait!" I scream in panic when my foot slips just a little over the edge.

"Are you going to tell me your secrets now?" he murmurs softly in my ear.

I bite my lip as I wrack my brain for something, *anything*, I can think of giving him.

"I didn't think so," he says way too soon, and then he pushes me into the hole.

I scream as I fall into darkness, my voice echoing around the concrete walls until my body crashes into something soft. I feel around me, and whatever I'm on shifts and sounds like rice when it moves. Is this...a fucking bean bag?

The entire room goes pitch black, and I gasp when my memories shove to the forefront. The cold, dark room. Alone for hours, *days*, with just me and my thoughts.

Then light bursts over me, and it snaps me out of it before my memories can fully sink their claws in. I squint up and find Aiden watching me with a pinched brow and a frown before he quickly covers it up with the clearing of his throat. "You ready yet?" he casually asks like he didn't just throw me into a terrifying hole and then trap us in complete darkness. He moves to another wall, shining the flashlight from his phone over it, and does something that makes it slide open like some Batman shit. Then he turns expectantly to me.

He really made me think he was going to lock me in here. I thought I was going to *die* or break something, at the very least from that fall, without knowing how far down it was. It wasn't far at all, considering how his hair is almost touching the ceiling.

Fury twists in my chest at his deception. Did he think that was *fun*? Or was it just a fucking power move against me?

As if reading my rage, he responds tightly, "I gave you a chance to go down the ladder, and you refused. Remember that the next time you think to go against my instructions."

"You're a sadistic *bastard*," I snap, pushing myself upright from the oversized bean bags. "I fucking hate you."

He gives me a sardonic smirk. "And I, you."

We travel downstairs in the dark with the flashlight to guide the way for a long fucking time. It's probably about thirty minutes, but with him, it feels like forever. I'm still in disbelief over what he'd done, what lengths he was willing to go to pry my secrets from me.

If only he knew my secrets would change nothing in this fight.

They'll just change what he thinks of me. What the others think of me.

It'll shatter whatever self-confidence I've built up over the last few years, the moment I see how they look at me after that. It'll destroy me.

We reach a large wooden door, and Aiden stops before it and turns to me. "Against my better judgment, I'm going to show you something. Whether I believe you're a sleeper agent or not is moot, as the others wouldn't let you go at this point, anyway. I will find out the truth, but until then, expect to be with one of us at all times so we can make sure you aren't communicating with the enemy."

I roll my eyes at him. "If this is your S&M room, then I'll just wait out here until you're done."

He stares at me, and I swear I see his hand twitch. Then he opens the door and ushers me in.

There are multiple doors in this empty room. All the same, stainless-steel appearance, so none of them look different from the rest. Except for the one he stands in front of, where there's a tiny sliding slot that opens after he knocks in an odd rhythm. The slot closes just as quickly as it opens, and then there's a loud thump, and the door opens.

The next room is clearly a security room with all the computers, monitors, and cameras on the wall. Someone greets Aiden, who he acknowledges with a smile and a nod, but we breeze through the room to another one. He moves so quickly that I barely have time to look at everything we're passing. We walk down more stairs, until I wonder how the ever-loving-fuck I'm going to have the stamina to get out of here when he's done with his "errand."

I see at least a medical area, offices, a greenhouse or growing area, and further down, we walk into a large, open room that has a similar feel to the Guild main hall. Only greener.

It's probably only a third of the size of the main hall, but its style and layout are roughly the same, with fewer tables and minus everything that had been under the half-dome. The place is flourishing with plant life. Trees, bushes, flowers, vines. There's greenery everywhere, like a jungle has overtaken the room, and the people are just living around it.

Though, if I look close enough, the plants aren't encroaching on any of the tables or areas where people are walking around. Organized chaos.

We walk by a mini waterfall coming out of a random wall in the room that then moves down a raised platform like a bubbling brook and then drops over the edge of the floor to another one, just like this, below it.

It's...beautiful.

My hands curl around the railing as I look out over the rest of the area and all the people eating and laughing at the various tables.

"Welcome to our temporary Guild."

"This is where everyone went?" I ask, unable to keep the amazement from my voice. I remember how he was working hard to fix the Tower to bring everyone back, and I had imagined they were all hiding away in an abandoned building somewhere. Kind of like we are in Old Red. But this?

"We're deep underneath the Tower. The bunker has its own separate utilities for everything. Air. Water. Electricity. All hidden underground and apart from the building above us."

Wow. Words aren't enough to describe the wonderment of this place. And the liveliness of the people in it.

"Follow me. I just need to speak with someone, and then we'll leave."

He's offering me a glimpse into what he's built—or expanded on—and what else he's fighting for. I've heard them all talk about the Guild, but I never imagined anything like this. It's humbling.

I nod.

We walk over to one of the occupied tables, and I immediately recognize one of the people there. Her red hair is vibrant amongst all the greenery, and her voice rings out with laughter.

Cassandra looks up when we approach, and her eyes widen and sparkle when she spots Aiden. "Aiden! I didn't know you were going to be stopping by today. Will you be visiting for a while?"

He smiles kindly at her, and I almost break a tooth off with how hard my teeth grind at the sight of it. "I'm not here long. I'm just looking for Claudia."

Her face falls with disappointment, and it's only then that she notices me. She makes a face, like she thinks I'm the reason he won't be sticking around. Which, maybe it's not entirely false, but I'm not against either.

"Cassandra, you remember Raegan," Aiden re-introduces us when neither of us says anything. I'd been in the van when she'd healed Jackson and the others, but it'd been easy to ignore each other when she was so focused on healing them. Thankfully, I hadn't needed her services.

"Of course." She plasters on a fake smile, just for his benefit.

Aiden gives me a look, and I think I hear my tooth crack. "Thank you for healing everyone the other night," I offer her stiffly. I am grateful, but I'd be a hell of a lot more grateful if she'd stop touching the guys and looking at Aiden like she plans to get herself pregnant with his baby so he'll marry her.

"Well, aren't you two frosty?" A voice chuckles from the other side of Aiden, but when I look, no one's there.

Aiden's hand snaps out to grab air. It closes around something, and then the chuckle returns. A wrist slowly appears in Aiden's grasp, and then, like a magic blanket being pulled away, a man is standing there.

He's closer to my height, with short blond hair and blue eyes that shine with mirth. His lips are spread into a wide grin as he looks past Aiden to me. In his grip is Aiden's phone, which he drops into Aiden's outstretched hand.

"I'll get you one day, Master," he chortles, as if stealing Aiden's phone is some sort of game to him. And it must be, because Aiden doesn't seem the least bit perturbed by it, and he would be *livid* if I stole his phone. I'm sure of it.

And also. *Master?*

"You're still breathing too heavily," Aiden replies calmly instead.

"So, who's this? A new member?" the man asks, moving around Aiden. He takes my hand and kisses the back of it before my brain can wrap around what's happening. I think it's still in shock at seeing Aiden's smile and then him *not* reprimanding an attempted theft.

I've walked into an alternate universe. We went too far underground.

It's the only explanation.

"She's a quiet one, isn't she?" he says teasingly, arching his eyebrow at me.

Aiden's dark stare falls on me, and I can see the difference in the way he looks at me compared to them. This must be the difference between being liked by Aiden and hated. "No, she's not."

"Hm, well then." He suddenly holds my chin and strokes his thumb across my lips. "Cat got your tongue then, sweetling?"

I smack his hand away at the same time as Aiden growls and positions himself between us. "Don't touch her, Harvey."

Harvey's eyebrows jump up to his hairline, and he whistles lowly. "Is this your girl?"

My pulse does a weird hopping beat, and my breathing shallows. I almost intervene to scoff that idea off and say something cutting to Aiden. It's better to ruin it myself than have confirmation of his hatred repeatedly. But masochistic curiosity holds my tongue, and I wait for his response instead.

Aiden looks at me, and I think he expected me to cut in as I normally would. When I don't, his gaze slides back to Harvey. "She can kill you with one touch. It's better you keep your distance."

Why. Why do I do this to myself?

Harvey laughs and plants his hands on his hips. "If she's yours, that's all you have to say, Master. No need to make her a pariah over it." He leans down to whisper in my ear. "If you ever want to just disappear for a while, you come find me."

Aiden fully moves between us, so Harvey is forced to step back, but he's still grinning at me like the Cheshire Cat. "I'll see you around...Raegan." He holds his hand up in a farewell and wiggles his fingers, and then he vanishes.

Raised voices shout behind us, and I spin around to see what's happening. A table flies into the air, and something, or someone, crashes into another table, and it breaks. Aiden sighs behind me like this is all so tiresome.

Vines lift someone in the air and more shouting ensues.

"Uh, are you going to do something?" I point to where four people are apparently fighting. Gifts in use and everything.

A tall, dark-skinned woman steps up on the other side of Aiden, where Harvey had been. Her hair is black and just long enough to frame her face, shining under the lights. She's wearing a pencil skirt with a white button-down blouse, stockings, and heels. She looks the part of a businesswoman, and her presence fills the room.

"I'll handle it. And dock their pay for the broken tables," she says softly. They're both watching it passively, and I hate that I don't understand anything that's happening here.

"Wait and see how they handle it first," Aiden replies.

She nods, and then her striking amber eyes fall on me. She smiles warmly. "I'm sorry you had to see this. I'd say that this is uncommon, but our members are a passionate bunch."

"Do they not get along?" I ask, because she seems kind enough to share something with me, while Aiden is happy to leave me in the dark. It just reminds me that I'm here as a tagalong, so I'm not unsupervised. Not because he was looking to share this side of his life with me.

And where do the others fit in with the Guild? Are they considered members?

"They do. They just…" she considers her words and then continues, "Have a bit more fun in their disagreements."

That doesn't make any sense to me still. How is fighting with their gifts, where they could hurt one another, just be fun?

The woman nods at my confusion. "In a world where we have to hide who and what we are, this is the only place they can freely be themselves. That means using their gifts when they're upset or happy or having fun. Just like you can use your hands to hold or to high five or to hit, gifts can be very much the same."

Her words almost echo what Kellan was trying to tell me earlier. Was this what he meant? But that can't apply to me. Sure, others might be able to do fun things with their gifts, but not me. I can't play around with my gift.

"I'm Cibrina, by the way. I run operations here at the Guild. I presume that you're Raegan?"

"You know about me?"

Her eyes slip to Aiden, and her smile deepens. "I've heard about you. And when you arrived in the city."

Aiden clears his throat. "Cibrina, would you mind keeping Raegan company? I have a short matter to deal with."

"Of course." She nods with a smile.

He disappears around a corner.

"So, how did you meet Aiden? Or find the Guild?"

Cibrina hums softly. "Well, I found the Guild first. I'm an attorney who likes to help gifted clients, in particular. When one of them mentioned the Guild to me, I joined and became its exclusive lawyer."

"Was that when…Thorne was in charge?"

"Mm. Indeed. Though, I can count on one hand the number of times I saw him, let alone spoke to him." Her gaze flicks around us before returning to me. She continues in a hushed tone, "He kept his distance from the members and used intermediaries to approve or post the jobs he wanted done. Distancing himself made it harder for anyone to catch on to what he was doing, so we're all grateful to Jackson for getting close to him and revealing his true goal."

I'm not so sure that Jack had gotten close to him on purpose like that, based on what Kellan told me, but I keep that thought to myself and merely nod.

She straightens and resumes her normal volume. "Anyway, I met Aiden when he stepped in to become the new master of the Guild. It started with me demanding to know who he was and what happened to Thorne and, for some reason, he decided to trust me and told me the truth. I helped smooth his transition in with the rest of the Guild, and he made me the director of operations once he saw what I could do with my gift."

"And what's that?"

She smiles and lifts her hands up as if there's a keyboard in front of her. Gold light in the form of lines fades in to the air around her, forming a glowing outline of keys and a screen. "It's called Archive." Her fingers dip and rise over the intangible keyboard. Golden text appears on the screen.

Raegan LaRoux

Age: 22 years old

Birth day: September 26th

Gift: Disintegration

Gift type: Tangible

I'm not sure what's more shocking; the fact that she knows my gift, or my birthday. I didn't even remember when that was. The text keeps scrolling upward and revealing more information about me. No! There's still a room full of people here who could read it. I swing my head back and forth to make sure no one is watching us, then step forward and reach out, as if I can swipe it away. The gold light fades out.

Cibrina gives me a kind smile. "I'm sorry. I hope I didn't upset you. Showing my gift rather than explaining it is easier."

"No, it's—I'm okay. I'm not used to sharing so much about myself with others. How did you know all that about me?"

"Well—" Her smile curls. "I may have gotten that from Aiden."

I draw in a frustrated breath. Aiden.

She must read my expression, because she waves her hand. "Oh, it's not that he specifically offered that information to me." She taps the side of her head. "Everything I hear and see automatically gets stored in my Archive gift so I can pull it up again later. Even if it's information made as a passing comment. And it's not something I can turn on and off."

"Oh," is all I can manage. That gift is...a bit terrifying. Does that mean this entire conversation is being recorded by her gift? Is it picking apart everything we're saying?

"Thank you, Cibrina," Aiden says, rejoining us. His dark gaze sweeps over me, and I press my lips together. "I hope I didn't keep you waiting too long."

"Not at all," she answers.

He turns to face her fully. "While I'm here, I wanted to let you know I've received your request, but I haven't changed my mind."

"They want to fight, Aiden. They have every right to join you," she pushes.

"Look at them. They aren't ready for what it might cost. This is my fight, not theirs. I won't involve them."

Cibrina purses her lips but nods. "I'll let them know."

Aiden's hand finds the small of my back. "Thank you. I'll be back again soon, but I have some things at home that I need to fix first."

Her smile returns, and she moves her attention to me. "Of course. I'll be here if you need anything. It was a pleasure to meet you, Raegan."

"You too. This has all been...uh, enlightening."

Cibrina laughs softly. "I'm sure it has been. Please come visit again." She walks away, her heels clicking on the floor.

When I look back at where the fight had been, it's already cleaned up and quiet. A woman, tall and lithe, with long, straight black hair, glances up to see Aiden and stands. She strides over to us with something in one hand.

"Aiden," she says to him with a respectful bow of her head.

Okay. I can't do this anymore.

I turn away and start walking back the way we came. I'll guess my way back and ask for directions if I have to, but I need a minute. I knew Aiden would be a great leader one day. That he would help and protect others like he had our little group. And I *know* why I've been excluded from his protective bubble. Why he left me behind on the island with our enemies rather than talk and figure it out.

But seeing what he's built...how everyone looks at him with respect and...almost reverence, as if he's somehow saved them from something...

Tears sting at the corners of my eyes.

I wish I had been one of them. Someone he'd helped or tried to save.

Not a lost cause.

Even though he knows what happened with Vera now...he still treats me like a traitor. He doesn't trust me.

I'm an outsider and always will be.

So, watching what it's like for those on the inside...seeing his protectiveness over others compared to his severe mistrust of me...

It hurts.

Aiden catches up with me by the time I make it up the first set of stairs, probably because I'm still too worn out to take them quickly. He doesn't say anything to me; just takes up the front to lead the way. We go through a different door after the security room and take a new route that lets us out at some bar in the city. I'd wonder about it if my brain wasn't already overwhelmed with information.

I don't even know how we made it back to Old Red. All I know is that not a single word was spoken between us. I go straight to my tiny-ass room and lock the door behind me so I can be alone.

Chapter Nine

RAEGAN

I ALMOST BACK OUT of Kellan's training session tonight, but I'm able to argue myself back into it. I can't just run away because I don't feel like it. GE could attack at any time, even if I'm in a mood like this. So, no excuses.

I rally myself up to find Kellan and get it over with. He starts me in the weight training room, saying I need to build up my muscle strength first, and then he works me to the bone until my body is quivering from exhaustion. But it's a good muscle burn that makes me feel like I'll already be stronger tomorrow.

He only poked at my sour mood once, and after I snapped at him to leave it, he thankfully let it go and got back to business as my ruthless trainer.

I make it through another day, another training night, before my skin itches with the need for something. I don't know what it is at first, and I wander aimlessly throughout Old Red. Dane is zoned into his laptop, and Kellan is playing his zombie game in the living area. Aiden is sitting at the dining room table with his phone.

Where is Jackson?

And I realize that's it. I've only seen him once since he woke up from his healing sleep, and it was such a fleeting encounter. I need to see him. He'll be able to calm the chaos in my mind, even if it's just while I'm with him.

I check his room, knocking first and then letting myself in when he doesn't answer. He's the only one I would do this to because I know he wouldn't mind. His bed is unmade, the sheets a tangled mess and half on the floor like he'd been caught up in a nightmare the last time he was in it. For some reason, it feels odd to see proof that he sleeps. He seems...superhuman.

When does he sleep? Aside from when a healing forces it on him. When was the last time I'd seen him eat anything?

A breeze sweeps through the room, and I hurry to the open window to look outside. "Jack?" I call out, searching around the yard and then up at the roofline. I can't see anything from here, but I can feel it. In the way my heartrate picks up and the rush of adrenaline in knowing he's nearby. Maybe it's a sixth sense, or my other senses are picking up on him at a lower level than I can recognize.

Carefully, I crawl onto the window, twisting around to sit on it, and then stand while holding the top trim. I reach up to the edge of the roof, pushing to my tiptoes, as my fingertips swat at the roof. I strain harder when I finally feel the rough tile, but then my foot slips, and I drop.

A hand grabs mine above me, and I look up. Jackson smiles at me with that dimple and says, "You knew I'd catch you."

"I knew." Butterflies are having a field day in my stomach, and I feel a little weightless in my chest.

His smile grows. It would be pretty on his full lips if his eyes weren't shining with wickedness. There's something different about them tonight. Like the mask he wears to appear human and good is slipping, and I'm getting a glimpse of the monster underneath.

Air pushes under my feet to guide me up to him. His hand isn't actually needed on mine, but he keeps hold of me anyway, even when my feet meet with the roof.

"What's wrong?" His blue eyes search mine, and his body tenses. It's like he's preparing himself to attack whoever or whatever's upset me just as soon as I give him a direction. Or a victim. Because they certainly wouldn't survive him.

"Nothing," I start, to which he angles his head to the side. "Nothing I want to talk about. Right now."

Jackson stares at me—no, *through* me, it seems—straight into my heart and soul until he finds whatever he's looking for, and then he nods. "What do you need, little one?"

My cheeks heat at what I want to say, but also don't want to admit. Does it sound stupid? Am I willing to tell him why I sought him out? That I've been drowning in my thoughts about Aiden and the Guild for the last day, and I can't get my head above water.

Jack draws me close and strokes my face from my temple down to my jaw, then back up to push my hair behind my ear. Closing my eyes, I take a deep breath of his fresh, fall scent. It hits me then how weird it is for me to compare his smell to autumn. To the smell of dead leaves. Would he be upset if he knew that was what I smelled when he was near?

"Say it," he commands, and I feel compelled to do anything he asks when it sounds like that.

"You. I need you." I hate feeling so vulnerable. So *exposed*.

The unfiltered obsession in his gaze shines through. I realize it's probably not healthy to want that amount of attention from anyone, but it's too late for me now.

I could get addicted to that look. In fact, I might already be hooked.

He doesn't need any further persuasion from me. His hand at my ear curls around to the base of my neck, sending tingles down my neck and body like pop rocks on my tongue, and his full lips take my breath away.

His kiss is languid but firm and coated in darkness. I couldn't tell just from talking, but when he kisses me, I feel closer to him. The connection we have between us comes into focus when we kiss. I can *feel* him in a way that I couldn't before. I feel the fine tremor in his hands that hold me. The overly-controlled ministrations of his mouth on mine.

It's like he's holding himself back, forcing his demons at bay.

I push his hood back, lacing my fingers through his obsidian locks and gripping tight. I yank his head back to stop the kiss. "You're holding back," I accuse him.

He smiles at me. Not sweetly or sarcastically. No, this one is sharp and dangerous. A smarter person would be afraid of him. But I've already come to accept that I have nothing to fear. Everyone else should run screaming. "I'm in a mood."

Well, that's an understatement.

"What happened?"

"I received another message from Thorne." I release him and take half a step back, but Jackson pulls me back into him. "I'll take care of it. It's just taking me a minute to get it out of my head." He kisses the side of my neck, and I instantly angle my head to grant him more access.

"What did it say?" I ask breathily.

"Nothing important," he murmurs, sending a throb of desire between my thighs. His voice sounds a bit off when he says it, but I'm too distracted by his touch on my neck, and when I go to reach for the thought again, it slips through my fingers.

"I don't know if I can hold myself back right now," he admits.

My pulse accelerates. "Then don't."

There's so much in his eyes when he looks at me; it would be impossible for me to pick out every single one.

"Show me. I want to see all of you, Jack. Not just the mask you wear for the world. Give me your demons."

His body shudders at the request. I can tell he's unsure, but I wasn't asking. And there's no way he'll deny my request, even if I can see the shred of doubt in his gaze. "You won't hurt me," I promise him, an echo of the one he once said to me.

Something knocks my feet out. I gasp when I fall, but a cushion of air catches me before I hit the roofing tile. I drop onto it from an inch above, and then he's on top of me and kissing me with single-minded intensity. His hips press into me, rubbing against my clit, and I groan and wrap my legs around him. We grind into each other until I'm soaked and quivering in his arms.

Jack rips his hoodie and shirt over his head in a single motion, and I hurry to follow suit with my own clothes. I'm desperate to feel his skin on mine.

He moves me onto my hands and knees and then shoves my shoulders down so my ass is up and presented just for him. The cool night air sweeps over my heated skin, and I shiver. His dick glides through my folds, coating himself in my natural lube while also running across my clit. He inserts two fingers without warning and curls them inside of me.

I moan and push back against them, opening myself deeper to him, and he takes it all without hesitation. They drive in and out ruthlessly, pushing me higher and higher at a rate too fast to keep up with until my head is spinning. My body shakes uncontrollably when my orgasm creeps up on me too suddenly, my muscles tightening almost painfully as I'm forced to take the pleasure he's feeding me.

Then a third finger joins the other two, and his other hand strokes and flicks my clit, and I shatter.

A scream tears from my throat at the intensity of the orgasm. It hits me hard and fast, rushing through me like a tsunami and then pulling back all my strength as it leaves me just as quickly.

There's a second where I feel the head of his cock pressing at my entrance. But his voice, rough and drenched in shadows, curses. "I don't have a condom." His fingers are brutally gripping my hips as he holds himself back, just barely. I'm sure there'll be bruises there in the morning, but I couldn't care less.

I'm shocked that he's able to stop himself. That he cares. Kellan's fucked me four times now and never once thought to wear a condom.

"It's fine. I'm on birth control." I'd rather not get into the how's or why's about it since that leads back to an ex and the skeletons in my closet.

Jackson pauses only for a beat and then impales me on his long, hard dick.

All the air in my lungs is expelled by that move that feels like I've been skewered. There's no room left except for him.

My body rocks forward with each violent thrust, my forearms scratching against the roofing tile to protect my face as I'm driven into them. Everything about this is wild, hard, and rough. There's nothing sweet or loving about it. This is fulfilling a base need, which just so happens to be me, while exposing the truth of Jackson's current emotional state.

He's furious at something, though I have no idea what could get my calm and confident shadow this worked up. All I know is that I'm *loving* every second of it as I see the real Jackson when his gloves are off.

He's violent. Arrogant. Obsessive. Angry.

Jackson shifts behind me, and his cock scours over a spot that has me seeing stars. I fall apart within a few strokes, and he pounds faster, pushing through my orgasm to chase his own until he comes, his fingers digging into me to hold me still until he empties himself completely.

I re-gather air in my lungs once I've come down from my high, blinking up above us and noticing that the clouds have all gone and revealed the stars. It's beautiful up here, in the woods, without any light pollution to corrupt their glow. When I glance back over my shoulder to tell Jack, he's watching me in the same way I'd just been looking at the night sky.

The violence I'd felt humming beneath his skin has softened.

But it's not gone.

He's not done yet.

He scoops me up in his arms to cradle me against his chest. Then he walks right off the edge and we drift down to his window. He helps me in first, using his gift to keep me from falling, and sets me down on the full bed. Then he hops inside, and our clothes follow him before he shuts the window.

It's the first time I've seen him without the layers of black that keep so much of him hidden. The light in his room shows me everything, including tattoos all in black and shades of gray. There isn't a single one with color.

I don't get the chance to see what they are before he drops to his knees in front of me, then grabs my face and kisses me. It almost feels like he's bowing down to me. Like I'm his queen, and he, my loyal servant.

But he's more than that. Doesn't he realize?

I see something out of the corner of my eye and break the kiss to turn and get a better look at it. There's a tattoo on the inside of his right wrist in the shape of a butterfly. It's just the outline, though, because inside of it is a skull with eyes staring back at me. Beneath the butterfly in thick, bold letters, are two words. *Memento mori.*

"*Remember that you will die,*" he answers my unspoken question.

He's watching me with laser focus while I try to muddle through my sex-addled brain to understand why he would have that as a tattoo. Is it a reminder for himself? Or for his enemies? But, of course, he knows exactly what's going on in my head and elaborates, "It's for me and anyone I meet. None of us are exempt from death. I'm prepared to meet my end, if that's what it takes to win."

I grip his wrist and bring it back to my face, where he automatically cups it in his palm. "Don't say that. You're not allowed to die on me, Jack. No sacrificial shit. You've found me. Now keep me."

His lips curve in his typical, enigmatic smile that tells me nothing of what he's thinking. He drops his head to my neck, kissing and tasting me all at once. His tongue trails a line down my sternum until he's crouched between my thighs. I realize then that the lights are still on, and he can see every bit of me.

Normally, I couldn't care less if someone sees me naked. It's only a body. But with Jackson, it's more than that. He can see right through me, even in all my layers of clothing. Being bare like this seems more intimate than with anyone else. Like he can see all the scars on my soul written on my skin.

"Turn off the light," I pant just as his lips and heated breath run along my inner thigh.

"No." With that, he bites down hard on my thigh when I start to argue, and I cry out instead. He sucks the same spot and chases it with his tongue to ease the initial sting, and I can't help but wonder if that was near or on the same area that Kellan had marked the day before.

He shifts my feet onto each of his shoulders, angling me back on his bed on my elbows to keep me upright enough to watch him as he paints a line with his tongue from my entrance to my clit, flicking it at the very end.

It's a brief tease before he drops all pretenses and sets in to consume me. His cerulean gaze flicks up to mine as he eats me with abandon, and I nearly come from that look alone. Like he'd do anything and everything to please me, and he'll enjoy the fuck out of it too. My arms are shaking from trying to hold myself up, and I finally give in for the sake of grabbing a pillow and holding it over my face to muffle the noises rising unbidden past my lips.

"No one is going to hear us. I'm keeping your sounds all to myself." He chuckles, then returns to licking my pussy like it's drenched in his favorite flavor.

Cool wisps of air tickle and tease along my skin, and I know he's letting his gift out to play. It circles and dances across my flesh in devastatingly slow movements that draw pleasure to the surface of my skin. Every square inch of flesh is caressed and fondled while his tongue works leisurely strokes between my folds, circling my clit with strengthening pressure.

I'm writhing and moaning for him to release me, my hands clawing at the sheets and hips grinding into him. I need *more*. "More. Please, Jack. Touch me. Fuck me."

His tongue rounds my entrance, and his air finds my clit, spiraling it repeatedly with a fine pressure. Then he sinks his tongue inside of me and rubs it along my inner wall, and another orgasm whips through me. Before I can recover, he's replacing his tongue with his cock and thrusting into me. My wanton voice echoes back to me in the room as if it's in stereo.

I think he's just going to take what he needs, but his thumb rubs through our shared cum and drags itself over my overstimulated clit. I jolt from the contact. "Jack, it's too much. I can't—" His lips fuse with mine, and I'm swept away in his kiss. I surrender completely to him, wrapping my legs around him. It hurts so good that I can't stop it.

I think it's impossible for me to go again, but Jackson proves me wrong once again that he knows me better when an orgasm detonates inside me, leaving me boneless and shaking. My body sets off his release and milks his cock dry, greedy to have all of him even as it drips down the base of his shaft and the edge of the bed.

I can't move. My body twitches and trembles beneath him. I have just enough strength to turn my face to look at him.

He looks at me like a man possessed. I'm not sure if I'm soothing the demons inside or just calling them out to play because he looks hungrier for me than before. Like he'll never get enough.

I drag myself backward on the bed, and his eyes track my every movement. "Jackson..." I start, my voice soft and breathless.

My voice stirs something in him, and he moves to follow me, crawling over me to cage me in. "I'll never be done with you, little one."

His tongue finds the pulse in my neck, and he sucks on it, and I just know there's no escape for me tonight until one or both of us passes out from exhaustion.

Chapter Ten

JACKSON

RAEGAN'S BREATHING SLOWS AND deepens beside me. She's lying on her front, arms tucked under the pillows, and her back bare until the sheets crowd around her waist. My hand grazes across her smooth, exposed skin.

She doesn't move.

I don't expect her to. I had no intention of letting her leave my room tonight, which she would have if I hadn't fucked her until she passed out from exhaustion. Now she'll stay in my bed, exactly where she should be, until I return from an annoying but necessary errand.

I push those thoughts aside for a few minutes more and just enjoy this moment.

My fingertips trace along her shoulder blades, following the lines of her body down to the sheet, then circle back up to explore the phoenix tattoo inked at the base of her neck and some inches down her spine. It doesn't take much effort to guess the meaning behind it when the words *"and still I rise"* are written alongside of it.

Another tattoo peeks out from beneath her blonde hair, and I move her locks up and back to get a look at the ink I've seen but never been able to study this closely before. It's a single feather behind her ear, right over where her barcode used to be from GE, that turns into tiny birds at the tip, as if the feather is transforming.

My lips curve into a smile, and I continue touching my fingers to her flesh. I can't help it. I've dreamed of a moment like this for so long. Where I'm no longer forced to watch from a distance and imagine the softness of her skin. I can feel it for myself.

Her warmth causes an ache in my chest and ignites a fire in my bones. I'll do anything to keep this. To keep her safe. I memorize the feel of her skin and her expression of peace and contentment while she sleeps. This is what I fight for. What I will *always* fight for. What I'd put my life on the line for.

For the girl who thinks she's the villain in this story when, really, she's its hero. I still don't know what happened to her on that island or the five years after, but I'm working on learning every detail. Whatever it was, it left her sense of self warped like a funhouse mirror.

My little one thinks she's the one who's changed. She doesn't see that she still has the biggest heart of all of us. That she would willingly put herself on the line for any one of us or someone she deems as innocent. She puts scars on her soul to save and protect others.

Now, it's my job to protect her and take every one of them from here on out. And I'll do it all with a smile.

She shifts a bit in her sleep, and I watch her like a man enthralled. My cock stirs at the sight of her lithe body moving. I'm tempted to sheathe myself inside of her one more time, promising that I'd finally feel like I'd had enough and could leave without looking back. But I won't lie. There will never be enough of her for me.

Rather than disturb her rest, I force myself out of the bed. There's no rest for the wicked, after all.

I dress quickly and silently, each motion deliberate and measured so as not to alert Raegan or anyone else that I'm up and about. I pinch the paper in my pocket and pull it out to look at it again. It's four words, nameless, but I knew exactly who it came from the moment the paper crane drifted in on the breeze.

The fact that he used the crane to send his message is a sick reminder of all the things he knows about me. It was a taunt, and seeing it still makes my blood boil.

I won't let him ruin the meaning behind the crane for me and Raegan. I lift the paper in front of me and then snap my thumb down on the lighter from the same pocket. A tiny flame bursts to life, tasting the air in flickering movements before I bring it to the crane. The fire licks the paper, blackening it as it eats away.

My eyes stay trained on the fire, and I take a deep breath of the burning smell that tempts my inner demons for more. It's too small, though, for me to fully enjoy it. I drop what's left of the paper to the floor, then crush it and the mini flames beneath my boot.

The window in my room slides open easily. I sit on the sill, one foot up in preparation to leave, when I hear movement at my door.

A single knock hits the door before I open it. I doubt anything short of screaming would wake Reagan right now, but I'll still do anything to make sure nothing bothers her.

Aiden's standing there, dressed down in sweatpants and a shirt with his feet bare like he'd either been about to go to sleep, or he'd woken up from it. His eyes glance over my shoulder at the bed and Raegan. I don't try to hide her, nor do I gloat, as Kellan likely would have.

I do lock the knob from the inside and then close the door behind me, stepping into the hall so that whatever conversation Aiden's hoping to have doesn't intrude on her sleep. Locking it won't stop him from trying to storm in and wake her up as he had in his room a week ago, but it'll slow him down to either reconsider or alert Raegan before he comes in.

He hears the click of the lock, and his forehead creases further with whatever thoughts are plaguing his head tonight. I tuck my hands into the front pocket of my hoodie, and I lean back against the door, settling in for whatever he has to say so we can be done with it.

Silence stretches between us.

I'm curious about what he plans to say. Is he going to comment on the fact that she's in my room? Or tell me he thought she'd escaped him, which he now knows isn't the case. I smirk the longer he seems at a loss for what to say.

"She's still keeping things from us."

I cock my head to the side as I study him. His jaw is pronounced from the tension there, and his face is drawn with anger. His hands are fisted at his sides. I can hear his breathing accelerate, telling me that his heart is likely racing as well. For all appearances, he's trying to pretend he's in complete control. But it's clear to me that seeing her in my room has upset him.

I know he's referring to her supposed birth certificate he found.

He told me not long ago, thinking it would win me back to his side, but that in itself is the problem for him.

I've never been on any side but *hers* to begin with.

He doesn't get it yet. There is no us without her.

The birth certificate is just another puzzle piece that I'm going to figure out. And when I get them all, I'm going to put them together until I know exactly what Raegan needs, so I can give it to her.

"Are you keeping things from *us*?" I ask in an almost bored tone. I know that there's more going on between Aiden and Raegan than either of them is letting on. Something happened on the island with them that will explain why there's still so much tension between them.

"What would I be keeping from you?"

I shrug. "I won't push. Just remember that the next time you accuse her of holding back."

When he frowns, I lean forward and lower my voice to a threatening level. "If you want trust, then trust that my loyalty has and always will be with her. And there are no lengths I wouldn't go for her. Even against you."

Her enemies are my enemies. And so long as he draws the line in the sand separating himself from Raegan, he'll know exactly which side I'm on.

I walk away from his stunned face and take the exit door at the end of the hallway.

It's time to hunt the hunter.

The elevator pings and jerks to a halt on the Guild floor. My boot pushes off where I'd been leaning as the doors open into the massive great hall. I pass by the long tables and members without a word to anyone and no one greets me after being gone for the last two weeks.

I'm not here to make friends and everyone knows it.

I do, however, cycle through the various conversations happening in the room until I hear something of interest.

"—and she hasn't returned your calls? That's the fourth person this month! What job did she go on?"

"It was helping someone move or something like that."

"Well, maybe Evie went with them to help unload, too?"

"For three weeks?"

Their conversation fades as I walk down a corridor that leads to the back offices. This isn't the first time I've heard of disappearances. I'd ignored it at first. There's likely a simple explanation for it, especially as some jobs can take time to complete, considering the variableness of requests.

But instinct warns me not to ignore it this time.

I skip the door that leads to my office, which remains perpetually empty, and reach for the one next to it instead.

"—where is she now? No, let them do what they want with her. Just make sure she doesn't come near this city." My hand freezes on the knob at Thorne's words on the other side. "And tell me if she goes anywhere else. I need to know where she is at all times, so he doesn't accidentally find her."

He'd better not be referring to my little one. If she's been found...

I wait for his call to end before opening the door and letting myself in. Thorne jerks his head up when he sees me, but there's nothing in my expression to indicate I'd heard him. He smiles at me as I take my seat on his desk and my eyes land on Thorne's current victim, bound and gagged in the middle of the room.

"Jack! Good timing. I've been having difficulty getting this one to talk. Do you mind working your magic?" He grins widely, no doubt laughing to himself at the play on words he made.

I shrug one shoulder with a look of indifference. "Sure."

He taught me the basics of torture, or "in-depth questioning" as he liked to sugarcoat it, but he was too impatient. Too easily swayed by emotion that he was prone to lashing out and killing his captives before getting the answers he needed.

That's where I come in now.

"What information do you think he has?" I ask in an almost bored tone, resting my face against my fist as I look the man over. He's in a suit, so some sort of businessman I'd guess, but nothing else sticks out to me to show his ties to GE. "Does he know where Raegan is?" I add in, setting the bait.

"He's an attorney that works for the board, so I doubt he'll know where one gifted person is." Thorne wipes more blood from his hands with a rag, then leers at me. "Though it never hurts to ask."

Damn.

He knows my loyalty to him only extends as far as our goals align. He wants to blackmail and use GE to make himself the most powerful man in the world. I want to find Raegan, who I thought had escaped the island from GE until my year-long search for her turned up nothing.

Thorne found me after his people reported someone with a similar gift to his being around. He offered to help find her and train me more on my gift, so I'd be able to protect her better...if I'd help him with GE. If she did get recaptured by them, I'd have a higher chance of finding her with Thorne's resources.

Or so I thought.

"Right," I agree simply. "Any updates since I left?"

He unties his plastic apron and tucks all his torture gear into his office closet. "Nothing new, I'm afraid. Unless this guy gives us something of use. A board member's name would be nice."

"I overheard someone mention another missing Guild member."

Thorne scoffs. "Do you think I keep tabs on everyone in the Guild? I'm sure they're fine and that person's being dramatic. Since when do you care about it anyway?"

"I don't."

"Hmph. Well, don't waste your time on it. See what you can get out of him and make sure you keep any noise contained. No one else should be back here, but you never know."

I give him the nod he's waiting for, so he'll leave the room. I wait until his footsteps are gone before hopping off the desk to approach the attorney. Tugging the gag free, I tilt my head to the side and give him the full weight of my gaze. "Are you an attorney for GE?"

"Please! Let me go. That man kidnapped me out of nowhere. I have no idea what this GE is" – he blinks repeatedly before he looks away – "but I will pay you to release me. I have money. I can help you find whoever you're looking for."

Lies. "I'll let you go if you tell me everything that happened on the phone call before I came in."

The man's face brightens with hope. "Yes! He was talking to someone about a shipment. Said something about having another batch ready at the drop-off location tonight. He was listing off a bunch of things that didn't make sense...what was it? Plants was one of them, mass something or other, invisibility..."

Gifts.

The missing Guild members.

He's kidnapping and selling his own Guild members.

"And?"

"And...Oh! A girl that he's been looking for is causing trouble somewhere. I think it was Ray...Ray something."

Little one.

"Where?"

His eyes round. "Oh, I don't—I didn't hear—"

I pull a knife from my hoodie, flipping it between my fingers, and then slice through the cloth gag. He shrieks when the knife gets close, then drops his head, panting for air when he realizes what I'd done.

Between what the attorney said and what I overheard, I can surmise that she's in the States somewhere with the freedom to move around. It's time I stop hanging around this city waiting for leads and go back out on my own. But before that, I need to take care of Thorne. As soon as he finds out I'm no longer an ally, he'll come after me as an enemy for knowing too much.

And while I'm stronger than I was before, Thorne knows my moves. I'll need help to take him down.

I pull out my phone and dial the first contact on the list.

Aiden.

The safe house is destroyed from the roof inward. The exterior walls are made of brick, so most of it survived intact, save for along the top where the fire had been concentrated. The windows are all broken, giving me a glimpse inside at the charred remains.

I know, without evidence, that Thorne is waiting for me here.

I can practically hear his egotistical voice when I think of the words he'd written to draw me out.

Let me help you.

Clearly, he wants to crow over what he's considering his victory at the safe house and use that to his advantage.

I've done nothing but stew over the fight that happened here two nights ago. When I'd almost lost everything. It should have never gotten to that point.

I'm supposed to be the best there is. Even with Thorne back in the world of the living, somehow, I'd beaten him once before without so many injuries. We'd had the element of surprise then, but there's still something off about him that wasn't there before. I'm loathe to admit that I may no longer be the biggest bad in the shadows as it currently stands.

I'll have to fix that.

There's no point trying to scope out the building to find him before he sees me. He called the meeting between us with his offer, and he won't jeopardize whatever scheme he has by inviting stragglers. I'd kill them without hesitation, just like he'd do the same for me, and all talks would be off the table.

I stroll inside through the open doorway, casually stepping around the larger debris until I find a nice open area that gives me some room to move if needed. My eyes scan the building, automatically running through offensive and defensive opportunities, should a fight ensue.

"You sure took your time." Thorne's haughty voice carries through the darkness.

I smirk in its direction and watch him slowly walk forward into the moonlight shining brightly above us. "I had better things to do first," I reply calmly, as if we hadn't almost killed each other right here two days ago.

His smile is tainted and skewed by the ugly creature he is beneath the skin. I didn't see it when I first met him, but killing a person apparently does wonders in exposing it. Now, it's all I see when I look at him.

My monsters may be violent and bloodthirsty, but they at least serve a higher purpose beyond myself. Thorne doesn't have anyone or anything to help curb his power-hungry nature. No compass to guide him or keep him in check from burning the world down around himself in his desperate grab for ultimate power.

I'd almost followed in his footsteps. I feel the same desire for strength. The obsessive need to be the best. To be able to take down anyone who stands against me if I so pleased. If not for discovering Thorne's true intentions and reminding myself of my purpose in this life, I may have done exactly that.

The world should bow at Raegan's feet for existing in this lifetime with me.

"Ah, your little one, yes?"

"I should cut out your tongue for calling her that, Thorne." My fingers twitch in my hoodie pocket with the urge to follow through on that threat. Years of practiced patience stays my hand. I need to hear what he's offering first.

Thorne drops his gaze to seek out my hands, likely checking to make sure I'm not readying myself to do it, before he laughs and looks back at me. "And yet, you aren't. Which means you're interested in my offer."

The curve of my lips remains fixated in place as I wait for him to get on with it.

He grins and then drags his hand down the large piece of building debris that's beside him. "I thought you might, after witnessing that failure of a fight." His one brown eye snaps back over to me, searching for any sign of anger or distress.

I don't react, and his grin drops a fraction in disappointment. "Now that you have your girl back, I'm sure you're recognizing the severe disadvantage you're in. Gordon is actively searching for her now that he knows where she is. There are waves of agents being dispatched to find and capture that other boy in your group. We are a company of hundreds, maybe even a thousand, and there are five of you. Five of whom I almost cleared the board of single-handedly, I might add."

I catalog everything he's saying and not saying for later inspection. He knows where we're hiding out since he'd sent the message directly to me. He could capture Raegan and Dane at any time, but he hasn't. His loyalty to GE only goes so far before his own personal goals rise above it. And, aside from power, what else would keep him from turning them in and earning higher favor with GE?

Me.

He wants something from me. So long as that fact remains, it will keep Raegan and Dane safe from him.

"Your point?" I ask coolly.

Thorne's wicked grin returns. "I see so much of myself when I look at you, Jack. The same arrogance. The same aptitude for cruelty." He lifts his hand from the debris and claps them together to remove whatever dirt or ash particles he'd picked up. "But you won't be able to protect her with your ragtag group. You and I both saw how close you all came to losing. The others will only drag you both down and put her at risk. Trim the fat that's holding you back. Come with me, and I'll swear to you that no harm will come to your girl. From GE or anyone else. You know that there is no one in this world that could take on both of us."

My head tilts as I peer at him. "You think I'd join Gifted Enterprise?"

He laughs. "Of course not. You'd be joining me and me alone. We'll put on a show for GE to get what we need and then take it over like your friend did with my Guild. We can mold it into whatever we want it to be, and your girl will be safe." Thorne holds out his hand to me. "What does it matter which side you're on, so long as she's safe?"

I stare at his hand and consider what he's saying. "There's a third option." I pull my gaze back up to meet his. "I do this myself."

He retracts his hand, but his expression doesn't change. He thinks he has me. "That may be better than letting the others stick around, but you're outnumbered. Arrogance can only get you so far."

I shrug. "It's only arrogance when my skills don't meet the expectation."

"You almost lost against me," he reminds me.

"And yet, I rose to the challenge to win, anyway. I'm two for two with you, Thorne," I remind him right back.

He smiles coldly. "For now. There will always be someone stronger than you or smarter than you out there. You won't be able to beat everyone on your own. Especially not in a fair fight."

"Then I'll make sure I'm always the deadliest piece on the board."

Chapter Eleven

RAEGAN

The smell of crisp leaves and air edged in winter tickles my nose. I reach out on instinct to pull the source of that scent closer, and my arm falls through air back to the bed. I open my eyes and frown.

Had I dreamed last night? I shift my legs, and the resounding muscle aches tell me it was no dream. Everything hurts. But in a deliciously used way. I've never come so many times in one night, let alone a single marathon session of sex. I can't even remember falling asleep or how it ended. Had I passed out at the end?

I tuck my arm under the blankets I'm cocooned in and slide it over the space next to me.

It's still warm.

I'm torn between wishing he was still here with me and grateful that he's not, so I can skip any awkward or overly intimate morning-after conversation.

Groaning, I drag myself from bed and the bundle of warmth I'm leaving behind to get dressed. I hurry to my room for a change of clothes, take a hot shower, and roughly towel-dry my hair before walking into the main room.

The three that aren't my missing shadow are sitting at the table eating lunch. They look up when they hear me coming, and Kellan grins at me. "Well, if it isn't Sleeping Beauty, awake in time for lunch."

I snatch the bowl of strawberries from the kitchen counter and bring it with me to the table. I've unofficially claimed the chair opposite Aiden's at the head. Dane and Kellan sit on the long sides on either side, and Jack's not usually around or ever sitting at the table, so I'm not sure where he sits. Probably in this seat, and he's been keeping it to himself when he's seen me in it.

I close my mouth around the strawberry as I bite to contain the juices that spill free. I don't know where they have been getting these from, but they are the sweetest and most delicious strawberries I've ever tasted. I can only hope that the bowl keeps refilling every few days.

Kellan shoots me a heated look when I lick my fingers clean. I give him a saucy smile while reaching for another one, then turn my attention to Aiden, who's been staring me down since I sat. "Did I miss something while I was asleep? Are we finally moving in on GE?"

I'm getting antsy sitting around here for so long. My attempt at looking for clues from Gordon the other day failed, and aside from training, I don't feel like I'm doing anything toward my goal.

It's no wonder I made better progress in my short time here alone than they had in the years they've been here.

"Has anyone seen Jackson?" Aiden asks instead, staring pointedly at me. I can't imagine why. The door to Jack's room had been locked from the inside when I left it. There's no way he could have seen me in it. Jackson also promised me that no one could hear us, and I believe him.

I take a bite of another strawberry and slurp the juice, this time while keeping eye contact with Aiden. His lips thin at my noise, and I smile at him. It feels like sweet satisfaction whenever I piss him off. I know it's childish, but it gives me some small burst of pleasure that I can still affect him.

"Nope," I reply, popping the "p" for good measure.

Kellan chuckles and then shoves his plate in front of me. "Haven't seen him since yesterday on the roof," he says to Aiden, even though he's only looking at me.

"What is this?" I point to the sandwich on the plate in a low murmur, just for Kell.

"Eat it. You missed breakfast, and I'm not letting you pass out on me during training tonight." He goes into the kitchen to make himself another one before I can argue that I can make my own.

A knot forms in my throat at the simple but meaningful gesture. I'm so used to doing everything on my own and not having anyone else looking out for me. This right here is just...Oof. I will *not* get choked up in front of them all over it, though. They don't need to know about my time on the streets when I struggled for food. I grab the sandwich and take a large bite to shove any feelings down with it.

When I look up, I catch Dane watching me. His face gives away absolutely nothing of what he's thinking as he stares away unashamedly. I swallow the food. I debate on whether or not I should call him out for it even though I know it'll only trigger his recent asshole reflex, but Aiden intervenes before I have to make that choice.

"I'm still getting the Guild situated for a longer stay and making sure they are secure. We got ourselves somewhere safe; now, it's their turn. We won't be moving on anyone until that is in place."

I work quickly through my sandwich as he talks, pausing halfway through when I realize that sitting around here doing nothing is his plan right now. "That's what *you're* doing. What about us? We can at least keep going at GE before all trails run cold, if they haven't already. My last lead died with the congressman."

"We don't move until all of us are ready, so we don't bring GE to our doorstep or the Guild's. You may not be used to working as a team, but this is the way we do things." Aiden's voice is firm, like he thinks he can shut down my questions, just like that.

I go for another strawberry and bring it to my lips, but don't bite down until after I've spoken. "And if I don't agree? Am I your prisoner here, or will you let me keep doing things the way *I've* been doing them for the last few years? Considering my success rate at getting their attention is pretty high."

He scowls. "We're not trying to get their attention. We're trying to take them down from the top without having to face everyone between us and them first. If we get into a battle of just numbers, we'll lose."

I switch tactics. "What about Thorne? What's our plan for him since he kicked our asses when it was five against one?"

"Keep training with Kellan." He turns to look at Dane. "You should start joining them when you can. Aside from the truck bays and the locker room, this place is livable. We can put a hold on any more updates if needed."

Dane flicks an annoyed look at Kellan, who's grinning at him in a look that spells 'I told you so' all over it.

I finish my sandwich and pick up the plate, stealing one more strawberry for my exit. Sitting still isn't really my style, and neither is following directions. I waited patiently. I heard his plan. It sucks and takes too long. So, I'm taking things into my own hands.

"Where are you going?"

I set my plate down in the sink and turn to Aiden, smiling sweetly. "To the lady's room, why? Did you want to come?"

He gives me an annoyed look and then turns his back on me without taking the bait.

Good.

He doesn't need to follow and see where I'm really going. I stride down the hallway, past the bathrooms and rooms to the very end, where there's a door leading outside and to freedom.

He can do things his way, and I'll do mine my way.

We'll see who gets to the top first.

The university's coffee shop is just as busy mid-afternoon as it is in the morning. With my last lead dead and no secret messages from Gordon, I'm back to square one. Well, almost. I still have everyone who attended the mayor's end-of-summer party who I can investigate, which is what brought me back to the north end of the city.

I'm sure most, if not all, of them have ties to Gifted Enterprise.

I sip the overpriced coffee and pretend to read something on my burner phone so that I look distracted. The amount of money I've spent today, including buses to get here, makes me cringe. I've been getting by at Old Red since the guys have been supplying the food, and I haven't needed to buy anything else, but now that I'm back in hunting mode, I'll need to replenish my funds again.

Hype is too dangerous for me to return to, so I may have to find a regular bar that has no problem hiring me off the books and without identification. It's doable, but a hassle to find the right one.

The bell rings over the door to the coffee shop as another patron enters. I glance up briefly to see if I recognize this one. Average height, brown hair cut short, stuffy professor suit, and a plastic smile. It's Ken Doll from the beach house, who'd been pushing me into taking up his internship opening.

See, Aiden? I'm like a magnet for trouble.

Which I realize isn't the *best* attribute for a girl to have, but I've made it useful for me, and that's what counts.

The last Ken Doll saw of me, I'd gone to congressman Joe's home for food. And neither of us made it back to the party. Luckily for me, the congressman was seen after that night, so his current disappearance shouldn't link anything back to me. He may suspect something happened between us and then the congressman tossed me to the side when he finished with me like the others.

Ken, because I can't remember his actual name, orders his drink at the counter. I push my phone in my pocket, trash my current coffee, and rise to get in line behind him. He shifts to the side counter to wait for his order while I ask for another overpriced coffee.

"I'll get that," Ken speaks up beside me as I'm fishing through what bills I have left.

Game on.

"Oh! Hi…"

"Steve."

"Steve." I smile. *Ken*. He hands the cashier his card while keeping his plastic smile on me. "Thank you."

"Of course." We move to the side counter. "I didn't see you back at the party after you left with Joe."

"I'm sorry. I still didn't feel well after eating and had my friend pick me up and take me home."

"There's no need to apologize. I'm glad we could see each other again then. Are you still interested in the internship at my firm?"

Both of our drinks are pushed across the counter. He takes them and hands me mine.

I blow into the small opening of the lid and the steam warms my lips. "I am, but I was hoping to ask you more about it." *And hopefully find some sort of tie between you and GE.*

His smile widens, and he withdraws his cell phone from his inner jacket pocket. "As you should. I have a meeting to attend, but if you'll put your number in my phone, we can work out a good time for both of us."

"That would be great!" If only I remembered the number of my current burner phone. I whip out my phone instead and start a new text. "What's your number? I'll send you a text so we have each other's numbers."

Ken recites it and I send him a simple message that reads: *Rebecca*.

His phone buzzes, and he checks what I sent him. "Perfect. It was good to see you, Rebecca, but I have to run." He waves with his phone.

"No problem. Thank you again for the drink!" I wave back as he leaves the coffee shop.

I smile behind my drink.

This is a good first step in proving to Aiden that my plans get results.

Something big and warm clamps down over my mouth, and I jolt awake. Fear shoots through my limbs like electricity and sets my heart racing at who could have found me.

"Calm down," a familiar voice says softly above me. Dane waits for the panic on my face to melt away before he moves his hand. My heart is still galloping a mile a minute, and I focus on convincing it not to jump off a cliff. *We're safe; we're fine.* Just another one of the guys breaching my personal space yet again.

"Either you're up and ready in two minutes, or I'm leaving to see Vera without you." Dane leaves the room but keeps the door cracked so I can see his back as he waits for me.

My brain scrambles to put two and two together between still waking up and slowing down the panic. Vera. Out.

Oh, not again.

I throw the blankets off me and dress as fast as possible, knowing that Dane would love the excuse to leave me behind. He's upholding his end of our deal but trying to find a loophole around it. I pack myself with knives and a gun. I know I promised not to harm Vera, but she might not come alone this time.

I'm ready in record time and open my door fully to let him know. Dane frowns when he sees me, his lips thinning to a flat line but staying shut all the same.

All their vehicles are parked in the truck bays of the firehouse. I open the main door, and Dane pushes the motorcycle through it and keeps walking it down the drive. It isn't until we're down a road that he climbs on and starts it.

He hands me a backpack. "Put this on."

"What is it?" I ask while tucking my arms under the straps. It's light, but I can still feel the weight of something inside it.

"It's for Vera," is all he gives me, then jerks his head to tell me to get on.

I frown at him, but I can't imagine that he'd give her anything that would put the others in jeopardy, so I let it go. For now. I hop on after him and tug the helmet over my head before leaning into him.

I feel awkward and guilty as my arms slide around his waist to clasp in front of him. I'm sure he hates this part, having me touch him like this, but it's a testament to how much his sister means to him that he's putting up with it. I try not to cling too close or let my hands move at all from the one spot. I doubt he even notices my efforts, but I try anyway.

The drive to his chosen meeting place is longer than last time now that we're further away from the city. I'm still worn out and tired from Kellan's brutal workout that I find my eyes closing to the lull of the motor. Just a bit of rest before facing off against Vera again, who I'm sure will try harder to kill me this time. No biggie.

Dane's hand slaps over mine and yanks it back in front of him. I jump and blink when I realize I must have dozed off for a second. "What are you doing?" he yells at me from behind his mask.

I lace my fingers back together and give him a quick squeeze in apology. He wouldn't hear anything I try to say behind this helmet while we're driving, so it's the only thing I can think of to communicate that I'm good again. Thank fuck he noticed—and said something—before I fell off the bike.

We make it to the same building and up the fire escape to the roof. "Should I hide somewhere this time or...?" I ask, while handing over his backpack.

"No. Stay where I can see you."

I scoff and shake my head. Does he really think I'm going to sabotage his meeting with Vera after everything I've said? *Apparently, he does.*

We both do our perimeter and roof check, looking for signs of people, traps, weapons, whatever, and then sit before the letter O like last time.

"So, what's in the bag?" I ask again.

Dane looks at me with his lips turned down. "It's nothing."

I sigh and lean back on my hands so I can stare up at the sky. The city lights are too bright, so I can't see any stars. Just endless black with the reflected glow of lights trying to keep pure darkness at bay. "I'm going to find out if you're giving anything to her. May as well show me now, since we have time to kill."

He doesn't answer me for a long time. I assume he's choosing to ignore me until Vera comes when he unzips the pack and pulls out a notebook. "Here." Dane hands it to me with a look of tired resignation.

"I don't have to—" I start.

"It's fine," he interrupts sharply. "I'd rather not give you any ammunition for doubt in our group about what I could be giving her in case this comes out."

I nod slowly. It's a simple, black-and-white composition notebook like we used to use at school on the island. I open it. There are taped-in pieces of paper with letters in no order to make actual words or sentences. I flip through them, unsure of what they mean, and then there are pictures and random drawings and doodles.

I don't linger on anything for too long. This looks like a book of memories between Dane and Vera. It's personal to them, and it feels wrong for me to be looking at it. I turn more pages and pause when I see a letter from Dane to Vera sometime after she died. I pass by it to find another. And another. Like he's been writing her letters every day or week or whenever he needed to talk to her after she was gone.

I close the notebook with shaking hands.

The pain of losing Vera that I thought I'd moved past circles and tugs at my heart. I hand back the notebook and rest my forehead against my arms. It's a harsh reminder that I'll never really move on from that moment in my life. I'll always keep it with me. There will always be a chance that it may rise to drown me again if I'm not careful. Knowing the pain it would cause Dane was one of the biggest reasons I wallowed in my grief after. Now, seeing how he's still dealing with it even years later, it all comes rushing back.

"I've been doing a lot of thinking lately. About everything. Vera being alive. What you said happened when she died. What happened on the island after, and even when you saw me again and still didn't tell me what happened."

I peek up over my arms at Dane. He's staring hard at the concrete between his feet, his fingers shoved halfway through his blond hair, so it sticks up. He looks lost in thought, even as he's speaking. I hold my breath as I listen, as if my breathing might somehow interrupt his train of thought, and I'd never know what he was trying to say to me.

"I can't believe your story. Even if I wanted to, I can't. That would mean that Vera isn't the sister that I remember growing up with. It would mean throwing away everything about her I thought I knew. And I can't—I *won't*—accept that."

I bite my lip and duck further into my arms. There's nothing I can say about that. Am I happy about it? Of course not. But I also don't blame him for it. Why wouldn't he choose to believe in his sister, his blood, over me? A girl he met on an island who, according to Aiden, is a secret GE plant.

"But…" he starts up again, and my chest squeezes. "If I were to believe you, that would mean you'd sacrificed everything to protect that very image of her that I'm holding on to. That you refused to tell the truth of what happened—of who she was—so that I could keep remembering her as a good person."

He looks over at me, and my breath catches at the pain reflected in his gold-green eyes. My heart breaks at the sight of it. At him trying not to fall apart at the revelation of everything that had happened on and since that day.

"Even if it meant that I would hate you, that the others would hate you, that you would lose us forever, and you'd be alone, you guarded that secret."

I tear my gaze away from his when I can no longer handle it and bury my face back into the safety of my arms. I force myself to take calming breaths. Once I think I've gotten myself mostly under control, I reaffirm what he said. "If you believed me."

Dane nods and gazes back to the city. "If I believed you."

Right.

I nod, and we fall into silence.

Hours pass without any more words passing between us. I keep changing my position to try to stay comfortable, but without getting so comfortable that I fall asleep again. Vera almost killed me because of that last time.

When I can't stand the silence any longer, I decide to poke Dane about something Aiden had said to me that affects us both. "You know, Aiden's pretty pissed off that we've been going out without the whole team. Or, without permission, maybe," I begin. Just throwing that out there at the wall to see if it sticks and a conversation comes from it.

Dane sighs and scratches his head. "Yeah. If this were anything else, I'd listen."

I shrug and tap my fingers against the cold concrete. I'm lying on my side now, my head being held up by one hand as I look over at him. Dane has barely moved in the hours we've been here. He's switched his legs in and out a couple of times, done a few perimeter walks, and then gone right back to sitting in the same spot.

"Why?" Dane sends me a look, and I hold up my hand for him to let me finish. "He seems too busy with this Guild to be dealing with GE. If we're going to beat them, it's not going to be like this. That's all I'm saying."

"Well, it's not going to be won with you running in there alone either," he argues with another follow-up look, like he thinks I'd do that.

I mean, it's not entirely out of the question. It's just not my first or second plan if I can help it.

"There are a lot of people relying on Aiden now. More than just us. Have a little patience, and then we'll figure this out. Together, this time. No going rogue."

"They seemed more than fine when we were there. Living in a jungle, but happy enough to pick fights."

Dane smiles, honest-to-god *smiles*, at that. Fucking hell, I forgot how jaw-droppingly hot he looks when he does that. My heart pitter-patters before I squash it down. "Of course, they were," he says with a hint of amusement in his tone. The fluttering in my chest burns like it catches fire with jealousy at his tone and expression toward the Guild. Gah!

He doesn't seem to notice my inner battle and keeps going. "I haven't been there in a while. Did you say it's a jungle? Like the new Jumanji jungle?"

My eyes narrow. "What do you mean, *new* Jumanji?"

Dane blinks at me. "You know, the new ones they did."

"They did a Jumanji 2?"

"No..."

I feel a twinge of anger. "A remake?"

"Not...no."

I stare at him with confusion. "Well, which is it? I'll be pissed if it was a remake because the original was too good to be redone."

"It's not a sequel, really, but they do reference Alan in it, so it doesn't overwrite the original. How haven't you seen it?"

My stare hardens, and I can see the moment he remembers my apartment at Hype, and it clicks. So, no, I don't watch a lot of movies in my spare time or collect them. Not like Dane and I had on the island, where we binged movies like they were chips and thought sleep was for losers.

The conversation ends there, and we settle back in for another long stretch of nothing but waiting.

Eventually, the sun appears above the horizon, and Dane admits defeat. We pack up and leave. I'm glad to live another day and avoid the risk of Dane being captured, but my heart is heavy when we leave.

I wish he could have at least given her the notebook with his letters.

Chapter Twelve

RAEGAN

"Is that you, beautiful? Hold up." Kellan tosses his video game controller away and jumps up from the couch. Dane glances over at me with a frown and pauses the game. I assume it's to wait for Kell to return and not that he's curious about me, since he doesn't move from his seat.

I tug my hood further down to cover my head and hurry to my room. Kellan runs by me and then slaps his hand against the hallway wall to stop me. I duck under it, ready to bolt, when he grabs my hood and pulls it back to reveal my dark brown hair. He uses the grip on my hood to yank me back and around to face him.

"What's this?" He lifts a few locks and rubs them between his fingers, then presses them against his lips. "A wig?" His brows raise with surprise, and an amused smirk slides across his face. "What have you been up to?"

I shrug with faux innocence. "Nothing you need to worry about."

He steps forward and leans his other arm over my head, so I'm surrounded by him. The smell of musk overwhelms my senses. All I can smell or breathe is him. He chuckles and slides the fake hair through his fingers. "It's never nothing when you're involved. Getting into trouble without me?"

I scoff and turn my face away. "Hardly. I'm just trying to make a couple of bucks."

His mood tanks in an instant. "How?" he demands, grabbing my face and directing it back to his. I purse my lips and wonder if he's going to try to stop me from going out. "Answer the question before I lose my shit, beautiful."

I roll my eyes and huff. "I'm working at a bar, Kell. It's nothing to get worked up over. It's not safe for Hype if I'm seen there, but I can't do anything to hunt down GE without some money."

"Since when are you hunting down GE without us? Aiden told us to wait."

"Oh, yeah? Aiden isn't in charge of me. I got this job a few weeks ago when I got tired of waiting for you guys to do something. I can't just sit here twiddling my thumbs because Aiden thinks he has better things to do."

Kellan frowns and releases me, then points to my head. "And the hair?"

I pinch some of the strands to look at it and then back to him. "It's my disguise. Do you like it?"

"I think you're sexy in any hair color, but you know I'll always like the original you best," he says with a grin.

"Good to know. Now, let me go so I can get changed into something comfortable. I'm in need of a drink. Or fifty."

I try not to think about Portia, which, of course, means that's exactly what I do. What I wouldn't give for her upbeat attitude and willingness to help me get sloshed when I need to black out from my troubles for a night. A twinge of loneliness stings in my chest, and I grip at it involuntarily.

Kellan grabs the back of my neck, and my attention snaps to him. He trails his nose up the side of my neck, his facial hair tickling behind it. "I can think of other ways to keep you distracted, if you want. Especially while you have the little wig on," he drawls in his deep timbre.

My thighs clench, a resounding ache building between them at the sound of his voice alone. We already have a problem of interrupting our training sessions with sex over the last few weeks. He's tried having me wear more clothes or baggy shirts and hoodies, but none of it has helped. So far, we haven't found anything to deter either of us when the mood's just right.

As much as I'd love to take him up on his offer, this isn't a problem I want to solve with sex for once.

"Mm, let's put a pin in that idea for another time," I hum, because I'm definitely down for it later. "I have other plans for tonight already. You're welcome to join me, though. Just give me a few to dress down, and I'll see you out there."

He chuckles and pushes himself off the wall. "I'll see about starting your fifty drinks in the kitchen." Kellan strolls back down the hall, and I bite my lip while watching him go. He's in gray sweats and a black tank top, exposing the web of tattoos on his chest, shoulders, and all the way down his arms to his hands. His hair is tied up in a knot, and I can see the tattoos extending up his neck in a tribal-looking design atop tanned skin.

Kell sends me a cocky grin over his shoulder just before he turns the corner, so we both know I was checking him out.

Considering how often we've been fucking, he should know better by now that I'm attracted to him. Cat's already out of the bag.

Once he's no longer distracting me, I escape to my tiny room to change. I've spent most of today in tight, form-fitting clothes, and I'm ready to breathe. I slip on the pajamas I've been wearing since staying with the guys—some pajama shorts and one of Aiden's shirts. I'm a bit of a fan of how I'd knocked the words off his tongue when he'd seen me in it before. Anything that makes him speechless is a win for me.

It also doesn't hurt that they are supremely soft and cozy.

I won't mention the small lingering scent of cinnamon on them that I *do not* breathe in at night when no one can see me.

Reapplying some ointment and a bandage to a piece of ink I got earlier, I ditch the wig and opt for a messy bun to keep my hair out of my way tonight. I'm ready to go, but take a minute to open my window and look up. "Jack?" I call out tentatively.

I haven't seen him in weeks. Not since the night we'd been together, and he'd been gone before I woke up. I didn't worry at first. He's always gone out to do his own thing. And he *is* the monster living in the shadows at night. I'm also convinced that he's been sneaking into my room at night to sleep with me.

Sometimes, the bed is still warm next to me when I wake up. Or the creases in the sheets look like someone had been lying beside me. Or a faint memory of someone's hand gently stroking my arms or my thigh.

I can't actually confirm any of those are true signs he's been here. I even tried to stay awake one night to catch him, but he never came.

Either I'm going crazy and imagining him because I miss him, or he's trying to keep his distance for some reason.

I don't know which of those options is worse.

I hate that he and Kell have been able to work their way under my skin and into my heart again so easily. I thought I'd locked that shit down, blocking it from ever being hurt again, but they walked right through my barriers. It sets off warning bells in my head that I need to get out now before it's too late. For them or for me.

I'm a curse that hurts those who get too close to me.

I slam the window shut and swear at myself for my mood. This is why I need drinks. And dancing. A lot of fucking dancing. I'll dance so hard and drink so long that I'll sleep like a baby tonight. There's no other way I'll get there with the direction my mind keeps going.

Kellan has a line of forties on the kitchen counter for me to choose from, along with mixers and add-ins if I need them. I don't. I'd rather not waste any room on extras if I can fill it with straight alcohol tonight.

I grab the first bottle of whiskey and twist it open with a snap. I chug it for a full thirty seconds and then gasp for oxygen.

"What the fuck is your problem?" Dane snaps out from where he's staring at me on the couch. He's in a simple forest green shirt and black sweatpants. His arms are crossed over his chest, one foot up on the couch, as he leans against the arm so he has a clear view through the dining area to me in the kitchen. The game controller is sitting on the table next to Kellan's, and the game is still paused on the screen.

"Life. What's yours?" I counter back, but with far less aggression than him.

Kellan snatches the bottle from my hand and takes a long swig. I watch his throat work the liquid down and find I'm already thirsty for more. He hands it back to me with a grin. "How drunk are we going for? A happy buzz, puking our brains out, or a complete blackout?"

"Whatever puts me to sleep the fastest," I answer before drinking again.

"Alcohol isn't going to fix your fucked up life," Dane responds instead, and I can't help but laugh at what almost sounds like attempted advice, even if it is in an irritated tone.

"Thanks, Dr. Phil, but I'm not trying to fix it right now. I'm trying to make sure I still have some fun now and then. You should try it sometime." I stalk over to the living room and grab the TV remote, flipping over to a music channel and cranking the volume up to full blast.

Whether he had anything else he wanted to say or not doesn't matter anymore. I wouldn't hear a thing.

My body moves to the music like we're back in the club with sweaty bodies closed in around us. It doesn't matter that I'm the only one dancing here. I close my eyes and throw my head back, gyrating my hips and running my hand up my body into my hair. I let the music overwhelm my senses so all I can hear, think, and feel is the beat. There's no room for stress or worries when I give in to the music.

I drink from my bottle while dancing, sucking it down until I feel the warm tingle of a buzz humming under my skin. My eyes open to check in with the room, and Kellan's convincing Dane to do shots with him on the couch.

"Have some fun for a change, Rapunzel. It's just one night, and we could all use it."

Dane eyes the dark liquid in his shot glass. He glances up at me, and I can't help the grin that stretches across my face while I continue to dance and observe them both. His gaze is hot and intense, watching me with a look that makes me feel like it may cause my alcohol-warmed blood to combust. He tosses the shot back, and Kellan follows a second later with his own. He tops both of their glasses off again for another round.

I don't know why I'm cheesing so hard at this, but I laugh to release the pent-up energy that produced my grin.

Time blurs after that.

Until the front door opens, and everything comes into focus for a single moment of clarity. Aiden's staring at me as I'm dancing on the dining room table. I grin at him and keep dancing. Dane and Kellan are laughing and watching me from the couch.

"What is this?" Aiden demands. He strides over to the table and looks up at me. "Get down."

"Just some fun," Kellan drunkenly drawls when he gets up to meet him.

"Fun? What were you planning to do if GE attacked right now?" Aiden asks him sternly.

I giggle and take a step in his direction. Except my foot drops without a table there, and my body follows it. Kellan and Aiden both jump toward me. Everything spins and whirls around me, and I squeeze my eyes shut. I land against something warm with a grunt. I take a deep breath, and cinnamon flavors the oxygen I take in. I burrow deeper against the warmth because the smell is comforting and settles the stirring alcohol in my gut.

"I would've had her," Kellan gripes beside me.

"Both of you, sober up," Aiden's voice rumbles against my ear.

Then we're moving, and my hands roam over his chest until they find his silken tie to hold on to.

"You're muscly," I mumble my observation into his chest. I never could tell from the suits he always wears about how lean he is, but I can feel the pure strength of his arms and the firmness of his chest. I guess he has to heft all those metal weapons somehow.

"Do you hit on anyone when you're drunk or just me?" His smooth tone glides over me like melted chocolate, and I shiver against him.

He places me down and tucks me in under the blankets. His movements are slow and almost gentle as he gets me settled in. I smile and mumble something incoherent while getting comfortable. Sleep drags me under just as Aiden whispers something to me. I struggle to grab and hold on to it, but I'm out before I can remember what it was.

My body slams back on the mat, and I groan. "Uuuugh. I'm going to be sick. You did that on purpose, you prick." I roll onto my side and hold my stomach as it roils from being flipped in the air. Bile creeps up my throat, and I slap my hand over my mouth and will it back down.

It's not that I care about throwing up in front of him. He can fucking clean it for making me do this first thing in the morning instead of after dinner. I just hate throwing up. And seeing or smelling it will make me hurl all over again once I've started. Ugh, I feel so gross. This is why I always sleep off my hangovers and wake up in the afternoon.

Kellan's an absolute *dick* for waking me up and then making me train with him while I'm still hungover.

"This was Aiden's punishment for you, not mine. Take it up with him," he says with a grin. Oh, he's definitely doing it a bit for him, too. His blue-green eyes are sparkling with his enjoyment of working me like this.

I groan and push up to my hands and feet. "And why am I being punished, exactly?"

He offers his hand to me, and I glare at it before sighing heavily and taking it. He lifts me up with ease, and I sway into his chest. "For letting your guard down." I can feel the rumble of his deep voice where my hands are pressed against him. His hands steady me at my shoulders, and then he steps back, forcing me to stand on my own two feet.

I swipe the hair that's framing my face out of my eyes. "So, I'm not allowed to drink or have fun if I'm with you guys? Are you trying to make me leave? Because all you have to do is say so."

This week's training has focused on fighting with weapons in close combat. Today, in particular, is working with knives. Before we reset to go again, Kellan hands me the knife back by its hilt. It's small and fits easily in my hand. I have to be close to my opponent to use it, but that's the point of him training me. I need to be able to fight when the element of surprise is no longer an option for me.

"You're not going anywhere," he growls at me. I raise an eyebrow at him while taking the knife, but he grips the blade and doesn't let go. "Drink all you want. But you have to still be able to fight while intoxicated. Or"—he looks down my body and back up to my face—"while hungover."

He releases the blade, and I frown at the drops of blood that fall from his hand. I know he's confident in his gift healing him, but I can't say that I enjoy how easily he hurts himself for no good reason. Especially when he told me he's made no progress with his own training and testing of his gift.

I adjust the knife in my grip; the blade directed out the back of my hand as I angle it to point at Kellan, and my other hand is up and at the ready. My feet shift into the stance he taught me to keep my balance and reduce the target areas of my body by angling to the side.

He smirks at me, taking in my pose, and makes slight adjustments until he's satisfied. Then he crouches into his own stance to show he's ready, and I attack.

I swing out to stab him in the ribs, but he catches my wrist and spins me around. I drop the knife to my other hand and try again, this time in a slicing motion, but he releases my other wrist and backhands my attacking hand so hard that the knife flies out of my grip.

Kellan grabs and flips me onto my back, his forearm pressing into my throat and his body pinning mine into the mat. His face draws close, until whatever air I can still taste is all him. Musk and sweat that's delicious on my tongue and causes a low throb between my thighs in response.

"Tell me what you did wrong, beautiful."

I squirm beneath him, but we both know it's futile. I'm well and truly trapped by him. But I also won't complain about rubbing against him if it means I might make a weak point in his hold on me.

He smirks, like he knows exactly what I'm trying to do, and leans closer so his breath can tickle my ear. "What have I been telling you about your non-dominant hand?"

"It's weak," I mutter.

Kell nods. "As soon as you switched your knife to that hand, I knew I could knock it free easily. Because it's not used to fighting. It doesn't pull the trigger. It's not the hand you've used to kill or fight with in the past. And that's a big weakness that's easy to exploit." His other hand reaches for my left and brings it to his chest. "You can't rely on just your right hand when you're fighting for your life. You're cutting your potential in half by picking sides. You need to use both *equally*, so it doesn't matter which hand has the weapon or which hand has been incapacitated. You have to be able to fight with every part of your body." He folds my hand into a fist and reenacts using that hand to stab into his chest. "Make it second nature, just like you have with your right hand."

"You say that like it's easy. As if it doesn't take people years as kids to establish which hand is dominant."

He shrugs. "Start with using your left hand for everything you normally do with your right. Writing. Eating. Washing your hair..." Kellan trails off as he drags my hand down his chest to the waistline of his pants. His smirk intensifies into a wolfish grin. "I'll let you practice on me, too."

I yank my hand back and shove at his chest. He howls with laughter and rolls off me and back to his feet in such a smooth move that I'm instantly jealous. How can a guy who is so big move that well? "Get fucked, Kell," I snark back at him, even though my lips are twitching with the desire to smile.

He grins at me and starts unraveling the tape on his hands, signaling the end to our session for today. I stalk over to my water and drink until I feel slightly hydrated again. Then get to work on unwrapping my hands as well.

"Do you agree with what I'm saying, beautiful?" he prompts suddenly.

I look up at him with some confusion. "Of course. It makes a lot of sense."

Kellan nods, and minutes later, he says, "The same is true for using your gift."

I freeze.

"You're not using every available weapon at your disposal if you choose not to use it."

Not this again. I don't understand why he's so hung up over me using my gift. Everyone else would probably be relieved if I never used it again. But Kellan has been trying to bring this up with me multiple times since the fight with Thorne. "I do use it," I snap, turning away from him to roll up my wraps for next time. "You've seen me use it."

"Only as a last resort. And even you admit that you don't think you have control over it. That's exactly like your left hand. You can use it, but there's no strength, no control there, and it becomes more of a liability than a strength. You *have* to train it too, so it can be something that you can depend on rather than be afraid of."

My heart beats erratically in my chest at the topic of conversation, and I fight to slow my breaths and regain control over my body. I close my eyes and take a long, drawn out breath before answering. "Maybe you should be grateful I don't use my gift more, Kellan. You have no idea what I'm truly capable of if I were to use it to its fullest."

I don't look at him when I leave the room. I don't want to see whether or not he believes what I'm saying.

I can't let myself become comfortable using my gift again.

Chapter Thirteen

JACKSON

Even if instinct didn't warn me that I'm being watched, the smell of something rotten on the breeze gives him away. The scent of death that follows him adds weight to my theory that we had killed him before and he was brought back to life. It's a concerning idea that I've been mulling over.

How did someone find him after we'd buried him?

Who found him and are they a part of GE, or someone new?

Are there any limitations or changes to Thorne after being brought back, or is he the same as he was?

All are questions I don't yet have the answers to.

I flip the phone open once again to check the time. Almost two in the morning. I'd stolen this old phone from a goon who picks up kidnapped kids and transports them to GE. The call I received earlier today had given me this address for the next delivery, so here I am.

Sitting on the edge of a six-story building rooftop and watching the butcher shop across the street.

The ripe odor intensifies. I pull the gaiter up to cover my mouth and nose, but it can only block so much. "Thorne," I say calmly, to acknowledge his presence. He's somewhere on the same rooftop as me by the strength of his scent.

There's a deep chuckle and then, "You got me." He moves closer.

I don't bother looking his way or shifting my position. I keep my gaze locked on the butcher shop and the curb before it while leaving it to my other senses to keep track of Thorne behind me.

Everything with him is about power. Even something as simple as keeping my back to him will be regarded by him as a power move.

Thorne steps up onto the short wall that perimeters the rooftop next to where I'm sitting. "You've been busy." There's a pause where he's likely waiting for me to say something back before he impatiently presses on, "And you've proven your point. But I can help lighten the load."

"I'm not going to work for you."

"*With* me," he corrects. "It would be a partnership."

"We already tried that, and you hid Raegan from me."

"I wasn't hiding her from you. I needed your focus on weeding out a spy in the Guild first before you went dashing off into the sunset. I clearly misjudged her importance to you then, and that's my mistake. I won't make it again." He moves his hand over his heart like that would mean anything to me. The man doesn't have one.

I also know he dropped a new piece of information to reel me in. This is the first time I've heard of a spy. "What spy?"

A smile curves his lips. "Oh, just someone in the Guild who

secretly works for GE. I caught the ones I suspected to interrogate them and send them back to GE, but someone decided to play hero and free them." He slants his gaze my way, but I still don't turn to look at him.

A spy in the Guild?

Or a trick to get us to turn on each other trying to find an imaginary enemy?

"So, you see, you gave up on me too quickly. Or was your little family that eager to steal the Guild from me that you betrayed me for them?" He sneers.

"It wasn't about them."

"Yeah, yeah. It was about her. But I'm sure you see my concern with any partnership so long as the others are around. Your little group has tried to kill me twice now."

My lips twitch into a small smile, though it's hidden beneath my face covering. "I haven't agreed to work with you, Thorne."

He chuckles. "No, but you're still listening, aren't you?"

"I'm waiting for my next target. You came to me."

"Well then, listen to my new offer while you wait. You clearly can do this on your own, but I need your help to take over GE. You help me take down the board and I'll teach you the next level of using your gift, so you'll never need weapons again. All those knives weigh you down. And of course my previous offer to help you protect your girl is included. Gordon's been relentless in searching for her, but I've been throwing misdirects in his way. If you want that to continue, you'll accept my offer."

This time, it's my turn to laugh. "Is that a threat?"

Thorne shrugs and smiles. "Only if you want it to be. I need some insurance that you and your so-called brothers aren't hatching a plan to kill me again. The only reason I haven't killed them yet is because I haven't seen you around them lately, and I'm curious. Trouble at home?"

Unfortunately, his intentions are exactly what I suspected they would be. The others won't be safe until Thorne's handled. "I don't have anything to do with the others anymore, so you have nothing to worry about."

"Oh? Did you get kicked out? So, you'd be fine if I killed them all?"

"Not while they're watching Raegan. And Dane's more useful to you alive than dead."

He crosses his arms over his chest as he considers that. "You have a point. He'd be a good bargaining chip." A dark van pulls up in front of the butcher shop and three men get out. They unload large black bags into the store. "The other two can live until they're no longer needed to babysit, then. Fair?"

I shrug with indifference. "Sure." I pull one foot up against the building and push off into the air. My gift controls my fall until I land at the glass doors to the shop. I crack the door open enough to buffer the air and sound around the bell above the door, then slip inside.

The storefront is dark and empty, but there's heated voices and crying coming from the back. Knives in hand, I creep to the next doorway. The room is vacant, but the freezer door is open.

"You text him?"

"I'm doing it now. Let's grab the cash and go."

The phone in my pocket vibrates softly as the three men exit the freezer and close it.

One. Two. Three blades sink into their throats at once and they drop to the floor. This one was quick and easy. I'm sure it won't be so simple after GE catches on to their transfer locations being attacked.

Stalking over to the bodies, I slash each blade through the rest of their throats. There will be no miraculous survivors. I grab a nearby towel and wipe the blood from my knives before stowing them away.

The thick scent of copper spreads through the room with the mess on the floor worsening by the second, but I can still smell Thorne when he arrives.

He takes one look at the three men on the ground and scoffs. Thorne kicks one of them. "Pathetic. At least hire people who aren't completely useless."

I ignore his childish behavior and scan the room. Ah. That'll do.

"What's your end goal with this?" He waves at the bodies.

Grabbing the black tarp in the corner, I shake and snap it until it's fully spread. "Remove any enemies in the city and get GE's attention."

"And then what?"

"Hopefully, earn an audience that'll get me closer to the ones in charge."

"I can help you with that now. There's no need to go around murdering half the city."

If GE makes up half the city, then that's exactly how many I'll go after. The entire city could be GE goons and I'd still eliminate every last one to know Raegan is that much safer.

I place the tarp over the bodies. "If you're here to help, leave a message with those three after I'm gone."

Thorne frowns. Probably displeased that we'll be separated so soon after our alliance. "And where will you be?"

I nod toward the freezer door and open it until I can see the two children inside. "Taking care of them."

"A waste, if you ask me." He bends down to lift the tarp, and I shoot a knife at it, pinning it to the linoleum floor. Thorne hisses and rubs his finger that I'd grazed.

"Not until we leave."

The girl sobs when she sees me. It's a good thing I'm wearing black to hide the blood, but seeing any stranger dressed as I am isn't comforting either. The boy sniffles and shifts himself protectively in front of her.

They're both shivering from the cold, even though I'd been quick. I can feel the chill on my exposed fingertips, but I've always been more resilient to cold than heat.

I hold up my lock picking tools so they can see what I have before I squat in front of the boy first. There are dried tracks of tears on his cheeks, but he's putting on a brave face for the girl.

"What was that noise out there? Who are you? What do you want with us?" His teeth chatter as he talks.

"You're safe. I'm getting you out of here." I slide the lock picks into his cuff and start working it. It clicks open in under a minute. The girl's still crying when I look at her cuffs next.

"Let him take the cuffs off, Annie," the boy tells her reassuringly.

"He's scary!"

I tug my gaiter down and reach into my hoodie pocket for the treat I'd brought just in case. Pulling the chocolate bar free, I hold it out between us and smile. "For one of these?"

"I'm not supposed to take candy from strangers."

Mm. I can't argue with that.

I peel the wrapper back and snap off a corner to toss in my mouth, then re-offer the bar to her.

My lips curve into a smile when she hesitantly reaches for it. She takes a small bite and the boy gently pulls her arms out. "I'm freezing and I wanna get out of here. Let him take them off."

The cuffs are released in seconds and the girl immediately shovels the chocolate bar in her mouth. I pull my gaiter back over my nose and hold out my arms. "Climb on."

Annie goes first, grabbing my neck and clinging like a sloth to one side, before the boy does the same on the other.

Thorne's head snaps up when we leave the freezer, but I'm already using my gift to propel us into and then out of the room. I kick both storefront doors open and get us outside. The girl squeals once we're airborne, her arms tightening around my neck.

I need to drop them off. Then there's one more stop I need to make before I return to Thorne.

Chapter Fourteen

AIDEN

A text message from Cibrina stares at me from my phone screen. Internally, I'm pulling at my hair and then punching something in my frustration. On the outside, I'm frowning at it.

It's been almost two months since the attack on the Guild and all its members moved to the bunker. Two months of members being forced to share bunk rooms instead of the privacy of their own rooms. Of having a limited menu of meal options and more restrictive curfews to ensure all members were safe every day. Two months with a tighter screening and approval process on jobs for members to pick from. And then requiring all jobs to be worked as a team of three or more, thereby reducing their income further.

Even with all those precautions in place, there are still weekly reports of members going missing.

Now that Gifted Enterprise knows we're here, and that there is an entire group of gifted people to choose from, they're picking us off one by one.

I don't want to lock down the bunker to keep anyone from leaving. I am *not* their prison guard. The Guild is here to support and keep them safe as much as possible, but it will never try to control them.

I can only warn them of what's happening and hope that they make the best call for themselves.

But that's not what's eating at me now.

> **Cibrina:** Two more children arrived through the tunnels this morning.

Cibrina's text is the third one in two days of this new problem that has arisen. Gifted children are suddenly showing up at the bunker on their own. We don't know where they are coming from or how they are finding their way to us. Are they spies? Seeking entrance to where the Guild is and looking for ways to lure members out or bring others in?

The very idea of them using children as spies is abhorrent to me, but not at all unexpected, if that is the case.

Of course, we don't turn them away. But they're being isolated on one side of the infirmary on the upper levels so that they don't have any real information to pass back, just in case.

Again, Cibrina's name appears on the screen. I swipe to answer it and bring it to my ear. "What else?" I ask automatically because I know she wouldn't be calling unless she'd learned something more that she didn't want to share over a text.

Her voice is calm and confident, even with this shitshow on our hands, and it only reaffirms that she's the best choice I could have made to handle operations. She's a fucking unicorn, and I'm grateful the Guild has her.

"One of the children from last night woke up and was willing to talk."

Finally. "And?"

There's a second of silence, and my focus narrows to a needle-point. Cibrina doesn't hesitate to tell me anything. So, whatever this is, is important. "Tell me," I prompt again, trying to keep the impatience from my tone.

"He was kidnapped by men in black in a van and taken to a butcher shop. He'd been tied up in the cooler when he heard a lot of screaming. When it stopped, someone came for him. A man, all in black, but not like the others. His face was covered except for his blue eyes. He unlocked his chains and then brought him through the back of a bar and told him to keep walking until he reached the doors. He was told the people there would help him."

"Jackson." He's been gone since that night I found Raegan in his room a month ago. His threat still lingers in the back of my mind like a bad smell I can't get rid of, and it sours my mood at the reminder. I'd wondered what he'd been up to since disappearing, but I hadn't gone so far as to try tracking him down.

He disappeared a lot in the last couple of years since we'd come back together, but he always came back. I'd thought Raegan being here would have stopped that habit, but apparently not.

I wonder idly what Raegan thinks of him disappearing on her after that night and then flick that thought away. I don't have time to wonder or care about it. It'll just bring up other thoughts and annoying feelings that I don't have control over or time for.

"I wanted to confirm with you, but yes, I believe it's him as well. Why would he be sending the kids here? We can't take them all into the Guild, especially if their families are still alive."

"Let's find out if they are first and go from there. If they are alive, we can't just send them home either and hope that GE doesn't try again and murder the family the second time."

"We can't just kidnap kids either, even if it is for their protection."

"Of course not." I tap my fingers against the dining table in thought. I know what I'll have to do, but I don't like it. I run through every other possibility and come right back to this one. "I'll take care of it if it comes to that. If their families are dead, we'll need to sort out how to safely get them into the foster care system under new identities."

"The system can't take care of them like we can," Cibrina states.

I sigh and pinch the bridge of my nose at what she's asking, but not asking. "I know that, but the Guild isn't equipped for minors long-term. We help those who were brainwashed if we can. We don't just take any gifted child on who still needs to go to school and can't work or live on their own."

"I'll draft up a proposal and submit it to you by the end of this week for your review," she says in a clipped tone, and I shake my head and fight back a small smile. This woman has a heart of fucking gold. Far better than mine.

"As you wish. Just find out about their families first. It may not even come to that." We hang up, and I set my phone down. The chances of their families being alive are slim. It's more likely that Cibrina's plan may be the one we're forced to go with, even if it's not what I want for the Guild. We've saved kids from GE before, but it was one here or there that we were able to get back into society. Now we have five kids in two days, and we have no idea how many more may be coming.

To say we are unprepared is an understatement.

Fucking Jackson.

"What's going on?" Dane asks from the couch. I look up, and he's got the television muted while his arm is resting over the back of the couch, and he rests his chin on it. His computer sits on his lap with two more screens pulled out to either side to give him three monitors. He's been beefing up the security here and the bunker for me, but I've also caught him researching topics like brainwashing when he thinks I'm not looking.

"I'll fill you in after one more call," I tell him.

If there was any other way to do this, I wouldn't be calling this person. But my pride won't impede helping children, so I swallow it like a lump in my throat and lift the phone to my ear.

"Adams," the voice on the other end calmly answers.

"Thorton," I mimic him by addressing the other by last names.

"To what do I owe this unexpected call?" the bastard says with fake politeness and unmasked curiosity.

I never ask this man for favors. Elias Thorton is a pain in my ass. His holier-than-thou attitude of doing "clean" business and the way he helps others is the complete opposite of ours. It usually means we're never on the same page on how to go about helping the gifted community, even if we're both against GE.

It also doesn't help that this man refuses to sell the Tower to me. He thinks he's clever and that I haven't noticed he's using it as an excuse to keep tabs on me and the Guild.

He also owns a private jet and yacht and has staff like a chauffeur for himself. He may use his money to help others, but not without helping himself first.

"Do you have any contacts in the FBI?" I cut straight to the point. I don't have the patience or fortitude to bother with niceties that this man wastes his time with. But then, he also rubs elbows with politicians, so I'm not surprised he knows how to blow hot air and charm others with no substance in the conversation.

Another way we differ.

"The FBI?" he repeats with surprise. I don't waste my breath repeating myself. "What sort of trouble are you in?"

He's lucky that I'm the person he deals with rather than the other three. I'm sure a loaded question like that wouldn't be allowed to slide by without comment, but I at least have a better perspective and can keep myself in check so long as I keep the Guild and my brothers at the forefront of my mind.

"I have gifted children in danger who need to return to their families, but it won't be safe for them to go right back to life as it was. Not until GE has been handled. I need them in witness protection."

"And you think I have access to the strings to pull to make that happen?"

My eyes narrow at him, even though he can't see it. "That's what I'm asking, Thorton. Can you help them or not?"

"How long until GE is 'handled'?"

"We're working on it. I don't have an exact date if that's what you're looking for," I bite out as my temper frazzles.

He hums through the connection, and if I could reach through the phone and strangle him, I would. "How is Raegan?"

My teeth snap together and tighten to an uncomfortable grind. I don't like his interest in Raegan. Even if it's not sexual, now that I know about his infatuation with the girl, Portia, I don't want him involved in anything to do with her. Period.

"She's fine," I finally manage coolly.

"Are you playing nice, or do I need to get her another place to stay?"

I grip the phone so hard it cracks from the pressure, and I have to consciously relax my hand. "As I said, she's fine. Are you going to help the families or not? I'd hate to waste your time while you're running around the world trying to find your girl who wants nothing to do with you."

There's a soft chuckle on the other end. "I'll see what I can do. By the way, your lease is overdue. Make sure it's paid in full by the end of today, or I'll have to add a late fee." He ends the call. It feels like my entire chest is on fire, and my insides are melting to molten lava with my hatred for Elias Thorton.

I know the lease isn't overdue. It's on fucking auto-draft. He's trying for a 'made-you-look,' but he's an idiot if he thinks I'd fall for that.

"—bodies discovered this morning."

My eyes cut over to the television that's been unmuted. "Turn that off. We need to figure out what we're doing with Jackson's newest hobby."

"Aiden." Dane's voice is tight and clipped. I glance at his face and then back at the TV. It's a news station showing a taped-off building in the city and lined with police cars and detective units.

I move into the living room to get a better view as they talk about a massacre in an office building that occurred this morning. While such violence is terrible, I don't understand why Dane has pulled my attention to it until I see a still image of the inside of one of the floors after the bodies have been cleared. The GE logo is on scattered paper on the floor.

It's just a bit of a letterhead, but it's enough.

"It's Jack," I murmur aloud for Dane. There's the possibility of another killer on the loose who hates GE or who just so happened to not like that office, maybe, but the chances are far higher that it's Jackson. He's been going after GE all this time, and it's apparently escalated beyond stealth.

It doesn't look like he tried to hide this at all. He wanted it to be seen.

A message, perhaps. But we aren't ready for any sort of backlash or response.

What are you thinking?

Dane mutes the television and turns to me. "He's lost his fucking mind if that was him."

I nod, the gears in my brain turning as I identify all potential outcomes of this clearly visible move and outright call to war. "I need to find out who was in that building. See if there was an actual target or what the purpose of that office was for."

"And if there wasn't one?"

I take a slow breath. If there wasn't any real meaning to this building, then it would mean Jackson is just killing GE indiscriminately now.

The clock strikes two, and I quietly leave my room. I don't worry too much about keeping my steps overly silent since Jack and I are the only light sleepers in the group. The other three could sleep through an earthquake.

I stop outside Raegan's room and listen intently for any signs that she's still awake. She came back from her bar shift at midnight, wearing another ridiculous wig that I want to yank off every time I see it. I know why she's trying to disguise herself, but I'd rather she not go out at all between Gordon, Vera, Thorne, and the rest of GE out there now. It's too dangerous.

When all I can hear is the sound of her breathing deeply, I grasp the doorknob and turn it slowly. I've been coming to her room almost regularly since she moved in here. I feel like a fucking creep for doing it, but watching her sleep seems to be the only thing right now that settles all the thoughts in my mind enough for me to eventually sleep.

I hate that I'm relying on her for this, even if she's completely unaware I'm doing it. It's just another sign that I'm completely fucked over this girl. When I learned what happened with Vera, I was so shocked that I couldn't even process what that meant with how I felt about her anymore. It was an accident. It possibly saved Dane's life. Could I be angry with her for that? Had I made a terrible mistake?

For a brief moment, there was hope that we would work this out.

And then she helped Dane escape and put him in danger without telling me.

Or I found her sneaking around the Tower, and I was reminded that she's still keeping secrets. We may know about Vera, but there's a lot more she isn't telling us.

I wish she would give me something. *Anything*, at this point, so we can get past this.

On top of that, she's a wild card who refuses to work with others. I need to know that she'll work *with* us. I brought her in, but she has yet to prove that she can be a team player. She enables Dane's obsession with his sister, who we all know is working with the enemy that wants to kidnap Dane again. She goes out on her own without telling anyone what she's doing or considering the potential fallout of her actions that affect us or the Guild.

I'm obsessed with her anyway.

I hate it. I hate myself for my weakness, most of all.

I close the door behind me. Just as it clicks shut, there's movement in the darkness of her room, and then I'm pinned against the door with something sharp against my neck. The light of the moon is faint but enough to provide shadows in the room so I can make out a silhouette in front of me.

"Why are you in here?"

I mold the knife in my hand at my side back into a thick metal band around my wrist when I recognize Jackson's voice. "Where have you been?" I demand in a low voice. The last thing I need is to wake Raegan and have her find me in her room. Jackson could probably care less.

"Hunting. Now, answer mine," Jack replies evenly, like he isn't still holding a knife to my throat. That in itself tells me that I need to tread carefully with him tonight.

"Checking on her." I won't admit that I was going to watch her sleep, but even saying this much ticks me off.

Jackson chuckles and taps the knife against my neck before finally pulling it and himself away from me. "What did I tell you about keeping secrets?" I can see the shape of him moving toward the bed, thereby getting close to the window and the moonlight. I can see more of him now between that and my eyes adjusting.

He crouches to the floor and then strokes the hair from Raegan's face. He watches her with single-minded intensity. Like everything else in the world, even me in the room with them, has completely fallen away, and she's the only thing he sees.

He leans closer to her, and I assume he's just going to whisper something to her, but then his mouth meets hers, and I jump forward to grab him.

A gust of wind knocks me back. Did he just...? I catch myself on my feet, and by the time I look back at him with shock, he's smirking at me while still in his crouch.

"Don't touch her in her sleep," I snap as quietly as I can, taking another step toward him.

Jackson shrugs and smiles back. "She wouldn't mind."

My jaw ticks at the reminder of them sleeping together. I had a feeling it would come to this, though I had expected Kellan more than Jackson. Jealousy writhes in my chest like a venomous snake wrapping around my lungs.

It shouldn't matter to me if she's with anyone. I had given up on having her a long time ago. Back when she could have been mine before anyone else's. When I discovered there was a bigger connection between her and GE, I kept it to myself because I let my feelings for her cloud my judgment. Vera died that same week, and I can't help but think that the outcome would have been different had I said something to the others right away.

Even if it was an accident, putting the others on alert might have changed things. As of today, I still don't have an explanation for her birth certificate. I also don't understand her connection with Gordon. What is he, to her? Why did she obey him when he'd attacked? If there was abuse involved, as I suspect, did he succeed in getting some sort of control over her? Am I putting everyone more at risk by having her around before I've determined if she'd still obey commands from him? If he hurt her, why would she think he'd left something for her at the Tower? What am I missing?

I can't choose her again. Not at the risk of everyone else.

That doesn't mean seeing her with the others makes it burn any less.

"I can wake her up to do it instead, if you'd prefer," Jackson adds with a knowing smirk. Of course, I don't want him to wake her up while I'm in the room. She can't know I've been sneaking in here. I also have *zero* interest in watching them kiss as she tells him how much she's missed him.

She hasn't said anything to us, but there are clear moments when she's looking out the window, and I know she's thinking about him.

"How did you do that before? With the wind? Only Thorne could do that." Jackson's been able to manipulate people and objects, even smells and sounds, with his aerokinesis since we were children. But creating a powerful wind or weaponizing the air itself takes a strength he's never been able to harness before. His strength lays in fine control using the air around something rather than the air itself. But to have improved this quickly to what Thorne can do while he's alive and out there is...concerning.

Jackson sits on the top corner of her bed, his fingers trailing through Raegan's hair while he watches her. "I've been practicing."

I move closer to them until I'm within arm's reach of her if I feel like I need to intervene. To which Jack raises his eyebrows at me with that enigmatic smile of his, as if to remind me that he's never a danger to her. Of the two of us, I'm the more likely one to hurt her.

"You practiced before, and it never worked," I remind him.

He shrugs again. "I'm more motivated this time around."

My lips turn down at the possible implications of that. "Does it have anything to do with the massacre at an office building this morning? Or those children you keep dropping off at the Guild?"

"Maybe," he answers cryptically.

"There's shit going on at the Guild right now, Jack. We don't need you to be hunting anyone down or drawing more attention to us. Why did you kill all those people this morning? You didn't even try to hide it."

Jackson smiles. But it's dark and twisted and stalls the breath in my lungs when I see it. "How do you call a shark to you?" he asks softly, dangerously. I don't think he means for me to answer him, so I don't. "You put blood in the water."

Tense silence fills the air between us.

"And who is the shark you're calling for?" I finally ask.

"All the ones that matter." Jack stands and then perches on the open window. "Keep her safe, Aiden. Or else I'll come for you, too." Then he slips out the window and is gone.

I look back at Raegan and her peaceful, sleeping face.

If she ever turns on us, we're fucked.

CHAPTER FIFTEEN

RAEGAN

IF STARES COULD BURN holes into people, I'd have two of them right through my cheek. I raise my brows in question at Kellan. What the hell did I do to cause Aiden to stare at me in a way that feels like a glare, even if his expression is stoic?

Kell looks over at Aiden and then back to me with a shrug. "Sorry, beautiful, but you'll have to ask him. I'm thankful I have no idea what goes on in his head all the time."

My face drops into a scowl at him for openly outing me in front of everyone.

He flashes me a grin and then goes back to devouring his food.

Dane finishes his orange juice and sets it down with an audible knock. "Why *are* you looking at her?" he directs to Aiden, who has since dropped his gaze back to his phone in front of him. His food is untouched, with just his coffee finished for his breakfast.

I eat another strawberry that's sitting on top of my pancakes while we all wait for him to answer. I pile the strawberries on my breakfast, but I always eat them off first and then eat the pancakes—or French toast or eggs—after. I love fruit for breakfast, just not with anything other than maybe whipped cream or chocolate.

Aiden finally looks up at Dane, then shifts his eyes over to Kellan before finally landing on me. "We need to talk about Jackson," he states.

I pause with the berry poised in my open mouth, then drop it back. Well, *that* has my attention. "What about him?" I ask defensively. I don't like the way he said it or the way he's looking at me. My sixth sense, or woman's sense, or whatever it is, is putting me on alert on Jackson's behalf.

He's done nothing but be there for me ever since I came here. The least I can do is have his back in return.

Aiden's eyes narrow at me and my tone, but I don't back down. I don't care how he feels about me defending Jackson. Even if I haven't seen him in a *month* and have no idea what he's been up to, I'm positive that he's been visiting me at night when he can.

A phone interrupts us, and he answers it. I go back to eating my fruit, annoyed that he'd answer his phone while we're all in the middle of a conversation. What was he going to say about Jack? The 'we need to talk' phrase always means something bad happened.

"We'll be right there." We all look at Aiden expectantly. "Two gifted persons from GE submitted an application to join the Guild. They're waiting to meet with someone at the city library."

"Let them wait," Dane immediately snaps. "Like hell, we'll let GE scum into the Guild."

Aiden looks at Kell. "They asked specifically to speak with you."

Kellan looks as shocked as I feel. Why would they want to talk to him in particular? Not that there's anything wrong with talking to him, but Aiden is the face of the Guild.

"Any idea why that is?" Aiden questions him.

Kell shrugs and finishes his coffee. "Naw, but I'm interested to see who these people are now. We all going, or just us?"

"I'm going," I speak up before Aiden can try to decide for me. "I've done nothing but hide out here for a month. If these guys can give us any information on GE, then I'm not missing out."

"You've been going into the city and working at a bar every night. I wouldn't call that hiding out," Dane unhelpfully counters.

"Don't be jealous, Rapunzel." Kellan grins at him. "If she comes, then you're coming too. So, there. Family outing."

I roll my eyes at Kellan and stand with my plate. I'm too excited to get out and make some progress on GE to eat now. "Don't call us that. Hurry up and put a shirt on, or we're leaving without you."

The city library is in the heart of downtown. We take Aiden's Aston Martin, which forces me and Dane into the back together because Kellan is way too large to fit anywhere but the front. I keep a clear amount of space between us because he still doesn't seem too keen on us making any contact. While we've made progress with him accepting my presence in Old Red, mostly at mealtimes or the random training sessions he chooses to attend, touching or casual conversations are still off the table.

It's more than I ever thought I'd get from him, even after my confession, so I take it without complaint and do my best to respect the boundaries he still has in place.

The librarian at the front desk startles when the four of us roll up through the front doors. I hide a laugh behind my hand as she looks us over. Kellan's both tall and thick with muscle, his tanned and tattooed skin on display across both arms and up his neck while his hair is tied up. Dane's dressed in jeans and a gray hoodie with his hood up to hide his face and his hands in his kangaroo pocket. Then Aiden looks the complete opposite of them in his three-piece suit and tie, his posture perfect as he scans the library with a critical gaze. Last, there's me, dressed in black jeans and a turtleneck sweater. My hair is down and around my shoulders to give the appearance of being relaxed, even though I'm internally ready for battle.

There are metal detectors at the entrance, so we're all unarmed aside from Aiden, who looks like some hardcore metal fan with the amount of metal "jewelry" he has on him under his suit. It's not enough to arm all of us, but it's something.

The expression on the security guard's face when the man in the suit pulls all his metal jewelry off into the bin is *priceless*.

We move to the back of the library reading corner, where Cibrina told Aiden they would be waiting until five o'clock tonight. My steps falter when I see who's waiting there for us, and then I look up at Kellan to check his reaction. His eyes widen, and then they find mine.

"You know them?" Aiden asks when we both stop.

"They were at the warehouse with the congressman," I tell him. The guy and girl who had fought with Kellan. "She's fast, and the guy can teleport." I report their gifts before they notice us, just in case this is a trap.

"I thought you killed everyone." Aiden's back to watching them with a calculating eye.

Kellan crosses his arms as we watch too, and they both jerk upright when they feel our gazes on them. "The guy wanted nothing to do with his assignment. He was just looking out for the girl. She...well, she seemed to have a fun time fighting me. But after she got hurt, the guy grabbed her and ran rather than fight me. I'd trust him more than her."

"We don't trust either of them," Dane reminds him sharply. "If they work for GE, then they're both a threat."

"I agree. Let's go." Aiden leads the way and pulls out the chair at the head of the table and across from them. Dane takes a seat to his right and Kellan on the other side of Dane, as if this sort of seating arrangement was pre-planned. And maybe it is. I just haven't been around them outside of Old Red enough to see how they work together without needing to say anything. I sit on Aiden's other side.

I wish Jackson were here to watch our backs, then squash the thought. We can handle this ourselves. Worst case, I can get up to scout the library more if needed. Until then, I plan to hear what's going on firsthand if I can.

"Your request said you're looking to join the Guild," Aiden begins, pulling a folded piece of paper from his blazer and then opening it.

The guy at the end has dark hair and blue eyes. He's wearing whatever loaner clothes GE probably gave him to wear when not in the military uniform, which is jeans and a plain, long-sleeved shirt. We haven't even started and his face is already tight and brooding.

It's completely unlike the ball of energy at his back. She has long chestnut hair and brown eyes. She's wearing a medium green turtle-neck and a white skirt with tan leggings. She, on the other hand, is smiling and looks excited.

Based on their history, it's a red flag for me.

I share a look with Kellan, who gives me the barest of nods. Good. We're on the same page.

"We're looking for asylum," the guy replies evenly.

"And why would you think we would offer it, considering where you're coming from?" Aiden asks.

The guy's eyes look to Kellan and then back to Aiden. "Because he offered." He jabs his thumb in Kell's direction, and we all look at him.

"What?" He scratches his beard, and then his face opens back up when it hits him. "Oh, right. I did." Kellan laughs like it's all no big deal, and I snicker behind my hand at the smallest twitch of Aiden's eye.

"He promised we had more options than whatever GE was giving us. And when we were ready to take our lives back, we could come to the Guild. So, here we are."

Aiden shoots Kellan a look, who merely shrugs. "What? Better at the Guild than with GE."

Aiden sighs. "Alright, let's start with your names. Then tell us about how you wound up with GE and why you're leaving."

The guy nods. "I'm Reid. This is Tinsley. We were both taken a few years ago under the promise of being able to use our gifts without fear or restriction. It wasn't until after we joined that we learned it was on their terms rather than ours. And..." Reid's eyes slide to look at Tinsley, and the affection in his gaze is palpable. He looks back at us. "Threats were made if we disagreed with them or tried to leave."

Ah. I know all too well how they target loved ones and use them against you. They must have used Tinsley to keep him in line. And it probably escalated to where it was safer to run away and hope for asylum than to stay there.

"Gordon?" I ask, since he was the one who did it to me.

Reid shakes his head. "Some crazy chick called Vera."

Dane's fist slams onto the table. "Don't call her that."

Reid scowls. "She's a psycho bitch who's threatened both of us more times than I can count. So, I'll call her as I see it."

Aiden puts his hand on Dane's arm, who growls and leans back in his chair with his arms crossed. Aiden shifts the conversation back to the two of them. "How can we trust that this isn't some ruse to gain you access to the Guild?"

Reid shrugs. "That's up to you, isn't it? You tell me what I have to do to gain the Guild's protection for myself and Tins. I'll answer any questions about GE or whatever." He looks over at Dane. "Like how they've been sending out multiple units to hunt him down, but they've pulled it back in the last week."

"Why?" Aiden questions.

"Don't know. They didn't share that with us. I just noticed not as many of them going out as before. They still want him, without a doubt, but they may be changing tactics."

I check Dane's face, and his lips have thinned into a flat line. I'm sure he hates being the target for GE, especially with his sister being one of the ones out there trying to bring him in now.

Aiden nods. "You'll have to accept being quarantined from the others for a time until we know we can trust you. And we'll have a lot of questions."

"As long as we're not separated. I need to know that no harm will come to Tinsley."

Tinsley rolls her eyes and squeezes Reid's arm as she leans into him. "I can handle myself, Reid. I'd run away before they could touch me." She turns to peg Aiden with an excited stare. "Is it true I can use my gift there whenever I want? I don't have to hide it?"

"No, you don't have to hide it," Aiden answers slowly. "But there are still rules that have to be followed for everyone's safety." Her face falls a little at that, but she doesn't look completely deterred. "We'll give you the rundown of everything if we've decided you can be trusted, and you'd be a good fit for the Guild."

"A good fit?" Reid asks.

"Yes. If you don't like the way things are done in the Guild, or don't mesh with our mindset, then it would be unfair on either side to try to force you to," Aiden replies coolly.

"And if we aren't a good fit?" Tinsley inquires next.

"Then we'll look for other places you can be among others like us where you fit in better. We aren't the only group of gifted people."

Reid and Tinsley both nod at the acceptable terms. It's Reid who speaks up first. "When can we start?"

I step out of my room with a towel and stride toward the girl's bathroom for my shower after a long training session with Kellan. I'd planned to hunt Aiden down and finish the breakfast conversation about Jackson, but apparently, he's still at the Guild making sure Reid and Tinsley are all set in their *quarters*.

That's the fancy term Aiden is using for a lockup, but it does supposedly look like a bedroom with an ensuite bathroom rather than a room with bars. It's just locked from the outside and has security cameras to keep an eye on them.

I just hope he's not asking them questions about GE without me. Shit.

What if he's doing exactly that?

I need to hurry and shower and head down there to make sure he's not back before I'm out.

I pick up my pace and gasp when I'm yanked into one of the empty dorm rooms. The citrusy scent from the body I'm being held against switches my momentary panic to annoyance. "What the fuck, Dane?" I snark into his hand over my mouth, so it comes out as just a muffled noise.

"Vera's willing to meet me again. But we have to leave *now* before we miss her. Are you in or out?" he whispers behind me, sending the stray hairs that came loose after training into a tizzy tickling my ear. I fight against the prickle of goosebumps that carve up my neckline at his breath and push away from him.

"Now?" I ask in a hushed tone. Aiden may be out, but Kellan's still around and would interfere if he found out. We don't usually go until after everyone's asleep, so leaving this early in the night when the others are still awake is suspicious.

"Now. Are you coming?"

I check my person. "I need to grab some weapons. I took them all off."

"You don't need them. You swore not to harm her."

Fuck. He has me there. I feel naked without them, but if I run to my room to grab some, I know he'll leave without me. "Alright.

Fine."

We sneak out to the truck bay again for his motorcycle, bring it down the road, and then take off to the usual meeting place.

I go up the ladder first to make sure the coast is clear, but freeze when I see Vera already there and waiting. She smirks at me like she's won something, and my gut clenches. Why does it feel like we're falling into a trap?

"Dane, I don't think—"

"Is she there?" His hopeful voice is breathy from the climb. He's wearing the backpack from the last time.

I remember the notebook and his letters to her. If anything or anyone is going to save Vera, it's Dane. Can I really take this chance away from him?

I turn my gaze back on Vera, who's seemingly waiting for me to give him my response rather than answering herself. To see if she can call me out for lying if I don't? Well, I've got Dane's back here no matter what. She's about to learn that very quickly. My eyes harden with determination while meeting her stare. "She's here."

He pushes at my legs to urge me onward. "Hurry up! Why'd you stop?"

I step over the ledge and then move to the side to make room for Dane while making sure I'm standing between them. She's in the middle of the roof, so as long as we keep our distance, we should be okay. Her ability to manipulate technology doesn't help her on a brick roof with nothing but big letters on it. Other than turning the lights on and off.

"Vera!" The hope in Dane's voice is soul-crushing. If she doesn't break out of whatever brainwashing or infatuation she has with GE, it is going to destroy him. *She* is going to destroy him. And I'm stuck standing on the sidelines to watch like a car crash in slow motion.

"Dane." I notice the smile she gives him is nothing like the look she'd had before he could see her.

Gah. Manipulative bitch.

"I figured out why you won't leave her to come with me. You don't know about all the horrible things she's done. You don't know where, or who, she comes from." Vera's smile turns sly as she looks at me before sliding back to Dane. "So, I'm going to tell you everything. And then you can decide if you're going to come with me or leave with *her*."

A wave of nausea hits me at her threat. *She can't possibly know*, I try to reason with myself. She wasn't there. She could be making up bullshit just to make Dane hate me.

She doesn't have to make anything up for that to happen.

"Vera, I don't want to talk about Raegan. I want to talk about you. About mom. And dad. They're both alive, you know?" He takes a step closer to her. When she doesn't immediately retreat like last time, he takes another. By the third step, I move next to him and touch his arm in a silent reminder not to get too close just yet. He gives me the barest of nods that he understands, and I drop my hand. "We could go back to them. I couldn't go back without you, but now that you're here, we could see them again."

"Why would we go back?" She sneers. "You don't care about them. I doubt you even remember them."

Dane's hand tightens on the strap of his backpack. "Of course, I do." He bends down and pulls his backpack forward to unzip it. "Here." He pulls out his notebook, and Vera laughs coldly.

"You may not want to hear about her, but I can't let you stay near her in good conscience unless you know this. Her mother was a terrorist. She blew up buildings full of people with her gift until GE captured her. What do you think Raegan's going to do on the loose?"

What did she just say?

This time, Dane turns to look at me. I can't give him anything, though. I have no freaking clue how to process that information. Is it a lie, just to catch us both off guard? Or is it the truth? Is that how I was born on the island? Did Grams know and lie to me about my parents' deaths?

You're dangerous, Gordon's voice bubbles up from my memories and pops, leaking pain and misery into my head like pus from an infected wound.

"Raegan," Dane's voice calls to me. My face turns instinctively to him, but it takes forced blinks to bring him into focus. I'm frozen on my feet, my hands grabbing my arms, as I see him now standing in front of me. I'm expecting fear, or maybe anger, in his expression. But all I see is concern as he calls me back to him. "Look at me. We'll figure this out."

"What's there to figure out?" Vera's voice practically screeches from behind Dane. Apparently, seeing him come to my aid was not what she had expected. "She's a fucking *whore*, Dane! A murderer and a whore! Don't waste your feelings on her. She doesn't care about yours."

"Did you kill me?" Dane's voice is soft, almost like he's not positive he wants to ask the question. When she doesn't respond, he turns to look at her over his shoulder and raises his voice. "Did. You. Kill. Me?"

"What? No, I'd never! You're my sweet younger brother. How could you ask me that?"

"Fine. Did you almost kill me? Over an experiment? Raegan said she was trying to stop you when...it happened. Is what she said true?" he tries again, his voice trembling.

Vera stomps her foot. "No! She's exaggerating. You weren't going to die. Worst case, the machines would have brought you back, so she was overreacting. I *told* her you would be fine."

"Worst case?"

Vera's eyes widen when he turns, fists clenched. I can't think about the literal bombshell she just dropped on me right now. Dane's right. We can look into it later. I can't even let myself absorb the words she'd called me in front of Dane, either. Right now, I need to make sure he's safe.

"You were *fine*, Dane." She takes a step away from us and starts digging into her pocket for something. "Did you hear anything I said before? She's the murderer. Hundreds of people, little brother. She killed her boyfriend and his friends, too. You could be next. You have to get away from her."

Jab after jab hits my psyche, but I hold them there. I won't let them sink in just yet. I can fall apart later, but for now, I keep my eyes trained on whatever's in her hand that she pulled from her pocket.

It looks...like a cell phone?

Oh.

Fuck.

A myriad of red lasers cover me from head to toe in an instant.

"Don't worry. I'll take care of her for the both of us. She won't be able to kill anyone anymore. I'll be doing the *world* a favor."

"Vera..." I start, but I trail off when I realize there's probably nothing I can say to stop her. I close my eyes and look inside to where my gift lives in my gut, calling it to me. The burn sears through my limbs, but I drive it on and concentrate it into my hands. I can hear Dane, too close to me, trying to talk her down.

"Stop! Don't do it, Vera. This has nothing to do with her. I just wanted you to read this." I hear something slapping on the ground close to Vera and assume he's tossed her his notebook. "Read it. Right now. Turn that off, and show me that my sister is still in there somewhere."

I open my eyes to see Vera kicking the notebook away. "What could I possibly read that would make me change my mind about killing the person who killed me first?"

I know then that she's going to do it. There is no getting through to her when it comes to me. Maybe not even when it comes to Dane. How much does she even want him back because he's her brother and not just as the lab rat GE needs?

Dane's standing too close to me for whatever's going to shoot at me and for what I'm planning to do, so my foot strikes out with all the strength I've gained from training with Kellan. He falls back on the ground, his expression wide with shock, but it's enough to ensure he won't follow me. I take two large steps away from him and then drop my hands to the rooftop.

My gift pulses and then strikes. It tries to rush out of me in a torrent of heat and disaster, but I clench my teeth and pull it back. It feels like scrambling at hundreds of threads and trying to keep them all together and reel them in, but I still miss a few that lash out and send cracks further out than I planned.

The roof drops out beneath me just as the sound of gunfire reaches my ears.

"Noooo!" Dane yells, but he sounds distant and soft.

I crash onto something metal and start sliding off of it, but I grab it and hold on tight, my gift thankfully back asleep. Vera screams, and I look up to see the roof beneath her feet caving in.

I pull myself up on what looks like a metal catwalk and run toward her just as she drops. My hand grabs hers, and then her body yanks down until I face plant into the metal walk. I groan, seeing fucking stars from the impact. It felt like someone wailed a heavy metal tray into my face.

Vera shrieks and jerks in my grip, and I have to squeeze tighter to make sure I don't drop her. I had a brief look down when I first fell, and the top floor is apparently two stories tall. A fall from here could kill or permanently damage us.

"Get off of me! Don't *touch* me!"

Her movements grow more frantic, and the stress on my arm sharpens. "Stop moving! I'm trying to save you, but I'm going to *drop* you if you don't quit it!"

"Fire! Fire!" she yells out, and I realize that the stupid phone is still in her other hand. I check my body over for any red lasers, but the nearest ones can only get an angle into the hole where neither of us are.

Bullets fly into the brick and cement, but it's the sharp ping each time it hits metal that sends my heart into my throat. They better not ricochet and hit us. Then small chunks of concrete and debris fall, and I realize a whole other way that she could kill us with this. "Stop it! If you actually care about being alive, then *turn it off*! You could hit Dane up there for all you know!"

Vera doesn't acknowledge me, but the shooting stops, and I drop my face back on the catwalk with a sigh of relief. Then something sharp burns across the back of my arm, and I scream in pain. I look back over the edge. Vera's changed out the phone for a knife. For *fuck's sake*, does she want to die that badly?

I should drop her. Fuck the crazy psycho bitch. She's gone. Completely lost to GE or Gordon. I don't know who this person is anymore, but she's not the Vera I once knew. I can't see any sign, any inkling, that we'll ever get her back.

"Vera! Raegan!" Dane shouts down at us from the edge of the hole I made now that the firing has stopped. "Fuck!" he adds when he sees the predicament we're in.

His voice brings back the promise that I wouldn't harm her. And I'd do whatever it took to save her.

Guess this counts as that.

I groan my frustration at what I have to do, even as my shoulder aches and the cut on my arm throbs. Blood trails from the cut to my hand on hers, and I know it'll slip before long. I reposition myself and reach down to grab her elbow with my other hand, making sounds of struggle and pain as I have to try lifting her with my one hand to make it to her elbow.

Vera's still screaming about me touching her, and I'm afraid she might stab me with the blade, but I'm able to grip her elbow, plant my feet, and then fall back. I use my body weight to heave her up until she's on top of me. She raises the knife up, and I shove her off of me and roll away.

She tries to swipe at me again, and I crawl backward far enough until I can get my feet under me. One foot slips on the blood I've been spreading across the walk from my arm. I cling to the bar before I slide right off, then right myself and grip at my arm to slow the bleeding.

"Vera, stop!" Dane yells on deaf ears. Her murderous glare stays locked on me.

The sound of helicopter blades snaps my gaze back up at Dane.

No. I must have misheard it.

The sound intensifies, and the wind behind Dane picks up.

"Dane! Run! Get out of here!"

He looks behind him, then at us. At the wicked smile on Vera's face as she advances toward me with her knife. "I'm not leaving you. I'll find a way down, and we'll both get out of here." Then he disappears from the hole, and I have no way of knowing if they've taken him or if he's evading them.

"This was a trap all along," I hiss at Vera.

She smirks. "I told you. I wouldn't come back unless he came with me or with your dead body. I just found a way to give me both."

"You're a complete psycho, you know that?" I offer her a sharp smile that tells her to go fuck herself, then turn and run. The catwalk ends at a ladder and then stairs, so I slide down the ladder and jump down the stairs. I need to get back to Dane as fast as possible.

I can hear her clanging behind me, but other than the faint light coming through the hole in the roof, it's pitch black in here. No technology or electricity for her to use, but also no light for either of us to see by.

It's just the sound of our heavy breathing, feet pounding the floor, and my heart stampeding in my chest.

My hand drags along the wall on one side while my other hand is extended out. I can't move at a full run without risking hurting myself if I bash into something, so I keep it to a light jog while I try to get my bearings. As soon as I feel a door, I turn the handle. I could cry with relief when it turns without needing a key. I close it quietly behind me, knowing that unless she has perfect hearing, she won't know where I've gone in the dark.

It also means I have to move quietly in this room.

I feel around, taking my time to place my feet somewhere solid without bumping into anything until I make my way to the windows. They offer a bit of light, so I can see exactly which one is in front of the fire escape. I silently break the window with my gift and put it away again.

I'm pretty sure there are tears in my eyes from the pain of everything, but I ignore them and pull myself out of the window. I climb up like my ass is on fire

I search for Dane before I'm even completely up the ladder and stare for a second when I see Aiden and Kellan up here fighting along with Dane. Aiden sees me first, his eyes dropping to the blood on my arm and then back up to my face.

"She's here," he tells the others with a raised voice. "Let's go!" Aiden's arm swings from behind, throwing the whipsword at the helicopters. The metal narrows and extends to make the distance before it slashes downward and slices one of the two helicopters clean in half. He flips it back to the other one and removes its tail.

Dane punches the guy he's fighting in the face, throwing his entire back into it, and the guy is lights out on the roof. He runs to me with Aiden and then Kellan at his back after taking care of the ones they'd been fighting. More agents hop out of the helicopter, but we're already hurrying down the fire escape to the ground.

"Dane and Raegan, in the car. Kell, take Dane's bike," Aiden orders before my feet can touch the ground. Dane tosses his keys to Kellan, and then we're all flying down the road.

My heart thunders in my ears as we make sharp turns again and again, then finally park under the cover of trees once we've reached the edge of the city. I check out the window to see Kellan right next to us and look up to make sure there's no sign of another helicopter that might have been out for Dane tonight.

"Let me see your arm," he demands, grabbing my hand and pulling it to him. I bite my lip as the adrenaline recedes now that we've escaped, and the pain creeps in.

"Do I need to call Cassandra?" Aiden asks from the driver's seat. He looks pissed, and I wonder if it has anything to do with me bleeding all over the back seat of his fancy car.

Dane answers for me since he's the one inspecting it, "It doesn't look like it'll need stitches, but—"

I pull my arm back to me and hold it against my chest to keep the bleeding to myself. "Then it's fine. I'll just wrap it when we get back, and it'll be good."

"Good," Aiden croons. The car moves again. "Now you can both listen to everything fucking wrong with tonight and how you will *never* do anything like that again."

Dane and I look at each other, but there are no words for how either of us is feeling right now. The things Vera said about me, about my mother, come back to me, and I rip my gaze from his with shame.

We remain silent the entire drive back through Aiden's reprimand and then some.

Chapter Sixteen

RAEGAN

THERE'S ABSOLUTELY NO WAY I can sleep after what happened tonight. I take a long, hot shower, re-wrap my arm in dry bandages, and then wait until everyone else is fast asleep before I sneak out. The bars are still open for another hour or two, so I go where it's familiar.

The bartender, Susie, recognizes me with a scoff. You'd think she's pissed I didn't show up tonight, but she's probably thrilled about that. It's my arrangement of showing up when I want and taking away tips from the working bartenders that make her and the rest of them hate me. "Really? A city full of bars, and you came to this one to look miserable?"

I give her my best I-don't-give-a-fuck smile. "Yes, a jack and coke sounds good. Light on the coke. You know what? Scratch that. Just jack."

My face falls. Where is Jack? He didn't come tonight. I'm not saying that I wasn't able to handle myself without him, but he's almost always appeared when I've been in trouble in this city. But tonight, my stalker was nowhere to be found.

Crap, that sounds stupid. I should not be upset that he's not stalking me like he used to. That should be a good sign. Definitely less toxic.

Instead, it feels like an omen. Like something bad must be keeping him from me. I didn't realize how attached I'd gotten to my shadow last month, but his absence is a tangible ache in my chest whenever I think of him.

Susie fills a glass—at least she's not dumb enough to think I was only asking for a shot—and slides it over to me.

I need to drink and see if I can make myself forget about everything Vera said tonight. If I can't forget, how am I going to look Dane in the eye again?

Then there's the news about my mom. I have no memory of either of my parents. She could be making it up, but what she shared about me killing an ex-boyfriend had been true. Somehow, she or GE found out about that. If she got that right, does that mean she's telling the truth about my mother?

I finish my drink in a couple gulps and flick the glass forward for more. Susie eyes me and then sets the entire bottle on the bar. "You're paying for this. But I'm not keeping up with whatever self-destructive mood you're in. Serve yourself."

I grab the bottle and start pouring myself another. "Thanks."

I finish the next glass and drop my head into the crook of my arm to take a long breath. I wonder if my mom is still alive. Or my dad. Does he have a gift too? Where is he? Does GE still have my mom?

Buzzing in my pocket startles me from my thoughts. *Ken Doll* displays on the screen of my phone. I'd tried texting him a couple of times to meet up, but it had always been a bad time. Now it's my turn.

Or this could be just what I need.

"Hello?" I answer before I can talk myself out of it.

"Rebecca! I'm so glad you answered. Is this a good time?"

"Yeah. I'm free."

"Great. Where are you now?"

"Right now?"

"Yes, I'll come to you."

"Oh. I'm at Porky's bar in the city."

There's a pause on the other end. Does being at the bar break Rebecca's character? "Are you with your friends? I thought you were free."

Is that annoyance in his tone?

"No, I'm alone," I reply, my voice tight.

"Oh, I see. I'm right around the corner from there, actually, so I'll see you soon."

Now I'm wondering if this was a good idea. He hangs up before waiting for me to respond, which means I'm now committed to the decision I made.

I can just leave if I'm not getting any worthwhile information.

With that reassurance in mind, I refill my glass. I'll need to slow down now that he's coming, but that doesn't mean I'm going to stop. I still need the warm buzz to keep my thoughts from spiraling over everything Vera said.

Ken doll wasn't lying when he said he was around the corner. I've barely had half a glass before he's walking inside. He scans the room and finds me in the first pass, his smile lighting up his face when our eyes connect. He looks around me too, I guess to verify that no one else is around me, before he waves and strides to the seat next to mine.

"I know we're meeting to talk about the internship, but if there's something else you need to get off your chest, I can be quite the listener." His eyes shine with mirth, like there's something funny about what he said, but I have no idea what it could be. Maybe I've had too much to drink to catch on to dumb jokes.

"Nope. I'm good. Just wanted to go out for a drink," I lie easily with a smile before taking another sip of my drink, as if to prove a point.

He chuckles and points to the large bottle of whiskey next to my glass. "All of that yours?"

Ah. That doesn't really help my case. I set my glass down and laugh softly. "Okay, you got me. But please"–I wave at the bottle–"help yourself. Susie!" I shout, then point between my glass and Ken doll. She rolls her eyes and brings another glass over to me. "Thanks, Suze."

"Whatever." She looks Ken doll up and down and frowns when she glances back at me. Then she must decide she doesn't care enough to say or ask anything and walks away again.

Ken grabs the bottle and the extra glass. "Is she a friend of yours?"

"No–oh!" I hold my hand up as he tops off my drink with a heavy pour that makes it splash. "Uh, thanks."

He lifts his glass expectantly. "A toast."

"To what?"

"To finally being able to meet. I'm sorry for being so busy before today."

Oh. That's...weird. He jerks his glass again and I raise mine to clink his.

"So, the internship," he begins. "There are only two spots open at my firm, but you'll get full access to the process of various cases. You'll have to sign an NDA, of course, to protect our clients."

Ken continues on in a long-winded explanation of the internship, and I find myself reaching for my drink more often just to give myself something to do.

"And that's everything. What questions do you have for me?"

The room blurs around me. I blink to bring him back into focus. "Hm?" What did he say? Questions? "Oh, um." I grab my glass to give myself more time and realize it's empty. How much more did I drink? Ugh, not good. I need to leave while I still have enough sense to get back to Old Red.

"Actually." I speak the words slowly, putting all my focus on getting the right ones out. "I think you've given me a lot. Can we call it a night? I can call you when I know all I wanna ask." Did that sound good? Shit, even thinking is becoming a struggle.

Ken smiles like he understands. "Of course. It is pretty late, so we can call it here. Do you need a ride?"

I shake my head and then freeze when the room spins. Nope. Don't do that, Rae. "No, but thanks." I carefully stand and reach into my pocket.

"I'll get the drinks. You get home safe."

I nod, but I'm not even looking at him. I need to call a cab and make it within walking distance of the firehouse before I can't walk straight. "Thanks," I mumble. I walk to the door and stand at the sidewalk, looking both ways for a taxi. They're still out at this time of night, right?

There's no yellow car in sight even after a few minutes pass. I should call a service at this point.

A black car pulls up at the curb in front of me. Wait. Did I already call for a car?

Ken gets out of the driver's seat and walks around to open the back door in front of me. "Please, Rebecca. I insist. It's no trouble."

Maybe not for him, but I can't get in his car with how I'm feeling. I open my mouth to refuse again when I'm shoved from behind and pushed into the backseat.

"Hey!" I cry out, then slap my hand over my mouth as my world tilts and nausea grips me. The door slams shut behind me, but I'm already sinking into pitch black.

I wake to hands groping my breasts and a tongue down my throat.

I gag.

My initial reaction is to shove whoever it is away from me, but my hands jerk in restraints behind my back.

I bite the tongue in my mouth, hard. A man shouts in front of me, and I take another slow breath, making sure I'm not actually going to hurl before I open my eyes.

Ken's holding his mouth and glaring down at me. I look down, and thank fuck I'm still wearing clothes. But I am tied to a chair. I check our surroundings, albeit slowly, because my head still feels like it's filled with cotton balls, and any fast movements make my stomach clench painfully.

It looks like I'm in a kitchen-dining area of an apartment.

His place?

Ugh.

"What. Did. You. Give. Me?" My mouth is dry as fuck. The only saliva in there tastes like *him*. My stomach rolls again. I gather whatever moisture is in my mouth and spit it out on the floor.

Ken either moves really fast, or my brain is still moving too slow because he's suddenly kneeling between my legs with his hand on my throat. "Just some sleeping pills, Becky. I didn't think you'd wake up so soon, but maybe I took too long getting everything ready."

Ew. That nickname sounds worse than anything else he could have given me. "Not. *Becca*."

"Oh, I know. You're Raegan. But I like Becky better. You're not the only one who can rename people to what they want."

Wait. What?

"And once I'm done with you, you can go back to being Raegan when I turn you in to GE."

Oh. Fuck no. I know this is bad. Really bad. I can barely get any words from my brain to my mouth, let alone get my body to respond to me right now. Wake up, stupid body!

And I *knew* he was tied to GE. But where does he fit in with them? He must be higher than a goon if he was at the mayor's house.

Ken chuckles. "A goon? That's cute."

Did I say that aloud? No, he said something earlier about renaming people too. As if he knows I call him Ken.

I drag my head up so I can see his face more clearly. He's grinning at me.

"That's right. I can hear everything you're thinking."

Shit. Of course, now all the things I *shouldn't* let him know about all compete to jump to the forefront of my mind.

"Yes, I know Joe is dead. And I suspected it was you, but it's good to know I was right."

No, no, no. Think of nothing. Or vomiting in his face.

"Hm. Yes. You've thought about Jackson and Aiden before. I'll look into them. Who's Old Red? Ah, a firehouse?"

Panic slips through my veins as he easily plucks information from my head. I squeeze my eyes shut, hoping that might somehow block him out. *Please, no.*

"Too much?" He laughs and straightens in his position between my knees. "That was fun, but we have plenty of time to catch up later."

His hand pinches my jaw hard enough to make me cry out, and then his tongue shoves back into my mouth. I try to fight against him, but he clearly has the advantage over me now. I fight to block out what he's doing and focus instead on calling my gift. I reach for it, and then his hand grabs my tit roughly, and it snaps my concentration.

He ends the sloppy kiss, and I spit him out again. Bile creeps up my throat, and I don't try to keep it down. Memories of my ex and his friends resurface unbidden, bringing me right back to that small apartment. Of being used and tossed aside like an object.

"Don't. Touch. Me," I spit out between heavy breaths.

Ken's pawing at my shirt and trying to move it up and out of the way so he doesn't see when something floats down behind him.

But I do.

I laugh uncontrollably. At least I can do that. I may not be able to form words well enough, but I can laugh like a fucking hyena right now. My body shakes with the laughter, or maybe as a side effect of the drugs, and it's enough that he stops what he's doing to look at me with confusion.

"Why are you laughing?"

I keep laughing while looking right at the small white paper crane on the floor at his feet. "Dead. So. Dead."

His face scrunches with more confusion. Something slices through the binds at my hands and feet without a sound. I grab the rope in my hands and then smile at Ken. He hasn't noticed I'm free yet, but it's not like that's going to do me a load of good while my body is still sluggish.

There's a scuffing noise from a room off the living area, and Ken spins around to look. I get up slowly, only because my body doesn't let me move as much as I want to, then step on the chair and launch myself at his back. I fall into him, knocking us both down, but I'm able to get the rope around his throat.

I get up enough to kneel on his spine while leaning back, forcing his head up.

Jackson enters the room steadily, his boots taking their time as he crosses the floor to us. He stops just in front of Ken and pauses to look me over. Then he smiles at me, but it's cold and void of anything human.

He's *pissed*.

My body shivers involuntarily at his smile. I know it's aimed at Ken, not me, but it's terrifying all the same.

"Hold him still for me, little one," his husky voice commands. He slides a knife out from under his hoodie and crouches before Ken. Even in that position, he still has to look down to see Ken's face, where it's angled up from the ground. He looks menacing as his body shadows over Ken's while he prepares to mete out his punishment.

Jackson grips Ken's cheeks in an imitation of what that man had just done to me. I can feel his body tremble with the effort not to open his mouth. Jack just keeps smiling and then lays the blade against his cheekbone with the sharp point angling into his eye.

"Open wide, or I'll take your eye out first."

Ken's body jerks and thrashes beneath me. I hold on tightly to the rope, but my balance still isn't where it normally is, and I fall off him. He jumps to his feet, breaking my hold on the rope, then screams and looks down.

There's a knife sticking out of his gut. He reaches for it, but Jack tsks.

"I wouldn't pull that out if I were you. Now, take a seat." He shoves Ken backward, who falls into the chair I'd been in. The rope I'd dropped hovers in front of me. I grab it and wrap it back around his throat without question.

He jerks in the seat, but something is keeping his legs against the chair because every movement is small and hardly moves him from his spot. "No, wait. Don't! I'm begging you! Oh my God, you're crazy! Stay the fuck away from me!" Ken struggles harder, refusing to give up. As if he knows the second he stops trying to escape, it's over.

I wonder if he's reading Jack's mind right now and what he found there.

"Please, don't do this. I'll do anything. I swear!" He snivels, tears and snot running down his face.

Jackson cocks his head to the side as if he's considering letting this man live.

I know with certainty that he won't be walking out of here.

It's not great, considering his ties to Joe, but this isn't on me. If he hadn't drugged me, stolen information from my head, or forced himself on me, then I wouldn't be killing him. Now he has to die. I don't let rapists live to do it to anyone else.

"What's your role with Gifted Enterprise?" Jack asks calmly.

"I'm—I'm their lawyer. I represent anyone in GE if a suit comes up."

Jackson taps a blade into the palm of his hand. "Joe?"

"Yes! Yes, he's—was—my current client. He had a lot of harassment suits I was taking care of before he could join the Board."

"Who are your other clients?"

"Let me get you a list. If we can just go to my office…"

"What do you know about where GE's headquarters is?" Jack asks instead.

"I-I don't know that! They come to me or call my office when they need something."

"What about their lab research facilities?" Jackson tries again.

Ken sputters. "I don't—Wait! I know they own a hospital here. Saint…St. Marks! They could be doing experiments there! It's where I was going to take her after—" He gasps and snaps his mouth shut.

Jack's dark smile returns. "I've already dismantled that hospital. Anything else? No?" He shoves his thumb into Ken's mouth and pries it open with the knife between his teeth. Ken's screams tear through the apartment, and there's a second of concern about being heard until I see the lack of reaction by Jackson. And then I forget all about that when I see Ken's tongue pinched between Jack's fingers before he drops it at his feet.

Ken's head lulls forward.

I look over him to Jackson, whose blue eyes are already fixated on me. I feel like a deer in headlights as his attention zeroes in on me.

He's giving off a lot of bloodlust vibes right now, and self-preservation tells me not to move and draw more attention to me. So I don't. I barely breathe.

Then his gaze drops back to Ken. His hand grips the back of Ken's hair and pulls his face back up. I realize that I'm no longer holding the rope at his throat, but I don't think it was doing much to begin with. "You touched her too, right?" Jack looks down pointedly at Ken's hands, which are still cupping the hilt coming out of him as if they might stabilize it.

"Jack," I breathe before I can stop myself. His eyes jump up to mine without hesitation, and the air suddenly feels thinner. Shit. What was I going to say? I don't have a problem killing him. It's just...something about Jackson feels...off. Something's not right. "He's my kill," I finally tell him.

He chuckles and shakes his head at me. Not to tell me no, but like he expected this from me. "You're still trying to save them, even after what he would have done to you." I don't answer him. I'm not sure why he thinks I'm saving him when I'm saying I want to be the one to kill him, but I also don't think it's wise to try arguing with him right now. He's been gone for a month doing, I have no idea what, but apparently, taking down a *hospital* is in there somewhere, and I can see the difference.

It's like he's shed the skin of humanity and left only the monster.

"You don't want me to hurt him anymore?" he asks me, his head tilted like a curious puppy wanting to understand what his master wants from him.

"No. I just want this over with."

He nods and takes a step back. He wipes his blade clean on his hoodie and puts it away, then yanks his other knife free from Ken to clean and sheath it as well. If he removes it rougher than necessary, I don't comment. Jackson finally settles his hands in his front pocket to show he has no plans to interfere. But he remains standing in front of Ken like he wants to watch this man's death front and center.

It takes more time than usual to call on my gift, even without distractions, but I can feel that my body is pushing through the sleeping pills. My head is clearer, if foggy, and my body is responding to me faster than before. I'm through the worst of it, though I'm sure I'll still sleep like the dead after this is all over until it's completely out of my system.

I flinch at the pain of my gift when it finally comes out. Hopefully, Jack doesn't notice, but I don't dare look at him in case he did. I focus on Ken instead, on thrusting my gift into him and watching him scream as it eats away at his insides. I keep both hands on his shoulders, pouring more and more of my gift into him and focusing only on the burn in my hands rather than the aftermath of Ken.

When his voice stops suddenly, I look up at Jackson. He's smirking at Ken, then lifts his gaze to mine. "He's dead," he confirms. There's blood on his face. I don't remember if it's from what he did before or what just happened, but the combination of blood spatter and the malicious intent in his darker blue eyes while he stares at me sends goosebumps racing down my neck and arms.

A moment of silence stretches between us, and then Jackson's kissing me in a frenzy. I'm still not one hundred percent, but I give him everything I can and let him take the rest. I fall into his kiss, letting him consume me as he tells me with his mouth and his hands how much he missed me. How we're not meant to be apart for so long.

My hands grab and claw at the back of his neck, as if I can somehow press myself closer to him if I have him in my hands just right.

He rips his mouth from mine, and the same frenzy is in his eyes when he looks at me. "Run, little one. Don't let me catch you."

My mind trips over his words.

What?

"Now." He licks his lips and steps back. His body is vibrating with the need to move. To *catch me.*

I feel a thrill of excitement rush through me, leaving me breathless, while a still-sane part of my brain tries to tell me this is crazy. Alarm bells are ringing in my head, but the hunger in his stare sends my heart catapulting out of my chest.

I'm doing this. It's insane. Sick. Twisted. We just killed someone. He has that man's blood on him still. There's every chance he might want a piece of me too, and I'm just setting myself up like a pig on a platter for him, apple in my mouth and all, but I'm convinced he won't hurt me. Just like I told him to stop torturing what's-his-face, he would stop right now if I asked him to.

I could.

But I won't.

I turn and run from him, my heart in my throat and a buzz of adrenaline electrifying my body as I run through room after room. This apartment is giant. I find a spiral staircase in a hallway and take it two steps at a time. I'm straining to hear if he's started hunting me yet, but the pounding of my heart and my harsh pants are making it impossible to hear anything else.

I run into what looks like a second smaller kitchen, then scramble to open the cabinets to find one that will fit me. I try to quietly shove some pots aside and then crawl underneath, closing the cabinet in front of me when I'm in.

The rapid beat of my heart makes me feel lightheaded, but it's like a new sort of high that I revel in as I wait anxiously for any sign of him. I think I hear a door creak open, and I cover my mouth to make sure my breathing doesn't give me away. The cabinet door swings open, and a hand wraps around my ankle and pulls me out.

I kick at him and flip over onto my hands and knees to try to get to my feet, but he deflects the kick and drags me back under him. Jackson flips me over on my back. All the while, I'm still playing the game of trying to get away. He told me not to let him catch me, and it clicks in my brain that I didn't know exactly what my punishment would be if he did catch me.

I fight harder, but his hips pin my legs down, and my wrists are captured over my head, stretching me out for him. Jackson kisses me, and my thighs clench with the desperate need for him to claim me. His hand unbuttons my pants and slips inside to feel just how much I need him. He drives two fingers into me, and my body welcomes him with easy, slick passage.

I groan into his mouth, my fight completely melting away under his touch. I whimper when his hand leaves me. In seconds, he's removed our shoes and pants, and lines his dick with my entrance.

I cry out when he slams into me, my back arching sharply. It's rough, but I love it. I feel alive and wild. Each thrust and grind of his hips has me moaning his name for more. His pace slows when he dips down to kiss me again, and it feels like he's claiming me in every way. He's tasting his name on my lips and drinking in my pleasure for his own.

Then he draws my wetness up through my folds and teases around my clit, and my body stutters against his. He doesn't let up, running his thumb in maddening circles as his pace intensifies until

I explode around him. I scream out as my orgasm takes me. Jackson rides through it and then hilts himself with a shudder.

He drops over me, his forearms on either side of me, and kisses me like I'm a glass of water he's parched for. My hands tug and grip his dark hair, loving the feel of it, of him, against me again.

Jack presses his forehead against mine as we catch our breath.

"I missed you," I tell him softly.

His eyes widen a fraction, then drop back down as he smiles. Admitting that to him is embarrassing and vulnerable. Two things I actively avoid. But I'd also regret not telling him if he disappears again for another month. Or...who knows how long next time? The only reason I'm seeing him now is because he came to save me. Again.

He strokes his thumb across my cheekbone. "I've missed you too, little one."

He's calmer now, almost peaceful, and I know that it's because of me. He needs me just as much as I need him. I calm the monster beneath his skin, just like he calms the demons in my head.

Jackson takes me back to Old Red and sneaks us into my room through the window. I wasn't sure if I'd planned on coming back here before, but now all I can think about is sleep. I'll figure out what I'm doing next after that.

"Is this how you've been visiting me? Sneaking through my window?" I smile up at him. We're both lying on our sides on my bed facing each other, his one arm wrapped under the pillow and me and the other tracing circles along my hip.

He smiles at me, bringing his dimple out for me to see up close. "You knew."

I nod my head, fighting my eyes to stay open as sleep calls to me.

"Get some sleep, little one."

"Are you going to leave again?"

His fingers stop their movements so he can tuck hair behind my ear. "Yes."

"Why?"

"I can't stay until I'm done."

"Will you tell me what you're doing?"

"No." I frown when he doesn't hesitate. He softens it by adding, "Not yet. It's almost time."

Almost time. For what?

"Go to sleep. I won't leave for a few hours still," he promises me.

I fight back a yawn and close my eyes, but try to keep our conversation going. "I shouldn't have killed him. Aiden's going to be mad at me," I mumble.

"He deserved worse." He kisses the side of my forehead. "Don't worry. I'll take care of everything."

CHAPTER SEVENTEEN

RAEGAN

I MAKE IT THROUGH two days without seeing anyone. Well, for the most part. I sneak into the kitchen for the replenished bowl of strawberries and sandwiches and smuggle them back to my room while everyone is asleep, then lock my door and close the curtains.

Kellan comes knocking first about our training session, but I'd only just woken up after falling asleep with Jackson, and I was not in the mood. I tell him I'm out of commission for girl reasons. He promises light exercises instead, but I snap at him to leave me alone, and he thankfully gets the hint.

Dane tries next, saying he wants to talk to me. He is the *exact* person I'm hiding from right now, so I tell him I don't feel well. Thankfully, he doesn't push it and leaves without a fuss like Kell.

Aiden comes the next day and even unlocks my door to peek inside. As if he thinks I have a recording or something in here. I chuck a book at him and yell at him to get out.

Kellan tries again, and through sheer force of my will over his, I get him to leave me alone.

It seems like they have no idea why I'm hiding, which means Dane hasn't said anything to them yet, but I'm too scared to test it. I'm too ashamed to face Dane and see the look on his face. I'm not even sure what I'm imagining. Disgust? Fear? Loathing?

Maybe a combination of all of it.

Whatever it is, I don't want to see it. Over the last month, I've worked hard for the begrudging acceptance from Dane. He still doesn't trust me, or believe me, or...*like* me, but he isn't going out of his way to be a dick to me either. If anything, he's quiet around me. Observant. Like he's measuring my every action and word against his previous vision of me.

Once he tells the others, and I know he will, then I won't be able to look any of them in the eye. It'd be better to skip out now before that happens. Then I can still remember the good times before it all went to hell. I can remember the way Kellan looked at me, teased me, and made me feel like I was strong. A fighter.

I don't think I can keep them back another day, or if I'll have the answer on what to do by tomorrow.

So, I do what I do best, and I run.

I stuff my backpack with as many clothes as I can fit. It's the middle of the night now, so I open my window and gently drop my backpack first, then carefully crawl out and hop down.

I creep out of the yard and down the drive, then relax once I'm on the road.

I walk toward the city while working on a plan as I go. I'm not sure if I'm ready to leave this city yet, not when all the GE activity is happening here. I tell myself it's not out of fear of Dane being taken and wanting to be close by, just in case. This city is just a hotspot right now.

Next is where I'm going to live. I could check for any hostels in the city and, if not, see if the bar owner where I work owns the apartments above it or knows who does. It's backward from how I usually barter, where I trade my off-the-books employment for the room. He's already getting that, so I'm not sure what else I could offer him. I can't give away my tips since that's my only income.

I hear a car motor behind me and dash behind the nearest tree. It slows and then stops on the road right where I was.

"Why are you hiding?" Aiden calls out.

Shit. He obviously saw me, so I step around the tree. "I didn't realize it was you," I answer with confidence I don't feel. GE is still looking for me, even if the cops aren't, so it should be a satisfactory response. He doesn't look convinced.

"Well, it's me. Come here."

I sigh and step closer to the door. He eyes my backpack, and I subconsciously shift it further over my shoulder and behind me.

"Where are you going?" he croons in his velvety tone that spells trouble.

I shrug nonchalantly. "To work." I lift the arm of the backpack. "This is for my disguise." He stares at me, and I smile back at him. See? Nothing to see here. Move along.

"Get in." I hesitate, and he leans over to shove the passenger door open for me. "I got a call from Cibrina about something at the Guild, and I'm going in. I'll probably chat with the two GE people while I'm there if they're up." He watches my face before adding, "I assume you want to be there for that."

I grip my backpack harder. If I go with him, he's going to bring me back to Old Red when we're done, and I'll have to try this all over again tomorrow. And get through another whole day without Kellan breaking my door down. Which I'm pretty sure is his next move.

If I don't go with him, it'll definitely set off a flag to Aiden that something's up, and he'll drag me back to Old Red, anyway.

So, really, there's no choice. At least pretending I'm making this call means I might glean some information from Reid or Tinsley. I'll have to work on my escape plan while Aiden's working on whatever else he's doing at the Guild to see how I can slip away as soon as we return.

Aiden raises his eyebrows at me, and I nod mutely. I walk around the car and buckle in.

There's almost no time between him hitting the gas on the car and diving right into questioning me. "Have you seen Jackson lately?"

Yes. "No," I lie. I don't know why I do. Jackson didn't ask me to hide that I'd seen him, but something in my gut tells me there's something going on between them. I need to get more information before I decide what I'm going to do with what I know.

Not that it's much at all. Jackson didn't tell me anything. Something about a hospital, I guess, but I don't know what that would have to do with Aiden.

Aiden keeps his eyes on the road ahead of us, but his jaw ticks with frustration.

"Why? Is something wrong?"

He purses his lips in thought, then gives me a careful side-eye. "He's been going on a killing rampage of GE employees. Groups of them at a time. And half of them aren't being cleaned up and are left for people to find. They're being plastered all over the news."

Oh. Well, then.

I bite my lower lip and stare at my hands in my lap. When he said he 'dismantled' a hospital, was that what he meant? Killing them and having it on the news? And for what? Why bring attention to it? We don't want the cops or FBI involved in the fight with GE. Most of the government is in GE's pocket, and who knows who else has been compromised.

"So...he's not working under your orders?" I check just in case. Maybe he took it a step too far by not cleaning up after himself like usual.

"No. Guarding Old Red was the last thing I asked him to do."

"Oh."

I glance up again to see him watching me out of the corner of his eye. "He's also been dropping children off at the Guild. No warning or heads-up. They just walk down one of the tunnels from different access points in the city and knock at the door."

I fold my arms over my chest. His eyes drop to the bandage on my arm from Vera, but it's already scabbed over and healing. It was a shallow cut. Bloody, but shallow.

"Isn't that a good thing? He's rescuing them."

Aiden exhales, and I feel like an ignorant child who doesn't understand the world yet. There's truth in that, though, because I don't have the faintest idea of *his* world. He gave me a taste of what else was on his plate, and before he could explain any more of it to me, I ran from it. How much more do I want to see proof of how deeply Aiden cares for others? It only reinforces the reminder that I'm the problem, not him, when it comes to us.

There is no us. There never was.

Just that one time. In the island library.

"The Guild is like a business. Everyone in it has a job or contributes in some way. No one is under the working age. What are we going to do with a bunch of children? We don't have the place or the resources to give them everything they need."

"You've saved kids before. Isabel, for one..."

"We have been working on ways to deprogram anyone we've saved from GE, but they usually aren't children. She was an exception, and it was one kid. Any others we found we planned for. We erased any documentation or GE people who knew about them before returning them to a family member. That was how we worked as a team. But Jack isn't doing any of that. He's doing all the killing and getting the kids away and then moving on without the follow-through that Dane and I would do."

"Then do it for these kids."

We pull into a parking space at a standalone bar downtown and park. Aiden's hands tighten on the wheel as he looks directly at me. "He's dropping off kids daily when we used to have two to three a month. Even if I knew who he took them from or if they told anyone about these kids, I couldn't be one hundred percent certain that GE doesn't still know about them to try kidnapping them again."

I chew anxiously on my lip when I realize how messed up this is now. The Guild has a bunch of missing children on them that they can't just return home. And he said they don't have the resources to keep them either.

Aiden turns the car off and unbuckles himself. "Now, you see the problem. If you see Jackson again" – he gives me a look that tells me he doesn't believe my previous lie for a second – "then tell him we all need to talk. If he's working on some sort of plan, we all need to be in on it. You and Dane already learned why going rogue is off the table at this point. Now, it's Jackson's turn."

I follow him out of the car. "Well, if you say it like *that*, he's not going to listen," I mutter aloud.

He shoots me a look, and I shrug. It's the truth.

We take the secret entrance in the bar to the tunnels that will lead us to the bunker. Something was definitely different with Jackson, but it wasn't wrong. He was still him. More like he's been letting more of the real him out lately.

The only reason I can think of that would have triggered the change is Thorne.

Is he hunting him down? Trying to draw him out? If so, I hope he would come to us to help him so he's not facing that terrifying man alone.

Once we're inside, I keep on Aiden's heels to make sure I don't get lost. We stop in front of a solid door that's within a wall of glass to expose the interior of the room. It looks like a bedroom. Could this be where Reid or Tinsley are staying? I thought we would interview them later.

Aiden pulls his phone out and types in a number, then the lock clicks loudly. He pushes the door in and waits for me to enter first. It would seem gentlemanly, if we weren't walking into a prisoner's cell where the first one in could be attacked. I glance through the doorway into the room and frown when I don't see anyone. There are a couple of doors in the room, so maybe they're in one of those?

I walk in slowly, everything on alert to listen for someone else.

The door closes and locks behind us, which I'm sure is a security protocol, so the prisoner doesn't try to escape while we're in here, but then a steel wall comes down in front of the floor-to-ceiling glass wall.

For privacy during the interview, I try to reassure myself, but my gut pinches in disagreement. There's another beep behind me, and I look up to see the lights turning off on the security cameras in the ceiling. Aiden finishes pushing all the buttons on his phone and pockets it in the inside of his suit jacket.

I swallow my nerves and step away from him so my back is to the wall, and I can see him and the rest of the room. "What's going on?" My voice comes out thinly, probably because my heart rate and breathing have both picked up.

Aiden slowly pulls out the cuff congressman Joe had put on me, that I'd stolen and brought to my room in Old Red but forgot about since then, out of his jacket. There's a new chain and cuff attached to the other end of it. "Put these on first."

I give him a sarcastic, if breathy, laugh. "You're joking." He stares at me. "Why would I do that?"

"This is me asking nicely, Raegan. Just like last time. Do what I'm telling you, or don't complain about how I make it happen anyway," he coos. I shiver. Not in response to the cool threat of his words, but the smoothness of his voice as he says them.

"What do you want, Aiden? Stop threatening me and just tell me," I snap angrily.

He holds the cuffs out to me on one finger, his other hand casually tucked into his slacks pocket. "I want you to put these on so we can have a conversation without you trying to destroy me or this room to run away. I want you to *do what I say* for once in your life, so this isn't more difficult than it needs to be."

I stare at him. At the cuffs. Him.

Does he really think I'd use my gift on him or this room to avoid some questions? I just won't answer them. Or is this a test? To see if I can ever listen to him or if he'll never be able to trust me.

My hand slowly extends out to his. I wrap my fingers around the cuff, waiting for him to drop it and then bring it in front of me. He watches me closely, but he doesn't rush me. Maybe this is just a test. If it is, I hate that he's using these. Anything but these. It feels...*wrong*...when my gift is muted. Like I'm missing a limb, and I'm no longer fully balanced.

I flip them over in my hands. "You found this in my room." It's not a question.

"I did," he agrees anyway.

"What were you doing in there?"

His lips thin, and he looks away. "I was retrieving my stolen shirts."

Hm. I'm not sure I believe him on that but let it go for now. I open one of the cuffs further in preparation to put one of my wrists inside and then stop. "There's no key for these," I say when I remember I hadn't grabbed them off Joe before leaving.

Aiden holds up a small key between his thumb and forefinger. "I made a new one. That's how they're open now."

I realize I'm dragging this out, but I'm dreading the feeling of being cut off from my gift. I'd ask if we could use rope or something else instead, but I know the point is to render my gift useless. If he only knew how much I hated using it in the first place, maybe this wouldn't be such an issue. Only Kellan really knows that. And Jack a bit, only because he knows how I see myself.

Finally, I bite the bullet and click my wrist on the first bracelet, then do the same for the other. The feeling is almost instant. I feel empty, hollowed out.

I may not like using my gift, but I have to admit I'd never want to be without it. It's like cutting out one of my senses that I've used all my life and making me walk around without it.

My face is tight with unease when I glare over at Aiden for making me do this. "There. Now, what?"

Aiden looks surprised. "I didn't think you'd do it on your own."

"Yeah, well, miracles do happen, but they're rare, so don't get used to it. Now, say what you want to say or ask, and let's get this over with so I can take them off. I hate feeling like this."

His brown eyes bounce back up to mine, and I think I spot a flicker of pity in them. "They aren't coming off."

My heart jumps out of rhythm.

"*Excuse me?*" I demand, my voice pitching higher than usual.

"You were running tonight, weren't you?" he asks casually. He takes several steps closer to me, but I have nowhere to go with the wall at my back. My neck cranes back so I can keep his face in my view when he draws nearer. I clench my fists and glare at him to hide the fear snaking up my spine.

He continues on when I don't answer him right away. "I heard you leave and followed you. There was no phone call from Cibrina. I'm not interviewing Reid or Tinsley in the middle of the night. We're here because you're running from something. You're going to tell me what that is so you can get over it and come back to Old Red with me, or you're going to move here permanently until you can be trusted again not to run off."

My back hits the wall, and he leans down to whisper. "I told you I'd lock you up if I could. Now that you can't run or break out of here, we have a lot to talk about, don't you think?"

I swallow.

Fuck.

His index finger lifts my chin to bring my face up to his. "Well? What spooked you?"

I try to keep the cringe and effort off my face as I work at pushing my thumb out of its socket. He doesn't know I got out of these cuffs before without a key. I can just do it again. Doesn't mean I don't hate doing this, but I'd rather that than open up to the person who's betrayed my trust the most. I don't owe him explanations for anything.

As far as he knows, he abandoned me on the island with our enemies. He doesn't know my roommate rescued me that day despite his efforts against me. And he hasn't said a *damn thing* about what he did since learning why I'd killed Vera. I don't think he even flinched. As if knowing it was an accident made no difference to him at all. He's already decided to hate me, regardless of what happens from here.

So, no, I don't think I'll be sharing.

"Fuck you, Aiden."

My thumb slips over the other one in my attempt, and my body jerks the tiniest movement.

He notices.

Aiden looks down to see what I'm trying to do, and his brows furrow. He snatches my hands and throws them over my head, lacing our fingers together in each hand as he now crowds over me. "Start talking, or this will be your new home for the foreseeable future."

I glare up at him. There's absolutely no way I'm being locked up again. My hands struggle against his to get free, but it's no use. I bring my leg up, but he blocks it with his own with a snarl.

"Fuck, you're infuriating! Why do you have to make everything so difficult?!" His hands shift to the chain, and then he drops one to point it at my chest. "Give me something. If you want me to trust you, then you can't keep running off on your own without telling us what's going on."

My arms jerk when I attempt to bring my hands back together, only to find that my arms are firmly stuck apart. I glance up and stare at the solid metal bar he's holding against the wall instead of the chain. Which means I can't reach my other hand to dislocate my thumb anymore.

Dammit.

"Well?" he demands in a low tone but no less angry.

I shift my face back to glare at him. "Why would I ever tell you anything? You're the *first* person who would use anything I said against me. Did you ever think that the reason I don't tell you anything is because I don't trust *you*?" I spit back.

Aiden yanks us both back from the wall and spins us around so my back is to his front, his hands gripping the bar in front of me, and his breath heating the side of my neck. "We seem to be at an impasse, then. I won't trust you until you share everything you're hiding, and you don't trust me enough to tell me any of it."

My heart thumps like I'm running a marathon as his arms trap me back against him. Cinnamon fills my nose when I take a breath to fight the shiver slithering down my neck. "Where does that leave us?"

I can feel his lips twist up into a smirk. "Right here. In this room."

He releases me suddenly, and I have to plant my feet before I fall over. The door clicks and locks shut behind him, and I'm left alone.

Locked up, just like he'd promised.

CHAPTER EIGHTEEN

DANE

I TAP MY FOOT continuously on the hardwood floor while leaning back onto the couch. I shove my fingers through my hair for the umpteenth time to relieve the headache that's slowly formed over the last thirty minutes of being awake while Aiden still sleeps. Kellan is punching a bag in the workout room while he waits, but it won't be long before he breaks.

Raegan was going to leave last night.

We'd all been on alert after the way she'd been hiding from us the last couple of days. So, when she slipped out her window in the dead of night, none of us had been asleep.

And then Aiden came back hours later. Alone. Said something about giving her a night alone to cool down, and then she would come back in the morning. He *swore* that she wasn't going to disappear.

But now it's morning.

And she's still not here.

It's bothering me more than I'd like to admit, but there are things I need to say to her still. Questions I have to ask her.

The other night showed me another side to Vera. A side I never thought I would see.

The *look* she gave me when I told her we could go home together. As if our family meant nothing to her anymore.

How *I* felt like nothing to her when she kicked my notebook aside.

What have they done to you, Vera?

We used to be so close that I could tell what she was thinking with only a look. We didn't need words between us, because we always knew what the other was thinking or feeling.

The person who I saw on the rooftop was a stranger to me.

"Did you know that she and Gordon were fucking?" I didn't believe Raegan when she said that. I'd assumed she was being petty and just trying to paint Vera in a negative light. She couldn't have known that. *My sister* wouldn't have slept with the people holding us captive. She was too young and too smart for that.

"She was going to kill Dane."

"You were fine, *Dane. Worst case, the machines would have brought you back."*

I've made a horrible mistake.

Raegan saved me.

And I tried to kill her.

Fuck.

I have to see her. I need to talk to her and...I don't even know what to say. Does sorry even cover how horrible I've been to her?

Will she even give me a chance to make it right, or have I fucked everything up too much? Is it too late?

Boots thunder across the floorboards, and I pull my hand from my hair to stuff in my pocket as Kellan stomps by. He doesn't bother looking my way as he exits the training room and storms down the hallway to what I'm sure is Aiden's door. He pounds on it repeatedly and then snarls, "Where is she?!"

Aiden must say something to him, because then his anger escalates. "Safe?! What does that mean?"

I'm tempted to get up and walk over there so I can hear what Aiden's saying, but decide to make myself and Aiden a cup of coffee in the kitchen instead. It brings me close enough to hear them both without officially joining the conversation.

"It means she hasn't gone anywhere. Calm down and let me put some goddamn clothes on. I'll meet you in the dining room to tell you what happened."

I hear Kellan's fist connect with the wall. "If you've done anything to her..."

"I didn't harm a single hair on her head, Kell. Now, get out." The door slams shut.

Kellan shows up at the table, roughly yanking out a chair, and then, glaring at it, knocks it to the side and opts for pacing instead. I'm watching him over the edge of my coffee cup when his eyes snap over to me, and he realizes I've moved from the couch. Instead of taunting me over it, he growls to himself and keeps pacing the floor.

I move to the table and set Aiden's coffee down before sitting in my seat. I rarely make the others coffee, but I feel the smallest smidge of guilt that Aiden's taking the heat from Kellan because of my issues with Raegan. I'm assuming that's why Aiden's been keeping his distance from her and is treating her in a way he never had on the island.

Another way I'm fucking up his life.

I take another sip of coffee, even though it scalds my tongue and burns the taste buds off.

Aiden strolls out in thick sweatpants and a plain shirt. He's barefoot as well, which means he really wasn't ready to wake up yet. If he even fell asleep. His face is drawn with exhaustion like he'd been up all night thinking instead of sleeping.

The second Aiden pulls out his chair to sit, Kell is spinning around and jumping down his throat. "What happened?"

"Give him a fucking second!" I snap. Nothing is going to change with her situation, whatever it is, by ripping the answers out in thirty seconds instead of giving Aiden a second to breathe first.

My heel pops off the ground again to bounce up and down. I keep it from touching the floor so no one else can hear it, but it helps me release the anxious energy coiled tightly in my chest.

Aiden sighs and lifts his cup of coffee. "Thank you," he offers me tiredly before bringing it to his lips.

Kellan's hands smack down on either side of the table as he leans over it from the opposite side of the table from Aiden. His body is quivering and tight. I think if he knew exactly where she was right now, he'd be running there.

"She wouldn't tell me anything," Aiden begins.

"I knew I should have been the one to stop her." Kellan grips the table in his hands. "She would have talked to me."

Aiden scoffs. "She would have given you a distraction and then slipped away while your back was turned. I made sure she didn't leave. That was more important."

"How?" Kellan demands.

"By locking her up in the bunker."

My foot flattens on the ground as I stare at him in shock.

"You WHAT?!" Kellan roars.

"Sorry, but how did you ask her what was going on? And go from that to locking her up?" I ask with feigned nonchalance. As if none of what he just said bothers me at all, even though my chest is tight and my fingers flex and then grip my coffee mug.

"I demanded she tell me, or she'd be staying there."

Kellan groans. "How can you suck at talking to Raegan so much? You don't have a problem talking with the Guild members, even when you're scolding them." He stands up and moves away from the table. "I'm getting her out and bringing her back here."

Aiden sets his coffee mug down abruptly. "No." Kell's chest puffs up, but Aiden's eyes snap to mine. "Dane's going to get her out."

My eyes narrow at him. "Why?" My voice comes out caustic, which sets off a growl in Kellan, but I keep my focus trained on Aiden.

"Because whatever her problem is, it has to do with you. Or Vera. This all started after your last adventure that almost got you both killed. So, you go let her free and figure this out."

My mouth tightens. I have an idea of what she might be upset about. No, not an idea. A slew of them. I just don't know which of them are the ones that made her think it was better for her to leave than stick around.

I have some things to say to her anyway, so I just nod that I'll do it without further complaint.

"I'm coming with you." Kellan crosses his arms over his chest, prepared to fight with me on it, but I haven't gone anywhere alone in a very long time.

"No shit," I snark at him. "You're driving."

"Pick up groceries on your way back. I won't be able to get them today, and we're almost out," Aiden slides in like it's nothing. "Oh, and you'll need this." His hand pushes something across the table to me and then returns to his coffee mug.

I pick up the key that's far too small for a door. "For what?"

"She's wearing the cuff she'd told us about that has your gift in it. So, she couldn't just break out and leave."

If looks could kill, Aiden would be dead. I rush Kellan out the door before that can happen.

"Give me the key. I'll get her out."

I roll my eyes and keep walking. "Aiden said it has to be me." My fist tightens on the small key I haven't let go of since I picked it up off the table. We're walking down the 'nice' prisoner corridor, which was originally meant for quarantine if needed, rather than as jail cells. It's why they have nice beds, a closet, a private bathroom, and a table and chairs. They each have a television, books, and other random things to entertain the guests staying in them.

It's sad that these rooms are bigger and nicer than the rooms we're currently staying in at Old Red.

Which reminds me, I need to get back to renovating the place. Once the main areas were done, I'd had to focus on training. But there's still the other half of the dorm rooms that need to be fixed up or torn down and used to expand our rooms. Then the truck bay and locker room after that, for whatever we plan on converting those into.

"He can say whatever he wants. But you are not manipulating her into talking to you. If she doesn't want to talk, then she doesn't fucking have to." Kellan stops in front of me and holds out his hand.

I jerk to a halt and then glare at his hand and the expectation that I'll just hand it over. I bring my gaze up to his face. "I'm not manipulating anyone."

Kellan grins arrogantly at me. "Good. Then you'll give me the key."

"Me unlocking her cuffs isn't manipulating her," I argue hotly, keeping my fist at my side resolutely.

"No? Then why do you care about doing it? Since when do you care about setting her free?"

"I don't—"

"Right. You don't," he interrupts before I can finish. Not that I have any clue what the fuck I was about to say anyway, so it's actually for the best. "So. Give. Me. The. Key."

My jaw clenches. He fucking has me.

Why am I clinging to the key so hard? Being the one with the key to release her gift makes them her hero in that moment. Is that what I'm suddenly trying to be? Or am I going to give that to Kellan, who's been at her side almost since she showed up here? He deserves it much more than I do.

But it's my fault she tried to run away in the first place. If I hadn't brought her out with me to Vera again...

I thrust the key into his hand and then move around him to keep walking.

Prick.

Movement in one of the rooms draws my attention, and I see Reid and Tinsley sitting in the same room together. Tinsley's watching something on the TV while Reid reads a book in the other chair, though it's pressed up right against hers, so their arms are almost touching. I pause to watch them through the glass and wonder if having them here was the best idea.

If Reid can teleport, he could leave that room at any time. He could scout out the Guild and report back to GE, and we would never know. They were both blindfolded and given headphones with loud music to block them from being able to track how we got here or from seeing anything outside of this room, but again, that doesn't defend well against a transporter.

"Piece of shit..." Kellan mutters a handful of rooms down while jabbing his finger at the screen of his phone.

I sigh and pull out my phone to open the app Aiden and I worked on together for this place. I key in the number on the door to pull up the options, then press the button to unlock the door and remove the steel wall over the window.

Raegan's still fast asleep in the bed. She's lying on her side on top of the blankets, her shirt hiked up to expose her side and lower back while her arms are tucked in and her hands out. It isn't until I'm inside the room that I see the cuffs on her wrists and the bar between them, forcing her hands apart from each other.

Her body rises and falls slowly in her sleep, and I'm mesmerized watching her. Like the sound of her breathing is hypnotic, or maybe just the peacefulness of her expression compared to when she's awake. Her hair is a sheet of blonde above and behind her, with some of it falling over her face.

She was always the prettiest girl I'd ever seen on the island. Cute and sweet, with a little she-devil in her that Kellan usually brought out, but I'd been enamored with her from the moment we met. She'd been sixteen the last time I had seen her. Her body was almost fully grown, but seeing her now shows how much more she's come into her own since then.

Strong. Beautiful. Fearless.

"Move," Kellan commands, and I realize I'm standing near the bed as if I'd been drawn to her from the moment I walked into the room.

I step back out of the way to give him plenty of room. "Are you going to wake her up? She looks tired."

"Well, I'm not going to stand here and stare at her like a creep until she wakes up on her own," he drawls at me in an obvious taunt for what I'd just been doing. "She can go back to sleep at Old Red in her own bed if she wants."

I move away even further so she'd have to look around the room to see me. I doubt she'd be happy to wake up to me. Kellan, on the other hand, I'm sure she's fine with. They are fucking, after all.

The reminder is like a javelin to my heart, piercing it through the center and leaving a gaping hole behind. The raw and intense reaction I have sets my teeth on edge. I fold my arms over my chest and try not to watch Kellan and Raegan out of the corner of my eye as he wakes her.

"Kell...?"

"Wake up, beautiful." His soft voice is a stark contrast to all the raging he'd been doing earlier. My fingers dig into my arms as I'm forced to listen to them, even if I'm doing my best not to watch.

"Are you breaking me out?"

"Yep. Let me get you out of those cuffs."

She inhales sharply. "How did you get the key?"

"Aiden handed it over. What he did last night was a dick move, but he was never going to keep you here long. He was just scared you were really going to take off."

Raegan huffs. "I seriously doubt that. I think he was getting off on locking me away."

Kellan cackles as I hear the click of a latch and a cuff popping open. "I bet you're fucking right. Maybe we'll lock him up next time. See how he likes it."

"Yeeees," she practically groans, and I can hear the smile coming into her voice. "Without his phone. And put a camera in Old Red that he can watch on the TV so he can see us having a fun party without him. Then he watches us sleep in until dinnertime the next day."

"I like the way you think, beautiful. We can Go Pro a joyride in his car too," Kellan adds with a loud snicker.

She laughs and then it grows quiet. I know I shouldn't look, but I do. Her hands are wrapped around the back of his neck and in his hair as she has him tugged down in a kiss. His hands are on the bed, his back hunched over in order to reach her because he's so freaking tall.

An incessant ache devours my chest as much as I try to ignore it. This shouldn't bother me. The feelings I'd buried beneath years of anger and grief shouldn't be rising steadily, day after day of being near her again. Would letting them back in make me a shit brother?

I'm such a fucking hypocrite.

Pain in my hand startles me away from them to find red crescents embedded in my palm. I stretch out my hand and almost make a noise to interrupt when they finally take a breath. About fucking time.

"We both know you don't give a shit about him watching you in his car. You just want an excuse to drive it again. Race with it, probably," Raegan teases Kellan.

Kell chuckles. "You've got me there."

She smiles, and then something catches her eye because she looks up over his shoulder and notices me for the first time. Her eyes widen slightly, and she freezes.

I hate that Kellan was right, that he should be the one to help her and wake her. One look at me, and she looks ready to bolt again. Everything in my chest feels tight, constricting the air I breathe and locking my body to stone beneath her stare. I don't like her looking at me like that. It bothers me, and then I'm pissed that it would bother me in the first place.

I frown back at her. "What?" I snap on reflex.

He cups the side of her face to bring her attention back to him. His hand is practically the size of her face, and I notice the way she leans into his touch. My frown deepens. "Don't worry about Rapunzel over there. We're all going on a field trip for some groceries and then heading home."

Her bright blue eyes flick over to me again, looking uncertain—and *nervous?*—before she casts them over to the door. Like she's thinking of running.

"Nuh-uh." Kellan helps her to stand and then wraps his arm around her neck and shoulders to draw her into a side hold. "No rabbiting on us again, bunny. Whatever Dane did, just forget about it. He's a drama king and blows everything out of proportion. None of us want you to leave, even him, so there's nothing to worry about."

"I'm standing right here, asshole," I bitch at him, and he waves his other hand that's holding the cuffs at me.

"See? Drama king. We can ignore him if you want."

Raegan sighs and shakes her head. "That's not what I want."

Kellan nods, ever the one to go with the flow. "Okay then. We can talk to him if you want to."

She sneaks another look at me out of the corner of her eye. I cross my arms and watch them with undisguised annoyance. I don't care for the way Kellan's so easily draped around her and she lets it happen. It was the same way they'd been before, with him finding any excuse to touch her, usually with different styles of hugs like this one. Sneaky bastard.

I also hate that they're talking about me when I'm standing right fucking here.

But I'm able to recognize what he's doing in trying to get her to talk, so I keep my mouth shut and tongue pinched between my teeth. Kellan shoots me a smirk over her head.

Asshole.

"Uh...maybe later. You said something about a field trip?" She changes topics, running away in a different sense, but I'd prefer not to have that conversation in front of Kellan, anyway.

The things I need to say are only for her.

CHAPTER NINETEEN

DANE

GOING OUT IN PUBLIC with Kellan and Raegan together is just asking for trouble.

We're in the one-stop-shop of the town where we're staying in at Old Red, so it has everything from groceries to clothes, electronics, and games. It's where we've gotten everything we needed since moving into the firehouse, including the home repair and update items I've been using.

It's outside of the city and in such a small town that the store doesn't even bother with security cameras. I keep my hood up, anyway.

I push the cart past the aisles of things that are not groceries with a look of murder. Kellan and Raegan grabbed their own cart as if they thought we were buying that much food or would be of any help. Then Kell thought it would be fun to toss Raegan in it and sprint her down the aisles before releasing her and then trying to race her in the cart to the end. He also has to *catch* her cart at the end before she crashes into one of the displays in the bigger main aisle, and they get kicked out of the store.

If they don't get booted for doing this first.

They've already had two close calls before I swore at them and left on my own to do the shopping.

I pass one of the displays of discounted movies and pause next to it. Something possesses me to grab one of them. I pick up my pace to the grocery section and start piling food on top of it with things from our list.

"Oh, my god! Dunkaroos?!" Raegan's voice cries out in disbelief.

My head swivels toward her voice, and I see that they, at some point, have caught up to me and are following behind. Raegan's still lying back in the cart, legs hanging in the air over the end, as she holds a turquoise box of children's snacks to her chest.

"I didn't know anyone still made these!" she adds gleefully.

It doesn't pass my notice that those were some of the snacks we used to steal from the kitchens at night.

Kellan reaches in to take the box, and she play-snarls and snaps at him with her teeth while curling herself further around the box. "Mine!"

He laughs and then yanks the cart back on two wheels, and she starts sliding out. She scrambles at the sides, clinging to the cart on either side to keep herself in it while also trying to hold the treat between her chin and her chest. Kellan snatches the box away from her and then sets the cart back down.

"If I knew this was all it took to bring out your teeth, beautiful, I'd have bought a pallet of these," Kellan drawls, dangling the box over her head for her to try to reach.

I turn away from them and move down the aisle. I don't even remember what I'm supposed to be going for next, but I can't watch them anymore. They're in their own happy bubble, and I'm just staring at them like some regretful idiot.

They've fallen right back into their playful ways as they had six years ago. I miss it. But I also don't think I could ever go back to how I was. To how *we* were together.

Now, I'm just an outsider who doesn't know the first thing about what to say or do anymore.

I pull out the list again to remind myself of what's left and then make it my mission to get it all as fast as possible so we can get out of here. It's good that Kellan's been able to cheer her up, especially with me around, and I don't hate seeing her smiling again or hearing her laugh.

Once I've finished the list, I call the other two over to the register and then frown at the boxes of junk food piled around and on top of Raegan. "We are not buying all of that crap," I snap at them.

"Raegan wants it," Kellan says with a shrug. "She hasn't had any of these in years, and who are we to deny her?"

"The tooth fucking fairy denies her. None of that is good for any of us." I caution a glance at Raegan, who's hugging the Dunkaroos to her chest like she thinks I'll pry it away from her to throw in the trash. The light in her eyes she'd had while goofing off with Kellan dies as I see her closing herself off from me. Like she's just remembered that I'm here and there's still so much unspoken between us from the other night. I sigh dramatically and hold out my hand. "Give me the fucking Dunkaroos. I'll buy them, but that's it. Put the rest back."

Kellan grins at me, and I flip him off behind my back, where she can't see it.

That fucking asshole was testing me.

As soon as the bags of groceries are dumped in a heap in the kitchen, Kellan bails to the living room. "Come on, beautiful. Let's play a game."

Raegan looks between the bags and Kellan. "You aren't going to help put them away?"

"Naw. I get yelled at for putting things in the wrong place. And I've been told I take up too much room in the kitchen. Better for me to stay over here and help like this."

I ignore them both and focus on the frozen and refrigerated items first, tossing the empty bags in a pile in the corner for me to clean up when I'm done.

"I'll help Dane then, you lazy ass," she teasingly yells at him. Then she smiles almost hesitantly toward me, like she's still trying to figure out how to act around me again.

I feel the same fucking way.

"You can do the pantry items," I tell her because she's looking at me like she's waiting for a direction. She nods and opens the pantry doors, then pulls items out of bags to bring into the L-shaped walk-in pantry.

After I'm done with the cold items, I pick up the rest of the bags in two hands and bring them into the pantry, so we don't have to walk back and forth, and set them on the ground.

"Oh. That's smart." She picks through the closest bag to her and takes what she can carry, then turns to put the cans on the shelf. "So...about what Vera said..." I can tell that she's trying to act like everything's cool, but there's a shaky undertone in her voice that gives away her nerves.

"You mean when she called you names?" If that's what she's worried about, then we are on completely different pages.

"Well...yeah, that and the other things she said about me. And my...mom."

I stop putting groceries away, hoping she'll stop too so we can look at each other, but she keeps going like she needs to keep herself busy while talking. I sigh and grab something else to help her, though I take my time with it so I can still concentrate on what I want to say.

"Look...I think we should call a truce," I start, but her nose scrunches with confusion when she looks up at me from grabbing the next item on the floor.

"A truce? But I don't hate you. There's nothing to forgive on my side."

"Like me pulling a gun on you?" I ask, raising an eyebrow in disbelief.

She shrugs again, not looking at me while putting something else on the shelf. "I understood. I didn't *like* it, but I get it."

She just...understood? That almost sounds like she thinks she deserved it. I don't like that at all, if that's the way she thinks about herself. But I don't want to get sidetracked from what I need to say and push those thoughts away for later.

"Okay, fine. Then I wanted to tell you that I believe you. After seeing everything Vera did and how she acted...I can't pretend that she hasn't changed. She even admitted that she would have let me die and brought me back to get what she wanted. So...I'm sorry." I take a long, shaky breath, and she stops to stare at me with shock.

"I'm sorry for the way I've treated you when you were only trying to protect me. I...still can't believe that you guarded Vera's memory for me, even though we all turned on you for it. Part of me wishes you hadn't. That maybe we could have figured things out back then, but I also know it might not have mattered to me then. I know now that she's changed from who I remember. But I'm still not giving up on her. My sister is in there somewhere, and I *will* save her."

Raegan rubs her arms self-consciously and doesn't look convinced. "Dane, I don't know how long before I found out about her that she'd turned. I don't know if she can go back."

I shake my head because there is no way I can believe that this can't be fixed. She's *alive*. That means there's still a chance we can get her back. That's all that matters. "I was going into this thinking I could change her mind with a quick conversation, but now that I see this has been going on for at least six years, I know I need to try harder and do more."

Her face tightens, but she doesn't argue.

"It doesn't matter," I say so I can finish. "My point is that I don't want to fight with you anymore. I still care about you, even when I tried to pretend I didn't, and I don't want to see you getting hurt, either. I'd like to try being friends again; whatever that means. I forgive you for what you did. So, if you want to talk about the other things Vera mentioned, then I'm here. And if not, I won't pry. I choose to believe in you because that's what I should have done from the start."

Raegan turns away from me and closes her eyes. "No."

No?

"You don't forgive me. You can't. I don't...think that's how for-giveness works. Just because you want to give it doesn't mean that you do. I don't think it's that simple. Even if you want to, in your heart, you won't truly forgive me until you have Vera back. I still killed her. I'm still the reason you haven't had the last six years with her." She sniffs, but I can't see her face while her back is to me. "Even if we get her back, you may not forgive what I did. And I...I would understand it. I promise you, I will do anything to get her back to you. And then we can see where we are and go from there."

I ball my hands into fists and the distance between us. She's two feet from me, but she suddenly feels a thousand miles away. Have I done this? Am I the reason she doesn't think she's worthy of forgiveness? But I can't deny that what she said doesn't resonate with me.

I wrap my arms around her from behind and tug her back into me. "I'm sorry." The words come out automatically, and I'm not even sure what they're for. For making her feel this way. For not believing her the first time or the second, or any time after. For all the piece of shit things I've said and done to her. For not really forgiving her in my heart like she said, but trying to give it to her anyway before I was ready. For all the bullshit that's been going on between us.

All of it.

"I'm so fucking sorry," I say again while holding her tight, because it will never be enough.

She turns into my chest and throws her arms around my back in the first hug we've had in years. I look down and see tears running down her face in a steady stream. Her eyes are closed as she tries to bury herself into my beige hoodie, where her tears are already dark-ening the fabric. For all her strength and fight against me, against the others, and against GE, I'd forgotten that she's still sweet little Rae underneath it all.

My hands stroke her back, and I close my eyes. I don't stop until her tears do, and she's taking longer, calm breaths.

"I got you something," I tell her once she releases me and tries to go back to groceries. She tilts her head, and I stretch my lips into a smile. I pull the movie from one of the bags on the floor and offer it to her. "The new Jumanji."

"You...today?"

I nod. "Want to watch it together?"

She smiles at me, and my heart somersaults in my chest now that it's directed at me. "I'd love that."

RAEGAN

THE SHOWER SQUEALS WHEN I crank the knob to turn it off. I close my eyes, my head falling back as I take a deep lungful of air.

Even after everything that happened today, Kellan didn't let me off the hook for training. As soon as the movie ended, he'd dragged me to the training room to get back to it. This is my first time alone since everything that happened with Aiden, and then Dane, and I'm still reeling from it all.

Aiden locked me up.

He broke my trust. Again.

I may be able to understand that he's always got the safety and best interest of the others in mind, but I've never had to be on the other side of that before.

I hate it.

And then Dane...

I never thought that there could be any sort of peace between us. That we could talk as friends. Share something between us. Watch a movie together again.

We didn't sit right next to each other like we always did, but still. It was more than I ever thought I'd have again.

I grab my towel and wipe the water off, then wrap it around myself. I leave the stall and head for the bathroom door, ready to wind down in something comfortable—that will *not* be Aiden's shirt—for the rest of the night while I try to sort through everything that's happened.

I open the door and freeze when I come face-to-face with a broad chest in a dark shirt and leather jacket.

"Well, hello there, beautiful," Kellan drawls above me. His arm rests against the door frame like he'd been waiting for me to come out. His other hand is hidden behind his back, his body filling the doorway so there's no chance for me to slip around him if I wanted to.

His blue-green gaze starts at my bare feet, tracking up my damp and flushed skin to where a single turquoise towel covers me from armpit to barely past the curve of my ass. He slows and then holds his stare on the towel like he's picturing exactly what's beneath it from memory before his eyes keep moving to my collarbone and finally to my face.

There's a heat in his look that causes my heart rate to accelerate and the air from my lungs to expel in a rush.

He looks every bit the big bad wolf here to gobble me up, and if that's the case, I don't think I could find the willpower to stop him.

"Kell..." I acknowledge slowly, wondering what he's up to now. We'd just seen each other in training. At least this time, he didn't barge in to interrupt and take over my shower. I'm a bit surprised he waited outside, though, which means he's got something else in mind.

I try to peek around his back, but his body's so large that he doesn't even bother pretending to shift and keeps whatever he's holding back there hidden. His teeth flash in a dangerous grin. "I know you've had a rough day, so you and I are going out to unwind."

A sardonic laugh slips out. "Right. Because the best thing for me to do right now after Aiden locked me up and told me how much he doesn't trust me is to go out."

His grin widens. "Exactly."

I huff and shake my head, though I can't help smiling at him.

"When has anything Aiden said or done stopped you from having a good time, huh? Naw. This is *exactly* the time that we stand our ground and show him that you and I? We're not afraid of anyone or anything. And we'll have some fun if we damn well please."

"A night of rebellion?"

"Of freedom," he amends, swinging a dress out from behind him. He holds it out to me, and I stroke my hand down the soft fabric. It's a navy halter neck short dress that's perfect for dancing.

A small part of me shakes her head as I take the hanger from him. It tells me I shouldn't go out of my way to piss Aiden off further, now that he's proven he'll do what he promised me. But I squash that part down.

Kellan's right.

This is what he and I do, after all.

Aiden can stick a straw in his juice box and suck it.

I'm distracted enough by my thoughts and the dress that I don't notice Kellan leaning forward until his beard tickles above my chest and his tongue drags over a stray droplet of water to my shoulder.

My heart stutters in my chest, and I squeeze my thighs together.

"Hurry up and get ready before I fuck you right here in the hallway and we don't make it out of the house tonight."

I lick my lips and barely have to turn my face to whisper in his ear. "Then move out of my way."

Kellan's chuckle is more of a rumble in his chest before he draws himself back and angles enough for me to slide by him. I keep the dress between us as a buffer to make sure we don't give in to what our bodies want.

Once I'm free of the immediate space around him, I can draw a full breath of fresh, less-charged air and hurry to my room to close the door behind me. I'm quick to get dressed from there with the excitement of going out with Kellan. We always have a good time, and I could really use this opportunity to unwind after what happened with Aiden and Dane. And Vera and Ken Doll, too.

And that all happened in the last week.

Fuck, yes, Kellan was right. This is exactly what I need—not sitting and overthinking everything in my room all night.

I'm able to do a rough blow dry of my hair and put on some make-up with the small picture-frame sized mirror in my room that'll have to do. Rather than styling my hair, I opt for one of the wigs I'd gotten for working at the bar that's already styled.

Besides, I already promised Kellan I'd wear one for him sometime. I'm excited to see his reaction to it when we go out.

Once I'm ready to go, I knock on his bedroom door, expecting him to be waiting for me there, but frown when there's no answer. I creep down the dorm hallway to peek into the open living area, hoping to avoid Aiden or Dane's notice, when I see Kellan sitting on the couch with Dane.

Well, shit. How are we supposed to sneak out when Kell's sitting right next to him?

I fake cough, hoping to draw only his attention, but they both look up and spot me, practically hiding against the hallway wall.

Kellan grins over at me. "That wig is hot, beautiful. I hope you've got it on tight for it to last all night."

My fingers reach into the reddish-brown locks as my face warms, and I slip a glance over to Dane. He frowns at Kellan, then looks over at me. He takes in my wig first, then my dress and the long exposure of my legs, thanks to the shortness of the dress and my heels making them look longer than they are. His gaze is scorching as it drags down my body, heating my blood and causing my pulse to race beneath his scrutiny.

Then he blinks, breaking the spell, and he brings his eyes back to mine. "The wig is a good call." He turns back to Kellan, and I notice his tone sharpens. "Don't do anything stupid like draw attention to yourselves. Have your fun and then come right back."

Kell laughs and stands from the couch. "Yes, dear." He places his hand over his heart. "We'll blend in and not do anything to alert GE that we're out and about. But don't wait up," he adds with a wink.

Dane scoffs at him and shakes his head.

"Aiden's on his way here from the bunker, so we need to head out before we cross paths," Kellan tells me as he closes the distance between us. I meet him halfway now that I know it's apparently not a secret to Dane that we're heading out. Just Aiden.

I'm setting myself up for another confrontation with Aiden, but that's typical at this point. He'll never trick me into using those cuffs again, so he can threaten me all he likes.

"You ready?" he asks, his big hand coming up to tease the fake strands of hair between his fingers while his eyes sparkle with mischief.

My body is alive and nearly vibrating with excitement at going out with Kell. Fun times. Drinking, dancing, and pissing off Aiden...what else could a girl ask for?

"Ready."

Kellan brings us to a nightclub that fills the second to fourth floors of a building in the city. We get in past the line with a nod from the bouncer when he sees Kellan, which reminds me of just how well-known he is in this city.

There are different dance floors and DJs on each level, with their own bars and lounges to enjoy and their own theme for the night. The first floor is filled with foam and bubbles floating in the air, covering the dancers in the slippery substance from head to toe. We move to the second floor karaoke theme, and then to the top floor of the nightclub with a more standard style of what I'm used to.

I'm relieved he didn't bring me to Hype, although I miss its aesthetic and vibe compared to this place. I move to the dance floor once it's clear this is where we're staying, but he grabs my wrist and orders us some drinks at the bar, then guides me to a table with stools to sit.

"Drinks first," he shouts over the music to me just as a server brings a tray of shots and two tall glasses of whiskey to our table.

I nod and pick up the first shot, waiting for him to follow suit before we clink them together and shoot them back. A question that's been niggling at the back of my mind since we left the firehouse pushes its way forward. "Why was Dane so okay with us leaving? I know Aiden was going to be there to keep an eye on him, but..."

"But you expected him to be pissed about us going out? Or jealous, since he can't?"

I shrug. "Well, yeah. Either of those. Or both, really." I take a sip of my drink and can't taste any soda behind the burn of whiskey. Which is fine by me, but reminds me of how perfectly Portia made drinks at Hype.

"He's not happy about it," he answers me, and I almost choke on the next shot.

"Then why didn't he put up a bigger fight? He didn't seem mad." And he didn't snark or call us both out for being idiots like he definitely would have done not even a month ago.

Kell finishes his next shot, and I notice we're going shot for shot as we respond to each other. "Let's just say that this is a one-time permission slip from him, where he'll cover our asses with Aiden. So we should enjoy it while we're here."

He holds up his glass to toast mine, and then we're racing to chug the drink first and clear our table. I still don't understand why Dane would cover for us, but decide to worry about it later. This is supposed to be us enjoying ourselves and having a good time, not trying to pick apart what Dane might be thinking.

Kellan walks around the small, circular table and holds his hand out to me. "Come on, beautiful. Let's finish what we started on our last date."

I roll my eyes at the reminder when I'd forgotten about our night out and he kidnapped me from Hype. "That wasn't a date. And this isn't either," I retort, even though my hand drops easily into his, and my stomach flutters at the arrogant grin that tells me I can say what I want, but he's calling them dates.

We move onto the dance floor that's less packed with bodies as Hype is, but considering there are three floors, I guess there's a bit more room. It's still busy enough that we have to move through the crowd to find a good spot for us where I can feel like I'm blending in with the other dancers.

I dance to the beat, doing what I always do, as I let the music run through my body and take control. I'm surprised by how well Kellan moves in front of me, using his arms and hips in a way that screams sex and strength. It isn't long before I see other girls eyeing him and trying to move in. It's easy to ignore them after the third attempt when Kellan clearly only has eyes for me, shifting himself away from them and closer to me to make his intentions clear.

I feel trapped in his gaze as we both move and bump and grind with the music, eventually drawn closer to one another by some invisible magnet until my arms are wrapped around his neck, my legs straddling one of his as I grind my hips against him, and our eyes lock.

I lose track of time as one song easily bleeds into the next. The dance floor is a sweltering mass of bodies and movement, heating my skin and making me sweat. My lips are parted to gather more air while we dance and watch each other as if the rest of the club doesn't exist.

Kellan's hand drags down my lower back to my ass cheek. He squeezes it firmly in his grasp and then uses that grip to pull my body further against him until I can feel the hard press of his cock through his jeans. His head dips down and I tilt my face toward his, grateful for the added height from my high heels which means I don't have to push up on my toes and he doesn't have to lean too far to reach me.

His lips crash into mine. My arms tighten around him, gripping his neck and moaning into his kiss as he eats me alive while I grind my pussy over his leg.

He breaks away from me and flips me around, my back to his front, with his hands on my hips and yanking me back against him as he moves us together to the beat of the music. I want to complain at the loss of friction, but one of his hands slips beneath my dress.

When his fingers find that I'm going commando, he nips at my ear and growls, "You're playing a dangerous game with a dress this short, beautiful. But if you were looking for me to fight any guy that gets close to you, then challenge accepted."

Kellan's finger slips inside me before I have a chance to respond, and all conscious thought leaves my brain in an instant. My body sinks onto his finger, taking it in greedily and desperate for more.

My arms move up over my head to wrap around his neck so I have something to hold on to as my body tries to take anything and everything he wants to give me. It doesn't matter that we're still in the middle of the dance floor or that there are hundreds of people around us who could see.

The very idea that we could get caught, that we're sneaking this in public, sends a rush through me that heats my skin in a different way than dancing never could.

"Fuck, beautiful. I really will kill any man who tries to touch you tonight. This better all be for me." He adds a second finger, pumping it in and out of me while his other hand somehow keeps us both on the beat of the music as if nothing's happening.

Thankfully, Kell can multitask, because I'm doing a shit job of focusing on anything other than the feel of his hand. I'm lucky I'm still standing, honestly, and when he brings his slick fingers to tease my clit, my knees shake and test my resolve to keep my shit together so he doesn't stop.

His mouth nibbles along my shoulder, which shoots straight to my cunt, and I can feel a warm trickle of desire before his fingers fill me up again. There are three this time, though, and I gasp and moan out without care. Kellan's other hand shifts in front of my dress, his hand pressing down against my clit and moving it in a slow but steady pressure while his fingers do the work of driving into me until I cry out once an orgasm rips through me.

I collapse against him, using his body and hands on me to stay upright while my jelly legs try to remember how to work properly. He draws me up against him, turning me like a doll in his arms that he can move as he pleases, then makes me watch him suck his three fingers clean in my daze.

"You'd better learn to walk fast, Bambi, because I'm not through with you."

Right.

I use him for support to test my legs, and as soon as he sees that I can stand on my own, he wraps his arm behind my back and propels us through the crowd to some planned destination. He snaps at a few people who don't move immediately out of his path, but we finally make it to...

The bathroom?

"Wait—" I start, suddenly unsure of what his plan is.

Kellan yanks the door open and brings us both inside. He lifts and sets me on the counter, then turns on the guy still pissing in one of the urinals. "Out!"

"Dude, I'm in the middle of a stream—"

"Then put a cork in it for later and get out." Kellan widens his stance and crosses his arms over his chest.

"You can't—"

Kell grins savagely at him, reaching out to grab the man by the back of the neck.

"Shit! Shit! Fine, just give me a sec…" The guy fumbles at his pants to zip up while Kellan's already moving him to the door. He barely finishes putting his dick away before Kellan throws him out of the room.

He stalks down the stalls, banging each door open to make sure they're clear, then shoves the table of courtesy condoms and body spray in front of the bathroom door to block anyone else from entering.

His gaze is dark when it finds its way back to me, still sitting on the counter between sinks where I've been too busy watching in shock at what he was doing.

"Kell, was that necessary—"

He grabs the back of my neck, reminding me of the way he'd taken control of that other guy before he kisses me into submission. My legs part on instinct, letting him stand between them, while he uses his free hand to work his pants open.

I pull his hair tie free so I can grip and hold his dark brown hair while he pushes me further back into the counter and against the mirror.

Kellan unties my dress at the back and then frees my breasts. His tongue swirls around one nipple, sucking it deep and then surprising me with a bite that makes my pussy clench.

"Fuck!" I curse, my hands gripping his hair while he tastes the mix of soap and sweat on my skin.

"Put your elbows down," he orders me. It takes me half a second to register what he's asking for as I see him shoving his pants the rest of the way down and off before his dick is free and thrusting into me. My forearms on the counter keep my head from crashing back into the mirror as he drives into me.

I can't do anything at this point but hold on as he fucks me on the bathroom counter like a wild animal.

Garbled sounds escape my mouth that I have no control over as he brutally brings me to the edge again.

My lower back coils and tightens, wrapping around my spine in a death grip that has me gasping for air until it finally snaps. Pure pleasure explodes through me, rushing through my body and limbs like water from a broken dam. I scream out for anyone on this plane or the next to hear me.

Kellan drops over me, though his hands keep his body from falling on me, as he catches his breath and watches me.

One hand tugs at my fake hair. "Take this off."

I forgot I even had it on.

I'm still panting beneath him, waiting for my soul to return to my body, but my hand moves on autopilot at his command and starts pulling the clips free so I can slide the wig off my head.

His hand moves to my hair, my *real* hair, before his hold tightens. "Before you overthink things, you're going to listen to what I have to say."

"Really?" I gasp out, still breathless. "Now?" It hasn't passed my notice that he's still inside of me.

"Now. You scared the shit out of me when you tried to run away last night. I don't know what happened or why you did it, but I need to know that you're not still planning on leaving."

"I-I'm not."

Kellan shifts, and I can feel him hardening again already. I bite my lower lip to keep my whimper quiet.

He slowly drags himself out of me, and I breathe a sigh of relief. But it's short-won because he's sliding me off the counter on my own two feet and turning me around before his cock buries itself back in me. The moan that breaks through my lips is low and deep. His fingers are slick as they slide and rub around my clit, and my body clenches instinctively to his touch, no matter how tired it may be.

He yanks my hair back, making sure I can't look anywhere else but in the mirror. My hair is a wild and tangled mess, my lips swollen and breasts bared above bunched up navy fabric. Kellan's wide frame is a looming shadow behind me, his own dark hair loose to his shoulders, his expression fierce as he watches my reflection.

"Tell me that again, beautiful," he growls in my ear.

His hips move back and forth in an agonizingly slow rhythm as his fingers circle and stroke and rub with the perfect pressure to bring my body to heel for him once again.

"What?"

"That you're not going to run away again the second I'm not looking. That if something is wrong, you'll come to *me* first. You won't pack your bag and leave without a fucking word."

"Y-yes," I agree in a low murmur.

"Look at me when you answer that, beautiful. I need you to look into my eyes and promise me you won't disappear on me without a word."

My eyes find his in the mirror. He's watching me fall apart like I'm on display for him. And there's nothing I can do about it. My hips rock back into him for more, but it's his fingers playing me so well that has my next orgasm creeping up on me.

I never realized how hot it was to watch yourself being fucked in a mirror. Or seeing the look in Kell's eyes as he watches me watch myself.

"Yes. Yes! I promise!"

My orgasm is coming faster now, ready to bring me to ruin in seconds, when his fingers and dick are suddenly gone in an instant. I'm shaking as it slips away, and I cry out with frustration at the loss and the smirk on Kellan's face.

"Good. And now you'll always remember that promise."

CHAPTER TWENTY-ONE

RAEGAN

My face drops when I stride out of the hallway and into the kitchen, where I can see Aiden sitting alone on the couch in the living area. The kitchen and dining area are clear of others, and I can't hear anything coming from the training room off to my right.

I debate turning around and searching the firehouse for Kellan, but as soon as Aiden's face turns and he spots me standing here, my stubborn pride won't let me leave. It seems too much like running away, and I have no desire to let him feel like he's won something if I do that.

We haven't been alone together since he locked me up at the bunker.

I steel myself with a slow, deep breath and clench my hands into fists before stalking over to the couch to face him. "Where are the others?"

It's only after I've stopped behind the U-shaped couch that I notice what he's wearing. Instead of his usual three-piece suit, he's dressed in sweatpants and one of the shirts I've been wearing to sleep. The shirt is loose over his chest, not tight like Kellan wears his, but there's a V neckline, offering me a rare glimpse of his smooth and solid chest underneath.

Somehow, that seems like more of a tease.

"Kellan took Dane into the woods for some training." His eyes take me in from my boots, up my leggings, to the sports bra tank top, and then my hair pulled back in a tie. It's almost time for my session with Kell, and I'm wearing the new workout outfit he'd bought me at the store to try out.

He's been not-so-secretly filling my room and wardrobe with things ever since we moved here and he'd seen the lack of *stuff* I had at my apartment. At first, I thought it was sweet. Now, my room is filled with clutter, and I'm ready to throw it all out the window.

Aiden's gaze darkens as it tracks upward, if that's even possible for brown eyes so shadowy to begin with. I don't know what to think when he looks at me this way. I can only imagine it as hate. Like he's picking what I'm wearing apart and is preparing a slew of insults to jab me with. Or he's trying to remind himself why he thinks it's better to keep me here rather than letting me go off to do my own thing.

His mouth opens, but I cut him off before I have to hear whatever barb he's decided on. "Great. I'll go find them."

I turn, but his words stop me. "Kell said he'd be in for your session, so just have a seat and wait for him."

Mm...nope. "And hang out with you?" I ask, vitriol dripping from my tone. "Hard pass."

There's a flicker of something across his face before it tightens. "It's not my first choice, either. But I've been asked to babysit you to make sure you don't run away again. So, sit down like a good girl and wait patiently for Kellan to collect you."

Anger swells in my chest like embers bursting into flames.

This motherfucking—

"*—serial killer still at large. Everyone is being advised to lock their homes and call the police at any sign of suspicious activity.*"

My face snaps over to the news station that Aiden had been watching. Faces fill the screen of the latest victims, and my breath catches in my throat.

I recognize almost all of them from the beach house.

Jack?

"You know them?" Aiden asks darkly, and I nod. He turns the TV off and smacks the remote down on the table, then stands. "We need to find him and get him under control. This isn't how we do things."

He storms past me, and I turn and grab his arm. He stops and looks over his shoulder at me with a stern expression. "Wait, what do you plan to do?"

"Whatever it takes to make this bloodbath end."

My grip on him tightens. "How? By locking him up, too? Is that your answer for everything?"

He seizes my wrist and yanks it from his arm, then turns his back on me and keeps walking. I chase after him, catching the door before it hits me in the face as we move into the truck bays and through the other side to the locker room.

"You can't just lock people up because they don't do what you want! Jack's out there *doing* something for our cause. At least he's not sitting around here doing nothing! He's working on something, I know it, so just let him finish—"

Aiden whirls on me. My face smacks into his chest, and I bounce back. "Do you know it? What he's working on?"

I frown and rub my face where it impacted with his soft shirt, but firm chest. "No, but—"

"Then how are you so certain he has a plan? That he hasn't just gone on a killing spree for the fun of it?"

I glare up at him, meeting his eyes with all the conviction in me. "Because I know him. And I trust him."

Aiden's eyes shutter and close. "You trust him," he repeats slowly.

"Yes. I do. I don't immediately assume the worst of the people I care about when they do something bad or when something doesn't add up," I snark at him, thinking of how that's *all* he's done of me, since everything went to shit. "I'll believe in him first."

His eyes open, but only to narrow at me when he catches the double meaning in my words. "And what did he do to earn your trust so easily? Your blind belief in him? You don't know who he became in the last five years. You have no idea what he's capable of."

"I know him better than you think," I retort breathily, not needing to use my full voice while we're sharing the same air between us. His smell of cinnamon is richer than ever now that his body isn't tucked away behind layers of fabric. It fills my lungs and flushes my skin with heat. I tell myself it's the anger that's making my body respond this way, but I'm also all too aware of his proximity.

He's being an arrogant asshole, and I want to simultaneously strike him and kiss him into submission.

"Do you think fucking him means you know him now?" The shock of him knowing that freezes me in place. The back of his hand strokes down the side of my face, and my breath stalls. His touch is soft, unlike the malevolent undertone of his crooning voice. "Would you know and trust me, then, if we were to fuck?"

I slap him across the face. He grabs me by the throat and shoves me back against the lockers, the empty metal boxes clanging and echoing through the room.

"You're a fucking asshole," I spit at him.

"And you're the most difficult, infuriating woman I've ever met," he counters, his lips hovering over mine.

We stare at each other in a charged silence, with nothing but the sound of our breathing between us. His hand and body keep me pinned to the lockers, but it's not tight enough to block my airflow. It is enough to feel the rush of my pulse beneath his fingers as I watch him with a heady mixture of hate and lust that clouds rational thought.

He doesn't say anything more, but he doesn't move either, as if he's waiting for me to decide what happens next. The mere idea that he's relinquishing control to me for something that could be catastrophic to both of us makes me dizzy.

My hands dive into his hair, sliding my fingers between his short cut, before yanking his lips down on mine. His mouth opens without hesitation, both of us fighting for control of the other in a tangled tango of tongues.

A part of me is yelling at me to stop this. That I shouldn't be giving in to him like this, but I shove her away. I'm not giving in to him. I'm taking control of what I've wanted for a long time.

Aiden was my first kiss. The first boy I'd fallen for back on the island, and I've never stopped wanting him. Even as much as I hate him today, I can't deny the bottled-up desire that only stokes my irritation toward him, just waiting for the passion of anger to turn into this.

I kiss him with all my fury, hate, bitterness, and craving bundled up as one. I'm ready to drown in this feeling and let it consume us.

He rips away from me, using his hand on my throat to keep me still while he pants and eyes me warily. "You make no fucking sense."

"Good," I retort haughtily. "I'd hate to bore anyone." My hands drag him back down to me, and he caves in to our kiss again. He tastes like mint and a bit of bourbon, and I wonder idly if he'd been drinking when I first walked in on him in the living room. My hands slide down to his shirt, rubbing against the soft fabric, and then sliding up his chest underneath it. They pause over his pounding heart. It's echoing the pace of my own as if they're connected or one and the same.

His fingers twitch around my throat, and my hips grind into him instinctively, as if urging him on. I push my body further against him, straining against his hold on me until he does exactly as I'd hoped and slams me back against the lockers for my defiance.

Aiden pulls away again, but before I can protest, he spins me around and shoves me back against the lockers with an arm pressed firmly across my shoulders. He yanks my leggings and underwear down roughly, and then his palm cracks across my right ass cheek.

I jerk from the sting and inhale sharply. Then he's rubbing the pain away, and all that's left is a heated tingle beneath my skin.

"You don't know how long I've been wanting to do that," he whispers. The tingle spreads between my thighs, and I squeeze my eyes shut. There was a second when it hurt, but then it softened to an almost pleasurable ache. Fuck. Me.

He just *spanked me* like some errant child. I'm *furious* but also confused as fuck by how much I liked it.

Aiden's hand is now brushing against the other cheek, and my thighs clench. I can't tell if it's because of his nearness or to prepare for another strike.

"I hate you," I muster from my lips.

He pauses his movements. "What was that?"

"I hate you!" I shout at him.

Another smack rings down on my ass, followed by a caress that makes my blood sing. "I hate you too," he growls back at me. "You're such a brat. You can never do anything the right way or just follow instructions. You have *no* patience."

His words breathe fire into my soul, and I struggle against him. The sound of his palm on my flesh is almost as embarrassing as the way my body is lighting up for him. I can feel my thighs getting damp and the delicious ache for *more* there. My chest constricts, and anger bubbles to the surface as if each slap is drawing it out like poison from a wound.

"You're a sadistic bastard," I pant. The cool metal of the locker numbs my cheek while the rest of my body is on fire. "An egotistical dick who's addicted to his phone and cares more about a building full of strangers than a girl who'd depended on him to keep her safe."

The hand stroking my backside pauses, and I take that opportunity while his defenses are down to duck out of his hold and spin around. I shuck my leggings and underwear all the way off and jump up on the bench in between the row of lockers. Aiden turns around to follow me, so I easily hop on board, wrapping my arms and legs around him before he catches me.

I grab the longer hair at the top of his head and pull it back, so he's forced to look up at me for a change. "Are you going to fuck me this time, or am I going to someone else?" I snarl at him.

Aiden scowls. "Jackson isn't here."

"I've had sex with Kellan, too."

His nostrils flare, and his eyes darken to pitch black.

Yeah. *Didn't expect that, did ya, buddy?*

His lips crash into mine, and I moan at his sudden avarice. I try keeping control, but he sweeps it out from under me like he'd only been playing with me before. The lockers bang again when he charges me into them, using them to keep me from falling as his hands work his clothes down and out of the way. I hardly feel any of it, though, too consumed by the slashing heat of his tongue and the feel of his body against mine.

His dick glides along my folds, taking up the moisture that has accumulated there for himself. I grind into it, desperate to fill the ache inside. The head of his cock pushes at my entrance in a split second of warning before I'm impaled against the lockers. I cry out from the sudden stretch, but it quickly changes to a groan of pleasure as he rocks and grinds his hips.

I clamp down on his shoulder at the rush of pleasure that has my head spinning.

He slams into me again and again, clearly furious over something, though I can't tell if he's punishing me or himself.

But I'm not here just for the ride, so I use my elbows to push off of the lockers and throw my body into him, and he falls a few steps back. It's close enough to the lockers on the other side that I plant my feet against them, grip his shoulders with both hands, and start fucking him right back. I throw my body up and down his shaft, my breathing hard and labored with the effort, but *fuck* yes. Now it's his turn.

"You've got to be fucking kidding me," he groans, clearly still enjoying it as much as he may be pissed about it.

"Yup. Fuck you," I rasp.

Aiden growls and uses the momentum from me shoving off the lockers to send us backward, then he drops me down against the bench and picks up where he left off. "No. Fuck *you*," he growls. I try to sit up, ready to try flipping the tables again, but his hand goes for my throat and squeezes tight, pushing my head back against the bench. My hands grab his arm on instinct when my air supply cuts off.

Panic rises in my chest, but the lack of air gives me a head rush. Then his slick fingers are massaging and playing with my clit, and my entire body tightens with need. He rubs it furiously, and it feels like my body is being stretched and bowed inch by inch on a pulley until his hand slaps down on it, and I snap at his command.

His hand loosens on my throat at the same time, and I feel like I'm free falling off a cliff as my orgasm explodes through me. Aiden groans above me, but he sounds far off in the distance while I'm still falling apart to pieces. My body collapses back onto the bench as I gasp for air and blink to clear the black spots from my vision.

He has removed his shirt and is wiping my stomach clean. I look down and see that he pulled out and came on me, then drop my head back on the bench to focus on my breathing.

Now that I'm coming down from my high, reality sets back in. Like it always does.

I remember the words we'd been throwing at each other. How he'd spanked me. I'd liked it, but that's not the point. He even won who was fucking who in the end, as much as I'd tried to prove to him I can't be tamed.

"Would you know and trust me, then, if we were to fuck?"

Losing isn't an option for me. I need to come out on top of this so he doesn't think he's won something.

"There," I murmur, my chest still heaving while I work to recapture the oxygen I'd missed. "I fucked you, and I still don't know and trust you. So, that's not why I trust or believe in Jackson."

Aiden stills. A tiny part of me panics, wanting to backpedal and fix it, but I press my lips together to keep quiet. I push myself upright to sit, straddling the bench while watching him.

"Excuse me?" he asks slowly, his voice soft but terrifying.

"You heard me." I double down, even as my heart gallops.

His eyes close. When they open again, there's nothing but contempt in his expression as he looks at me. "Is that all that was? You fuck people to prove a point?"

I bristle at the implication, even if he's not entirely wrong. It's not why I wanted that. But it was the only way to protect myself from him if he were to think it was anything else. We both hate each other. How could I pretend it was anything more? "No, just *you*," I snap. "I apparently can't find any way to make you trust me other than proving you wrong."

"And you thought having sex was the answer?"

He's making me sound more and more like an idiot, even though I was lying about why we just did that, which just pisses me off further. I snatch my clothes from the floor, tugging them on angrily. "Of course not!"

"If you want me to trust you, then just tell me what you've been hiding. It's not that difficult."

"Yes, it is," I grind out. "You don't know *anything* about what I've been through!"

"I would if you'd just tell me!"

"It's none of your business! It has nothing to do with you. You stopped deserving any explanation the second you knocked me out on that island and left me for dead. You want to know why I almost left the other night? Because I know the moment you all learn anything more about my past, you'll do the same thing you did last time. You'll turn your backs on me. You'll call me all the words that hurt me." Tears threaten to spill from my eyes, but through sheer force of will, I hold them back. "You'll go out of your way to give *everything you have* to complete strangers at your Guild, but when I needed help, you abandoned me!"

My throat constricts, and I swallow past a lump. "You want my trust enough to tell you my secrets? You have to *earn* it. Because as far as I'm concerned, *you're* the one who can't be trusted. *You* didn't believe in me or ask questions when you found out about Vera. *You* are the one who left me defenseless and alone on the island while lying to everyone else that you didn't find me. *You* threw me into a hole in the floor while letting me believe you were trying to imprison me. And *you* used the smallest trust I had left in you to trick me into putting those handcuffs on, only to lock me up because I didn't do what you wanted."

Liquid brims my eyes, and my hands shake at my sides. I fist them to get control, even as my soul cracks while I list out every time Aiden has failed me.

His eyes are wide as he stares at me. I don't know if I've finally gotten through to him, if he's just taken aback by me finally opening up this much to him, or what, but I don't give him the chance to respond.

I've opened up my heart to him, and I can't bear to let him cut it again. He's already proven to me he can't be trusted with it. I take the scraps of myself that remain, bundling them close to my chest, and walk out.

Chapter Twenty-Two

AIDEN

My fist slams against the white subway tile of the shower wall. I hang my head under the scorching heat of the water as it cascades down my hair to the drain at my feet.

She had me.

She played me like a fucking fiddle, and like a fool, I fell for it without stopping to question it.

Why would I believe she wanted anything to do with me after all the horrible things I've said to her? When she has Jackson, and apparently Kellan as well?

I was just a means to an end. A way to prove her point. To show me I can control her about as well as I can hold the steam from this shower in my hand.

I thought we'd made a breakthrough. She would finally share something real with me. And while I was weak and hopeful, she ripped my heart from my chest and squeezed it in her grasp until it burst.

I should have known better.

We were never meant to be anything more to each other than spiteful allies. If that. Even when I'd almost had her all to myself, when I'd taken the leap and kissed her back on the island, it wasn't meant to be. We were over before we could really begin because fate decided that I find her birth certificate the next day.

I had one kiss with her. One night of hope and excitement before it was ripped away from us.

Now, the most we can share with each other is who can hurt the other the most. Now, any interaction we have just proves to me that any possible relationship between us would be toxic.

Even when I try to help her or open up, nasty digs and undercutting remarks fall from my tongue on reflex. I don't even think about them, and they're there. Past my lips and attacking her, to keep her at a distance.

I stare at the water circling the drain. I soak in the heat of the shower and the ache in my chest until they are both a part of me. I don't hide from it; I latch on and breathe it into me so that I remember this moment.

I won't be making that mistake again.

The bathroom door squeaks open, and I hear a curtain slide across the metal bar in a stall further down from mine. I take another long breath, drawing the steam into my chest one last time before slipping the mask of casual indifference over my features like a second skin. It's a talent I learned a long time ago to keep my emotions buried deep and away from others' notice.

Except when it comes to *her*, and it all comes out with the smallest provocation.

A quick glance over the stall confirms Dane is in here, as I'd guessed. Kellan would be training Raegan now, so Dane's showering after his session. The stalls are just tall enough to reach his chin, but my entire head is exposed above the cheap plastic walls. I have no idea how Kellan showers in these when my head barely fits under the shower head if I duck. He must have to squat under it or bend over to get his hair and face clean.

Seeing Dane just reminds me of what she'd thrown at me on her way out. She ran once again because that's what she's good at, and left me with bricks of ambiguous information that gave me more questions than answers. If only I could restrain her again, keep her from running away so I could get the information I need. She seems to open up more to me when she's angry than anything else, and I have a knack for getting her there.

But there was something she had given me this time that I might be able to work with. Something that I'd need Dane's assistance for.

I clear my throat and step back, so the shower is hitting my upper chest. My palm drags back over my hair to push the dripping water from my face, and then I check that I have Dane's attention. "What did Vera say to you about Raegan? She said she almost ran the other night because she was scared of us learning something about her, which I assume has to do with Vera sharing something with you. What was it?"

Dane's brows pinch together. "What did she say to you?"

"She didn't tell me more than that. I'd like you to fill me in so I know better what I'm dealing with."

His lips firm into a flat line, and he shakes his head while reaching for his soap. "If she isn't giving you that information, then I can't tell you anything."

My hands curl at my sides, but I force the tension in my body to relax before he can see it. This is getting ridiculous. The only reason there's division between us is poor communication. And every chance where I try to *fix it*, I'm denied. Now, by the very person who should hate her the most.

"Dane. I'm serious. We can't move forward until we get past this. I'm trying to help all of us."

"I'm serious, too. I promised her I wouldn't tell anyone or talk about it until she was ready. It's not mine to tell."

Deep, controlled breaths. "Since when are you standing up for her? Why wouldn't you ask her about it? What am I missing?"

He scrubs the soap into his hair with rough fingers and a pensive look that's so at odds with the scowl he's been wearing for years that I'm wondering what I've missed these last few weeks while helping the Guild. Has she changed the others this much just by being around us?

"We're...starting over. Vera showed her true colors the other night, and I have no choice but to believe Raegan. No," he corrects himself, then pauses to consider his next words. "I have a choice, but I choose to believe her now. She's protected me all this time from knowing what Vera's turned into, even though we all hated her for it. If Vera wasn't still around, she would have died with that knowledge, and I would still think that Raegan killed my innocent sister."

"She still killed your sister," I remind him flatly. Something that would once trigger a temper tantrum from him or make him pull his hair from grief.

Instead, he simply nods. "I know. I haven't forgiven that completely. But I know why she did it."

"So, what? Now you're pals again?" I fight to keep the sarcasm from my tone, but hearing that another one of us has worked something out with her has me livid. I'm the only one left. The only one she refuses to talk to, to hang out with, to tease. I see the way she looks out the window for Jackson. And now I better understand the looks she gives Kellan. The small smiles she's beginning to share with Dane.

She'll never look at me that way.

"We're figuring that out," he tells me at last, but I've already moved on from caring about his answer. I need a stiff drink. And fresh air.

Every time I come back to Old Red, I feel like I'm suffocating. Maybe that's the real reason I've been avoiding it. Why I've been coming up with excuses for them to hang tight and not move on GE. I want Raegan to be constantly around me and under my control, but then, when I have her in arm's reach, all we do is poison the air between us, and she runs away.

I turn off the shower and grab my towel, wrapping it around my waist and leaving the bathroom without another word to Dane. I don't know what else to say to him until I can get this shit figured out in my head first.

I go right for one of the suits that fill my closet, picking out a black one this time rather than the usual gray. I take my time pulling on each item of clothing, and I can feel my self-assuredness returning to me. It's like I'm putting on my armor for the world, for Raegan, for the thoughts and feelings that constantly haunt me, with every layer. Confidence oozes from me once I've finished the getup with my silk tie.

I run my hand down the tie to the buttons on my jacket and smirk into the mirror.

Much better.

I'll go get a drink, breathe in the crisp night air, and gather a fresh perspective before coming home with a new game plan.

I park my Aston Martin in the reserved spot at the bar the Guild owns in the city. A member of the Guild owns every establishment that holds one of the secret tunnels to the bunker. The Guild isn't listed on the ownership papers, of course, but it is the Guild that funds and supports the business, and the member just manages and runs it without worrying too deeply about the financials.

When I walk inside, half of the patrons are members who each catch my eye and smile or nod at me while I'm scanning the room. The rest are regular people of society who don't look twice at the man in the suit entering a bar at this hour. It's just after nine in the evening, so it's still early by bar and drinking standards.

I stride over to an open booth to sit rather than the bar. I'm not looking to chat with anyone tonight. I need to drink and process everything Raegan and Dane said to me so I can decide our next steps of how we move forward.

Jack's the first problem we need to solve before we can re-focus on GE.

I haven't told Raegan yet, but he's completely lost it. He may say that he's on Raegan's side, but all I've seen is him killing people left and right with no rhyme or reason. He's leaving nothing but blood and terror in his wake. He must have become so consumed by bloodlust that he's forgotten his original goal.

The last time I saw him was when he'd been in her room the other week. There's been no sign of him coming back to see her since.

Yahaira places a glass of bourbon before me with a smile. "I'd ask if you wanted someone to talk to, but seeing as you're here and not at my bar, I'll assume that's not what you want." She places a hand on her hip and tucks her brunette hair behind her ear. "But I can kick everyone else out if you change your mind and need some privacy for it."

My hand wraps around the glass, and I raise it in a salute to her. "I appreciate it, Yaya. But I need to work this out on my own."

She nods. "Understood, Ma—Aiden," she finishes after the look I give her, then leaves to return to her post at the bar.

I never wanted to be master of some Guild. I wanted to keep my brothers safe and take down the organization that took our lives from us. It had always been about us. It still is. But, I'll admit, it's become more than that.

While I never planned on this, I don't hate it. I like looking out for the others. And now I'm not just taking down Gifted Enterprise for myself and my brothers, but for them, too. And for the non-Gifted, who don't know that this shadow organization plans to rule the world without them even realizing it.

"You'll go out of your way to give everything you have to complete strangers at your Guild, but when I needed help, you abandoned me!"

She's wrong, I remind myself. I'm not choosing the Guild over her, if that's what she thinks. She's choosing herself over depending on us. On me. She would have everything, too, if she would just talk to me.

"You stopped deserving any explanation the second you knocked me

out on that island and left me for dead."

I take a long drink of my bourbon as her voice, full of pain and sorrow, rings in my ears. The sound carves a hole in my chest, shredding my heart to ribbons as I remember the day that's burned in my mind.

I catch her with one arm before she falls, dropping the debris I'd used to knock her unconscious and then swinging her legs up. A trickle of blood escapes the scrape I've inflicted on her temple. Tightening my hold, I draw our foreheads together and force myself to take a calming breath. To remind myself why I'm doing this.

I try to breathe in her vanilla scent, but it's nowhere to be found. Maybe it's the copper and sulfur in the air that's hiding it from me, and I tell myself it's for the best. That it'll somehow make what comes next easier.

The ground rumbles, another aftershock jarring the island and reminding me that I have to hurry. The adults were busy trying to save their equipment and their own lives at first, thinking the kids wouldn't see a way off the island. The idiots had a book on boating in the library, and I made sure to read it. I wonder how many others had the same idea. It won't be long before the adults realize some of us are escaping and they come after us.

There's another pier close to here, so I break into a run, seeking out any other brave prisoners trying to leave. I catch a small group of students on a boat and angle toward it, stopping in front of it with gasping breaths. "Tara!" I shout when I see Raegan's roommate. The one who always covered for her when she'd slip into our room.

The red head turns, the frown on her face changing to surprise when she sees Raegan in my arms. "Shit, is she okay?"

The boat jerks as I step onto it, and I turn so my back hits the cabin to catch us. My teeth clench as I brace myself against it through the strong rocking motion. "I need you to take her with you," I manage once she's standing in front of me.

"Are you not coming?"

"I've got another boat to catch."

Tara's brow pinches. She knows how close we all were, but I don't have the time to explain everything to her.

"Her Grams is in Alaska. I need to know that you'll help get her home."

"Why can't you—"

"–Can you help her?"

"Uh, yeah. We're all trying to find our homes anyway. We can do it together."

I breathe a sigh of relief. "Thank you. I'll put her in the bed below, if you can check on her injuries once you're out at sea."

"Sure."

I'm not thrilled by Tara's answers, but there's no time to find anyone else. I'm lucky enough that another group is trying to escape like us.

Carrying Raegan below deck to the tiny captain's quarters, I lay her carefully on the bed.

"I hope you lied," I whisper, stroking the hair from her face. "I hope you don't work for GE and you didn't kill Vera. I hope you go home to your Grams in Alaska and live a happy, quiet life away from all this." Leaning forward, I press a kiss to her uninjured temple, holding it there with eyes closed as I say goodbye. Because this should be the last time I ever see her again.

If she makes it home, there's no reason for us to ever run into each other.

Or else there is no Grams, and she told the truth about being with GE.

My chest tightens to an unbearable chokehold now that it's time to walk away. To leave her forever.

I wish...

No. Don't do that. This is for the best. I'm getting her away from GE. Getting her home and somewhere safe.

Leaving this island isn't going to be the end of GE for me and my brothers.

Shifting back, I trail my hand down her torso to her skirt, wanting to see her injury for myself so I can make sure Tara knows what to do for it.

The boat lurches to the side, and I slap my hand on the wall before I fall onto Raegan. Shouting starts outside, and it sounds like my time is up.

I rush above deck, not allowing myself to linger anymore. If I let myself, I'd stay on the boat with her. I have to force myself to leave, to get back to the others and hope they aren't under attack because I've taken too long.

A few scientists are running this way, and I curse to myself.

Jumping onto the dock, I cut the last rope holding the boat at the pier and toss the student who'd been trying to untie it onto the boat as the motor kicks on.

Goodbye, Raegan.

She should have been safe. She should have gone home.
What aren't you telling me?
Now that I know killing Vera was an accident, I'm forced to wonder if I made the right choice. If I brought her with us, would

she have told us about Vera? Or would she have kept that secret while she thought Vera was dead?

What would our lives look like now if I'd taken her with us?

Did she ever make it to her grandmother? Did Tara keep her promise?

What happened after I left her on the boat? And what happened to her that year she was separated from us on the island? I'd thought it was the same classes and training, just isolated from the rest of us. But then her reaction to Gordon...

What did he do to you?!

That question alone triggers a visceral rush of anger through my veins, throwing all rational thought and action from my mind. It's what drives me every time I see her, clogging my lungs and spewing sharp demands for her to tell me.

I *need* to know. I won't be able to rest until I know everything about her. Every detail that she guards like her life depends on it.

I need to make it right.

"You want my trust enough to tell you my secrets? You have to earn it."

I'd thought bringing her with us to Old Red would have been enough, but hearing her list out every time I'd failed her rings like a death knell in my head.

I don't know when I stopped caring about her birth certificate. At this point, it's clear she's not working for them. I think I always knew. It was just a convenient excuse to push her away. To keep her from getting too close before she could work her way back into my life. Into our lives.

But it's too late now.

If we ever had a chance.

"Oh, Aiden! Funny to see you here!" A sharp giggle follows before Cassandra slides into the bench seat across from me without my permission. "Are you meeting someone here?"

I take in the fiery red curls spilling from her head to her woodland eyes and freckled nose, and then the oversized beige sweater she's wearing. She's small and pixie-like and always tries to keep an upbeat attitude around everyone she's with. She's been an invaluable member of the Guild, especially as of late. She's a sweet and nice girl if I put aside the repeated advances that I've been forced to fend off.

I sigh and shift back against the thick wooden booth. It's a strategic move on my part to add more distance between us while she leans over the table. My hand is still latched around my glass of bourbon, and I suddenly feel as if I've traded places with Kellan somehow and the drink has become an extension of me. "No. I'm here by myself."

Her smile stretches across her face. "Can I join you?"

"Maybe another time. I need to think alone tonight."

Cassandra's face drops into a pout, but I can see the wheels turning in her mind when her brow furrows. "Is this about *her*?"

"Who?" I ask casually. She can't be talking about Raegan. I've been very careful to keep my history with her a secret outside of our group and Cibrina, who I know would never break my confidence. I consider each encounter Cassandra has had with Raegan, between healings and the Guild, and I had been sure to be visibly distant from her.

She laughs softly, like she thinks I'm messing with her, and settles herself more in the seat. "Raegan, silly. Is that why you came out here to think? Because she's staying with you?"

My face remains stoic as I take another sip of my drink to give myself more time to think. Apparently, I've been more obvious than

I thought. Though Cassandra is the only one to have seen her with me more than the one time when I'd brought her to the Guild. I often show newcomers the Guild, so to the others, there would have been nothing odd about that visit.

Cassandra smiles at me when I don't answer right away. "You know, a woman's intuition is pretty accurate, so I wouldn't be so hard on yourself. I would've been able to tell you had a thing for her even if I'd only seen you together the one time." Her fingers trail over the lines and cuts in the wooden table. I follow them with my eyes and then look back at her face.

"I don't have a thing for her," I deny, lying through my teeth without hesitation.

She shrugs, and I take it as if she's agreeing to disagree without trying to start up an argument. "So, what's the problem?" I raise an eyebrow at what she means by that, and she adds, "The one you came all the way out here to solve by yourself? Maybe I can help."

"No. I appreciate the offer, but this is a personal matter."

"Did she reject you? I mean, she stormed off on you when you showed her the Guild, right? Seems kinda childish of her, if you ask me. And she got snippy when I was healing Kellan. *And* she wouldn't let go of Jackson the entire time I healed him. Seems a bit possessive and controlling for a girl who showed up out of nowhere. I think you'll need to keep an eye on her with them if you're trying to go for her, and be careful she doesn't fuck your friends behind your back."

"Enough!" I stand and slam my glass down on the table hard enough that it shatters in my grasp. I don't even feel the glass cutting into my palm past the burn in my chest while I turn a heated glare on Cassandra. "Talk about her like that again and I won't be able to hold myself back. You have no idea who she is or what she's been through to spread slander like that."

The rest of the bar has gone quiet, but she doesn't bother looking around at anyone else. Cassandra smiles up at me and then takes my hand in both of hers. I jerk it back, but not hard, because she keeps her grip on it and shoots me a look. Then she turns it palm up and lightly picks out any glass there. "Maybe if you were more honest with yourself about her and how you feel, then she would be more honest with you."

I frown at that. She holds her palm over mine once the glass is gone, and her healing warmth fills in the cuts until there's no sign of what I'd done.

"Is everything alright over here?" Yahaira appears at our table.

"We're fine," Cassandra answers without looking her way.

Yaya glances over at me for confirmation, and I give her a curt nod. She nods in return and cleans the glass from the table with her wet rag. "I'll get you a fresh drink then," she says before turning and leaving us be.

I realize then that Cassandra has yet to let go of my hand, even though there's nothing more to heal.

"Cassandra..."

Her fingers tighten as she gazes up at me. "I know you've told me you're not interested in me that way. And now I know why. But, if it's too hard for you and her to be together, won't you try with me? I swear, I would be a good partner. I can cook, I'm great to have around after a fight, and I can take care of you. I'd listen to anything you had to say, and I wouldn't give you any trouble. I would love you better than anyone else could, Aiden."

I pull my hand free of hers, and her face falls. "Stop selling yourself short. You deserve to be with someone who will care about you just as much as you care about them. But that person will never be me." It's blunt and callous, but I've tried letting her down softly before, and she still comes back. I'm ready for her to realize that this is never happening between us. I gave away my heart a long time ago, and I don't think I'm ever getting it back.

I also know it's not me that she really likes. It's my power and position. She's hunting for safety and security, and right now, I'm fitting that image for her.

She sighs and leans her face into her hand. "Alright. I give." Yahaira delivers another bourbon to me and a glass of red wine to Cassandra without a word before Cassandra continues, "Do you think Kellan might—"

"No," I interrupt before she can even finish that thought. "And no to Dane and Jackson, too."

She huffs, and the curls on her forehead scatter. "Fine." She raises her wineglass at me and waves her hand at the seat to remind me that I'm still standing. I sit and raise my glass, but I don't move to clink it against hers until I know what she's toasting to. "Here's to a night of drinking, reflection, and unattainable love."

I fight not to roll my eyes at the last part but meet her glass halfway before taking a long swig of bourbon.

Because she's not wrong.

Chapter Twenty-Three

RAEGAN

The door slams behind me as I power through the firehouse. I'm not even sure where I'm heading, just so long as it's far away from Aiden. If I tell him what Gordon made me do, he'd call me the same names that Vera spat at me, and I know it would break me. He already shot close to the mark before, and I almost lost it then. I can't trust him not to verbally and viscerally rip me to shreds once he finds out.

Dane hasn't asked me about the names or accusations yet. I'm both surprised and relieved at his patience, but I know I can't keep hiding it from him forever. He's going to want an explanation about what she meant.

Killing GE goons who kidnap and harm children is one thing. But anyone else? An ex-boyfriend and his friends? Innocents? It's unforgivable.

She's dangerous.

Terrorist.

Monster.

Villain.

You're worthless.

The words circle in my head on a loop, taking bites out of me with every round. My lungs tighten, and I gasp for air, stumbling forward because I can't let myself stop and fall apart where anyone can see me. My legs move on autopilot, taking one step after another even though my entire body feels numb to the motion.

Then my face impacts with something warm and hard, and all my momentum halts before I'm ready.

"Where do you think you're going, beautiful? It's your turn," Kellan says. His hands grasp my upper arms to steady me, and I stiffen in his hold. "Hey." He tries to tilt my face up to look at his, but I don't want him to see whatever broken expression is on there and jerk it away.

He growls and grabs my face to make me look at him, and anger sparks in my chest at him for not letting me run away. "Let me go," I snarl, shoving at his chest. His hand on my arm drops behind my back to draw me closer to him instead.

"Never. You don't get to run from me, beautiful. I already told you that you have me. I'm yours whether you want me or not, so don't you fucking dare try to hide from me. You got a problem with me? I'll fix it. Got a problem with someone else? I'll ruin their fucking day, their year, their *life,* until it makes you happy. So, tell. Me. What's. Wrong."

His words are like a balm on my aching soul, and the anger melts enough to make me pause. I gnaw on my lip in thought. Should I tell him what happened? Or will that just open up more questions that I'd have to answer?

"Come on. Let's move to the training room." He shifts me around with his arm and leads us out of the open living area before either Dane or Aiden can walk in, and I'm grateful he realized I wouldn't want either of them seeing me right now.

He grabs a roll of gauze and sets it in my hand. "Wrap up. You can talk and train at the same time."

I take it, letting the familiar action of wrapping my hands set me more at ease. I draw a long breath once I'm done and seek out Kellan in the room.

He smacks the punching bag in the corner twice and then curls two fingers back to summon me over to him. "We'll start with the bag first. Pretend whoever or whatever upset you is right here. You can say or do whatever you want to them until you get it all out. If you have any energy left after, then you and I will keep working on your handwork."

I shift my legs apart in my fighting stance, internally pleased when he doesn't kick them immediately to show that I went too wide or too narrow, and raise my hands into fists in front of me. I stare at the large black punching bag that's bigger than me and picture Aiden.

I hear the insults that glide from his tongue as easily as breathing. I picture the contempt on his face or the hatred in his dark eyes when he looks at me. The way he gets close to me, setting my heart racing and my thoughts spiraling before he knocks me down again.

It's worse with him than anyone else. His words don't just burrow under my skin. It's the way I react to him and how he seems completely oblivious to it. To me. His words wrap around me in that smooth-as-chocolate cadence, lulling me into a sense of safety before he drives the needle home and leaves me devastated on the floor.

And still, every time he draws me in, I fall for it. Again and again. Like some masochistic sheep who craves the pain just as much as this stupid dream of acceptance from him.

My fists pummel the bag in different routines of strikes that Kellan has taught me in our nightly sessions. He stands behind it, holding it still for me as I go, but shouting out corrections that I hear more as a faraway echo while my own thoughts are at the forefront of my mind.

"Harder! Straighten your back! Use your legs! Don't drop that hand!"

I make the adjustments as he calls them out, but I don't let them interfere with where my thoughts go.

"Who are you hitting right now?"

"Aiden," I answer without thinking.

"Why Aiden?"

"He says he doesn't trust me, but he's broken my trust more than I've broken his," I growl, listening to the firm smacks of my fists against the plastic. The sound is therapeutic in the rhythm I've picked up. "All he does is tear me down, but he expects me to share shit with him that has *nothing* to do with him. It's none of his business. Or anyone's but mine."

"More!" Kellan shouts, and I don't know if he means with the punching bag or what I'm saying, but my body reacts automatically.

"He's the selfish, arrogant, sadistic asshole who won't admit when he's wrong! I hate him!" I gasp and swing one last punch at the bag before stumbling back to catch my breath. I drop to my knees and then fall back on the mats, stretching my arms and legs out while my chest heaves.

Kellan crouches beside me, his eyes taking me in from head to toe. His nostrils flare, and his lips twist into a frown. "Aiden, huh? Are you sure he's the one you're really angry with?"

My head rolls on the mats so I can look at him. "What do you mean by that?"

He shrugs, setting his chin in his hand as he gazes at me from higher up, which reminds me of Jackson. My chest twinges with the memory of my dark shadow, who I haven't seen or felt in a while. Where has he gone? Did he leave me behind on this mission he's on?

Kell smiles at me, but it's tight and doesn't reach his eyes. "You and Aiden fucked." My eyes widen and snap over to his before I can stop them, and he nods like that was answer enough.

"That and what I'm talking about have nothing to do with each other," I argue hotly.

His eyebrows raise slightly. "Oh, no?" he counters almost sarcastically. "So, are you thinking about doing it again, even when he pisses you off like this?"

I push up to my elbows on the floor to glare at him. "What does it matter?"

He moves over me in a heartbeat, his knees straddling either side of me while he leans forward and forces me back against the mats. "It matters," he breathes darkly, his large hand coming up to touch my face. "Everything matters when it comes to you, beautiful. I just need to know if I'm going to have to up my game at winning your favor if I have competition."

"There is no competition," I murmur between us because he's so close. "I already told you I don't do relationships. I do what I feel in the moment because I never know when it might be my last. I don't plan for the future or worry about tomorrow, in case it never comes."

"You will have a future. I swear it. And when GE is gone and you realize you could settle down with someone, give your heart to someone, then I'll be there to make sure that someone is me." My breath catches at the declaration, then releases slowly. I can't see any future until GE is gone.

Kellan smirks cockily and continues, "I didn't expect Aiden to get in the way, but I think he'll fuck up his chances all by himself. So, I think my odds are still looking good."

I chuckle and shake my head at him. "You can't forget about Jackson."

He raises a single brow. "What about him?" I give him a knowing look, and he huffs a laugh. "Of course, that sneaky guy got to you, too. I knew it would always be between the four of us." Kellan pushes himself back to his feet and holds out his hand for me. I take it and pull onto my feet.

I realize then that he said the four of them. "There's nothing between me and Dane. And Aiden...that was a *mistake*."

He chuckles and grabs a wipe off the wall to clean the punching bag, but doesn't argue with me. I can't tell if that means he agrees or if he's just choosing not to push his statement.

I sit on a bench against the wall and grab a bottled water from the pack. The idea of a future and what I would do with my life rolls around like the water in my mouth. Is it even worth dreaming about?

What about Portia?

I promised to take down Gifted Enterprise so that I could see her again. I have to have a future to make that happen.

"Hey, Kell?" I ask quietly, still somewhat lost in my thoughts.

He tucks the last bit of gauze into his wrap, then secures it with a bit of tape before punching a fist into his palm. "Yeah?"

"Did we miss Christmas?"

Kellan cocks his head to the side, and his face furrows with confusion. Probably at the sudden topic change, or maybe he is as unsure of date and time as I am. "I saw decorations and lights out at the store earlier, so probably not. Why? I don't need a gift, beautiful, if that's what you're worried about. I can think of a few things that don't cost anything you could give me instead," he teases with a wolfish grin.

I chuck my water at him after an eye roll and a smirk, and of course, he catches it easily in one hand. "Like you'd wait around for Christmas every year for that."

His grin widens. "Oh, but I'd put a bow on it to make it special." He snaps his fingers together in an ah-ha moment and points to me. "Actually, if you could dress yourself up in a bow...that would be my favorite gift."

"Duly noted," I reply with a smile, and his eyebrows jump to his hairline. "I want to get some white lights to hang around the firehouse," I speak up before he can distract me again with the main reason I'd asked about Christmas. The white lights will look really good against the exposed brick and wood that takes up the main living area through to the kitchen.

Kellan takes a swig from my water bottle and then wipes his lips with the back of his hand. "Alright. We usually put a tree up every year, but we don't decorate aside from that. The Guild does the bigger deal for the holidays."

I nod slowly, taking my time to share this with him. "I, uh, can't remember the last time I celebrated a holiday. Something about being here makes me want to experience that again…if it's not a big deal, I mean."

"Not a big…" Kellan stares at me incredulously and then scoffs. "Fuck, beautiful, we can do the whole kit and caboodle then! What about the last five—" He stops himself at my look and shakes his head. "Yes. We'll decorate, sing carols, you and Dane can watch those corny classics, and then we'll eat some Christmas turkey and ham."

"I don't need all of that. Just some lights and the tree will be great, Kell. We're still fighting in a war, and I'm not trying to take away from that."

"Too bad. We're also still living our lives here. There's no reason to put the holidays on hold for GE. If anything, we're showing them we'll continue to live our very best lives despite them being around. I've already missed the last five years of holidays without you; we're not skipping it this year." He crosses his arms and pinches his chin in thought while he nods to himself. "Christmas Day will be for us, but we'll need to take you to the Guild for all the shows and events the members put on for Christmas Eve."

"Shows?" I'm partly excited but mostly concerned with how much work and time this seems to be turning into. Shouldn't we still be hunting down GE? And would Aiden really approve of us wasting our time on this?

Well, it's not like we've been doing much else the past six weeks anyway for him to suddenly give a damn.

"Some of the members perform. There's a talent show where most of them use their gifts in some way, followed by anyone who can sing. Then a Secret Santa and some games, unless you want to just relax with a drink and listen to the music."

Oh. Wow. That all sounds incredible. "Are you a member of the

Guild?"

Kell shrugs. "Technically, yes."

"Does that mean you'll be performing?"

He throws his head back into a raucous laugh. "You want to hear me sing, beautiful?"

I imagine his deep timbre singing "Blue Christmas" and, uh, yeah. I really fucking do. "Maybe."

He chuckles and tosses my water bottle back to me. "I'll start working on a song for you, then."

I smile and nod, trying to picture the moment in the bunker surrounded by all that greenery and the people there. I wish I could bring Portia with me to see it.

The thought sucks the brief happiness from my soul.

Has Elias found her yet? Will she be celebrating Christmas with him, at least? What if I could take down GE before Christmas so she could come home?

My face is turned upward, and I see blue-green eyes staring down at me. "Now, where did you go?"

I try to smile at him, but it's small and melancholy. "Do you think Elias found Portia yet? I don't want her to be alone for Christmas. She should be here, coming to see the shows with me."

His lips turn down, but I don't expect him to know anything. Elias hasn't contacted me, and I'm sure he'd have found a way if he had her. At least to tell me she's safe. Which means he's still out looking for her.

"I'll talk to Aiden. But enough of that. I think it's time we tested the results of your training so far. And have a bit of fun. We've been cooped up in these walls for too long."

"What do you mean, test the results of my training?"

Kellan's grin turns feral. "I'm taking you to the Pits."

Chapter Twenty-Four

RAEGAN

He drives us into the heart of downtown and parks on the street. The car doors slam on either side as we get out, then Kellan guides me to a set of stairs directed downward from the sidewalk. There's an old neon sign hanging above it that says Cactus Jacks.

I give Kell a look over my shoulder. "A dive bar?"

"Not what you expected?"

I shrug. I'm not sure what I'm expecting from this trip. Does he want me to get into a bar fight to check my progress?

His long arm appears from behind me to shove the door open and let us inside. The constant hum of the city disappears instantly beneath rowdy voices and rock music. My minimalist life over the last five years makes me cringe at the clutter and disorganization of the bar.

The walls are covered in newspaper articles, pictures, license plates, and string lights dangling in front of them. The booths are worn and cracked leather along one side, a few high tables and chairs down the middle, and then the bar itself takes up three quarters of the room.

Kellan's hand on my hip encourages me forward, and I realize I'd frozen in the doorway to take it all in. I can feel the rumble in his chest when he chuckles since I can't hear him unless he yells at me, and I don't swat away the possessive arm around my back to my hip because I'm a tad overwhelmed.

He waves at some people at the bar, who look so relaxed and comfortable that I'm guessing they're regulars. The entire bar looks filled with regulars, though, if I'm going by those two requirements.

We pass by a couple of pool tables and dart boards in the back, and then Kellan opens another door that leads from one hallway to another, eventually bringing us to a bouncer-type guy at the top of a set of stairs.

"Evening, boss." The beefy guy nods his head in respect to Kellan, who's since taken up the front position for all the doorways while keeping a firm hold on my hand. "Miss," he adds with another distinct nod my way. I'm pleased he didn't ignore me as if I'm some temporary side piece to Kellan tonight. Does that mean he hasn't brought a lot of girls here before?

Ugh, stop thinking about it. It doesn't matter. I didn't even keep track of the guys I'd been with in the last five years, so it shouldn't bother me if he'd done the same thing. We were dead to each other, and we each had moved on in our own ways.

It still fucking bothers me.

"You fightin' tonight?" The bouncer's gruff expression cracks enough to reveal barely restrained eagerness.

Kellan's hand squeezes mine. I'm not sure what he's looking for with that squeeze, but then I see the look in his blue-green eyes, and it's nothing but pure excitement. He's pumped over whatever's about to happen.

"Naw, I'm here to watch my girl tonight."

The bouncer turns to look me up and down, sizing me up in my black leggings, tank top, and jacket. He merely nods. "If you're with him, then I'm sure you're a fighter. I'll put my money on you, darling," He shoots me a wink.

Kellan laughs and pats his hand on the guy's shoulder. "Good call, Lorcan. Hopefully, your shift is over soon, so you can watch."

Lorcan digs a wad of cash from his pocket. He flicks through a few bills and hands it to Kell. "In case I'm late, put my bet in for me, will ya?"

Kellan raises his hand with the money and tilts his head. "You got it." He turns his face to me. "You ready, beautiful?"

"No, but when has that ever stopped me?"

Snickering, he pulls us down the stairs. I can already hear the echo of shouting and cheers from here, even though there's a thick door between the stairs and the next room. Once it opens, we're walking into a large, open room full of barrels for seats and small round tables. In the center of the room is a platform with a metal cage around it in the shape of a dome. It goes as high as the ceiling and is twice as wide.

It's huge.

The room itself is packed. Money is held up in hands, and I spot staff serving drinks and taking bets every ten feet. Kellan uses his large frame to push a pathway for us to a guy in the corner with the microphone.

The guy sees us and stands on the stool he'd been parked on. "Oh, hells yes! Folks, count your lucky stars because I see the Dragon is here!" he cries out into the microphone over the din. Cheers from every corner of the room erupt in a deafening roar. "If you think you're fierce, I dare you to take on the Dragon! This is your chance to claim the title of champion while he's here, so sign up against him while you can!"

Kellan drops my hand to cross his arms over his chest while smirking up at him. "Get your dumb ass down here, York. I never said I was fighting tonight."

York jumps down and tosses the microphone back behind him. "Well, you can't disappoint your fans and competition now, can you?" He grins. "It's been too long since you were here last, man. You owe me some of that hype we've been missing." He looks past Kell to me. "Evening!" He salutes me with two fingers. "You a watcher or a fighter?"

"A fighter," I shout back at him, even though we're only a couple feet from one another, because the crowd still hasn't calmed down from his announcement.

Pride glows from Kellan, and my heart trips over itself. It's like a shot of adrenaline and dopamine all at once, and a girl could get addicted to the feeling.

I can't remember the last time I'd ever wanted to do something for someone else like this. I better not fuck it up. He clearly thinks I can do this, but what if I fail in front of everyone here?

"You're worthless."

Shut up, Gordon. Kellan believes in me, and I'm not going to let him down.

"Fucking fantastic! This is going to be a great night, Kell. You'll see in your bank account when it's over."

Kellan waves his hand at that like he couldn't care less. "Make sure she's got some time to watch the fights before you stick her in the line-up. This is her first time, so she'll need to see what we're about first."

York whips out his phone and nods seriously. "Yes, yes. Oh! What's your calling card?" he directs the question my way.

Uh... "My what?"

"Your nickname that they'll call you," Kellan leans down in my ear to answer.

"Oh. I don't know..."

I recall Kit's nickname for me and snort. Well, if Kellan is Dragon, then maybe this name isn't as silly as it sounds.

"Ruin. Call me Ruin."

Kellan's eyebrows pop up, and I shake my head. I'll tell him about Kit and the moniker he dubbed me with at another time.

The emcee cackles. "Alright, Dragon and Ruin. I'll call you out when it's your turn to fight. Now let me take care of this line behind you of new contenders so I can redo all the match-ups." He waves us away, and Kellan loops his arm around my shoulders to keep me close while leading us through the throng of people to the cage.

It's large enough that we find an open spot against it. The ring is empty, probably while that guy York rearranges the fights, and I turn out of Kellan's hold and grip the unzipped sides of his leather jacket in each hand.

"Are you going to tell me what exactly you've gotten me into, *Dragon*?" I tease with an arched brow.

Kellan gives me a wolfish grin and crowds me back against the cage. His fingers grasp the metal on either side of me as he hunches over me. "A gifted fight."

My eyes widen. Did he say gifted?

"Yup. This isn't your regular pack of ragtag thugs and fighters here. Everyone here has a gift and uses it in the fight."

Shit. He couldn't start me with some normal fight club to see how far I've come? We didn't train with gifts.

"If you want to face GE, then this is how you train. I can train you with your gift if you'll let me, but the only way you'll be able to practice against others who have gifts is going to be here."

I bite my lip. "But Kell, I can't use my gift in there. What if I kill someone by accident?"

He's so close now that the heat from his body instantly warms me as I draw in a breath of his musk and motor oil scent.

"Then don't," he replies simply with a quirk of his lips.

"Gee, thanks," I snark back at his lack of help.

Kellan angles my face to look at him. "Not today, but we *will* start training with your gift, so you aren't afraid of it anymore. And then you'll find a way where you can use it that won't be just for killing."

York's voice blares through the speakers overhead as he calls out the next contenders before I can say anything back to him. My gift does nothing but kill. There's no other way for me to use it, not like how Jackson can do so many amazing things with his, or Aiden. I'm a one-trick pony. Death and destruction.

"Just watch." He spins me around to face the cage, and his body tucks in behind me. The first two in the ring, or dome really, are a girl who's smaller than me and a guy around my height. They're both lean and look nimble rather than strong, and I find myself pressing my nose between the cage bars in anticipation of their gifts.

A horn sounds, and they immediately move. The girl jumps back but lands on air a few feet up. She keeps hopping up some invisible steps until she's above the guy. If I squint and angle my head, I can see the faintest shimmer in the air.

"She can solidify air," Kellan murmurs, his facial hair tickling my skin and sending a rush of heat through me.

I watch as she jumps around the dome, and now I can see why they needed a cage all the way around and so high. It gives her far more room to move in instead of just the platform.

Her competitor seems unphased and jumps onto one of her air platforms, beginning his ascent after her by following the same path she took. His head rears back when he gets closer, and then something flies from his mouth at her.

She dodges, but whatever liquid he expelled is aimed at her feet and hits the air she'd hardened instead. The girl drops, but she catches herself with another translucent circle of air before she hits the ground.

"He can create all types of acids and poisons in his body," Kellan explains while I look on in awe.

The guy shoots acid in rapid fire at her, and she creates a shield of air that blocks it, but disintegrates almost as quickly as she's able to throw it up. I realize then that they are relying primarily on their gifts for this fight rather than hand-to-hand. He works best at a distance, firing off his acid where she can't touch him.

She, on the other hand, keeps trying to find an opening to reach him. The girl jumps from one platform to the next. Then, from behind him, she flips upside down for her feet to plant on a platform above his head. She launches herself down at him, and he turns in time to spit acid at her, but she conjures a shield in seconds. It melts away, and her body crashes down on his, and the impact knocks him out.

The bell rings and York's voice carries over the crowd's hollers. "Float wins by knockout!"

The girl raises her arms up to her fans and grins when their cheers heighten. Someone enters the cage and presses two fingers to her contender's forehead, and he groans and pushes himself up. They all leave the cage, and York calls out the next match.

I watch fight after fight of people using their gifts with their fighting skills. It's amazing to see just how different some gifts are while also seeing some familiar ones as well. The fight is won by either a knockout or yielding, and there's a healer just outside of the door to take care of any serious injuries or wake up those who are knocked out.

After what feels like a lifetime, I hear my name being called.

"Next up! Knight versus a brand-new, first-time fighter...Ruin! Don't let her inexperience fool you, though! She came hand-picked by our very own Dragon."

Kellan squeezes my shoulders and walks around the dome with me to the one and only door that leads inside it.

"Give it up for your next fighters!"

I take a deep breath and flex my hands. I can do this. I've seen what some of the others can do, but if I can somehow bring the fight back to hand-to-hand combat like a few of the fights I'd just watched, that's my chance.

"You've got this, beautiful. Just remember everything I taught you, and don't lose your head in the moment. If you need to stop and think, then make that time and do it. This isn't a battle of strength. It's a battle of thinking on your feet with what you have, what they have, and whatever's available around you."

I nod and take another breath. "Okay."

He grins and opens the door for me. "Go be a badass, Ruin."

I smirk while walking through the door and shoot over my shoulder, "Try not to nut in your pants while watching."

Kellan howls with laughter and smacks his chest. "Sorry, but no promises on that."

I laugh and keep moving to the marker on the floor for the start position. The guy across from me takes up his spot and assesses me from head to toe.

"Ruin, huh?"

I shift my feet for better balance and raise my hands up at the ready. "That's me. I hope you're not too knightly to just let a lady win."

He scoffs and drops his hands at his sides, his fingers open but curved as if they're ready to catch something. "There are no ladies here. Just warriors."

My lips tug into a smile. *Damn. I like this guy.*

The horn blasts, and I watch as glowing red weapons appear in each of his hands in an instant.

Well. Fuck me.

I silently curse Kellan for not preparing me better for this before throwing me to the wolves, but there's no more time for that when Knight rushes me with his weapons.

I do the only thing I can do when unarmed and run. When I keep my distance, sadly just running from him with no move to counterattack, he switches up his swords for a halberd that crosses the distance between us. He swings it at me, and I dive over it, then roll to dodge his strike downward.

Shit on a stick. I'm literally a sitting duck, just waiting for him to hit me with one of his weapons when I lose all stamina from running around this huge space. I need to find a way to switch to the offensive.

He comes around with the halberd again, and this time, when I dodge, I bend myself out of the way and then take a chance and grab the pole. It's warm and feels like micro zaps of electricity against my skin, but it's not unpleasant. Best of all, I *can* touch it.

I shove it back at him, trying to dislodge his hold on it, but he doesn't relent. We're both tugging on the weapon between us and then I move down it toward him to close the distance.

The halberd vanishes, and two more short swords appear in his hands. His arms sweep down at me in alternating patterns, and I'm forced back, but he tosses something behind me, and just as I turn to look at it, I trip on it instead and fall on my back.

Knight pounces over me, holding the one short sword left in his hand and holding it at my neck. "Yield!"

I growl and thrash under him, but he's sitting above my waist where my legs can't reach him. I can't lose like this. I've barely even showed them what I'm capable of.

My gift heats in my gut and snakes up to my hands. I grab his blade, and it shatters as soon as I touch it.

He jumps back from me and my hands, and even through all the surrounding noise, I can hear Kellan's deep voice whooping from one side of the cage.

I get back on my feet, holding my gift in my hands and raising them up in front of me, open and waiting for his next attack. Knight has called in another short sword and flips it in one hand in a circle.

"Took you long enough to reveal your gift," he shouts.

I smirk and shrug. "I was hoping to not have to use it."

He crouches, and I mirror him. "Kind of arrogant, aren't you?"

"Nope. It was just wishful thinking," I quip. He looks confused by that for a second, and then he's running toward me. I spread my gift down my arm, feeding it more and more until my arm's glowing a faint red and it feels like I've buried my arm in hot coals.

I grit my teeth together through the pain, praying that my idea works, or else I'm going to have to hope that these healers can reattach body parts.

Knight swings his sword down, and I raise that arm up between us, concentrating on strengthening my gift there. His blade touches my skin and then turns to dust in an instant. He falls forward when it disappears, and I take that opportunity to use my legs to knock him all the way down.

More weapons appear in his hands, but I grab one with my charged right hand to make it disintegrate, while my left hand, which no longer has my gift in it, knocks the weapon from his hand and snatches it up. I hold the blade against his neck, the same as he'd done to me, while my charged hand is held up and ready as a threat.

"Yield," I command softly.

He doesn't give any attention to the dagger at his neck, since he can probably make it disappear at will, but he's eyeing my hand with wariness.

"Yield!" I don't want him to think about his options. He doesn't know that I don't have full control over my gift and that I can't use it against him. He has no idea what it would do to him if I were to touch him with it, so he has to decide if he's feeling lucky today and wants to test it.

Knight frowns and then his blue-gray eyes jump to mine. "Alright. I yield."

I breathe a sigh of relief and fall back on my heels. The room goes wild around us. My heart is jack hammering in a mixture of adrenaline and panic while I focus on reeling my gift back in. My hands and arms still burn after it's gone, and I'm now dreaming of drowning them in a cold bath when we get home. I touch the floor with each hand just to be sure there are no remnants of it that stick around, then get to my feet.

Knight holds out his hand for me. "Good match," he says when I accept the handshake. "Now that I know your gift, though, it won't be so easy next time."

I think about whether or not there will be a next time and decide that, yeah, maybe that was fun. And crazy. Seeing everyone using their gifts freely and in creative ways only makes me want to know what else I can do. A smile breaks free despite myself. "I'll be better than this next time, too," I promise.

He nods and stalks off, waving a hand up in the air as a farewell before exiting the ring. "I look forward to it!"

Kellan dashes over to me, and I'm suddenly airborne as he lifts me by my thighs. I squeal and grab onto his shoulders. "That's my fucking girl! I knew you could do it."

"Kell! Put me down!" York is already calling the next fighters into the ring, and Kellan seems to give zero fucks that there's anyone else around but us.

He chuckles and loosens his grip so that my body slides down the front of his. His mouth stamps over mine, and then I'm right there with him, where there's nothing left outside of us. I moan into his kiss that feels like fireworks exploding in my chest. My arms wrap around his neck, and I press further into him as my body melts and liquefies just for him.

"Ahem!" York's voice cuts through my momentary loss of brain activity. "Please clear the fighting dome if you aren't Bubbles or Spitfire!"

I jerk back and cover my mouth and then my face as embarrassment floods under my skin.

Kellan laughs and flips the bird in York's direction, then guides me out since I'm too fucking mortified to open my eyes and see myself out. I have to assume, to *hope*, that I wouldn't have fucked Kellan on a stage in front of a hundred people because I was too doped up on adrenaline and lust to notice.

We find another spot along the cages to watch the rest of the fights and wait for Kellan's turn. I'm not gonna lie. I'm now excited as hell to see his fight. By the time his turn rolls around, my thighs are clenched, and I'm gripping the metal of the cage with bated breath. York runs through a *list* of people who want to take on the Dragon, and I turn worried eyes on Kell.

"Can they do that? Make you fight all of them in a row?"

He shrugs. "They could fight me all at once, but they want the glory of taking me on by themselves." Kellan bends down to nip my ear. "I can't wait for you to cheer for me, beautiful. Your voice is the only one I want to hear."

I push him playfully away from me. "Only if you promise to win every single match."

And he does.

Every.

Single.

One.

Chapter Twenty-Five

KELLAN

I'M NOT SURE HOW I managed to fall asleep last night while Raegan laid in my arms, but somehow, I'm peeling my eyes open at the intoxicating smell of vanilla while sunlight peeks through the slit in the curtains.

Raegan is sprawled over and around me like a baby sloth. There's absolutely nothing ladylike about the way her limbs are tangled up in mine, and her body is pressing into me as if she could sink into my skin to steal my warmth.

The covers are gone. I can see the pile at the foot of the bed like she couldn't handle the heat of both me and the blankets, and she chose me.

I tilt my nose into her hair and breathe deeply. She has no idea how much she drives me wild. Everything about her draws me in.

She mutters something incoherent in her sleep and burrows her face into my chest, and my arm tightens reflexively around her back to encourage that closeness. My cock stirs when she moves, but I ignore it. I'm not ruining this moment just yet. She already thinks that our relationship is made up only of sex and adventures.

Which, fuck, if that's the worst of it, then we're doing pretty fucking well.

But I want more.

I want to sleep in with her like this and see what she looks like when she wakes up. I want to steal those quiet moments she doesn't share with anyone else and covet them like a dragon hoarding his treasure. I want her wild and crazy times, and I want her soft and vulnerable times.

All of it.

All of *her*.

Mine to love. Mine to cherish.

Her breathing changes and her eyelids flutter as she wakes up. I wrap my other arm around her and hold her close one more time before she wakes, then bring my hand up to stroke over her lower lip.

"Morning, beautiful." My voice is husky and thick still from sleep. I'm only grateful that I could wake up before her so I could have that moment first.

Raegan's eyes snap open at my voice, and then her memory of last night must kick in because they lower again, and she hums. "Morning, Dragon."

I chuckle and run my fingers through her washed but sleep-dried hair that's now formed a few small nests. "Shall we get up? Dragon's gotta eat."

She smiles into my chest and then stretches her arm over to the other side. "Fuck, you're comfortable," she groans. "And Aiden's out there. I don't wanna."

I grin at the easy compliment that's worth far more to me than she'll ever know, then tug lightly at one of her nasty tangles. "You're not hiding from him. Let's get it over with so you're not trying to hide from us again. I *will* break down your door the next time you try it."

"What if you stayed with me?" She pouts so prettily that I almost fucking cave. She's way too good at that. Or I'm just a sucker for her.

"As much as I would seriously love that, we're all in this together. I won't shut my brothers out."

"Ugh, you suck." She rolls away from me, and I bite my tongue to keep myself from snatching her back. I can't risk her running again because of this shit with Aiden. They need to get it out and find some common ground so we can work together.

Raegan tugs her clothes back on at the edge of the bed, and I sit up and straddle her from behind. My arms wrap around her waist and pull her back against me. "Kellan, what—" Her breath catches as my tongue paints a line up the side of her neck and circles at the sensitive spot behind her ear. Her entire body shivers, and I tighten my arms around her and chuckle.

"You should sleep in my room again tonight," I breathe into her skin while pressing fervent kisses along the crux of her neck and shoulder.

Her head tilts to grant me more access as she sighs. "If I did that, you'd think that this might become a regular thing. Or you'd ask me to stay every night."

"Well, I'd be lying if I said that wasn't my end goal," I drawl and then bite down on her shoulder.

She hisses, but I lick and suck the pain away so there'll be a mark left when I'm done. "You're incorrigible," Raegan huffs, and I smile at that. Damn right I am. The sooner she learns it, the better, too. She turns in my arms and kisses me. It's warm and languid. Hot and sweet. And everything I could ever ask for in a kiss.

She cups the side of my face, stroking my beard in such a way that brings my dick right-the-fuck to attention. She pulls away, and a growl rumbles in my chest.

"Like you said. We need to get up and eat."

When the fuck did I say that?

She laughs at whatever face I'm making and stands up to finish getting dressed, then slips out of my room to leave me to it.

I should've kept my damn mouth shut this morning.

Everyone else is already at the dining table when I get there, excluding Jackson, of course. Haven't seen him in *weeks*, which wouldn't be odd except for the fact that Raegan is here with us, and he isn't.

Not to mention the blatant and unrepentant murders.

You know. Just two really big deals for it being Jackson.

I pull out my chair, letting it loudly scrape across the floor before I plop right down. Dane has made a large plate of pancakes and bacon, and there's a bowl of mixed fruit as well. Considering it's past lunchtime, and he's still made us all breakfast, I'm wondering how many of us had a late night and just recently woke up.

I pile a load of each onto my plate and then pour myself a large glass of orange juice.

My fork stabs into the fruit first, shoving it into my mouth before I look around the table. Dane's plate is already empty, and he's just watching me with unguarded disgust at my eating habits. Aiden is scrolling through his phone as usual, while Raegan's trying to look anywhere but at him. If I didn't know what happened yesterday, I wouldn't think much of it since they normally aren't very chatty with each other in the morning. But now I feel a bit like Jack as I pick apart the details I would normally overlook.

Aiden's wearing a black suit that's wrinkled and rumpled. His tie is missing, and the first few buttons in his dress shirt are undone. It looks like he slept in it and then came straight here when he woke up.

If I paid any attention to clothes at all, aside from Raegan's, I might know if he wore that suit yesterday or not. There's also a light smell of bourbon wafting from him. Again, is it from last night or this morning?

At minimum, he's definitely still going through some shit from Raegan last night. Even if he's acting like nothing's happened.

"Out late last night or early this morning?" I shoot Aiden's way with a smirk. Some might ignore it or give him his privacy, but that's not me. I just call it as I see it.

Aiden sets his coffee mug down and frowns at me. "Since we're all here now, we need to come up with a game plan for our next steps. Where are we with Gifted Enterprise?"

I chuckle at the topic shift and lounge back in my seat, one arm hooked over the back of the chair and one leg sprawled out.

"I haven't made any progress on finding the island. Or, islands," Dane begins. "I think Vera's blocking me, so it's almost wasted time at this point to keep trying." His eyes snap up to Aiden. "I think we should prioritize getting Vera back. Not just because she's my sister, but we're stuck in this holding pattern because of her too. Getting her on our side means we don't have to worry about technology or the Guild anymore, and I can get the exact locations of the islands."

"You would say that." I scoff, and he slashes a glare my way. I shrug back. "What? I'm just saying that getting her here and on our side is going to be just as time-consuming. You really think she'll just hand herself over to us and cooperate?"

"I'm with Kellan," Raegan chimes in. "There has to be a faster way to take down GE."

"Reid and Tinsley weren't much help in the information they had," Aiden admits. "They were brought to other locations by someone with the ability to create a portal between two places, so they never knew where exactly they were. And they weren't high enough up the chain to know more than a couple names of lead agents." Aiden finishes the rest of his coffee before he continues. "Hopefully, those names can give us somewhere to start. Otherwise, we're back to square one. Jackson usually sniffed them out for us, so we need a backup plan."

"I can do it. I'm a magnet for trouble, so I'm sure I'll run into something we can use," Raegan volunteers.

My hand smacks down on the table. "I'll come with you."

Her eyes cut over to me, and her mouth opens. To argue, I'm sure, but Aiden talks as if he didn't notice.

"Good. Next, we need to figure out what to do with Jackson. We need to bring him in, detain him, and figure out what he's doing and why."

"We haven't seen Thorne since Jackson took off," Dane muses accusingly.

"What's that supposed to mean?" Raegan's head whips around to him.

He gives a slight shrug. "Nothing. Maybe something. I don't know. I just think it's odd that he tried to draw us out over a month ago, he ran, and then he never tried coming back at us?"

I frown at that revelation.

"In any case, getting Jackson will be our priority. Has anyone seen him?" Aiden looks around the table.

"Nope," I offer once he's looking my way. Dane's shaking his head, as is Raegan.

Wind out of nowhere sweeps through the room, knocking décor off the walls and sending any loose papers flying. It comes in a steady torrent, increasing in speed as if a tornado's about to pick up within the walls of the firehouse.

"Get under the table!" I shout at the others, jumping over to Raegan first to help her duck under the table. The chairs are whipped away from us before I can grab them, so I hold either side of the table from underneath and keep it in place instead.

Our dishes fly off the table and crash against the wall. Anything lighter than the chairs and not mounted to the floor or wall has been picked up and is now spinning around the room.

Aiden curses. "It's Thorne. I don't have enough metal on me." He raises the small shield he's made from whatever metal he'd had on him, but it's barely the length of his forearm.

"Where's the rest of it?" I shout over the wind.

His jaw clenches. "In the locker room."

Great. So, the complete opposite side of this building.

I look out at the room just in time to see shards of broken glass and ceramic flying our way. I drop the table on its side to take the hit with a curse, then turn to see more coming from the other direction.

"Get behind me!" I yell at the others, then widen my arms and chest to take up as much space as possible. I reach out to grab or knock into the shards further out from me, then position myself to take the largest group of them.

They hit me all at once, slamming into my chest, my stomach, and my arms and legs. The pain is nothing if I can take it for the others. I'll take every one of them to keep them safe. I roar with defiance as the last of them hits me. I drop to my knees and growl when a shard there snaps and burrows deeper.

"Kell!"

I turn my head back to try offering her a smile, that I'm alright, but my vision swims from the pain, and I lose control of my balance. "Shit."

I crash down on the floor, miraculously on my back, and I can feel hands yanking the projectiles out of me. As soon as the first one leaves, my gift kicks in there. Then the next. And the next. The furious flow of regeneration and scales starts taking over enough that I blink my eyes and see Dane and Raegan hurrying to remove every last piece. Aiden stands guard behind them with his small shield.

It's what I see standing beyond them that shocks me.

"What is this, Thorne?" Jackson's voice is cold, dead. He's asking a question, but it doesn't sound at all like he actually cares about the answer. He's standing on the kitchen island looking out over the room decimated by Thorne's personal tornado. His hands are tucked in his hoodie pocket, and there's an odd look as he takes it all in.

Thorne's voice answers from the living area, but I can't turn my head yet to look at him. I'm not even sure I would if I could. Because there is no way I'm looking away from Jackson right now. "Just keeping things interesting until you arrive."

I'm about halfway healed now, but both Dane and Raegan freeze when Jack appears.

"Jack?" Raegan queries slowly.

His head slowly turns until his eyes fall on her. "Little one." Jackson hops from the counter to the floor, and then he holds his hand out for her. "Come with me."

She looks at his hand, and then Dane stands up in front of her. "Like fuck!"

"Jackson, what's going on here?" Aiden asks calmly, as if he's treating Jack like a rabid dog. He steps forward, trying to draw his attention when it doesn't stray from Raegan.

"You know me," Jack says, still talking directly to Raegan as if none of us are in the room.

She moves to stand, and I snatch her wrist. "No, beautiful. If he has something to say to you, he can fucking say it right here. There's no reason for you to go anywhere with him." What hold does he have over her that she would willingly go to him after something like this?

All I know is that I can't let her leave with him. *Them*. Because while we can't be sure of whatever dynamics are happening between him and Thorne right now, there's something there. Thorne hasn't moved or attacked since Jackson arrived.

Raegan smiles softly at me, and my grip on her wrist tightens. *No.*

Her hand touches mine. "He won't hurt me, Kell. I'll be fine. Let me go."

"Never," I growl. "I told you that before, and I fucking meant it."

Dane spins around and takes her elbow. "He's clearly working with Thorne now. You can't go with him. What if he takes you back to GE? I can't—"

"Enough of this," Thorne snaps and swings his hand. Everyone's thrown apart from each other, and I grunt when the table flies at me, and I have my scaled forearm block it from crushing me.

I shove it off, only to see that Jackson now has his arm around Raegan, and they're both standing on the kitchen counter. Thorne blasts wind above them to create a hole through the roof outside, and he leaves first.

"Jackson, don't make me do this," Aiden calls out to him before he can leave, too. His shield is now a spear that he has aimed at him. "Tell us what's going on, and we can help. But you're not taking her."

Jack just smiles at him. Something clicks, and then I see the lighter in his other hand right before he tosses it on a pile of scattered papers on the floor. The fire catches and grows instantly, too fast, like he's stoking it with his gift.

And then he and Raegan are gone.

Chapter Twenty-Six

RAEGAN

Jackson takes us onto the roof, then sweeps his other arm under my knees so I'm cradled against his chest. "Hold on tight, little one."

Thorne is standing there with his hands on his hips, smirking at me like he thinks this whole thing is too damn funny. I flip him the finger and then wrap my arms around Jack's neck.

Just because I'm putting my trust in Jackson doesn't mean I plan on playing nice for Thorne. Maybe I'll find a chance to kill him while his guard is down.

Jackson leaps into the air, and I gasp and cling tighter to him once we're airborne. A smirk tugs at his lips, telling me he caught my reaction, but he says nothing.

I'll wait until we're alone before finding out what the fuck Jackson's gotten himself into and what the plan is.

I wish I could say it was a smooth journey, but both Jack and Thorne don't waste their gift simply flying us through the sky. Instead, it's like they give themselves a boost every time they touch down, then soar through the air until their feet land on something—a building, tree, whatever—and then shoot back up.

At first, I try to keep track of where we're going. But the city looks completely different from up here, and after only five minutes, I've already lost where we've come from, let alone where we might be going. I bury my face into Jack's neck instead, soaking in his scent and grounding myself against him while my stomach rides this roller coaster over and over again.

Eventually, I doze off. I don't know how long we'd been flying for. An hour? Two? It feels like forever, and with nothing better to do and coming in so late this morning, my body conks out.

I wake up to the smell of salt and brine. I prepare to open my eyes, but stop when I realize we've stopped flying.

"We can chat after I've gotten her settled," Jackson tells someone, his dark voice vibrating against my ear.

There's a loud scoff. "I'm not sure what you see in a girl who falls asleep after being kidnapped." *Ugh. Thorne.*

"Good," Jack retorts calmly. "There's nothing for you to see in her other than your lifeline."

We start moving, but I keep my eyes closed in case there's anyone else around. I focus on my other senses instead. The smell of the ocean isn't as strong now, like we've gone inside, but I'm sure we're on the coast somewhere.

The air outside felt cool, with the usual ocean breeze, but I didn't feel any sunlight. So, is it after dark now?

"I know you're awake," Jackson interrupts my thoughts. A door creaks open and then shuts behind us. He sets me down on my feet, and I blink to gather my bearings.

We're in a small room with a twin bed against the far wall under a circular window. There's a desk next to a closet on one side and then a door on the other that's most likely a private bathroom.

"Where are we?"

"On a cargo ship."

"Uh-huh," I murmur, looking out the window to check that we are, in fact, out at sea. Trapped in the middle of the ocean with no escape. Again.

I close my eyes and take a deep breath. I can feel Jackson come up behind me, even though I hear nothing when he moves.

I spin around to face him with my mouth set in a firm line and anger blazing in my eyes. My hand slaps across his face.

He doesn't flinch or try to stop me. He lets me get that slap in and then just smiles knowingly at me.

Well, that's not good enough for me.

"What the *fuck*, Jackson?! You'd better fill me in right *now* or else I'll find a way to leave this and you behind. You owe me a really big explanation for what happened back there!"

He nods and crosses his arms over his chest while leaning against the wall that cuts into the room for the bathroom. "I'm using Thorne to infiltrate GE."

"And you had to hurt the guys to do that?"

"Thorne got ahead of me. It wasn't supposed to happen like that, but looking back now, he was testing me. He wanted to make sure I wasn't going to care about them. It's why I started the fire before I left too. To make sure I proved to Thorne that I didn't plan to have them follow us. I'd keep them busy with the fire before they could see where we went."

Kellan got hurt because of all that. I know he can heal, but that doesn't mean I like seeing him hurt more than anyone else. And what if Kellan hadn't been able to protect us? What if those hit Aiden or Dane? If Thorne had hit me, what would Jackson have done? Keep up the charade?

"He saw that you care about me. How does that factor in?"

Jackson tilts his head. "He knows about me and you. You come first, for me, which was why he decided he would come with me to pick you up. To...give me backup," he finishes with a smirk.

I'm still not finding any of this funny. "So then, what's the plan? You've got me out in the middle of the ocean on a boat, with one of our biggest enemies."

He stalks toward me. I hold my ground, even though instinct tells me to back up and keep the distance between us. He stops just in front of me and cups my face. "I'm sorry, little one. I had to use you, too, but I won't let them have you."

My eyes search his, but it's always been impossible for me to read anything from him that he doesn't willingly give. "What do you mean?" I ask, my hand coming up to the back of his to hold it there.

"I got GE's attention by taking out everyone tied to them in our city. I killed every last one of them. Every supporter, partner, sub-sidiary, employee. There's no one left there that belongs to them." Something flickers in his gaze. "Thorne agreed to back me, then, once he realized the winning side. He got me a meeting to pretend that we'll both join their side in exchange for your safety."

He really did it. He wiped the board clean in that city by himself. Holy fuck.

"What is Thorne getting out of this?" I'll never trust that man, even if he says he's chosen to back Jackson. I'm sure his loyalties will flip the second it may look like Jackson's not in complete control.

Jack's thumb strokes along my cheek. "He plans to take over GE for himself. I kill the board for him and then let him take it over to do what he wants with it. But he leaves us and the others out of it."

I huff at the audacity of that man. As if Jackson would put in all this effort to take down the organization just to let Thorne take it over instead. Jackson easily reads my line of thinking and smiles.

"All Thorne sees is my obsession with you. He believes that as long as I know you aren't being hunted any longer, I'll back off. He also thinks he can convince me to join him by the end of this. That I'll see the power he holds and want some of it, too."

"Well, that's ridiculous." He nods in agreement. Apparently, Thorne is only seeing what he wants to see in Jack. "So, what are we doing next?"

"We're waiting for a helicopter to pick us up and bring us to the island. Thorne's likely called them to confirm that I have you. But I want you to stay here when it comes."

"What? Why?"

His hand moves down my jaw to my neck, his cerulean gaze following his hand until his thumb pauses over the pulse point there. "You're my ticket in with them, little one, but I have no plans to bring you with me. I'll tell Thorne I want to meet first to make sure they're going to hold up their end of the deal before I bring you with me. You being here was enough for them to send the helicopter. You've done your part. And once we go, the captain will send you and a couple of his crew on a boat back to the mainland."

Fear drops like a rock in my gut. I grab his arm in both hands. "You can't go there alone. The entire island would be against you.

And Thorne is just as likely to stab you in the back as he is to help you. I have to go with you."

Sneaking around the city and taking out all the people related to Gifted Enterprise is one thing—a crazy, terrifying thing, yes, but it's not the same as this. He could be walking into a trap. He just murdered an entire city of their people. Who's to say their plan isn't just to off him the second the helicopter lands? He doesn't know the island, and he has no allies.

"Getting you involved this much is more than what I wanted. If I could have left you and the others out of it completely, I would have."

"Well, I'm here now! So, let me help you! I can help keep up the charade until we find a good opening. They could suspect something if you suddenly refuse to bring me with you."

Jackson smiles at me again, like his mind has been made up. "This is the only way, little one. Once I'm there, I'll find a way to get into their computers and upload everything there to the cloud. Dane at least taught me how to access our personal drive to upload important things to. So, in case I don't make it—"

I yank my sleeve down from my wrist to shove it between us so he can see it. "Don't you dare finish that sentence, Jack. I'm coming with you, and there's nothing you can say or do that's going to stop me. Because of this."

On my wrist is a black and gray butterfly filled in with a skull, just like his. But instead of *memento mori*, mine says *memento vivere*. Remember you must live.

"We're going to do this together, and we're going to win. We're going to survive it. Together. Because where you go, I go."

Jackson holds the back of my forearm and looks at the tattoo with surprise. It's the most expression I've ever seen from him, and I think I've shocked any words right off his tongue.

His other hand snatches the back of my head, and the two of us are crushed together in a blistering kiss. He drops my arm in favor of wrapping around my waist to pull me tighter against him, even though I don't think a single sliver of air could fit between us. My hands drive his hood back to grip and cling to his black hair, fisting it so hard, like I'm afraid he'll disappear if I were to let go.

He's mine. My shadow. My demon. And I won't let him sacrifice himself for me. We're in this together. I'll stalk him right back if I have to, just to be sure he comes home safe and sound.

We fall back on the small bed, and my legs lift and wrap around his waist the second my feet are no longer on the ground. He drags me further up the bed until my head hits the pillow. He slowly coaxes my arms up and over my head, his hands covering mine to close over the narrow piece of wood for a headboard.

Then he presses a long kiss to the tattoo there. I watch him as he does it, breathless, and a heady feeling washing over me when his eyes close and he holds his lips against it. Almost like he's taking a moment to pray or promise something in his head that I can't hear, but I can feel in his kiss.

He pulls away and starts trailing kisses down my body. He licks, sucks, and kisses, every bit of exposed skin, and then finds more by pushing my clothes up and out of the way. Every touch is like a spark against my skin, echoing down to my core.

Jackson takes his time in his descent down my body. His touch is soft, but demanding. Reverent, while edged with obsession. He makes me feel like an angel fallen from heaven that he's sworn to worship and please until we're both ruined. I'll gladly fall from grace if it means having him touch me this way forever.

He moves to the side to slide my pants and underwear down, but stops them at my ankles before pushing my knees up and then leaning over them. I try to shift my legs, but they're trapped by my pants and his weight on them.

"Jack," I pant, because I can't shift myself the way I want to.

"Shh," he breathes against my folds. I shudder with pleasure at him being so close, and then a whimper falls from my lips when his tongue splits me open.

"Oh, fuck," I whimper, throwing my head back.

His fingers pull me apart to give him more access, and then his tongue firmly glides between me. My body convulses when he flicks my clit before moving back down to make sure there's no area forgotten. My pussy grinds down on his face, desperate for the release that he's been teasing me with as his tongue and lips lick the soul from my body. I whimper and writhe against him, needing more.

"More," I beg. "Please, Jack. I need—"

He slides his fingers into me, and it feels like all the air leaves my body in a rush. *Yes!* I don't know what garbled sounds are coming from my throat now as he strokes my inner walls at the same time as he plays more with my clit.

My lower back tightens, and I grip the wood above my head so much that I don't know if my hands or the wood might break first. "Fuck! Yes! Yes! Ungh...Jack!"

He adds a third finger, and I'm done. Destroyed. My orgasm takes me over completely until I'm nothing but nerve endings and pure fucking pleasure that I scream out to the world, not giving a fuck that other people live in it outside of me and him. It rushes through my limbs in an instant and then drags itself back and strips me bare of my strength.

My body sags against the bed when it finally passes, leaving me breathless and boneless all at once. Jackson's crawling over me, and I instinctually turn my mouth to his because I know exactly what he wants, and I'd give him anything right now.

He kisses me slow and deep, stroking me with his tongue once again into submission as I fall deeper and deeper for him. I kiss him like he's the one who supplies my oxygen, and I need nothing else. I can taste myself in his kiss, and it's like he's mixing me with me because he wants all of it at once and can never get enough.

When he finally breaks away, he barely raises his face above mine so my eyes are captured in his. And they are. I latch on to his gaze and couldn't look away if I tried, with the way he's staring at me.

Like I'm the entire world, right here in his arms.

"I love you, Raegan," he whispers above me. "More than oxygen or air. More than every star in the sky. I have always loved you, and there is nowhere you can go where I won't follow."

My lungs freeze, and I think I've forgotten how to breathe. Jackson kisses me again, and fuck it; I don't need oxygen either.

A knock bangs against the door, and Jackson snaps backward to swing his head around and look at it. His face tightens, and then he's up and moving. He wets a washcloth in the tiny bathroom to help clean me up before he opens the small port-hole window to toss the cloth out. He spins a few fingers, and there's a quick breeze that rushes through the room and back out the window while I pull my clothes back on and stand.

Jackson looks me over to make sure I'm good, which I give him a quick nod to, and then he crosses the room to open the door.

"I'm *so* sorry. Did I interrupt something?" Thorne sneers from the doorway.

I move up just behind Jack so I can see him and cross my arms.

His one good eye drops to look at me, and his face twists with disgust.

"Were you hiding yourself from me?" Jackson asks, his tone unperturbed, but I can tell from the tension in his stance that he's angry about it. "How long were you standing there?"

Fuck.

Did he hear Jackson's plans?

Thorne looks back to Jack. "Long enough to hear you wasting your time with sex when we have plans we should prepare for."

Gross.

I mean, yay that he didn't hear our plans, but did he just stand there and listen to that?

I need a fucking shower.

Jackson's hand grips the door frame while he leans against the other side, effectively blocking me from Thorne's view. But I'm staring at the white knuckles of his hand as he holds himself back from attacking Thorne.

"Eavesdrop on us again, Thorne, and I'll cut your ears off and stuff the holes with cotton balls." I can't see Thorne's reaction now that Jackson has changed his position, but Jack doesn't let him respond to that. "The plans have already been made. We're waiting on the chopper. Is it here?"

Thorne's voice is slightly raised, and he bites the words out in his anger. "It's five minutes out."

"We'll meet you up there, then," Jackson says right before slamming the door in his face.

I tie my hair up in a ponytail when he turns back to me. "Guess our time's up, huh?"

Time to prepare for entering the enemy stronghold.

Chapter Twenty-Seven

JACKSON

It's time.

All my planning, the blood I've spilled, everything has led up to this moment. And I'm ready for it. I had every intention of tucking my little one away while I took care of GE once and for all, but my arrogance at this all going according to plan was outclassed by her stubbornness.

And her love for me.

I know she didn't say it, but she doesn't have to. I see it in the way she looks at me. The way she fights for me, for *us*. Seeing her matching tattoo is all the proof I'll ever need, and now I feel like I'm invincible.

That tattoo will be our talisman, our good luck charm. I don't usually believe in that stuff, but when I saw it on her, I knew I could believe in it. It's our bond given physical form for the world to see that we can't be separated.

So, even though the plan has changed, my determination to see this through doesn't waver. Raegan was never meant to sit back and let others take care of her problems for her. She's a warrior. A fighter. I should have known she wouldn't cower and run from danger. She'll run right to it if someone she cares about might be in trouble.

That strength and bravery are only the tip of the iceberg of why I'm so obsessed with her.

The helicopter is already waiting on the pad by the time Raegan and I get there. We climb in, buckling ourselves next to one another across from Thorne. My hand immediately seeks out hers, intertwining our fingers together.

And with that simple gesture, any annoying flutter of concern dissipates. Her touch brings my feet back to the ground, reminds me of who I am and why I'm here. There is no end to this other than getting what we need and escaping together. Whether we kill everyone on the island to do it or not; it doesn't matter. Only that I'll protect her at all costs.

Thorne tries to have a conversation through the bulky and uncomfortable headsets he has us wearing. He didn't offer one to Raegan, so I almost declined mine, but I was too curious to hear what he had to say to me.

Nothing.

He blabbers on about what we're going to accomplish, and I tune him out. I know I need to keep him from being too upset with me while I'm pretending to be on the same side, but the fact that he listened to Raegan's pleasure still has rage burning in my gut. I turn my face away from him, casually dismissing him and whatever he's saying, to lean over to Raegan and press a kiss at her temple.

She bites back a smile, flicking an annoyed look at Thorne before her ocean blue eyes soften once they reach me. I smile back, constantly enamored with her reactions to me. I want to learn every single one. If I could spend an entire day drawing each of them from her until I'm satisfied, then I would.

Maybe after this is all over.

Soon.

Thorne's glaring at me when I look back at him, and my smile twists into a smirk. He knows, has always known, about my feelings toward Raegan. There's nothing he can say or do about it because she's the only reason I'm supposedly helping him right now. He's forced to swallow that bitter pill, and it's a pleasure to witness.

Thankfully, that puts an end to any conversation or haughty remarks for me to have to endure, and the remainder of the flight is silent between the three of us.

It's only an hour or two before the island appears ahead. As we draw closer, it looks mostly un-lived in, apart from a few small buildings maybe a mile inland from the southern beach. If this is supposed to be one of their strongholds, I expected far more buildings, more activity, more...*everything* from what I'm seeing now.

Raegan squeezes my hand in concern.

It wouldn't be entirely unexpected if they were to make us meet at a lesser island for their protection, so I don't let any negative feelings cloud my thoughts. We stick to the plan. They should have computers connected to the rest somehow, so there will still be a way in. I'll reach out to Dane if I have to in order to help us once we're online.

Worst case, there's always a paper trail.

I rub my thumb over the back of her hand to reassure her that everything's going to be okay.

The helicopter lands, and there's a man with a clipboard waiting off to the side. I have Thorne get out first, and then I follow behind him with Raegan behind me. Before I'm even out of the helicopter, I'm scanning the area around us for signs of danger. Like the sound of a gun cocking. I check the helipad is clear, and there are no buildings at this height around us.

Just the man with the clipboard, the helicopter pilot, and us.

When I'm certain that we're not under immediate threat, I jump down and turn to offer Raegan a hand down, recapturing it in the process once she's clear of the chopper.

"You made good timing!" the man with the clipboard shouts over the helicopter, which departs once we're all out of range. It means we no longer have that as our escape, but I've seen plenty of boats around when we were landing.

Thorne approaches the man and shakes his hand. "Yes, we did. Is the meeting still running on schedule?"

The GE employee pushes his glasses up his nose and nods emphatically. "Yes, yes. I'll bring you to the meeting room and then let them know you've arrived."

Thorne smirks at me over his shoulder. "Shall we, then?"

When I don't react at all, waiting for him to get on with it, he scoffs and indicates to the employee to lead the way.

We stroll through hallways and stairs, winding through the building to the far side, but still a few floors up from the ground. Once the hallways narrow, I shift to the back of the line with Raegan in front of me.

The employee opens a door at the end of a long hallway to a meeting room. There's a single table with chairs, a short counter with drinks, and one wall of windows overlooking the ocean.

"Please, have a seat. Thorne." He indicates a chair on the opposite side of the table, which Thorne takes. He tries to pick out seats for me and Raegan next, but I take her to the other end of the table. "Oh, well, I'll just let him know you're here." The man leaves the room through the only door.

"What game are you playing at, Jackson? We're supposed to be a united front to show that I've convinced you to join their group." Thorne leans forward on the table with his fingers laced in front of him; his head turned with narrowed eyes on me.

I'm too preoccupied looking for signs of deception to worry about Thorne's feelings. My hands twitch with restless energy in my lap, fingering the blades through my hoodie.

Something's off.

I don't know what yet, but I can smell it like something foul hanging in the air.

There's a low, barely audible whirring sound behind me, and I jump forward, knocking the chair back while effortlessly hopping up onto the table and spinning around.

"Shit!" Raegan's voice instantly brings my attention to her without thought. Her wrists are clasped against the arms of the chair, and there's a metal collar around her neck.

My chair on the ground has the same cuffs and collar out, though they're wrapped around nothing but air.

"My gift...it's blocking my gift," she grits through her teeth, her hands clenched tight and jerking against the restraints.

Thorne's still in his seat, but now he's smiling and leaning back in it with no sign of the same trickery on his chair. "You should've stayed in your seat," he voices haughtily. "It would be much easier for all of us if you didn't fight it."

Anger and bloodlust slip and burn through my veins, my body tensing with the need to follow through on all the promises I've made to Thorne. The only part of this plan where he stayed alive was so long as Raegan was safe. Now, all bets are off.

My hands fist at my sides, but I turn away from him and drop next to Raegan's chair instead. The only thing, and I mean the *only* thing, that will delay his death is making sure she's safe first.

She struggles against the unforgiving metal, trying to slip her hands out or break them free. "Jack, it's on my ankles, too," she tells me.

"I'll get you out." My voice comes out steady, despite the monster in me chomping at the bit to be released on Thorne. We're on the clock now, but getting her free is my top priority. I'll carry her chair with me to escape if I have to, but it'll be far easier if she's unrestrained and can move freely.

My lock picks are always handy in my pocket, so I get to work on the first cuff. Thorne moves, as I expected he would, but I get the first cuff free in record time.

"Jack!" Raegan shouts to warn me, but I'm already leaping forward to meet him before he can reach her.

He sends a blast of air at me, trying to knock me away, but I counter it with one of my own. The two opposing winds swirl and clash between us.

"Just keep to your end of the deal, and she won't be hurt," Thorne calls out. "I needed an insurance policy to make sure you didn't turn on me. GE gets what they want to make them trust us, and you and I still do what we planned. I've received their word that she won't be harmed so long as you follow your orders."

My orders. They plan to make me their dog of war. And probably their scapegoat if I'm ever to be caught. Then call me an unhinged serial killer and lock me away for life while they find their next beast to do their dirty work.

It's a solid plan, actually, that my ruthless side is able to admit to.

I'd do anything they asked if they dangled Raegan's safety in the balance.

The problem with that plan is that they'd have to kill me first to get to her.

I drop from the table and throw a gust of air under it. The table flips over and sails through the air at Thorne, and I take those seconds to return to Raegan's side. The picks are back in my hand, working on her other wrist.

The table smashes against the wall, and I know my time is up.

"Go. I'll dislocate my thumb to get out of this one," Raegan urges me while looking over my shoulder, most likely at Thorne closing in.

I can feel his approach behind me like a breeze at my back, raising the hairs on my neck. The air around me shifts like it's being sucked away from us. It reminds me of a tidal wave, when all the water is pulled back, only to crash forward with devastating results.

The second cuff clicks open. Spinning around, I dive to the side, throwing air and knives at Thorne to bring his attention around to me. There's no sign of the air I'd sent his way, and my knives are thrown back before they can get within a foot of him.

I reach out to draw the blades back to me before they can be used against me or Raegan, grasping them in hand. Thorne smirks at me, then turns and keeps walking to Raegan rather than me.

Anger swells in my chest, threatening to blind me in a red haze, but I shove it down and out of my mind. This isn't the time for me to lose my head. I need a clear mind while Raegan is still restricted and in danger in this room. Once I know she's safe, I can let it out.

I flip a blade between my fingers, resting a foot back against the wall behind me, and then use my gift to help propel me across the room at Thorne.

I hit an invisible wall between us, but use my gift to keep me airborne and pushing against it. My hand shakes with the effort and strain to shove my blade through whatever whirlwind of protection he has up around himself. I'm almost through when Thorne grunts and shoots me a look before I'm blown back.

My gift catches me before I slam to the ground, and I try again.

And again.

Each time, he tosses me away.

I can feel the pressure in the room shifting. Whatever attack he's been building up is almost complete, and there's nothing between him and Raegan. She's trying to pull at the collar around her neck, but it's futile until I get the lock picks to her.

Thorne smirks at me, raising his hands, and there's a rush of wind around us. He looks back at Raegan.

No.

I use the air around me to shift my trajectory to Raegan instead of Thorne this time, stopping just in front of her chair and widening my stance before her. I throw a shield of air around us that I know will only lessen whatever blow is coming our way rather than stop it. I barely get the shield in place before the second of silence, like the room is holding its breath, warns me that my time's run out.

His attack hits me from behind like a sledgehammer. I throw my hand out to catch myself on the back of her chair before I crash into her. White-hot pain sears across my back, and I'm momentarily blinded from the pain of it.

"Jack! *Jack!*"

I focus on her voice like a lifeline. I can't pass out. Whatever Thorne threw this way, he didn't lessen it just because I'd stepped between him and his target. That, or he expected this and wanted me down for good.

Thorne's footsteps get closer. I keep my eyes closed and my body still. It's torturous to keep my body immobile while drawing in ragged breaths through the pain. But I do it. So, when he sighs from above me, and I can feel his presence within reach, he doesn't have time to react before I slam a knife into his chest.

I yank it out with a grunt from the strength and motility needed for that move while my entire back seizes in agony. My arm slashes in an arc on autopilot, seeking his throat but missing entirely when Thorne uses his gift to hop back and add some distance between us.

His face is contorted with more anger than pain, and I'm forced to wonder again how he's even alive. Is he alive? There's blood, but it doesn't seem to flow as heavily as it should where I've just stabbed him. Or I'm only thinking that's the case because something has felt off about him since I first saw him again.

Whatever method he used to survive or come back last time, I'll have to be sure there are no third chances.

I look at my little one's collar next, and when I see it isn't attached to the chair like her other cuffs, I pass her my lock-picking tools. "Your ankles first." She can work on them while I finish this, and then I'll remove that collar from her.

"No!" Thorne shouts when he sees Raegan halfway free already. His hand reaches out to her, readying to cut off her air, but I shove off the ground and use my gift to propel me through the air without having to move my body.

My knife swings at his arm. He's forced to drop it to dodge, stopping his attack on Raegan and bringing his focus back to me.

He catches my wrist and tries to turn my knife on me. My back screams as I fight to hold him back, my arm trembling as I keep the blade from touching me. I open my hand and drop it into my other hand, where I thrust it up into his gut.

Thorne's fist smashes into the side of my face. I bite my tongue, and blood fills my mouth and flows freely from my nose. My body hits the wall from the force behind his punch, and my back is pounding to the rapid beat of my heart. I lost my grip on the knife in that attack, and Thorne pulls it free from his midsection and holds it in his hand as he stalks past me toward Raegan.

"You're blinded by that woman. Once she's gone, then you'll remember what you were born for. You won't have any excuse anymore not to stand by my side."

No.

I don't feel the pain when I turn and launch a gust of wind at Thorne, throwing him against the wall and holding him there. I see the knife already flying at Raegan and use my other hand to catch that, too, redirecting it to Thorne so his body catches it in the throat instead.

I walk over to him, even as I can feel his gift pushing against mine and trying to get free. It feels like a kitten batting at my sides. Like nothing. My hand flexes and his gift dies beneath the pressure of mine. Not even a whisper or tickle of it left.

I always had the stronger gift between the two of us. We both knew it, though Thorne tried to play it off that he would always be better. Just because he'd mastered power before control. But now I have both.

My head cocks to the side to study him once I'm standing in front of him. He has three stab wounds now that, for any normal person, would have put them in critical condition if not killed them by now. The throat wound, in particular, should have been the end of this.

Thorne makes a gargling sound. It looks like I won't be getting any answers from him since I acted too rashly with that knife and cut into his vocal cords. I can't regret the action, though. He'd dared aim the knife at Raegan.

Now, all I care about is his death. And the promises that I need to fulfill.

I drop him to the ground and get to work, divesting him of his ears and tongue as I'd once sworn to do. I remove his head last, using a collapsible bone saw I brought with me for this trip.

When I'm done, I stand above him and wipe the blood from my mouth and nose with the back of my sleeve. "Let's see you come back from this."

Chapter Twenty-Eight

RAEGAN

It's not every day you see a man you think you're falling in love with cutting off the head of your enemy. I try not to think about the sound the metal made against bone, and shiver, anyway. Is it any more disgusting than breaking someone down from the inside out? No. Is the sound going to still spring up out of nowhere to give me nightmares in my future?

Probably.

As soon as he's done, I call out his name. I need to see his face. To look upon my shadow and savior. My nightmare and hero.

He turns. His face and neck are covered in blood. His hood dropped from his head at some point, so his black hair is exposed and disheveled. I'd put money down that there's blood in that, too, but his hair does just as well as his hoodie and pants at hiding it.

I'll need a closer look if I'm going to find and assess his injuries.

His expression is serene, and that's what worries me most when I look at him. He's just brutally killed a man, and I know he's hurting from that first attack Thorne threw at him. But one wouldn't know it by looking at his face. It's like he's above all of that and is now content with all that's happened, as if it had all gone to plan.

"Jack," I say again when he doesn't move more than that. His deep blue eyes snap to mine. Then they run over my body, like they're seeking any injury or if I need anything. I was able to get one ankle free during the fight, but I'm not going to lie. I stopped everything I was doing when Jackson turned the tables on Thorne.

He takes a step toward me, and then he flinches, and his face tightens.

Shit. He's really hurt.

I bend forward to try working on my other ankle.

"Let me." His husky voice is even lower than usual, but he's crouched at my feet, so I hear him clearly all the same. Jackson takes the picks from my hands and gets to work on my ankle.

Copper fills my nose at his proximity, and I have to take a slow breath through my mouth to keep from gagging. Is it from Thorne or...?

My fingers move on instinct to the back of Jackson's hoodie while he's bent over my foot. I lift them up after a simple touch of his saturated hoodie, knowing the moment I make contact that it's his blood. I stare at the bright red liquid on my fingers.

This is bad.

His head pops up to look toward the wall, and his eyes narrow. "They're coming," he tells me right before focusing back on my ankle.

I mentally curse that we don't have more time. I shouldn't be surprised with all the noise likely coming from this room between him and Thorne. Or had they watched it all through some cameras to wait for a victor before coming in?

"Got it." Jackson directs my foot out of the cuff. He uses his gift, I think, to help himself stand because I feel a soft breeze around my legs when he does so. His fingers rub against the collar, and his lips purse. "I'll get this off once we're hidden somewhere. We need to get out of here first. Can you use your gift?"

I close my eyes and reach for it, seeking that burning sensation in my gut that usually jumps at the chance to be used, but the container there is still empty. My eyes open. He nods like he can read the answer in them.

He takes my hand and guides me to one of the large windows. There's something small in the grasp of his other hand, but it fits in it so well that I can't really tell what he's holding. Only that there's a small metal point sticking out from one side that he pounds into the window. Cracks spider from the impact, but they're small and tight. He does it again and again, and the cracks widen and spread until my hair flies about while he brings his gift into play and the window shatters.

Jackson knocks a few more bits of glass away to give us a wide enough opening. We're still a few stories off the ground, though, so I'm not sure how he plans on us getting down there with him injured as much as he is.

He uses his gift to swing me up into his arms, and then he gives the barest of grunts when my weight settles into him. I hate that he has to do this, but I don't see another way out.

The door to the meeting room opens. My eyes lock with Gordon's a second before Jack jumps out the window, and we sail down to the top of a palm tree. We hop a few more times before he brings us to the ground.

Jackson's knees buckle as soon as his feet hit the ground, and I drop onto his thighs. I scramble off of him so I'm not weighing him down any longer, then turn to help him up. His jaw is tight, and there's sweat sliding down the side of his face. His eyes are glazed, and he blinks rapidly. He's going to fucking pass out.

I hurriedly check around us for somewhere to hide and find a shed maybe a hundred steps away. About a hundred too many, but it's the only option to give me the time I need to get this damn collar off. If I can get my gift back, we'll still have a fighting chance.

I duck under Jack's arm and try to lift him, but it takes him putting weight back on his feet before I can get him standing again. It's not just his weight, but the weight of all the weapons he carries on him. Speaking of, I slide a hand under his hoodie and snag a knife for myself to hold in my other hand in case we run into any surprises, so I'm not completely unarmed.

Technically, so long as I'm close to Jackson, I have my own armory. I'm just nowhere near as good at using them as I need to be to go up against an entire island.

"Boat..." Jackson manages out roughly after a couple of steps.

I keep us moving and shake my head. "We won't make it. We'll barricade ourselves in here long enough for me to get this stupid collar off and let you rest."

The building we landed on was in the middle of the island. The docks are at least a mile away, and I have no idea which side of the island we're on after flying out the window.

The arm I have wrapped around his lower back is covered in blood where it's touching him, and I panic that he may not make it at all without medical help soon. We can't hide out for long without risking his life.

And being on a boat in the middle of the ocean? I have no idea what direction to travel to get back to land or how long it would take.

I chew on my bottom lip for any scenario that doesn't end up with Jackson losing his life.

Then it hits me. Medical supplies. They have to have some sort of medical room or supplies here on this island if anyone were to get hurt. If I can get us there and patch him up a bit, then it'll give us more time.

I just...have to find it. And not let them find us in the process.

His weight suddenly doubles, and I stumble, catching us both with shaking knees as I struggle to keep us vertical. "Jack! Jack, please, don't pass out. We're almost there. Just a few more steps."

It's more like twenty, but he forces his eyes open and takes another step forward. I keep pace with him, encouraging him quietly as we go to make sure he doesn't lose consciousness.

I reach out to the door handle as soon as it's in reach and breathe a sigh of relief when it turns. Thank fuck it isn't locked. I help Jack inside, getting him comfortable before his eyes close, and I know he's out.

Should I leave him here and bring back what I find? What if they find him here while I'm gone, completely alone and defenseless?

I curse and start working on barricading the door. This is the only building nearby from where we dropped, so it's only a matter of time before they search here. It really wasn't the best option for us to go to, but it was the only one we had where we could have some sort of defensible position.

I pull the lock-picking tools from my pocket and start feeling around the collar for the keyhole.

I bite back a scream of frustration when I find that it's at the back of my neck. It's a super inconvenient location for me to work on, not to mention uncomfortable. I stick the tools in anyway and get to work. It feels like I'm doing everything backward, which means the tools slip and fall out of position more often than not. The fact that I know we're on a ticking clock doesn't help my patience or control.

My arms ache painfully as time passes, and I'm nowhere closer to getting the damn thing removed. But I refuse to take a break. I'm our only hope, so I can't give up or stop trying. There will be time to rest after we get through this.

Electricity buzzes through the collar in an instant, and every muscle in my body seizes. My hands unwillingly grip the collar as the shock thrusts through my entire body. It's over in seconds, but I drop to the dusty wood floor in a heap, my body still twitching and tingling.

I've been shocked before, so I know instantly what this is, but that knowledge does shit-all to help me do anything about it. My body suddenly feels weak and numb, and it's slow to respond to any direction I'm trying to give it. Not to mention that my neck feels like it's on fire, and my entire nervous system is screaming in pain.

"Oh good, you do still have it on."

Panic lodges in my throat, and my body freezes. It's Gordon's voice talking from above me. They not only found me, but they're already inside.

Jack!

I force my arms to move. To push myself off the ground and to look at the man who single-handedly brought me to ruin six years ago. The man of my nightmares. I finally make it to my knees and look up at him. He's smiling down at me like a master recovering his lost pet.

It brings me back to the girl I was under his control. Like I'm sixteen again and powerless against him. Small. Worthless. Alone.

But I'm not alone now, am I?

I tear my eyes away from Gordon to make sure Jackson is untouched in the corner behind me. He's still unconscious to the world, which means it's up to me to get us out of this.

Gordon grabs my jaw and jerks my face to look back at him with a snarl. "Look at me!" His tongue clicks as he looks me over. "You're even more useless now than when I first had you. Might not even be worth the effort."

"Then just kill her, and let's get off this shitty island." Vera steps into view behind Gordon. She looks at Jackson with cold eyes before returning to me. "The other one's dead anyway. Kill her and leave 'em both here for someone else to clean up."

"Enough, Vera. I'm taking her back with us. I'm sure her training will kick back in once she's separated from the others again. I refuse to let my invested time with her in the past be a waste."

I smack his hand away from my face. He scowls, and Vera's smirk intensifies. "I'd rather die than go back with you. Take this collar off and let me fight you to show you I'm not that scared little girl anymore. If I win, then you let us off the island. If you win, then you'll take us with you and get Jack to a doctor. He's worth more to you alive than dead."

I'm making this up as I go, but all that matters is protecting Jackson. Even if they have him, too, I know he'll be okay. They won't be able to hold him for long, and at least he'll get treated first. My chances against Gordon are pretty slim, but it's a chance I'm willing to take rather than give in. Kellan's taught me a lot in the months I've been with them, and I'd rather go down fighting.

"You bring her back, and *I'll* kill her," Vera snaps to Gordon. "She owes me her life."

Gordon frowns at her. "Are we going to have a problem?"

The sound of feet pounding on sand draws all of our attention to the opening of the shed. I stand and move in front of Jackson on instinct. Two others I don't recognize are already standing in front of the shed, blocking me in with Gordon and Vera, but they aren't the ones coming this way.

"Raegan!"

I startle at the deep voice that I'd recognize anywhere. How did he find me? Kellan, Aiden, Dane, and the teleporting guy—Reid—all stop a few paces back from the shed.

"Vera!" Dane shouts when he sees his sister in the shed.

Aiden looks at me with a pinched brow. I'm probably covered in blood, but none of it is mine. His gaze moves past me to Jackson, and his face tightens further as he realizes the predicament we're in.

"Holt," Gordon says in a bored tone. The man in front of the shed steps forward and raises his hand to the sky.

I watch the second they all look up before lightning crashes down on each of them. They fall to the ground when he doesn't let up, the electricity turning their muscles to jelly and keeping them from moving or fighting against it.

"Stop! You'll kill them!" I rush at Gordon and grab his arm to turn him to look at me when he ignores me. He's grinning until he's forced to look at me, and then it drops to a smirk. "Make him stop. *Please.*" I know how much he likes begging, and I'll do anything right now.

Gordon snickers like he's won something. "Ah, good to see you haven't forgotten everything. Holt, that's enough."

The lightning stops, but all the guys are still twitching and lie immobile on the ground.

Vera's watching Dane with an unreadable expression, and I wonder if she would have tried to stop it for her brother or if she would have just watched him die without feeling anything.

"Let them go," I plead, my brain scrambling to figure out what I can even offer him for their freedom.

"And why would I do that?" Gordon asks.

"New deal," I begin hurriedly, my voice breathless in my rush to keep his attention and somehow turn this in our favor. "We'll trade. Vera doesn't want to be around me anyway, so me for her. You let her go home with them, and I'll come with you." He doesn't look convinced so I add, "Willingly. I won't try to run or escape. I'll stay with you and do your training or whatever you want, so long as Vera is with them."

"No!" Kellan shouts from outside. He and the others have crawled back up. Some on their knees with Aiden working to stand. "Fight him, beautiful. Don't just hand yourself over."

He doesn't know that my gift is blocked, but it doesn't matter. Even with that, I can't touch Gordon. Not if he doesn't want me to. I'd never win against him.

I ignore him and lock my gaze with Gordon's. He likes that I didn't answer Kell and that I'm keeping my focus on him. Even if he doesn't like me looking him in the eyes, it's enough that I see him considering my offer.

No running away. No trying to escape. No trying to kill him to get away.

The perfect pet.

It's everything he could want. He just has to give up Vera and the guys.

Gordon looks over to Vera, who gapes at him. "Are you serious?"

He gives her a look. "Don't you want to spend some time with your dear brother again? Without her around?"

Vera shoots a glance my way and then over the other side to Dane. Then back to Gordon. "Yes."

"Good. I like this deal. It's a waste to kill gifted folks, and I'll be leaving with what I came to this awful island for."

I plaster a fake smile on for his benefit, even though my insides are twisting with panic at what I've done. He probably thinks he'll brainwash me enough to get Vera back in the end, anyway. This deal will get me, and once he sinks his claws back in, he can do whatever he pleases from there.

He holds out his hand. I don't hesitate to take it. I have to show him that I'm all in on this deal. Because if anything happens to the guys or Vera leaves them, then the deal is off. I'll uphold my end of the deal so long as he does his.

His fingers wrap tightly around my hand, and he turns to walk us to the opening of the shed. The other two step aside to let us through.

Kellan and Aiden lunge forward to try grabbing me, but lightning strikes down and immobilizes them.

I start toward them on instinct, but Gordon's grip on my hand tightens painfully. "He'll release them as soon as the rest of us are through. So don't dawdle, or their brains will be piles of mush for taking too long."

The woman who'd been standing in front of the shed waves her hand at the air before us. It shifts and darkens in a long oval in the air.

A portal.

I always wondered how he popped in and out of places so easily.

We step up to it, and I look back at each of the guys for one last look. One last memory of how they all came for me. Dane's eyes are wide, and he's slowly shaking his head at me to avoid drawing the lightning guy's attention to him. He's urging me to stop. Not to go.

Even with the promise of his sister returning home to him, he doesn't want me to do this. And it breaks my heart that I have to leave so soon after what he and I just went through together. But this is for the best.

Tears brim my eyes, and I smile softly at him. This is his chance with Vera. I promised him I'd do everything I could to bring her back, and this is as far as I can go. Now, it's up to him to bring the sister we all knew and loved before back.

I pull my gaze from him as a single tear falls. And then I walk through the portal and leave the life I knew behind.

To Be Continued in Ramshackle

Raegan of Ruin Book 3

Thank you for reading Raze.
Please consider leaving your review.

Turn the page for access to a **<u>bonus scene</u>**!

BONUS SCENE
Boyfriend - Elias POV

One year since Portia lost her memory; One year before Raegan shows up at Hype.

The door to my office bursts open, stopping me mid-sentence on the phone.

"Elias! I'm leaving!" Portia announces excitedly as she runs inside, pulling someone behind her.

Not again.

"Change of plans," I mutter into the phone. "I won't make the meeting. Reschedule it." I hang up without waiting for confirmation.

"This is Frank." She pulls him up beside her with their interlocked hands. "He's my boyfriend!"

My hands jerk with the impulse to choke out the man touching my woman, but I clasp them together on the desk instead. Shifting back in my chair, I regard them with a calmness I certainly don't feel each time this happens.

We've been through this enough that it shouldn't bother me. I know the final outcome and ought to take comfort in that, but the fact that it continues to happen is beginning to fray my patience.

Portia's wearing a new crafted outfit that I would have sent her back to her apartment over if she'd checked in with me like she was supposed to prior to her shift. Beads of all shapes, sizes, and colors are glued to a bra so densely I can't tell what color it once was. More beads dangle on strings from the bottom to roll and move along her exposed torso. Her flared, rainbow tutu has more beads glued haphazardly along the top over bright red booty shorts, and then thigh-high rainbow-striped socks cover more of her skin than anything else she's wearing.

Half of her chocolate brown hair is split into two space buns while the rest of it falls over her shoulders and down her back. She's grinning at me as if this *news* is the best thing since sliced bread, and her green eyes are damn-near sparkling.

"He says he's been looking *everywhere* for me, but I've been in the wrong city! He just happened to stop by here with some friends for the night when he saw me. We started talking and I told him how I lost my memory, and that's when he said he knew it was me! He wasn't sure at first since I didn't remember him, but now he's positive. Isn't that great?" she gushes on.

My gaze perches on their hands for a solid beat before I force it to drag up the male's attached arm and stop on his face. He looks relaxed, if not a bit confused, while Portia fills me in on each important detail of what transpired between them. I listen to her every word, filling in the blanks for myself where needed, so that I can make a complete assessment of the situation and therefore a fitting...resolution.

The moment I make eye contact with him, his confidence falters.

He likely thought she was here to gossip with a co-worker or maybe tell her boss that she's quitting. It's not until he's pinned beneath my stare that warning bells likely go off to tell him that there's more going on here.

I smile at him. Under ordinary circumstances, it might be seen as a polite smile, but I do it to show acknowledgement of his failing confidence.

Of his *lie*.

My gift doesn't go off to tell me he lied to her. He did tell her everything that she's repeating back to me, so there's no lie in that. I would need to hear the words from his lips for it to react. But I don't need the gift of Truth to know that everything this man said to her was made up with the intention of taking advantage of her.

It sounds like he's luring her home with him. Then what?

That's the million-dollar question.

How long does he plan to continue this ruse with her? For the one night? Since he can easily fool her into saying what she was like and what they did together, does he intend to keep up the charade for as long as he can so long as she goes along with it?

The very thought of someone doing that to Portia makes me question my moral high ground, and if I should cave to the more animalistic instinct in me to see his life ended. She's the only person who can make me consider leaving my principles at the door. Who can tap into the basest parts of me and draw emotions and actions I'd never known existed.

"Elias?"

Her voice snaps me from my train of thought, anchoring me back to the present.

The male, *Frank*, is beginning to fidget and check the door and only exit to this room.

Well, at least he's not so dumb as some of the others. He seems to recognize that I know what he's doing.

My gaze flicks back to Portia, dismissing him in favor of her requested attention. "My apologies. If Frank is who he claims to be, then he shouldn't mind answering a question."

Portia nods vigorously on Frank's behalf. "Yes, of course!"

Frank balks. "W-wait—"

When he doesn't say anything more than that, I tilt my head to the side to regard him with faux interest. "Is there a problem?"

"Uh…" he looks between us. "Aren't you her boss? What would you know?"

"Oh! Right!" Portia removes her hand from his and then proceeds to wrap herself around his arm. My fingers tighten their hold on each other, but I force my expression to remain unperturbed by the way she so freely touches this stranger. "Elias is the one who found and saved me! And he's been taking care of me ever since. I owe him a lot."

You owe me nothing, sweetness. Nothing I've done or could ever do will be enough for what she deserves.

She beams at me, and it sets my chest alight. Then I catch her bulging chest press harder into his arm and a blood vessel nearly pops in my forehead.

Time to end this charade before I do something uncharacteristic and chop the man's arm off.

"The question is simple. What is her favorite food?"

"Her favorite food?" he parrots back with a mixture of surprise and relief. I don't understand why they always seem relieved by the question at first. Perhaps they believe they have a chance at guessing the correct answer. But I would never allow that to happen.

"Well, you had a lot of them. Ice cream was one…"

Portia's face falls. "What?"

"Or…was it cake?" he tries again, laughing nervously. "You had so many."

Her arms pull away from his and she takes a step back. I'm compelled to shove him further away from her but maintain my seat as it all falls into place.

No stranger would look at her and think of anything other than the sweetest things.

The truth is, she loves meat. Ribs, in particular, are her absolute favorite.

"That's not right at all." She shakes her head. "So then…everything else you said…"

"No, wait. That was a dumb question anyway. You can't write everything off just because of that."

I make a short call to my head of security, Bryant, to come to my office. Frank reaches out to Portia, and I stand abruptly. My sudden movement startles him enough to stop and bring his attention to me. I casually button my jacket, then move around my desk to step between them.

Frank glares at me, then tries to look around me to Portia. "You're really using your boss as your gatekeeper? You think your pussy's made of gold or something? I'm out of here." He turns and runs face first into Bryant's chest.

It's another mark against him for referencing her body. And one more for the mean words. His tally so far isn't looking good.

"Yes, you are," I agree with him, then look over his head to Bryant.

My head of security has already grabbed Frank by the arm to keep him in place while he waits for my order.

"Please escort Frank to the exit. Make a copy of his driver's license on the way out to pass around to security to get a look at his face. He's banned from the club."

Bryant nods. "Yes, Boss."

"Oh, and round up his friends as well. They don't need to be here any longer, either."

He drags Frank out the door and closes it behind them. Portia picks at the beads on her skirt, clearly avoiding my eyes when they land on her.

"I'm sorry. I really thought I'd found someone who knew me this time. It's been a whole year and I still don't remember anything. I just..." Her hands fist the tulle of her skirt, revealing more of her shorts than should ever be seen in public. My mouth waters involuntarily, making me swallow it and any urge to wrap her in my arms.

I can't have her like that.

She may be mine in my heart, but I can never act on it.

I'm the reason she can't remember anything.

I'm the one who clipped her wings by making her so dependent on me to live that she doesn't dare go out and explore the world on her own. I give her anything she might require so that she has no need to go looking elsewhere.

It's selfish and cruel, and I'd be a bastard to take the next step with her.

I also swore to Noah that I wouldn't.

The joke is on me, though, because Portia hasn't been subtle with her crush on me. I can either lie and reject her, or pretend to be completely unaware of her feelings to avoid it.

I chose the latter option.

It spares me the lie and her hurt feelings, but it also means I'm now subject to the tease of having her so close.

"I understand," I offer soothingly, lifting her face with a finger until her eyes are looking at mine. "I can't imagine what that feels like. But remember what I told you before. Don't--"

"--force it," she finishes with a sigh. "I know, I know." Portia gives me a small smile that begins to grow while pushing her hair behind her ear. "Just...don't get tired of me, okay? I don't know what I'd do without you."

Never.

It takes all my willpower to keep me from grabbing and kissing her. From showing her everything I feel about her until she has no doubts about it.

I'm never letting her go.

Even if I have to stay at a distance that eats me alive inside, I'll be by her side.

My hand drops from her face before I lose control, and I return her smile with my own. "Of course not. I could never get tired of someone as vibrant as you."

Her cheeks flush. "Good!" Portia spins away before I can watch anymore of her reaction, stealing my prize from me. If she were mine, I'd spin her back around and make her show me everything. There'd be no hiding from me.

Instead, my hand runs down the front of my jacket to smooth away invisible wrinkles to keep busy. "How about you head home, get in some cozy pajamas, and watch a movie for the rest of the night? I'll have Ethan walk you to your apartment."

I pull my phone from my pocket and see various notifications I'd missed in the short time since she arrived with that stranger. But it's the one from Bryant with Frank's driver's license that catches my attention.

Perfect.

"I can walk home by myself." She rolls her eyes and I stare at her, unamused.

"I insist. Frank may be blacklisted from this club, but he could still be lurking outside." I open the app to the Hype staff comms, dial in Ethan's ID, and wait for his voice.

"Yeah?"

"Portia's just leaving my office and requires an escort back to her apartment. See that she gets there safely."

"Roger that, Boss. I'm heading to your office now to pick her up."

Portia glares and crosses her arms. "You're unbelievable."

The door opens and Ethan pops his blonde head in, looking around until he spots Portia. "You ready?"

She holds her glare, and I smile. "Thank you."

"Wait, what? That wasn't a compliment!" she sputters, but I'm already guiding her to the door and Ethan.

"Have a good night." I close the door behind them.

Well.

Time to ruin Frank's life.

Want to receive a bonus scene?

Or maybe stay up to date on the newest releases?

How about early access to ARC or giveaway opportunities?

Sign up for A. L. Rook's newsletter to stay in the know of all things

Rook's books.

Scan or click the QR code below, or go to the website to sign up

@

www.alrookauthor.com

Join the A. L. Rook Reader Group on Facebook

The Rookery

@

www.facebook.com/groups/rookery

Or scan the QR code below

STALKING LINKS

amazon.com/stores/author/B0CYQJ2GWL

facebook.com/groups/rookery

instagram.com/alrookauthor

tiktok.com/@alrookauthor

WEBSITE: https://www.alrookauthor.com

NEWSLETTER: https://subscribepage.io/rooknewsletter

SPOTIFY: https://open.spotify.com/user/31g47djeh3oqclz7y
yaag2hwvtom?si=ca7e308dc7ec4b2c

FB PAGE: https://www.facebook.com/61557109453545/

About the Author

A.L. Rook is an avid reader and has been dreaming of becoming an author since the first grade. She's been thinking up and writing stories ever since. Her favorite stories are dark contemporary or fantasy romance with strong characters that leave a lasting impression. When not drinking exorbitant amounts of coffee while writing, she can be found reading, binge-watching various shows, or traveling.

If you want to stay up to date on release dates, news, or for a chance at extra teasers and giveaways, follow Rook on her socials and join her newsletter.